The Nine Lives of Rose Napolitano is Donna Freitas's first adult novel. She is the author of *Consent: A Memoir of Unwanted Attention*, as well as other works of non-fiction and novels for children and young adults. Donna has written for *The Washington Post*, *The New York Times*, *The Wall Street Journal*, and *The Boston Globe*, and appeared on NPR's All Things Considered and The Today Show. She is currently a member of the faculty at Fairleigh Dickinson University's MFA program.

Donna lives in Brooklyn and Connecticut.

Also by Donna Freitas

Consent: A Memoir of Unwanted Attention

THE NINE
LIVES
OF ROSE
NAPOLITANO

THE NINE LIVES OF ROSE NAPOLITANO

DONNA FREITAS

HarperCollins*Publishers*

HarperCollins*Publishers* Ltd
1 London Bridge Street,
London SE1 9GF

www.harpercollins.co.uk

HarperCollins*Publishers*
1st Floor, Watermarque Building, Ringsend Road
Dublin 4, Ireland

First published in the USA by Viking, an imprint of Penguin Random House LLC 2021

First published in Great Britain by HarperCollins*Publishers* 2021

1

A catalogue record for this book is available from the British Library

ISBN: 978-0-00-837067-1 (HB)
ISBN: 978-0-00-837064-0 (TPB)

This novel is entirely a work of fiction.
The names, characters and incidents portrayed in it are
the work of the author's imagination. Any resemblance to
actual persons, living or dead, events or localities is
entirely coincidental.

Typeset in Adobe Caslon by Palimpsest Book Production Ltd, Falkirk, Stirlingshire

Printed and bound in the UK by CPI Group (UK) Ltd, Croydon CR0 4YY

MIX
Paper from
responsible sources
FSC
www.fsc.org
FSC™ C007454

This book is produced from independently certified FSC™ paper
to ensure responsible forest management.

For more information visit: www.harpercollins.co.uk/green

To my mother,
who gave me this life

March 2, 2008

Rose, Life 3

S HE IS BEAUTIFUL.

I am awed by her perfection. The heady scent of her skin. 'Addie,' I sigh. 'Adelaide,' I try again, a faint whisper in the sterile air. 'Adelaide Luz.'

I raise her little head to my nose and inhale, long and needy, ignoring the sharp pain in my abdomen. I smile as I admire the soft fuzz of her hair.

How I resisted having this little being in my arms! Before the pregnancy and the birth, I would rage about the pressure to have a child – to Luke, to Mom, to Jill, to whomever would listen. The stranger next to me on the subway, the unsuspecting man on the sidewalk. I was just. So. Angry.

But now?

The snow falls in wet clumps against the windowpanes of the hospital room, everything around me shades of gray in dim light. I inch to the left, shift into a better position. The temperature drops and the snow turns papery, thick and dry like paste. She sleeps.

My eyes are hers.

'How could I not have wanted you?' I whisper into her tiny, curling ear, a pearly shell. 'How could there be a life where you and I never met? If there is such a life, I wouldn't want to live it.'

Her eyelids twitch, pale, veined, transparent, her nose and mouth and forehead scrunching.

'Did you hear what I said, sweet girl? You should only listen to the second part, about how your mother wouldn't want a life without you. That's all you need to know.'

Part One

Rose, Life 1

1

August 15, 2006

Rose, Life 1

LUKE IS STANDING on my side of the bed. He never goes to my side of the bed. In his hand is a bottle of prenatal vitamins. He holds it up.

He shakes it, a plastic rattle.

The sound is heavy and dull because it is full.

This is the problem.

'You promised,' he says, even and slow.

Uh-oh. I am in trouble.

'Sometimes I forget to take them,' I admit.

He shakes the bottle again, a maraca in a minor key. 'Sometimes?' The light through the curtains forms a halo around Luke's upper body, the hand held high with the offending object outlined by the sun and glowing.

I am in the doorway of our room, on my way to pull clothes from the drawers and the closet. Mundane things. Underwear. Socks. A top and a pair of jeans. Like any other morning. I would have folded the clothing across one arm and carried it to the bathroom so I could shower and change. Instead I stop, cross my arms over my chest, the heart inside it mangled with hurt and anger. 'Did you count them, Luke?' My question is a cold snap in the humid August air.

'So what if I did, Rose? What if I did count them? Can you blame me?'

I turn my back on him, go to open the long drawer that contains underwear, bras, slips, camisoles, riffle through my things, disrupting the order of my clothing, everything growing more and more out of control. My heart starts pounding.

'You promised me,' Luke says.

I grab a pair of my granniest underwear. I want to scream. 'Like promises mean anything in this marriage.'

'That's not fair.'

'It's perfectly fair.'

'Rose—'

'So I didn't take the pills! I don't want a baby. I never wanted a baby and I don't want one now and I won't want one ever and you knew that before we got engaged! I told you a thousand times! I've told you a million times since!'

'You said you'd take the vitamins.'

'I said it to stop you from tormenting me.' Tears sting my eyes even as the blood inside me pulses with fury. 'I said it so we could have a little peace in this apartment.'

'So you lied.'

I turn. The underwear falls from my hand as I march my way to the other side of the bed to confront my husband. 'You swore you didn't want a baby.'

'I changed my mind.'

'Right. Sure. No big deal.' I am tumbling down a hill, we are tumbling, and I don't know how to stop us from crashing. 'You "changed your mind", but I'm the liar.'

'You said you'd try.'

'I said I'd take the vitamins. That's all I said.'

'You didn't take them.'

'I took some.'

'How many?'

'I don't know. Unlike you, I didn't count.'

Luke lowers the bottle, grips it between both hands, palm pressing down on the top, twisting, removing. He peers into the opening. 'This bottle is full, Rose.' He looks up at me again, head shaking left, right, his disapproval pouring over me.

Who is this man before me, this man I love, this man I married?

I can barely see a resemblance between this person and the one who used to look at me like I was the only woman in the universe, like I was the meaning of his entire existence. I loved being that for Luke. I loved being his everything. He has always been my everything, this man with the soft, thoughtful gaze, with the friendliest, most open of smiles, this man I was certain I would love for the rest of my days on this earth.

The words *But I love you, Luke* are trapped moths banging around inside me, unable to find their way out.

Instead of disarming the bomb between us, in one swift motion I explode, swiping the bottle from Luke's hand, my arm like a club, knocking it hard and high, the huge, oval pills becoming an arc of ugly green Skittles flung across the wood floor, scattering across the white sheets on the bed.

7

This action freezes both of us.

Luke's lips are slightly parted, the sharp, clean edges of his front teeth visible. His eyes follow the trail of pills that have come to represent the success or failure of this marriage, tiny buoys I was meant to ingest to keep our marriage afloat. I've spilled them, so now we are sinking. The only sound in the room is our breathing. Luke's eyes are wide. Betrayed.

He thinks I am the one to betray him, that the proof lies in that stupid bottle of vitamins.

Why doesn't he see that he is the one who betrayed me? That by changing his mind about children he's only shown me that I am not worthy enough on my own?

Luke returns to life, walks to the corner of the room where the rolling bottle came to a stop. He bends down and picks it up. He plucks one vitamin from the floor, then another, pinching them between his fingers before dropping them back inside. The pills clatter to the bottom of the bottle.

I stand there, watching as Luke bends and straightens, bends and straightens until every last prenatal vitamin is back in its rightful home, even those that went skittering under the bed. Luke has to lift the edge of the comforter to see them, has to lie down on the floor to retrieve them, arm straining.

When he's finished, he looks at me, eyes full of accusation. 'Why did I have to marry the one woman in the world who doesn't want a baby?'

I inhale sharply.

There.

There it is. The thing that Luke's been thinking forever, finally out in the open. Not the part about me not wanting a baby –

that he's known since the very beginning. It's the clear ring of regret in his voice that makes me wince, the way he singles me out as unique and only in the worst of ways.

We stare at each other. I wait for an apology that doesn't come. My heart is pounding, my mind is racing from Luke's question, piling my own on top of his. Why can't I be just like every other woman who wants a baby? Why am I not? Why was I made this way?

Will this be the summary of my life at its end?

Rose Napolitano: *Never a mother.*

Rose Napolitano: *She didn't want a baby.*

Luke looks down at his feet. He picks up the bottle cap, closes it with a hard snap of the lid.

I reach for it – I reach for him.

2

March 14, 1998

Rose, Lives 1–9

I DON'T LIKE having my picture taken.

'Can you look up from your lap?'

My eyes, my head, my chin all refuse this request.

I'm the kind of person who runs from a camera, who hides behind whomever is next to me. Who puts up my hand to a lens if one shows up in my face. All the more reason I should not be here right now, having a portrait done in my cap and gown. What was I thinking?

'Um, Rose?'

I hear footsteps. A pair of navy-blue sneakers, worn at the toe, laces ragged, appear on the floor in front of me. I take a big breath, let it out, and look up. The photographer is youngish, maybe my age, maybe a year or two older. His eyes blink, he bites his lip, his brow gathers.

'Sorry,' I say, hands fidgeting in my lap, fingers clasping and unclasping. 'I must be your worst subject ever.' I look away, off to the side, into the dim space beyond this bright, portrait setup

10

where I sit, a gray background scrolled behind me. A row of boxes, the kind you buy if you are moving apartments, is stacked against the wall. A blue jacket is draped over the top, and a hockey stick lies on the floor along the baseboard. 'This was a dumb idea,' I go on. 'I just thought . . . I mean, I wanted . . . but then . . .'

'You wanted?' the photographer asks.

I don't answer, I guess because I don't really want to talk to this stranger about the inner workings of my heart. Besides, I'm still taking in the junk piled everywhere. This must be the photographer's house. He called it his 'studio', but it looks like he lives here. Or maybe just moved in.

'You wanted what?' he presses.

There's something about the sound of his voice – gentle, patient – that makes me want to cry. This whole situation makes me want to cry. 'I shouldn't be here, I'm not good at this.' Now I do start to cry. 'This is so embarrassing, I don't like getting my picture taken. I'm sorry, I'm really, really sorry.' I cry harder, even as my inner feminist scolds me for so much apologizing.

The photographer – I can't remember his name (Larry? No. Lou? Maybe.) – squats down next to my chair so we are almost at eye level. 'Don't worry. Lots of people hate having their picture taken. But are you crying because of the portrait, or because of something else?'

I study this man, the way his right knee presses through the rip in his jeans, the way his body sways ever so slightly in his crouch. How does he know that my reason for crying isn't because of the picture? Has he also sensed that this is really about my parents, who sometimes have a hard time understanding my choices? The woman I've become as an adult?

I cross my arms, press them into my body. This black gown with the velvet trim is thick and stiff. I bet it would stand on its own if I propped it just right. I pull the puffy beanie from my head and shake my hair out. It probably looks awful after sitting under the weight of this thing. The beanie is also velvet, the same blue as the gown. I was so excited when it came in the mail, the symbol of so many years of hard work, of the doctorate I am about to receive officially on graduation day in May. My PhD in sociology, the one that will turn me from just Rose into Professor Napolitano. Doctor Napolitano.

'Who's that picture of, over there?' I ask the photographer instead of answering his question. I point at it, extending my arm to the right.

Hanging on the wall above the stack of boxes is a large, framed photo. It seems out of place, given the transitional state of everything else – fixed and permanent. Two people, a man and a woman, are sitting side by side on a porch, each one with a book open in front of them. The expressions on their faces are so alive, so engaged, like the words before them are the most exciting words ever written.

The photographer turns in the direction I point and chuckles. 'Those are my parents. I took that when I was ten. I'd gotten my first real camera for my birthday that year. I was taking pictures of everything around me, flowers, blades of grass, the grain of the floorboards in the living room – very artsy.'

He turns back, looks at me and shrugs. Rolls his eyes at himself. They are green, with flecks of brown.

'I took a lot of excellent shots of the dog, too.'

I laugh a little. Some of the tension in me releases. 'And so . . . ?'

'Yeah, right.' This time he doesn't turn away. He keeps his gaze on me. 'Well, that photo, I was just arriving home. There was this monarch flying above the tall grass and I went running after it, trying to get the perfect shot.' He covers his eyes with his hands.

I find myself wanting to reach for them, to pull them away from his face, touch his smooth, olive skin. I don't want him to be embarrassed.

His hands fall back to his knees. He bobbles a little. 'I was such a nerd. So there I was, grass plastered all over my jeans, tired, sweaty, and suddenly I looked up and saw my parents reading on the porch. And I could see something on their faces – something I had to capture. I stopped, lifted my camera, and snapped a single photograph.' He smiles.

'That photograph?'

He stands again. He's so tall. 'Yup. It was the picture that made me want to become a photographer. When I saw it, I just knew. My mother had it framed, so I could always remember who I am and what I want to do, even when times get hard. It's not easy starting out in this business.' He pats the camera that's next to him on the floor with affection, and he shrugs again.

My head tilts, studying him. 'Thank you for telling me that story.'

He nods. 'Thank you for asking about that photograph.' He taps his foot. 'Now it's your turn.'

'My turn?'

'Tell me what the deal is. I told you a story, so now you have to tell me one, about why you're really here.'

'Um.'

13

'Um, yes, well?'

'Um, okay. Fine.'

He crosses the room and retrieves a chair, parks it next to mine, and sits. Leans forward. 'I've got plenty of time. You're my only appointment.'

I breathe deeply. 'Before I tell you, I have one more question.'

'Sure, go ahead.'

My cheeks grow hot. I stand up, unzip my graduation robe before sitting back down. This thing is melting me. 'It's embarrassing.'

His eyebrows arch.

'I forgot your name, and since we are telling each other life stories, I figure we should probably be on a first-name basis. I know it's not Larry. But is it – Lou, maybe?'

He smiles again, laughs again – he has such a nice laugh, low, but rich, like he enjoys laughing, like he is easy to laugh. 'Well, Rose Napolitano, my only appointment of the day, I agree that we should know each other's names, and since I already know yours, you should also know mine.' He sticks out his hand and I take it.

I feel it across my skin, everywhere, a rush.

'My name is Luke.'

3

August 15, 2006

Rose, Life 1

MY HAND HANGS in the air, reaching, empty.
Instead of giving the bottle to me, instead of taking
my hand, Luke returns the vitamins to the bedside stand where
I usually keep them, hidden behind the stack of novels that makes
its home next to my pillow. He is quiet.

I speak in my defense. 'I have been trying, Luke. Really.' I let
my arm drop, let my husband's question go unanswered. I want
to bury it from view, erase it by piling other words on top of it
until we can no longer see it. 'But sometimes those pills make
my stomach hurt, and you know I can't work while I'm sick. I
can't present at conferences, I can't do my research interviews. . .'
I wait for my husband to join in, help me paddle away from the
dangerous place where this fight has taken us.

We can fix this. My eyes are pleading.

Luke hesitates, only for a second, and I hang my hope on this
single breath.

But then his eyes narrow. 'I don't want to hear about your

15

work anymore, Rose. I'm tired of hearing about your work and how, because of it, we can't have a baby.'

There it is again. Exposed. The problem we cannot solve.

My impulse to try to fix this turns to ash. I glare back. 'It's not just because of my work that I don't want a baby and you know it. I don't want a baby because I've never wanted a baby and it's my right not to want a baby! But Jesus, Luke, what's so wrong about loving my work? What's so wrong with making it my priority? What's so wrong with *me?*'

'What's wrong is that you love your academic career more than you'd love a baby even if we did have one! What matters is that the baby would always come second. I don't know why I ever thought it might be otherwise.'

'Oh, and like you don't love being a photographer. But you get to be as happy and obsessed with your work as you want because you're a man.'

Luke presses his hands into the sides of his head, elbows all sharp angles. 'Stop spouting the feminist crap. I'm sick of hearing it.'

'Well, you stop spouting your parents' words!'

His hands fall back to his side, ball into fists. 'Fine. I'm tired of defending you to them anyway.'

I grit my teeth.

Luke's parents wish he'd married someone else, someone traditional, someone who would give up everything to become a mother. Someone who would put a baby over her career. It's a fight Luke and his parents keep having about me – which means it's a fight he and I keep having about us.

Last year when I found out I got tenure, I called Luke from

my office and he said all the right things, like how we would go out for drinks and dinner to celebrate. But when I got home, Luke was on the phone with his father. He didn't hear me come in.

'Yeah, Dad, I know, I know,' Luke was saying. 'But Rose . . .'

I stopped moving, the front door not quite shut. I held it open so it wouldn't make a noise and Luke would continue to think he was alone.

'Yes, I know, but Rose is coming around. She'll be fine once she has a baby.'

There was a long pause.

My chest hurt, my rib cage hurt, the heart behind it hurt. If there was a glass nearby, a plate, anything breakable, I would have picked it up and smashed it to the ground. I wanted to scream.

Finally, Luke spoke again. 'I know you think work will always come first, but I think a baby will change that.' Pause. 'I know you disagree, but I wish you'd give her more of a chance.' Pause. 'Dad, she gets tired of talking about it.' Another pause, then a heavy, frustrated sigh from Luke, followed by an angry outburst of, 'Dad, stop, please!'

A book fell from the lip of my overstuffed bag, hitting the floor with a heavy *clunk*.

'Rose?' Luke called out. 'Is that you?'

I shut the door with a loud slam, tried to make it seem like I was just arriving. 'Yup, I'm home! Ready for cocktails!'

'I've got to go, Dad,' he said. By the time I was one step into the living room, Luke had hung up and his phone was resting on the table.

He studied my face.

I studied his. Luke's cheeks were red.

'Hi.' I tried for a happy smile, to muster the excitement that had been bubbling through me all afternoon since I'd gotten my news. I wanted those feelings back. I felt cheated, my moment ruined by Luke's conversation with his father.

'How much of that call did you hear?' Luke asked.

I stopped with the false smile. 'Enough. Too much.'

'What do you think you heard?'

I set my bag onto a chair. 'Don't do that to me, Luke. I know what you guys were talking about.'

'Tell me.'

'It was yet another version of the conversation you keep having with your parents. That because I don't want a baby I'm a bad, deficient woman and always will be.'

'That is not what we were saying.'

'Right.'

'I also heard how my husband refuses to stand up to his parents and tell them to butt out of his marriage and stop maligning his wife!'

'I defended you.'

'Yeah, but why do you even need to? Why do your parents have a place in a conversation that has to do with our marriage? It's none of their business!'

'I'm doing my best! You know how strongly they feel and they're my parents and I love them!'

'Well, you know how strongly I feel and I'm your wife and I love *you*!' I yanked at the scarf around my neck and tossed it onto the table.

Luke took a breath, let it out. 'You know I love you, too.'

I kicked off my heels and they went clattering across the floor. 'You also told your parents that I changed my mind about having a baby.'

Luke picked up the scarf and began to fold it, pressing his hand along the delicate fabric. He'd given it to me as a gift the year before and it was my favorite. He held it out to me now. 'I was just trying to get them to back off,' he said quietly.

I didn't take it. Didn't move.

'Rose, please,' Luke said. 'Let's not do this tonight. We're supposed to be celebrating this amazing accomplishment in your life. Let's just go out.'

My eyes turned hard, everything about me grew harder and harder. My muscles, my cells, my limbs, my cheeks especially, calcifying as I stood there looking at my husband with something like hatred. Maybe it was hatred. The first ugly seeds of it. Seeds that would grow and grow like vines until we both suffocated. 'Somehow I don't feel like celebrating anymore, Luke.'

'Don't be like that.'

'What – a bad woman? A difficult woman? An *angry* woman?'

My voice, my tone, it rose until I was shrieking. What I wanted to do was stand there yelling. An endless cry of anger that would release the trapped feeling that imprisoned everything about my life. I wanted to let it out, exorcise it, but I didn't.

Instead, I stomped off to the bedroom like a petulant child, opening and slamming closet doors and drawers as I changed from my work clothes into sweats and those thick, ugly socks that are like slippers.

Congratulations to me, I raged.

*

'This is impossible,' Luke says now, breaking our silence. 'You're impossible.'

I watch as he passes me on his way out of the bedroom, hear his footsteps cross the living room, bare feet pattering against wooden planks. I listen as he opens the coat closet at the front of the apartment. On his way back his steps are trailed by the sound of wheels, low and constant. A suitcase.

He passes me a second time, suitcase dragging behind him, the biggest one we own, big enough for a dead body, we've always joked. He stops in front of the drawers where he keeps his clothing, folded, neat, organized, so unlike my drawers, which are overflowing, pajamas and bras balled up and mixed, a cocktail of silk and satin. He hoists the suitcase onto the bed, the rich sound of the zipper circling, followed by the slide and *thunk* of his hands pulling out a wooden drawer, hands that I once loved all over my skin but not in a long while, hands that are lifting tall stacks of T-shirts, jeans, boxers into the open roller bag. He empties a second drawer, then a third, socks, more boxers, followed by the closet full of shirts and sweaters, until there is no room left for any more clothing, for another piece of Luke. He has taken all that he can carry.

His gaze never meets mine.

My eyes drift to the photograph of me on Luke's bedside table. My head is thrown back, my mouth is open, and I am laughing. Snow sparkles across my thick gray sweater and throughout my dark hair – Luke had just surprised me with a snowball. He took that picture the day we got engaged. It's his favorite photo of me.

He doesn't touch it now, doesn't look at it.

I think about the other photos he's taken of me, of us, how he turned me from a person who hated having her picture taken, into one who is capable of enjoying it – well, as long as the picture is taken by him. I think about the very first time he took my photograph, how a photography session meant to last half an hour turned into an entire day spent together, a single day that extended into a lifetime of days. My rage, my anger, begins to melt.

I'd wanted a special gift for my parents for my graduation, something physical, something they could hang on the wall of the house, something that would create a conversation about my doctorate. I'd chosen Luke as the photographer because he was cheap, because he was close by my apartment. During our session, he and I got to talking. He was trying to make me relax for the camera, and eventually convinced me to tell him the real reason I started crying during our session.

So I told him.

I told Luke how, after defending my dissertation and having it bound, I'd presented my parents with a copy and they looked at it, read the title on the cover, and stopped there. How my mother said the right thing. 'Well, Rose, congratulations on such a big accomplishment! We have a doctor in the family!' But underneath her words, I could tell she wasn't sure what to make of the kind of doctor I'd become. How my parents struggled to understand why I'd wanted my PhD so badly when a college degree should have been plenty, especially since my carpenter father wasn't lucky enough to get even this. How even though my parents and I were close and even though we talked and saw each other regularly, grad school was something we didn't much

21

discuss. Whenever I brought up what I was studying, especially with my mother, she would listen with interest at first, but then her attention would fade and she would say something like, 'I don't even understand half of the words you're using, Rose' – embarrassment in her tone. I told Luke how much I loved my parents and how much they loved me back and how much I wanted us to connect on this thing that had become such an important part of who I am, and yet this connection had remained elusive. I wanted to bridge the distance between us, so here I was at his studio, getting pictures taken as though this would somehow erase the gap.

'I have an idea,' Luke said, when I arrived at the end of my story.

He took my doctoral gown and hung it up in a closet, set my cap on the chair, and asked me to take him to the university where I attended graduate school.

'Okay,' I said, thinking, *Why not?*

It was a fine afternoon, not great, a bit chilly and gray, but dry. Luke told me that clouds offered better lighting for photographs than sunlight. When we arrived on campus, I felt awkward taking him around.

'I want you to show me everything,' he assured me. 'Every classroom, your favorite spot in the library, your favorite bench on the quad, the room where you defended your dissertation. I want you to give me Rose's grand tour of her graduate experience and why she loved it so much.'

The longer we were there and the more we talked, the more I was able to forget that Luke was taking photographs. Our session lasted four hours and it turned into dinner afterward – my treat. I insisted.

There are photographs from that day of me walking down the hallway of my department, eyes glancing at the bookshelf that holds the faculty's monographs, of me hugging my dissertation inside the room where I defended it, of me searching for books in the sociology section of the library, talking to a few of my beloved professors, and a beautiful, happy photo of me and my dissertation director. They are goofy and fun and totally me. I couldn't even believe it when I saw them. Luke compiled the best ones into an album with an inscription that read: *To my parents, with love, Rose Napolitano, PhD* on the cover.

My mother and father sat down on the couch with the book perched between them. They asked me about every single photograph and I told them.

'Sweetheart, this one is my favorite,' my father said, pointing to the picture of me and my director. 'Maybe we can pull this one out and I can make a frame for it, so we can hang it in the living room.'

I took Luke out to dinner a second time to thank him for his hard work, for making something so special, for helping my parents better understand who their daughter had become. And because, well, I wanted to see him again. When I explained how much my parents loved the album, how they'd asked me so many questions about graduate school, Luke nodded.

'I've never been the biggest fan of portraits,' he said. 'I think the best photographs are the ones where we are just living and being in the places where we're most ourselves. And you are most yourself at your university, Rose.'

I looked at Luke right then. I loved him already.

*

23

Luke puts one last pair of jeans on top of everything else and zips the bag.

'Where are you going?' I manage. The words are dry and dusty in my throat. My body sags, everything hunching over toward the floor, shoulders curving, neck bent.

He is staring at his suitcase, at the shine of navy-blue vinyl. 'I can't, Rose. I just can't.'

'You can't what?'

'I can't stay. In this marriage.'

I straighten then, the movement sudden, knees, shoulders, the knobs of vertebrae along my spine, elbows tightening, wrists, fingers. 'You're leaving me over a bottle of vitamins?'

He turns to me, eyes sharp. I've seen this look many times in the last year. The look of righteousness, of determination, of tragedy for marrying a woman who refuses to have a child at all costs.

The cost, I see now, is him.

'No. I'm leaving you because I want a baby and you don't and I don't know how to fix this.'

'We used to understand each other,' I say, voice hollow. Defeated. 'You used to understand me.'

Luke swallows. Followed by a nearly imperceptible bob of his head.

He hefts the bag from the bed to the floor with a loud thud. Then he takes the handle, tips the suitcase, and wheels it past me and out of the bedroom.

I follow behind him, or I float, I'm not sure, my body, my brain, detached from each other. But I move, of this I am certain. I move as Luke moves, across the living room, past the long kitchen island we had built two years before because I love to cook, because I needed more room to chop and to prep.

Eventually Luke reaches the short hallway by the front door. He slips his feet into his shoes, reaches for the lock, turns it, a loud sharp note.

'Bye, Rose,' he says, his back to me, the light blue of his long-sleeved shirt the flag of surrender, signaling that this is the end. The battle over.

'Where are you going?' I ask one more time.

'It doesn't matter,' is all he says.

Then I watch as Luke walks out of the tall metal door of our apartment and it swings closed. I hear the sound of the latch clicking shut, listen to the elevator as it rises to our floor, the slide of it opening, Luke's footsteps entering it, the whirring of its descent to the lobby, followed by the quiet, by the unending silence. No more footsteps, no more whirring, no more suitcase wheels sliding along wooden planks and concrete hallways. This is the noise of being alone, of being left by one's husband, of being left to one's work. This is the sound of not being a mother, of refusing motherhood, the antinoise of my life to come. It is a long time before I am used to it.

4

September 22, 2004

Rose, Lives 1–9

'ROSE, THERE'S SOMETHING I want to talk to you about.'
Luke says this after popping a piece of tuna roll into his
mouth, chewing it, his chopsticks poised to pick up another. Tuna
rolls are his favorite. Spicy crunchy, not crunchy, inside out, outside
in. Luke will sometimes order only tuna rolls. 'One spicy, one
regular, another regular,' he'll say to the waiter. I always make fun
of him for it and then we laugh. It's one of those silly things you
end up loving about a person, just because they are also the person
whom you love more than anyone else in the world.

I am so absorbed in my own array of sushi – lots of salmon,
some eel, some yellowtail – that Luke's serious tone doesn't
register. 'You need to share some of that tuna with me,' I say,
distracted, chopsticks pointing at his food. 'You've got, like, twenty
of them.'

Luke picks up a spicy-crunchy roll and sets it down on my
plate. 'Rose, did you even hear what I said?'

I smile. 'Um, maybe?' I am relaxed, enjoying this celebratory

26

dinner. Last week, Luke had his first photograph picked up in newspapers across the country. Since then, invitations for higher-profile assignments have started pouring in. 'Sorry, what's on your mind?'

'I've been thinking a lot about children,' he says.

I jerk backward in my chair. 'Children?' I'm shocked, as if the mere mention of such creatures is like spotting a unicorn among the other diners. Unbelievable.

Luke sets his chopsticks across the tiny dish for soy sauce. 'Do you think you might ever change your mind about having one? You know, so we'd have something more in our lives aside from work and friends? I thought maybe we could – uh – talk about it again.'

The way he says this is bumpy, with the kind of wordiness that, if written by one of my students for a paper, I might flag and tell them to revise for clarity.

The worst part is I hate getting questions like this.

Luke knows how much I hate it.

Whenever I tell people I don't want children, that Luke and I don't plan to have any, people always give me this look. Then they'll say something condescending, like how I'll only discover my real purpose after I become a parent. As though we women are, by definition, just mothers-in-waiting. As though growing up into womanhood is simultaneous with growing up into motherhood, a kind of latent genetic condition that only shows up once a person reaches a certain age. Women eventually realize it's been there all along, it just hadn't presented itself yet.

It makes me so mad.

People never say things like that to Luke.

My eyebrows arch, I can feel them pulling upward into my forehead. 'Change my mind about a baby?' My voice rises an octave. 'Have you ever met me?' I laugh. My joke falls flat. Once again I notice how serious Luke is. 'Why, have *you* changed your mind about it?'

He takes a long time to respond. Enough for my stomach to be at sea, for me to set my chopsticks down too, but hastily, and one rolls off the table onto the floor. I don't bother to bend over and pick it up.

'Well, I've been thinking I might like us to have a baby,' Luke says.

My lips part. The breath coming in and out of me begins to dry out my tongue, my teeth. 'Might?'

He shrugs once. 'I worry that, as we get older, if we don't have one, we'll end up regretting it.' He says this slowly, pronouncing each syllable carefully.

The waiter breezes by and places another set of chopsticks on the table. My body heats up. I don't know what to say back to him. Or, I do know, but if I actually say it out loud, it will start a fight.

Though, when I see the sadness on my husband's face, I reach my hand across the table. 'You know how I feel about this, Luke. I don't want to end up arguing tonight.' I stare into his eyes. 'I love you so much.'

'Rose.' Luke sighs so heavily I think he might slump forward onto the table. 'I don't want to fight either.'

What I really meant was that I want this subject dropped. But what Luke understands seems to be something different.

'Can you just think about it? About having a baby? About changing your mind? Because back when we were dating and I told you I didn't want kids, I really believed it was true. It never occurred to me that my feelings might change. But then Chris had his baby,' Luke goes on, explaining how watching his best friend from college become a father really had an effect on him. 'And then, I've been doing those photo shoots for my other friends now that they're having kids. All I can think is what it would be like if I had a baby with you, Rose. Wouldn't it be amazing to meet our child? Don't you think we'd have this incredible baby together?'

No, no, no. Because I've never wanted a baby.

'Don't you want that, too?'

No. No way. Never.

I am trying so hard to hear my husband, to consider his arguments about why he's changed his mind. And his arguments seem totally reasonable. They *are* reasonable. I can understand how you might believe one thing in your twenties and realize you believe something else entirely as life moves forward.

The problem, of course, is that Luke needs me to see his reasons in such a way that I will go back on all of my reasons that tell me to do the opposite. That for Luke to fulfill his new hope of having children, I need to become the person who has the children for him.

I should have known this conversation was coming. There'd been signs before tonight. They were practically flashing. But what had I done? I'd closed my eyes to them, that's what. But then, the shift in him had been gradual, too. Subtle enough that it allowed me to live in denial – so that's what I did. What I'd been doing for a while now. Luke would raise the subject of children indirectly, angle it far enough away from our potential reality that I could decide to ignore it – and I did. But it was like someone deciding that if they just ignored the cancer spreading through their body, then it wouldn't kill them.

I remember when Luke and I were walking hand in hand through Trastevere, in Rome. We were on a much-needed vacation. Restaurants with lovely outdoor terraces lined the streets around us, people were drinking wine and eating delicious plates of pasta. It was hot out, humid, but I didn't care. Luke and I kept bumping into each other, in that pleasant way couples do when they are strolling along, not in a rush, enjoying the afternoon.

The apartment where we were staying was tiny, high up on the rooftop of a building. It was practically all terrace and we loved it. We'd been married for a few years by then and it was nice for us to have this break from work, to do nothing other than relax on the terrace with books and magazines, eating and drinking all afternoon until we were stuffed and dizzy with satisfaction. Earlier that same day, I'd been lounging outside in the shade, reading a mystery, when Luke came out to join me. The kiss he gave me turned into a make-out session that turned into a lovemaking session. At first, we worried that someone would see us, but then we abandoned caring whether they did.

It made me feel like we were on our honeymoon again.

'We should do that more,' I said to him as we wandered the street. Luke and I hadn't been like this in a long time. I was thinking about how this was exactly why we'd come on this trip, to reconnect, to make love in the middle of the day if we felt like it – so that maybe we *would* feel like it. 'We should do that, like, every afternoon that we are here.'

Luke's eyes gleamed. 'The neighbors might not like that.'

'We can be discreet. We were discreet!'

'We'd need to be more discreet,' Luke said, but I could tell that he liked my suggestion. That he loved it.

We looked at a menu posted outside of a restaurant, read it, moved on, considered another. My stomach was already growling for my afternoon dish of pasta, my throat thirsty for the wine we would drink.

Then, 'Look at that,' Luke said. He was pointing at a group of children, all of them boys, maybe seven or eight years old, playing soccer in the middle of the street. 'Kids don't do that in the US anymore, really. Play like that.'

'I guess not,' I said.

I didn't say anything else.

Luke stopped in front of a bench. 'Do you want to sit?'

'Sure,' I said, though what I really wanted to do was eat.

A low current of anxiety had entered my bloodstream the moment Luke began talking about the boys playing soccer. His parents had been pressuring him about us having children by then – and the more he tried to put them off, the more they took it upon themselves to pressure him. For a while he'd been complaining to me about it, how annoying they were being, but then his reports about these conversations stopped. At first, I assumed he'd gotten through to them, that they'd given up and finally decided to respect our decision not to have children – they'd known we didn't want them from the beginning, from even before Luke and I had gotten married.

What neither one of us had realized at the time, was that Luke's parents hadn't believed we meant what we said. They believed that we would change our minds. I think Luke's mom,

Nancy, assumed I would be the one to start clamoring for a baby, and she'd try to work on me when we'd visit. But I would shut her down, explain to her – forcefully, vehemently – no, *no*, this was not up for discussion. When I didn't budge, she and her husband, Joe, went to work on their son instead.

At first, this was a relief. I thought that I'd rather Luke be the person who was subject to their treatises about the joys of having children. But after a while I began to wonder if all of their arguments and pressure were actually starting to change his mind.

He started pointing out the children he'd notice around us, their parents, what they did, how they interacted, commented on them, trying to get me to comment back. Trying to start a conversation about children, raising children, how parents raise their children. Did I think they were happy about their children? How their children were behaving? Did I agree with the way they were talking to their children, allowing their children to act?

I could feel Luke fishing inside of me when he did this, dropping the line straight into my own body, my brain, trying to see what he might pull out of me. I didn't like him prodding, poking around in this place that already felt settled with that sharp hook. I was hoping that if I didn't really respond, eventually he would realize he wasn't getting anywhere with me. I was determined to believe that Luke wouldn't do this to me.

The two of us sat on that bench for a long time, Luke watching the children play soccer, me observing the adults at the restaurants as they sipped their wine, ate their pasta. I tried to stop the sinking feeling inside of me, but then a mother would walk by with a baby strapped to her chest, and then another, this time holding two children, one in each hand. Suddenly mothers and babies were everywhere. I closed my eyes.

'Would you rather raise a child here than in the US?' Luke was asking. 'You know, if you were going to have a child? In theory?'

Every time he did something like this, the effect on me was immediate – I would shut down completely, our afternoon of lovemaking erased, replaced by an urge to put my arm out, warding Luke off. Didn't he realize how it pushed me away? That the one reason we didn't have more afternoons of joyful sex was because of this? Why didn't he notice how distant it was making me? What he was doing to me – to us?

I shook my head at him but didn't say what I was really thinking. *No, because I don't want to raise a child in either place and you know that because I don't want a child, period.*

'Maybe if we left the city it would be different,' Luke went on. 'Easier. You know, like if we lived in one of the towns where you and I grew up.'

Still no. 'Hmmm.'

I refused to give any real reply. Luke knew how I felt and it didn't need repeating. Or at least, I thought it didn't.

I guess I thought wrong.

'I'm not sure if photography is enough for me in life,' Luke says. 'You know?'

I am nodding on the outside. But inside I've been shaking my head back and forth this entire time: *No, no, no. I do not know.* And, *I thought I was enough for you, Luke.*

Luke's face opens up, it *lights* up. He seems to breathe again.

'I'm so glad you understand, Rose. That you'll try to be open about this.'

My eyes are wide. 'Fine. Fine,' I say stupidly. 'I'll think about it,' I say. *No. No. Never.*

'Thank you,' he says, finishing his last piece of tuna. '*Thank you.*'

Meanwhile, my sushi has remained untouched. I nod again, but barely. I almost can't move. I think I might vomit.

'So you think you have a good shot at this grant, huh?' he asks happily, switching topics. 'That's so great!'

I search for words. Eventually I find them. 'Yes. It seems like it. It would be great.' I am robotic.

Our conversation continues, stilted on my side, Luke having to do all the work of maintaining it. After we pay our check and go home to our apartment, Luke chatters on about work, about a trip to Boston he'll leave for at the end of the week, about how much he truly loves the tuna at that restaurant, how the fish is always so fresh.

'Rose, I'm so glad we talked,' he says as we get into bed.

I stare at him, can see the corner of the photograph he keeps of me on the table next to his side, the arc of his prone body slicing my happy face at an angle. He waits for me to say something. That I agree with him, I suppose. Once again, all I can manage is a slight nod before I turn out the light. My eyes remain open in the darkness. I feel alone even with Luke lying next to me. As though our future is determined, as though he and I have already disappointed each other and he is already gone.

5

February 2, 2007
Rose, Life 1

'PROFESSOR NAPOLITANO?'
'Yes?' I halt the putting away of papers and books and look up from the desk at the front of my classroom. I've just finished teaching a course on feminist methodologies in sociology. Twenty students are enrolled, nearly all of them women, eager, engaged, earnest. Sometimes I want to gather them into a huddle to shout words of encouragement and fortitude before I let them back into the less sincere world outside the classroom doors.

My student, Jordana, is standing before me, speaking. 'I was wondering what you thought of . . .'

I hear her words but I also don't hear them, not enough to grasp their meaning. I am thinking about Luke, our marriage, how he still hasn't returned home and how this fact is always looming the moment my class ends, the moment any distraction is over. I am always thinking about this.

Jordana's brow furrows as she waits for my answer, but I have no idea what she's asked me. Her wide, owl eyes are big behind the equally large frames of her glasses.

'Professor?'

I turn toward the windows of the classroom to break the stare, to collect myself. The bare branches of a maple tree, once red with fall, press against the glass, the gray gloom of rain clouds fill the rest. Jordana's father died last year. I remember when it happened, how I could see it in her eyes afterward, his death, like a pinprick at their very center. Grief, loss, pain, the endurance of it.

I force myself to look at her again. There it is, I can still see it. The sadness. A permanent addition, even when Jordana is caught up in other things, like our class.

Do I have that on my face, too?

'Are you okay?' she asks me.

I open my mouth, close it. I don't know what to say.

Professor Napolitano is not okay. Professor Napolitano goes back to her office after class each day, shuts the door softly, and cries at her desk. She's taken to keeping large boxes of tissues hidden in its deep drawers. No, not those perky, square, small boxes of tissues designed for amateur hour. We're talking the long, rectangular, industrial-sized boxes that should come with large-print instructions on the side: *The perfect accompaniment for when your husband leaves you.*

'Jordana, you are sweet to ask how I am. But I am fine.' *I am not. Not at all.* 'Really. Thank you. Now what were you saying before?'

*

36

Later that afternoon, I am sitting in my office, reading through student essays, trying my best to focus, when Luke's number comes up on my phone.

I pick up quickly. 'Hi,' I say, barely a whisper.

'Hi, Rose,' he says, just as softly.

'How are you doing?' I ask him.

'I'm doing all right. How are *you*?'

I hesitate. Then, 'I miss you,' I say.

'I know.' He hesitates. Then, 'I miss you, too.'

'You do?'

There is silence at the other end.

And I wait. I wait for Luke to tell me yes. Yes, Rose, I miss you so much. Yes, Rose, I've realized I can't live without you. Yes, Rose, I'm coming home, I can't wait another day. I want Luke to change back into the man he used to be, the man who only needed me and not a baby, too, the man I thought I married. I want this so badly. So I keep waiting for him to come back to me, the Rose he used to love so much. I'm still here, I'm right here.

Last August, after Luke walked out of our apartment, I went through all the motions of starting school for the semester, preparing my syllabi, making sure to get them copied before the first day of classes, when the copy machine inevitably breaks, then breaks again. I began teaching, kept teaching, commuting from our empty apartment to my office and back home each night to go to bed alone. Then this January, I did it all again. Wrote my syllabi, got them copied. Still hoping that Luke and I could find a way through. February has begun, another new month, and we haven't found that way. Not yet.

On so many occasions I've gone back to our fight and those vitamins, rerunning it in my head, each time doing something slightly different, which always provokes a slightly different outcome. Most of these outcomes involve Luke staying. But in nearly all of my replays the reason Luke stays, the reason he comes around, is because I capitulate. I say I'm sorry, that I'll take the vitamins, that I'll have the baby he dreams of us having.

But would I? Would I really? Would I do that to myself in exchange for having my husband home again?

Maybe. Maybe I would. Maybe I should.

Luke's reply finally comes after a long wait and a heavy sigh. 'There's something I need to tell you, Rose.'

My stomach plummets. His words are nearly the same ones he used when he first confessed to me that he wanted a baby. The sound of his voice – gentle but firm, sad but determined – scares me. I can't speak. I know this voice. It's *that* voice. The voice he uses to break things to me.

Then Luke says, 'I met someone. I'm dating.'

'Dating?' This simple word, uttering it, lodges a great steel ball in my neck.

'Yes.'

'Who?'

'It doesn't matter who.'

'How doesn't it matter? Are you in love with her?' The ball squeezes up into the back of my throat.

'Rose, I don't know. But what I do know is that I want a baby just as much as you don't want one. And I want to find some-one who wants to have that baby with me. And this person wants one.'

'But—'

'You don't really want a baby and we both know it,' Luke says. 'It would make you unhappy. You said it yourself a million times.'

He's right. I did say it. At least a million times.

I start to cry.

Luke does, too. I can hear him on the other end of the line.

'But I said all of that before I knew it would mean I would lose you.' I whisper this. I can hear Luke breathing, thinking.

'I know you don't believe me right now, but one day you are going to wake up and be glad that I left.' Luke's tone is regretful. He sniffles. 'I'm not good for you. I haven't been good for you in a long time. You're going to be okay. We both are.'

'No.'

'Yes.'

'I'll never be glad that you left,' I say after a long silence. 'We're the loves of each other's lives. We've known this since the moment we met.'

'Yes,' he says, his own voice cracking. 'I'd always thought that, too. You know I did.'

Thought. Did. Past tense.

'I don't want to let go, Luke.'

'I don't want to either. But I have to. And I am.'

Part Two

Enter More Roses,
Lives 2 & 3

6

August 15, 2006

Rose, Life 2

L UKE IS STANDING on my side of the bed. He never goes
to my side of the bed. In his hand is a bottle of prenatal
vitamins. He holds it up.

He shakes it, a plastic rattle.

The sound is heavy and dull because it is full.

'You promised,' he says.

'Sometimes I forget,' I admit. I take a step closer to him.

Luke's shoulders slump. 'Rose. You *promised*.'

'I know I did.'

'Then why aren't you taking them?'

'I do take them. Just not every day.'

Luke shakes the bottle again. 'It's nearly full.' He opens it,
peers inside.

I walk over to the bed and sit down on the edge of it, a heap
of exhausted wife, the question of my future motherliness always
looming, ever on the horizon. The wooden planks of the floor
shine in the light. 'I guess I only take them once in a while.'

Luke pads over to the bed, sits down next to me, the mattress dipping under his weight and pulling us toward each other. 'I thought we were going to try to do this, Rose.'

'I said I'd take the vitamins. That's all I said.'

'But I thought it meant you were open to the possibility of a baby.'

'I was trying to be open.'

Luke eyes me. I can feel his gaze, warm on my already warm face.

'I was trying for *you*,' I clarify. 'And then I stopped trying.'

'Why didn't you tell me?'

I blink. A tuft of Luke's hair is sticking up in this way I've always loved. The sight of it hurts my heart. I want to smooth it down as I've also always loved to do. But I don't do it. Not now. 'I was afraid to tell you. I knew you'd be upset. I was worried what you would say.'

The sigh from Luke is heavy, long, and something else. Accepting? Frustrated? Despairing? The bottle of vitamins is cradled between his palms. 'What do we do now?' he asks.

'I don't know.'

'Yes, you do.'

This time it's easy to detect what's in my husband's voice: anger, sarcasm.

'Don't be like that,' I say.

'Don't be like what?' he snaps.

And suddenly I am divided, a woman, a wife, torn in two. One side of me wants to snatch the bottle from his hand and throw it with all my might against the wall. But the other wants to fix this unfixable thing growing between us, this chasm that neither Luke nor I have found a way to cross since it began to open.

One side wins out over the other.

I reach over and take Luke's hand in mine and I can feel it, how the second we touch, the second that *I* touch *him*, his anger retreats.

Hope, a small surge of it, flows between us.

'Do not think I'm going to come around.' I told Luke this for what felt like the thousandth time. By then, we'd been dating for more than a year. 'I've never wanted children and I'm not going to change my mind.' I wanted this to be clear – unmistakably, irrevocably clear.

We were at Luke's parents' house. Upstairs in the little guest room that doubles as an office. This was not my first visit, and each time we returned my relationship with Luke seemed a little more serious, a little closer to forever. Luke and I were about to go down to dinner that night, which would be fun and wonderful because that was back when his parents liked me.

'I don't want children, either,' Luke said. He, too, had told me this many times before.

'But you have to mean it.'

'I do mean it!'

'Do you?'

'Yes. Stop doubting me, Rose. It's annoying.' He wore a pained expression. 'Besides, photography is important to me. If we had a child, maybe I'd have to do something else. Making ends meet as a photographer is tough enough – you know that.'

'That would be unacceptable,' I said. 'You changing jobs.'

'Yes, which is why you need to stop warning me about the kids thing. You have to trust me.'

Luke and I were standing in the small, carpeted space between the big desk and the pull-out bed. I didn't want this to turn into a fight, but whenever I brought this subject up, something else would take over, this surge of anger would rise and tighten in my throat, until I spit it out. 'It's not that I doubt you, Luke. But I know from years of being me that whenever I tell people I don't want children, no one believes me. It's like *The* fucking *Yellow Wall-Paper*, where nobody trusts what women say!'

'Rose, don't get frustrated—'

'People actually have the gall to tell me that maybe I haven't met the right person yet, if I don't want to have a baby with you! But I am one-hundred-percent certain that I am not having a baby *and* that you are still the right person for me!'

Luke's face reddened in this way that meant he was happy. 'I am the right person for you,' he said. A statement, a declaration full of confidence.

We were both so confident.

'You are,' I told him. 'You are the only right person.'

'That's all that matters,' he said, smiling. Beaming.

Which made me beam, too.

He slipped his arms around my waist. I gazed up at him. If only I had known how easily adoration could turn to resentment. Would that have helped us? Or would that have stopped us from getting married at all?

'I love you so much,' I said, just as his mother was calling us to dinner.

We were engaged two days later.

If only. If *only*.

If only love was all that mattered.

Stupid. We were so stupid.

Or was it simply me who was stupid? Why should Luke believe me about what I wanted when no one else ever does? Why should he be the one exception?

Luke leans all the way down and places the bottle of vitamins on the floor, in the space between the bed and the wall. It looks strange there, out of place. Lonely. 'This is my fault,' he says.

'What is?'

'I promised you.'

My eyes land on Luke's profile, his cheek, the one eye that I can see. *You did, Luke. You did promise.* 'You promised what?' I ask. Am I a terrible person to want my husband to say it out loud? To remind himself and me about all those talks we had before we got engaged?

'I promised you I didn't want children. That I understood that you weren't going to come around after we were married.'

I am perfectly still as I wait, holding my breath, needing Luke to say more, to keep going, to arrive back in the place where we used to be, the place where this marriage began and where we agreed that I did not have to become a mother for this relationship to work, and he did not have to become a father for it to work, either.

'And I know it isn't fair that I've asked you to change your mind,' he says. 'But I've gone and done it anyway, and it's destroying us.'

The word *destroying* makes me flinch. I turn away from Luke, eyes down, and they catch sight of the lonely bottle, that little plastic island adrift and vulnerable. I could reach out a toe and kick it over, capsize it.

'Do you think we're destroyed?' I ask in a whisper.

Luke is silent a long time. Too long. Enough that my back begins to curve, vertebra by vertebra, folding over into a slump. Luke turns, stretches his arm, reaching for the frame sitting atop his bedside table. He returns with it, with the photograph of me that he keeps there, and holds it between us.

Is this a taunt? A prop for pointing out all that we've lost? My stomach clenches. Is this the moment when Luke and I break up, even though when we married we told each other that one of the best parts of getting married was knowing that we'd never have to go through a breakup again?

Then, 'No,' Luke says. 'I don't think we're destroyed.'

I turn to him, to that profile I've always admired, the way his forehead curves just so, toward the gentle slope of his nose. 'No?'

He shakes his head. His eyes are on me and they are full of pleading. 'I'm sorry, Rose. Can you ever forgive me? Can you be patient while I try to work my way back to the place I used to be about kids?' His gaze drops to the photograph of me. He runs a finger along the edge of the frame – lovingly, longingly. 'Maybe it's my turn to come around again – not yours?'

I am nodding as Luke is saying these things. A tear runs down my left cheek. 'Yes, I can. I can do all of that. I can be patient. I love you. I love you so much.'

He turns back to me. 'I love you, too, Rose.'

Then he sets the frame to the side and his arms are around me and we are in the tightest embrace we've managed in ages. That tiny surge of hope I felt a moment ago widens into a river.

7

December 20, 2012

Rose, Life 3

'ADDIE, PULL UP your little stool.'

I watch as my four-year-old daughter, determined, serious, goes over to the wall where her special cooking chair lives, right next to the shelf crammed with books and novels and where a mess of magazines is piled and teetering. She drags the chair made especially for her by my father over to the island – a slow tug of bright-pink-painted wood, her favorite color no matter how many times Luke and I have tried to convince her that blues and greens and lavenders are just as nice as the fuchsias and pastels she's always gravitated toward. Her hair shines in the overhead light – it's dark brown like mine, a halo of wild frizz like Luke's. I resist the urge to run my hand through it, because I know she'll give me a big, protesting *Mommy!* The longing to touch her is sometimes overwhelming.

A big, heavy bag of flour is waiting for us on the counter, the canister of warm water, the eggs at room temperature.

'Okay, Mommy,' she says. 'Ready.'

Addie places her small, chubby hands – less chubby every day – onto the wooden island. It's early, so early that Luke is still sleeping, and Addie and I are both in our pajamas. Hers are dotted with pink giraffes because she loves giraffes. Every time she sees a giraffe on television she squeals and laughs. There are giraffes all over her bedroom, even a great tall one whose neck serves as a coatrack. Her grandma, Luke's mother, got it for her fourth birthday in March. Christmas music plays softly in the background. Addie's expression is one of deep concentration, brown eyes focused, little red lips pursed, breaths audible through her nose.

She is such a serious child.

Just hear those sleigh bells jinga-ling.

'Do you remember what we do first, little Gnocchi?' My mother gave Addie this nickname and it stuck.

'We have to, we have to make, the *well*.' Addie's voice, sharp and small, carefully enunciating each word.

'Yes, good! And how are we going to do that?'

She leans over the counter as far as she can, reaching for the bag of flour. Before she can knock it over I shift it closer. She sticks a hand inside and it comes up coated in white, clutching a fist of flour that she dumps onto the counter. She promptly begins swirling it like she's seen me do a hundred times. I reach my hand in the bag, grab some more flour, and sprinkle it onto the counter, which prompts Addie to give me a look – NO.

'I can *do* it, Mommy.'

'I know you can. All right.' I raise my floured hands and back away, cracking up as she earnestly works to ready the space where we'll make the pasta dough. Back and forth, back and forth she goes, painstakingly slow, adding more and more flour until there is a mountain, peaked at the top. *Jack Frost nipping at your nose*, Frank Sinatra sings, providing the sound track to Addie's process.

I've never been a patient person, one of the realities I thought would make me a terrible mother. But it's strange, the resources you discover inside yourself when suddenly there is a child and she is yours. When you become a parent, everything about who you are, your personality, sense of self, your body, it's as though it's been shaken up and fizzed, but it never settles back to what it once was. If anyone else was taking this long to get enough flour from the bag to make the pasta dough, I would have shoved them aside and finished the work myself. But because it's Addie, I can stand here in my Doctor Chef apron that Luke gave me last Christmas and watch her doing the smallest, most insignificant things as though I have endless patience available.

'All right, Ms. Gnocchi, I think that's enough flour. Good job! Now let Mommy shape the well.'

Everybody knows a turkey and some mistletoe.

'I wanna help.'

'You can definitely help.' I lift her up – she's getting so heavy – and dangle her above this Mount Everest of flour. 'Now take both hands, flat, Addie, flat, yes, like that, and press down so the flour starts to spread out. Just like that! You're doing it. Now the sides. Okay! Now I'm going to put you back on your chair and I'm going to do the rest.'

'But—'

'Gnocchi dumpling, you need to be a good watcher of Mommy

so next time you can try this part on your own, all right?' Referring to myself in the third person, as Mommy – check that off as yet another item on the list of things I said I would never do in my lifetime.

Addie sighs, long, breathy. Nods her head.

I go to work, salvaging the pasta making from Addie's lopsided efforts, and Addie's favorite Christmas song comes on. 'Addie, can you sing with me? *Ohhh, way up North where the air gets cold!*'

'But what if we wake up Daddy?' Addie interrupts, but she's smiling, liking the thought of being loud in the morning when people are still sleeping.

'Oh, don't worry about Daddy. He won't wake up,' I say. 'He could sleep through a bomb going off.'

Luke is a good father – he is.

Or, he tries to be. He means to be.

But strangely, Luke, who so desperately, pleadingly wanted a child, isn't the man I expected him to be now that we have that child. I mean, I love him, he's wonderful, cheerful mostly, works hard, but he's not available that much, not really.

Practically every morning since Addie was born, I've had to battle to get Luke out of bed, battle to get him to help me with her.

'Luke – *Luke*,' I'll say, followed by a big, frustrated inhale. '*Luke!*' This will be me, next, shrieking in his ear, using both hands to shake him awake, wishing I had one of those air horns people use at football games.

'Hmmm.' This will be Luke, nearly always, unable to open his eyes, comatose, blissfully unaware that there is a baby in our house, a baby who would soon become a toddler and who by now had become a vibrant, talkative little nursery school student, a child who isn't going away, ever, who needs our care and attention, who will *always* need our care and attention.

Back when I finally agreed I'd try to get pregnant, Luke and I said we'd split the duties. Luke promised he'd do more than his share to compensate for the fact that I would have to bear the child no matter which way we tried it. He was going to make it up to me, he swore.

But no one and nothing can prepare you for the reality of that first year. The woman does it all. I mean, it's your body, and this sets the tone for everything to come. All those months of pregnancy, the chaos of the birth, the intense, blaring blur of it, followed by the unforgiving reality that you've just endured the most major physical trauma a woman can experience in a lifetime and pretty much the second it's over, you're responsible for taking care of this helpless person who wants to *feed off you.*

I insisted that I was not, was never going to breast-feed. Luke and I fought about this endlessly. Luke gave me every argument from every magazine and newspaper he could find as to why breast-feeding was essential, was practically criminal not to do. I was like, nope, no way, I don't care, our child will live. Luke and I were both formula babies and we've managed fine. But when I saw Addie, even after all that craziness – emergency C-section after twenty hours of labor – I had this weird, unexpected urge to do it. Who would have thought?

Maybe if I hadn't had that moment when I first looked into Addie's perfect little scrunched-up face, which led me to agree to breast-feed, Luke and I would have figured out the fifty-fifty thing. But I did have that moment and we didn't figure out the fifty-fifty thing and Luke is, well, a good dad, but not as good as I thought he would be.

Soon after Addie was born, he started going on so many work trips. When I commented on this, he laughed and said, 'No, I'm not. You're imagining things, Rose. It's probably the lack of sleep.' Then he came over to where I stood in front of the stovetop, supervising the broccoli and garlic simmering in the pan, and kissed my neck. 'I love you, you know. So much.'

'I love you, too,' I said back, because I did and I do. But it wasn't just lack of sleep. I knew he was taking more trips than he used to.

When I confronted him about this again a few months later, his reply was less loving.

'Not everyone gets promotions every time they publish something,' he snapped. 'I'm trying to provide for us, all right?'

'I know you work hard,' I said. 'But I'd rather have you home with us. It's not easy being with Addie on my own.'

He opened his mouth to say something else, but then he seemed to change his mind. 'You're so good with her, though. Better than I am.' He laughed, but it was a sad laugh.

'Luke,' I protested, my frustration ebbing, 'you're great with Addie. You *are*.' *When you're around*, I added privately.

'I try,' he said.

Not enough. 'And it's not a competition. You just need to be with us more. You need to be with *me* more.' I couldn't resist adding this. 'You and I barely spend any time together alone lately.'

He didn't respond. Instead, he said, 'I'm going down to the deli to buy some bagels. Want anything?'

I shook my head.

He walked away, grabbed his coat, and left.

I went into the bedroom, and stared for a very long time at the two photographs that live on Luke's bedside table – the one that has been there forever of me laughing in the snow, now joined by a second one, far more recent, of Addie and me laughing in the snow. A matching set. Luke looks at them before bed each night. He says it makes him content with the life that he's living, reminds him of all that is good. Seeing those photos helps me to remember that I have a husband who loves us as best he can.

Later that same night, Luke apologized, said that he would try to be home more. The next day he came home bubbly with excitement, a great bouquet of peonies, my favorite flowers, in his hand. He kissed me and explained that he had arranged for his parents to babysit for the weekend, that he was taking me somewhere special, just the two of us. He'd realized we hadn't had a weekend away since Addie was born and we needed one. That it would be good for us to go away, to be Rose and Luke again, not Rose and Luke and Addie.

Yes, I thought. *Yes.*

The little inn where we stayed was right on the water and our room had a view, so close to the ocean it was like the waves were next to us the entire time. We sat at the bar like adults who weren't parents, sipping our wine, chatting, laughing like old times; ate a wonderful, long, and luxurious dinner; and then went back to bed and made love with the kind of freedom we used to enjoy before we had Addie – freedom from the worry of being interrupted, of making too much noise. I remembered the things I used to love about the man I married, things that parenthood can make a person lose sight of. I think he remembered all those things about me, too. I hope that he did.

Luke's parents didn't call us, not once.

'You two have a good time,' Luke's mother, Nancy, said to me, when we were leaving.

I was so grateful to her that I did something I hadn't done in years – I hugged her. Nancy gasped when my arms went around her small frame, obviously surprised. Then she hugged me back, hard.

I never quite recovered from the way Luke's parents treated me when I was resisting having kids. We manage now because they are Addie's grandparents, but Addie aside, my relationship with them is shrimp cocktail at best – chilled and not as good as you hope it will be.

And yet, in that moment I felt such a surge of warmth at this spark of generosity in my parents-in-law that I couldn't help myself and I hugged Luke's father, Joe, too.

This made Luke start off our weekend smiling. It was always a hard thing between us, my anger at his parents, 'my refusal to forgive', as Luke put it, even as he failed to notice their continued awkwardness around me.

Our weekend only got better from there.

When things get hard, I try to remember our time away at that inn on the ocean; as it becomes more and more impossible to get Luke up from the bed to take Addie to the park like he promised. I tell myself that all it takes is one weekend away to fix everything. Poof!

*

The doorbell rings.

'Who is it, Mommy?'

Addie and I are covered in flour, sticky with dough, on our hands, our forearms. There's even some on Addie's cheeks and in her hair. She looks as though she's been rolling on the countertop. 'You stay here,' I tell her. 'Don't touch anything.'

We've just broken the well, which is a tricky moment in the pasta-making process. Meanwhile, Mariah Carey is belting out my favorite Christmas tune. I am singing to it as I wash my hands in the sink – it's not easy to remove pasta dough. I'll find it dotting my forearms, my neck, my foot, later tonight when I'm going to bed.

The bell rings again, then again. 'I'm coming, I'm coming!' I call out. I shut the faucet and dry my still-caked hands. Bits of dough are stuck to my palms, my fingers, peeling halfway off, like zombie skin.

'Maybe it's Christmas presents,' Addie says, sounding hopeful. She is standing on her little chair, bouncing her bum to Mariah. Luke and I managed to convince Addie that sometimes Santa sends his helper-delivery-people early with gifts. They can't dress up as elves because they need to disguise themselves as UPS workers.

My best friend, Jill, a psychology professor at my university, is standing outside my apartment when I open the door, holding a big brown shopping bag. 'I was trying to call you but you weren't picking up!' She takes in my flour-covered self, my apron, and adds, 'Doctor Chef!'

'I have my phone on silent.'

She heads inside and immediately puts on the slippers she keeps at the apartment for her visits. 'Oooh, Mariah Carey! My favorite! *I just want you for my own, more than you could ever know!*'

I follow her, cracking up at her off-key singing, loud and exuberant. 'Besides, I'm not exactly in a position to touch anything,' I say, but Jill's not really listening.

She drops the bag onto the kitchen table. 'Hello, my little Gnocchi,' she cries, giving Addie a big squeeze, mess and all, producing a squeal of laughter from her. Jill doesn't have any children. She's like me, she doesn't want any. Like I *used* to be. 'Sorry to interrupt the cooking extravaganza, but I have important business with your mom.' Jill gives Addie a noisy kiss on the cheek, followed by a little hip bump to the music, and turns to me. 'Where's Luke? Still asleep?'

'Where else?' I watch as Jill starts taking things out of the bag. She's dancing as she does it. A box of donuts. Chocolates. A buttery bag of croissants from my favorite bakery.

'What is this?' I ask. 'A party?' Next comes the fresh orange juice, followed by champagne. Something jolts inside me. 'What is going on?'

'You haven't been online this morning. Checked your email?'

'No. Tell me.'

Jill is grinning. She opens the orange juice.

'Oh my God, did I get it, did I, did I?'

There is a pause from Jill, she drumrolls the countertop. Then, 'You did! You got the grant! The list of recipients went up online this morning!'

'No fucking way!' I am shouting. Then I clamp a hand over my mouth when Addie's head snaps toward me. 'Wow, wow, wow! That's so amazing! Holy shit!'

'Mommy!'

'Sorry, sweetie. It won't happen again.'

Jill points the champagne bottle away from herself, and expertly pops the cork, the noise provoking a sharp cry of surprise from Addie. I pull down three glasses from the cabinet. Probably a bad idea to give Addie a flute, but I can't help myself and besides, hers will only have juice. I place them in a row on the flour-covered island and Jill gets busy pouring our mimosas.

'Is that soda?' Addie asks, referring to the champagne. She's leaning forward, studying the bottle intently.

'It's Mommy soda,' Jill says.

'Ohhh.' Addie sounds disappointed. Childhood is full of terrible disappointments, an ongoing series of nos – no, you can't have this or that, or say this or that, or do this or that. Addie is always bemoaning this, and pointing it out to us. *Why is the answer always no?* she asks. I used to ask that, too, my mother likes to remind me. It drove her crazy, too, she'll say, with a great satisfied grin on her face.

Jill picks up her flute from the other side of the island, the half-made pasta dough a great heap between us amid an explosion of flour. 'To you, Rose!'

I pick up my glass, help Addie raise hers. She teeters a bit, tipping the long stem, juice splashing onto the counter.

'Woohoo!'

Addie adds her laughter to our toast.

We clink glasses. More of Addie's juice spills onto the island, this time a bit onto the pasta dough, and I don't even mind. The fizz of the champagne bubbles out through my fingertips and down through my toes.

'And to the little Gnocchi!' I nudge Addie. 'That's you, sweet thing.'

She smiles, bits of caked, cracking pasta dough falling off her cheeks.

I give her a big noisy raspberry on her forehead.

'Mommy!' she protests, and wiggles away.

If you had asked me five years ago what would happen if I had a child, I would have said that having a baby is a career killer. It's true, the first year I thought I would never feel rested again. I was so tired all the time.

Then one night, a few months into the long hallucination that was Addie's first year, I couldn't get back to sleep after nursing. I opened my laptop and just started writing. What came out was all of my anxiety about becoming a mother after being resistant for so long. Did the *before* make me a bad mother? Did the *before* matter now that I was firmly in the after? Did people judge me harder, view me with more suspicion? Did they worry for my tiny daughter, that her mother might be unfit? *Was* I unfit? Were there other reluctant mothers in the world like me, who felt similar worries, or was I all alone?

Jill came over one evening, promising not to notice the spit-up on my sweater, bearing wine, whiskey for after the wine, and snacks. I'd pumped ahead of time, done the good-mommy thing, so I could drink with her. I'd gleefully ordered wine at dinner while I was pregnant – just one glass but I stared back at people's judgmental looks with a defiant smile on my face. Luke and I fought about that, too. His parents threw fits. Their fits and everyone's dirty looks only made me want to get a second glass and follow it up with a shot of tequila.

I explained to Jill that I'd been writing a little, but only a list of anxious questions. I told her about how I wondered if I was the only one who felt like this – that because I hadn't wanted a baby, that it was inevitable I'd do a bad job raising Addie.

Jill's eyes lit up. 'Well, Professor Napolitano, why don't you try to find that out?'

'What?'

'Those sound like really good study questions, Rose.'

'They do?' I asked, my reflexes dulled by exhaustion. Then that old feeling, the one that always reminded me of why I'd gone and gotten my PhD, suddenly it was there again, faint yet familiar. Exciting. 'Oh my God, those questions could ground a study. They *are* a study!'

Jill was nodding.

She was right.

That night felt like ages ago, and it was. It took me a long time to get that grant proposal together, longer than normal. But I did it. And now, here I am in my kitchen celebrating, drinking champagne and shoveling donuts and chocolates into my mouth. Addie has already eaten at least four caramels. Her cheeks are smeared with goo on top of the pasta dough.

'I'm so excited,' I say to Jill for probably the tenth time. 'I can't even believe it.'

Luke emerges from the bedroom right then, rubbing his eyes, his blue terry robe tied around him. 'What can't you believe, Rose?'

'Baby! Good morning!'

'Hey, Luke,' Jill says.

'Hi, Daddy.'

'Uh-oh.' Luke comes over and picks Addie up from her chair and gives her a squeeze. Then he turns to me. 'You never call me Baby in the morning. What happened?'

'I got the grant, Luke, I got the grant!' I can't help squealing, and Jill joins me. The two of us bounce up and down, the remains of our mimosas sloshing around in our flutes, spilling onto the floor.

'Wow. That's so amazing, Rose! Congratulations! You did it!'

I am still looking at Jill when Luke says this, when he exclaims it with great force. My head snaps in his direction. I study my husband. A shade of the excitement and nearly all of the breath inside me is knocked from my body. I stare at Luke, see the big smile on his face, hear him saying all the things a proud husband should say. And yet, underneath those right words and behind that proud smile I can detect that Luke is lying as he speaks, as he grins. He's not happy for me. He's the opposite of happy. I can tell. A wife always can.

8

September 19, 2008
Rose, Life 2

LUKE IS HAVING an affair.

I am sure of it.

This is my punishment, isn't it?

This is what I get for not wanting children. For depriving my husband and his parents of a child and a grandchild. For digging in my heels, for being unwilling to come around. I once had a loving husband, a happy life, and now, because of my choices, my loving husband is loving someone else.

So how do I know?

Well.

The better question might be: How could I not know?

How could any wife not know, when it is happening to them?

It's not that Luke is getting suspicious phone calls or anything. It's more of a general sixth sense I've had around him. The way he's behaving. No, it's the way he's been looking at me. Or rather, *not* looking at me.

A distance. There is a distance between us, ever since we had that stupid fight about vitamins, the one that ended with him promising that he would stop pressuring me to have children. Things improved for about a minute, but then . . .

He's always distracted, but not by tasks around the apartment or even his job or his emails. He's up in his head all the time, in a place I can't seem to reach. When I try, he comes back from wherever he's been in this exaggerated way. There's a forced cheerfulness, a sudden affection from him. *Too much* affection.

He'll say something really intense like, 'Rose, you are the only woman I've ever loved – you know that, right?' After I've asked him something innocuous like, *Luke, have you seen my favorite T-shirt?* Or *Luke, how do you feel about mushroom risotto for dinner?*

Guilt. He's guilty.

It's like an odor permeating our apartment. The ugly perfume of it, wafting around his body, trailing after him like he's Pig-Pen. All of this amorphous evidence and then, well.

There's a photo.

Not *that* kind of photo.

A different kind. Far worse. More telling.

It went by in a flash on his phone. He wanted to show me a photo he'd taken of some fat cat lounging that had made him laugh. He was always taking pictures of cats, which would prompt us to have yet another discussion of whether we should get a cat of our own – a consolation prize for the child we would never have. I wanted a cat, I was pressing him for one. I would try to make this joke, or sometimes even Luke would, that a kitten would surely fill the hole in our childless marriage. It never worked, never seemed to disarm the grenade that rattled around our lives like some loose ball, threatening to explode.

Luke was scrolling past photos, there were so many of them. I was peering over his shoulder.

He was chuckling already, telling me how hard I was going to laugh once I saw this cat.

My finger shot out to the screen of his phone, trying to catch this image, pause it, so I could see it better. 'Who's that?'

'Who's who?'

'That woman. The one in the photo you just passed.'

'Woman?' Luke tried to scroll upward, but my finger was pressing onto the screen. He tilted his head in my direction, eyebrows raised. 'I can't find it if you don't let me.'

'Oh.' I snatched my finger away. Luke's tone was laced with annoyance. 'Sorry,' I said, but I didn't move back, kept my eyes on the screen. I didn't want to miss it, didn't want Luke to pretend it wasn't there. The photos flew by too quickly for me to see them clearly. 'Slow down! I think you passed it.'

Luke scrolled the other way, this time at a turtle's pace, and I thought, *We are getting into a fight. I didn't want this to become a fight.* At first it was photos from work that I saw on the screen – a press conference with the mayor, an engagement shoot from last weekend, and then a series of random images. Luke was always taking photos on the street, at a store, any time he saw something interesting.

My finger shot out again. 'That one.'

'Oh, Cheryl?' He said this so nonchalantly, as though I should know Cheryl, or maybe to convey that obviously he should have a photo of this woman on his phone. But as soon as he revealed that he knew the woman's name, that the name Cheryl could roll off his tongue as easily as Rose, I could tell he regretted it. 'Or at least, I think that was her name,' he added.

'That *was* her name? Is she dead now?'

Luke was eyeing me. 'No, Rose, though why would I know or care one way or the other? She's just some woman.' He tapped the thumbnail, and the image filled the screen. He angled it so I could get a better look, like he was more than happy to show me, like this photograph was as benign as any other.

A hole opened in my stomach as I studied this woman's face, her expression, the posture of her body. It wasn't simply her beauty causing the cavern to open at my center, her long and wavy red hair and that translucent, freckled skin that only red-heads possess. It was the fact that she was laughing, the *way* she was laughing, head thrown back, hair cascading past her shoulders, eyes half closed, red-lipped mouth open in a round *O* of unself-conscious joy.

It was just like his favorite photograph of me.

'So who is she?' I asked, walking away as I spoke, heading into the kitchen. I was doing my best to be unconcerned, turning on the faucet, rinsing plates, and beginning to fill the dishwasher. 'I don't think you've ever mentioned her before. Cheryl.' Now that I'd heard the name, I couldn't stop saying it.

'I told you, she's just this person I saw in the park.' Luke walked over to the shelf where we keep the liquor, pulled down a bottle of whiskey, followed by a small glass. He unscrewed the top of the bottle and poured himself a shot. He never drank whiskey, but suddenly he was. 'I thought maybe I could use the photo on my website, you know, to help get more portrait bookings.

I only know her name because of the release she signed. Don't you think it's a good photo?'

I was arranging and rearranging plates and bowls and mugs, trying to make them fit better into the slots for the dishes. 'It is a great shot.'

'Yeah, I thought so, too,' Luke said, as though I were the one to first notice this and he had agreed. He walked toward me, whiskey in hand, still nearly brimming. He took a small sip. 'Let me do that.'

I moved aside and he handed me his glass. He bent over the dishwasher rack, shifted a bowl, slid another one into one of the tall slots, dropped a detergent pod inside and shut the door. He pressed the on button, looked over at me, reached for his whiskey again, and laughed.

It was empty.

While he was moving a plate, I had drunk it down.

I look at the clock. Luke is probably taking his lunch break by now at his studio.

I pick up the phone and call him.

It rings through to his voicemail. Yet another sign he's having an affair. He used to always pick up when I called. I wish I'd never seen that fucking photo. Now every single thing he does seems like a sign that he is cheating.

'Hey, Luke,' I begin, 'I was just calling to say hello and because I miss you. Also, I was wondering if you were in the mood for anything particular tonight for dinner? Just call me back or text what you'd like to eat. I know you're busy. Love you so much!'

The syrup I can hear in my voice gives me a stomachache and a headache. Too much sugar all in one gulp.

This is why people go crazy and hire private investigators.

I dial Jill next.

She picks up on the first ring. 'Hey! What's going on?'

At least someone in this world is eager to talk to me. 'Can you come over?'

'To your office or the apartment? I thought you were working from home today.'

'I am. Well, I was. I'm not, though. Not really. I can't concentrate. I need you. Please.' I hate how pathetic I sound as I say these things.

There is a long silence. Then, 'Rose,' Jill says, her voice descending, my name low and drawn out, 'what happened?'

I take a deep breath. I haven't said it out loud yet, because that will make it real. But I do it. 'Luke is having an affair.'

This time, Jill doesn't keep me waiting. 'I'll be right there,' she says immediately, followed by a click.

When I open the door, Jill pulls me into a hug.

'Let's have some tea,' she says as she heads into the apartment. She goes straight to the kitchen cabinets where we keep the mugs and sets two onto the island, then takes two pouches of chamomile and hooks the tags over the sides. I put the kettle on the stove to heat, and to give myself something to do.

While we wait for the water to boil, Jill says, 'Tea will help your nerves.'

'I didn't say I was nervous.'

Jill gives me a look that says she doesn't believe me.

'Fine. I'm anxious or I wouldn't have called.'

'Why do you think Luke is having an affair? Did you find something? A hotel receipt? A message?'

'Not exactly.'

Jill crosses her arms. She is wearing a bright, royal-blue top that matches her eyes. 'Then what?'

'Well.' I try to decide how to describe what I'm feeling. 'Luke's been acting . . . different. He's distant – not always, but some-times.'

'Husbands get distant. Wives get distant. Maria gets distant all the time.' Maria is Jill's partner. 'That doesn't mean there's an affair.'

'I know. But' – I pause, I breathe – 'he's distant but then he's the opposite. He's overly affectionate, as though he were trying to make up for something. As if he were feeling guilty. And then, there's this photo.'

Jill's eyebrows arch. 'Uh-oh.' She kicks off her shoes, one by one, then goes over to the wall and steps into her slippers. She pads back to the island. 'Tell me about this photo.'

'You know the one Luke has of me laughing in the snow?'

She nods.

'Well, he was scrolling around on his phone and I saw that he'd taken nearly that exact photo, but of this woman I've never seen before. He said her name is Cheryl.'

'Cheryl! Then it's not some random person.'

'He claimed she was random. But I think he said her name automatically, without thinking. Then he tried to cover it up.'

The kettle begins to shriek. Jill pours the water into our mugs and hands me mine. The bag bobs up to the top and I shove it down to the bottom with a spoon.

Jill grips her mug with both hands, the steam rising up around her face. 'Maybe you're interpreting this the wrong way. Maybe he took that photo because it reminded him of you and he was having wistful memories. Maybe he did it in a fit of nostalgia.'

I shake my head. 'There's something else that made me think she was somebody important.' I sigh. 'You're going to think I'm crazy.'

'Tell me.'

'Luke has always kept that photo of me angled toward him so he can see it when he goes to bed and when he gets up in the morning.'

There is a mock-choking noise from Jill. 'That's a sign he loves you, Rose, not the opposite, and that he's a pathetic romantic.'

I keep going. 'The other day I noticed it was angled away from him – so I angled it back. The next morning it was turned away *again*. Luke must have done it on purpose. He didn't want to look at my photo when he went to sleep that night. He moved it so he didn't have to see me!'

'You don't know that. Maybe he knocked it that way and it's just a coincidence. Maybe he's changed the way he's getting into bed.'

'You're reaching,' I say, even though I want to believe her. 'It's more likely that he's feeling guilty because he's having an affair with a woman named Cheryl.'

Jill pulls the tea bag out of her mug, squeezes it with the spoon, and sets it on a dish. Then, 'Evidence,' she says. '*If* he's having an affair – and this is a big *if* – then we'll find something that proves it.'

'We will?'

'Oh yes. We're going to look right now. When will Luke be home?'

'Not until seven.'

'Perfect. That gives us plenty of time.' Mug in hand, she heads straight into the office where Luke and I each have a desk.

I take a deep breath and follow her.

Jill is already rifling through Luke's drawers. 'Where do you think he'd keep something he doesn't want you to see? Or that he wants to hang on to?'

For a moment, I am stuck in a kind of vertigo, as though any movement backward, forward, sideways, will have me tumbling down a cliff. Am I really going to do this? Rifle through my husband's things? Search for evidence that he's having an affair?

Yes, I decide. Because maybe we'll find something definitive and then I'll know I'm not crazy. Or maybe we'll prove it's all in my head and then I can let it go.

I pick up a book from Luke's desk. Flip through it. Put it down. 'I'm not sure. We'll just have to look through everything, I guess.'

As I am sorting through Luke's things, stacks of mail, receipts for tax purposes, I suddenly feel like one of those wives who go on talk shows, revealing all of the desperate things she did when she suspected her husband of an affair. But then, letting my guard down and capitulating to my worst impulses is kind of freeing. I start to giggle.

'Why are you laughing?' Jill asks, opening a drawer and sifting through it.

'Me. Us. This.' I take a stack of papers from one of the shelves and paw through them. 'I mean, what's the difference between doing this and actually hiring a private investigator? Not much, right? I'm just one tele lens and a camera away from it. It's kind of funny,' I say.

'Well, it's only funny until we find something,' Jill responds, and my laughing stops.

I remember the first moment I realized I was in love with Luke, like, irrevocably and hopelessly in love with him; how it felt like my heart had been hijacked.

It was ten years ago. I was on a writing retreat with my graduate school friends Raya and Denise, who'd dragged me away with them so we could churn out articles from our dissertations and be in better positions on the job market.

But really, my friends had dragged me away from Luke.

Luke and I had only been dating for three months by then, but since the night of our second dinner, we were inseparable. We went bike riding together, we went for walks in the park together, we went to the grocery store together. All of it, even the mundane things like buying milk and cereal, were heightened somehow. Everything we did seemed significant, like we were getting a glimpse into the future we'd share, the endless afternoons of domestic life that would eventually grow to seem normal, like we'd been doing it forever.

Denise, Raya, and I had been sitting on the deck of the house we'd rented all afternoon, trying to work, when I got up from the couch where I'd been lounging, walked over to the chair where Denise was reading, and announced, 'I can't concentrate on anything!'

I remember how Denise looked up from her book and smirked at me. 'You can't concentrate because you can't stop thinking about Luke,' she said.

'That's not true!' I protested, but I was grinning because she was right.

Luke was always there in the back of my mind. I imagined him standing amid the pathways of my brain, waving hi constantly. There were moments when this scared me, like I might lose myself entirely to Luke if I wasn't careful. But mostly I tried to just let myself enjoy the feeling, let myself be carried along with the current of it, secure in the knowledge that somewhere deep I would always still be me.

Right then, the phone rang inside the house and I ran inside to grab it. I could hear Denise and Raya laughing at me on the deck. We all knew it would be Luke. 'Hello?' I said, breathless. It was an old phone, the kind with a windy cord.

'Hey,' Luke said

'It's so good to hear your voice,' I told him. I couldn't help it. 'I miss you,' he said.

I was giddy. 'Me, too.'

'How's writing going?'

'Okay. Well. Mostly I'm distracted.'

'Oh? Why?' Luke asked, but I could hear the smile in his voice.

'You already know.'

'I do.'

We both did. He didn't have to say it out loud for me to know either.

'What are you doing?' I asked him.

'Trying to drum up some business. The usual.'

'It will get easier.'

'Will it?'

'You can't give up,' I told him next. 'Someday we'll both look back on this time and laugh, because I won't be on the job market anymore and you'll have more work than you can handle and the kind of work you love, not just wedding gigs.'

'That sounds nice,' he said. 'Especially the part where you said, *Someday we'll both look back*. It makes it seem like you think we'll have a long life together.'

I walked across the room and stood by the window, stretching the cord as far as it could go. 'I do think that,' I said. 'Don't you?'

'Yeah.'

In the silence that stretched between us, our times together began to flash through my mind, how Luke would sit at my kitchen table in the tiny studio I rented, going through his photos on his computer, while I worked on articles I wanted to publish. How sometimes, for no reason, we'd stop what we were doing and have urgent, passionate sex, like maybe it would be for the last time, like one of us might die in the night or get murdered on the street and that would be it for us, so we'd have to make it count that one time. How I both loved and hated these feelings. How could I possibly survive without this man if I lost him? How did this feeling that my life wouldn't be complete without him happen so fast? But mostly I loved it. I loved *him*.

I loved him.

'Hey,' Luke says. 'Where did you go, Rose?'

'Nowhere. Just thinking.'

'I hope good things.'

I smiled. 'Yes, good things.'

'Things you can tell me now?'

'Things I'd rather tell you in person.' *Things like 'I love you, Luke.'*

'Okay.' He sounded disappointed.

'I'll be back home soon.'

'Not as soon as I wish you'd be back.'

'You can live without me for a couple more days.'

'I don't know – can I?'

We both laughed then. I glanced out onto the deck to make sure Raya and Denise weren't listening. They'd been making fun of me all day about my mushy conversation with Luke last night before bed. 'I should go. You know, I have articles to write, runs to go on with Denise and Raya, and things.'

I remember how Luke got quiet. How we both did.

I love you. This was what I wasn't saying.

I love you, too. This was what I was pretty sure that Luke was not saying back to me.

But it was there for both of us. I could feel it, that these words had settled deep into the chambers of both our hearts.

My love for Luke was still nestled there in mine. But was his love for me still in his? Or had someone else dislodged it from that privileged place in his body, sent it rolling away, far enough that he could no longer see it or feel it?

*

Jill and I find nothing.

I want to let my suspicions go, but I can't. I know he's cheating. I can feel it in every molecule, in the same way I've always known that motherhood is not for me. As if it is a basic truth.

Or maybe the problem is mine. Maybe I haven't yet learned to trust Luke's grand gesture of letting go of the child question. It just seems so impossible, how Luke went from desperate for a baby to *Okay, Rose, I'm so sorry for torturing and nearly destroying you and us, I'll stop now,* in the span of one measly fight about vitamins. I almost didn't know how to walk after that, didn't trust the ground of our marriage, filled as it was with crevasses and ravines and crumbling earth.

Have Luke and I simply bought ourselves a little more time?

Or have we found a way across that great gap for good?

Something in my stomach tells me, No. No, we haven't.

It's all I've been able to think about since Jill left the apartment, saying over and over on her way out the door, 'Rose, there's no evidence! Not a single scrap! Stop worrying!'

But Cheryl is real. There may not be evidence in our apartment, but I have a feeling she's here anyway, swirling between us, a phantom in the air. She's probably a baby maker. She's probably obsessed with having babies, which is what attracted Luke to her. Ugh.

I pick up my phone and scroll through the contact list until I find what I want.

Thomas.

There he is. Just a first name. Seeing it makes my heart jump.

My finger hovers, then I tap the screen.

I begin to type.

I know it's been a while, but do you still want to get that drink?

The cursor blinks after the question mark, waiting for me to say more, or to simply hit send. Do I do it? Do I dare go down this path, take this next step?

Yes, *yes*, Rose. Do it.

Thomas and I met at a conference. We were at a reception, and he was talking to my colleague, Devonne and a few other people from my department. The wine came in great goblets, accompanied by pigs in blankets, cheese and crackers. We stood around in a group, drinking, eating, chatting about our research. I was the only woman, which was not unusual since men outnumber women in sociology by a lot.

I talked to Thomas all night. He was fun, smart, interesting, attractive. I was trying not to think much about that part but it was difficult to avoid since we were facing each other, and his face, specifically, was very pleasing. Thomas was also so distracting and I needed distraction. I hadn't slept the night before because all I could think about was how Luke was likely at home alone, having sex with the woman from the photo, Cheryl, in our bed, the two of them thrilled I was away, making babies on our nice white sheets.

For some reason, I'd thought that Thomas was from Chicago, that I would likely never see him again so it didn't matter that we were locked in conversation for hours, everyone else going their separate ways to other receptions and leaving us alone.

'This was fun,' he said when we'd finally decided to say goodnight. His words were casual, but his tone said something else.

'It was,' I said, unable to erase the subtle acknowledgment of the current running between us.

'We should get together again,' he said.

I smiled. 'Same time next year?'

He laughed. 'No. Well yes, but I meant at a bar after we get home.'

'Don't you live in Chicago?'

'No, I teach in Manhattan.'

My stomach bottomed out. I hadn't told Thomas I was married. It was there, nagging at me all night, the urge to tell him this very important fact, to mention Luke's name in conversation, but still I held the information back. Maybe he'd noticed my wedding ring but maybe he hadn't. Maybe he didn't care one way or the other whether I was married. I was suddenly standing at a precipice, an infinite drop inches from my feet, as he stood there, waiting for me to say yes. Yes, Thomas, I'd love to see you again.

I am swaying now as I stand here in my kitchen, staring at Thomas's name, backlit, glowing on my phone.

I tap the screen. Erase the message.

I can't do it. I just can't.

I love Luke.

9

November 10, 2007
Rose, Life 1

'ROSE, ARE YOU all right?' my colleague, Devonne, asks, materializing in the doorway of my office. I'd been staring out into the nothingness of the hall, right through him, really – I hadn't noticed him there until he spoke.

'Hmmm – what?' I force my eyes to focus, and Devonne takes shape, tall, a bit rounded in the middle, his teeth visible in that big smile of his, bright against his skin.

Devonne is a hulking man, with a sweet and generous heart. Everyone loves him in our department and loves his wife just as much. They are always throwing dinner parties and inviting all of us, planning outings for drinks. Sociologists, academics in general, can be vipers – unfeeling, mean. But not Devonne.

He takes several steps inside my office, plants his hands on the back of one of the chairs for visitors on the other side of my desk. 'What is going on with you lately? Seriously. You haven't seemed yourself.'

I have to stop drifting into the dark depths of my brain while people are talking, fixating on the image of the divorce papers sitting on the kitchen table under a pile of other mail I try not to see when I get home at night. I want to be me again. Normal Rose. Not Divorcing Rose, Lost Rose. 'I don't know, Devonne. I'm just . . . I'm fine.'

He stares at me a beat – stares hard, stares like he doesn't believe me. My colleagues don't yet know about Luke. I've been avoiding telling them. Devonne lets out a big breath. 'So, there's this departmental happy hour next Thursday.'

This provokes a laugh from me. It isn't what I am expecting Devonne to say. His 'so' sounded weighty, like something heavy was about to come out of his mouth instead of an invitation to drinks. 'Yeah? I didn't know. I guess I've been kind of out of it.'

'You should go. Why don't we go together? I'll come by and—'

'I see what you're doing, Devonne.'

'Oh? What am I doing?'

'You're doing that thing we do with our students when we're concerned about them. We try to walk them to the counseling center from our office, to make sure they go. But you're trying to walk me to the happy hour.'

It's Devonne's turn to laugh. 'Maybe. But it looks like you need to hang out, you know? Have some fun. Maybe it will do you good.'

For a second, a surge of hope shoots through me. I have one of those precious moments when the possibility of *new life* opens inside me, flashes like a brilliant sun, warming my body. But then it's immediately erased by the doubt that always follows, doubt that without Luke I will ever feel happy again, doubt about myself after the failure of my marriage – a doubt that is much stronger than these fleeting moments of hope, more powerful, like a supervillain who's built his lair somewhere deep in my mind.

The smile on Devonne's face, though – kind, hopeful enough for the both of us – provides me just enough motivation to say my next words. 'All right. I'll be here in my office, waiting on Thursday afternoon for you to come get me, and then off to the happy hour we'll go.'

Devonne's smile takes over his face, the hills of his cheekbones rising. His is glowing, like a light, a beacon, and I think, *Why not? Why not follow that friendly light? You never know, Rose Napolitano. Good things might be just around the corner.*

But then, as Devonne turns and tosses a 'See you Thursday, then,' over his shoulder on his way out of my office, the super-villain lurking inside me shows up again, cackles his evil, self-sabotaging laugh, and all that light from Devonne blinks out.

On Thursday the restaurant for the happy hour is packed. I go back and forth, trying to decide whether I've made a mistake, letting Devonne bring me here.

'Hey, Rose!' My colleague Jason, expert in the behaviors of religious groups and other cultish things, tips a beer in my direction as we reach the long marble bar. 'Where've you been hiding this year?'

Devonne puts his large arm around me and gives my shoulder a squeeze. 'What can I get you to drink?' he asks, saving me from answering Jason.

His question stymies me – I never drink when I'm sad, it just makes me sadder. I've nearly forgotten what I do drink when I am drinking. 'An old-fashioned, I think?'

Devonne nods, leans into the bar to get the bartender's attention.

Jason is watching me, still waiting for an answer, I suppose. 'I'll be right back,' I tell him, and head off to the ladies' room.

My phone is full of unread messages – probably from my mother. She's worried about me, calls every day to check up on how I'm feeling. I've stopped returning her calls because my answer is always the same – I am sad, I am lonely, I am grieving. I dial Jill's number instead, but she doesn't pick up. 'Jill, if you get this and you're free, come rescue me at Maison's, please. I let Devonne convince me to come to the departmental happy hour and I already regret the decision. Maybe?'

Women jostle back and forth on their way to the bathroom stalls. I stare into the wide, gilded mirror in front of me, leaning over the sink, and have another one of those flashes – the ones I wish I could bottle and drink down when I'm particularly despondent. I see a woman reflected there, attractive – no, pretty – who's having a good hair day, who may indeed be a professor but a fashionable one. Before I can decide otherwise, I dig for the lipstick at the bottom of my bag and put it on, then I march back out to the bar where Devonne, Jason, and now Brandy, Sam, Winston, and Jennifer, my other estimable colleagues, are standing around, chatting alongside a man I don't know.

I put a big smile on my face. 'Hey guys, good to see you all!'

There is a chorus of 'Hey, Rose,' that comes back my way, and Devonne hands me my drink. I take a big swig of it, the warmth in my throat seeming to confirm that, yes, Rose, it *is* good that you are here at this bar. You are out in the world, being a person again! A person wearing lipstick! Hanging out with your colleagues! Being a professor – a fashionable one!

Devonne nods at the man I don't know and I look at him now, really look. 'Have you two met before?' Devonne asks us.

Something races through me, a familiar but faint sort of rush, a long-ago memory pushing to the surface. For a second I can't figure out what it is, but as I take in the sight of this man, the wave of his dark hair, the bright look in his brown eyes, I recognize it. I hold out my hand to him. 'No, we haven't met. I'm Rose.'

The man smiles, just a half of one, the left corner of his mouth turning up, a sly, playful look in his eyes. He takes the hand I offer. 'I'm Oliver.' He says this with a wonderful British accent.

'Oliver is from London, obviously,' Devonne explains.

Oliver laughs, I laugh, the two of us laughing like Devonne is the funniest person ever.

'But he's here for the year on sabbatical,' Devonne goes on, 'teaching over in the Lit Department.'

Oliver is gorgeous, my brain, my body, adds, the notion strange, forbidden, since it's about a man who isn't Luke. This thought is followed by other, more encouraging ones: *Rose, you are allowed to think this other man is gorgeous. You are getting divorced. You are supposed to think such things.*

These new thoughts linger, no, they solidify into something lasting, something that begins to grow and soothe and heal, even after our hands let go.

10

October 10, 2008

Rose, Life 2

'MOM?' I ASK.

My mother, adorned in a pumpkin-colored sweater for fall – she always dresses for the seasons and their holidays – looks up from her novel. She is doing her daily afternoon 'relaxing', which generally involves a book or the newspaper and a glass of white wine on the table next to her chair in the living room. The wine is there more as a prop. She likes the idea of the wine with her book more than actually drinking it.

'Yes, sweetheart?'

'Can I ask you something?'

The turn of her head is sharp, brown eyes peering at me over the rims of her reading glasses. I can see the interest in her angular face, her stare intense, focused, but trying to seem casual. She crosses and recrosses her legs, then decides to curl them underneath her. She takes the glass of wine, settling in. 'Of course you can. That's what mothers are for!'

I nod. But inside, I wonder, *Are they? Are they really for that? Is this the job?*

The woodsy smell of the room, with its red-grained cedar chest and the other furniture, courtesy of my father the craftsman, is familiar, consoling, the smell of home. I sit down on the couch. Get ready to get my question out, give myself a little pep talk, then go for it. 'Did you ever feel like . . . Dad might want to leave you?' I ask, then swallow hard. 'You know, get divorced? Like, maybe for another woman?'

My mother sets her glass down with a clatter, missing the coaster. 'What could possibly make you ask me that?'

Uh-oh. The horror and judgment in her voice should dissuade me from moving forward. But it doesn't. 'I just . . . it's just that Luke, maybe, I don't know. I think he might be unhappy. With me,' I add.

'Sweetheart. He would never leave you. He could never love someone else. He loves you.'

'But did you and Dad ever have . . . difficulties?'

'Of course. Every marriage has troubles. But you work through them. That's what you do.'

'Well, how did you and Dad work through things?'

My mother's bobbed hair sways slightly, a perfect slide toward her chin as she shifts positions. 'That is not really the issue, Rose. You shouldn't be worrying about your father and me if you and Luke are having trouble. You should be worrying about what you can do to make Luke happier—'

'But you just said that he loves me.'

'—and we both know what that is, even if you don't want to talk about it. Don't you think it's time we did? Do you really

86

want to lose your husband over your stubbornness? You've been avoiding the subject with me for a long time now.'

'Mom—'

'A baby. You need to have a *baby*, Rose. How do you think your father and I worked out all of our problems over the years? We did it because of you. We were – we are – invested in you, your well-being, your future. You are the glue between us.'

I inhale a long, hoarse breath. The urge to bend forward, put my head between my knees, is strong. 'Mom, I'm not going to do that, and Luke came around – at least that's what he said. Besides, it's not the life that I want – it's never been the life I've wanted. And you know that.'

My mother is blinking quickly.

Oh no. Have I made her cry? 'Mom—'

'Was I such a terrible mother?'

And here we are. Somehow, I knew we would end up in this place, which is why I usually avoid the subject. Ever since Luke and I married and my mother realized I was serious all those years when I said I wasn't having children, she can't stop talking about my resistance to motherhood as somehow a resistance to her motherhood of *me*.

'Rose, you're late.'

I was sixteen and I'd just walked in the front door from a date with Matt, my boyfriend on and off throughout high school. My mother was sitting at the kitchen table. It was just after midnight and I'd been kissed thoroughly. My father was likely asleep. I hoped he was asleep. I hated when my mother waited up for me. 'Like, by two minutes.'

'We need to talk about the Order of Things,' she said, as though I was supposed to know what this meant.

I approached her, full of dread. My mother pulled her reading glasses from her face and set them aside. Turned her book over, open to mark her place. There was a long-haired man embracing a scantily clad woman on the cover. Gross. I hated having to witness my mother reading racy romance novels. She kept a stash of them in an unmarked box under the bed. I knew this because I went and found them when I wanted to learn more about sex at age twelve. For some reason she believed she could read bodice rippers around the house, but never leave them on the bookshelves where she kept her other, more acceptable reading, like her collection of Jane Austen novels. As though they simply disappeared after she finished them.

My mother patted the space next to her. 'Sit.' She slid her chair back a few inches, shifted it so it was diagonal to the table, then did the same with the one that had my name on it.

'Fine, let's talk about "the Order", whatever that is.' I glared at her to make sure she knew I did not want to be there, having this discussion at midnight. I plopped down and folded my arms across my chest.

My mother perked up as she began speaking. 'Rose, you know that your father and I want a good life for you, easier than the one he and I have had.'

I nodded. I knew this story. I'd heard it before, many times. I leaned my elbow onto the table and propped the side of my face with my hand, already bored.

'Your father didn't go to college and your mother didn't go to a real college.'

'Um-hum.'

'Your father had to start his carpentry business without any help from our families, and for years he did odd jobs, whatever work he could get, while I taught elementary school for practically no money.'

'Yes, Mom,' I droned. Though whenever I heard these things from her, especially the stuff about my dad, there was a sharp pinch inside me. I'd always hated to think about my father struggling.

'But you are going to do things differently,' my mother was saying. 'You are going to go to college – a good college. A real college. And you are going to study business, and you are going to graduate and get a good job in finance.'

My mother was convinced that because I happened to be good at math, I needed to work in finance. She never wondered whether I wanted to work in finance.

'And after you get your job in finance, you are going to spend a lot of time working hard at that job and establishing your career and saving money in the bank.' She stopped, stared hard at me, like maybe I hadn't been listening.

'I heard you, Mom. When are we going to get to this "Order" stuff?'

'I'm telling you about it now.'

'Oh. I just thought you were telling me the story of how my life is going to be different than yours and Dad's.'

'It's part of that story.'

'Well, can you be more specific because obviously I'm missing the point.' I yawned big and wide to emphasize that the clock was ticking and I was sleepy.

My mother pulled her chair closer to mine. 'Rose, "the Order" is that *first* you go to college, *then* you graduate from college, *then* you get a very good job, *then* you spend time working hard at that job and saving up lots of money, *then* you meet someone, *then* you fall in love, *then* you get married, and *then and only then* do you have sex and children.'

At first, I'd felt a laugh bubbling up in me as my mother spoke. But the second she mentioned sex and children my eyes slid away from her and across the rest of the kitchen, the old rotary phone stuck to the wall for as long as I'd been alive, the radio/tape deck that sat next to the sink, the mobile of beach shells that still hangs at the center of the window to this day. 'Mom, please tell me this is not your version of a sex talk.'

She began shaking her head.

No? Yes? I couldn't tell.

'I just want you to understand that if you are to have a better life than your parents, then I don't want you to go falling in love with some boy in high school and getting yourself pregnant. That can't happen until you've done so many other things.'

My eyes were glued to the basket of fruit sitting at the edge of the kitchen island. Hills of apples, bananas, oranges. We always had so many bananas in this house. 'You have nothing to worry about, Mom. There's no way I'm getting pregnant.'

'Rose, don't just dismiss what I'm saying! Girls get pregnant all the time when they don't want to! And then' – she snapped her fingers so loud I was startled – 'all those dreams they have are gone!'

I let my gaze return to my mother. 'Well, you don't have to worry about me getting pregnant, like, ever, because I'm not having children. I've decided I don't want them. Period.'

My mother reared back in her chair, like I'd just confessed to murder, or as if I were about to hit her. 'Rose, you don't mean that!'

'I do mean that.'

'But you're too young to make that decision!'

'I am not,' I said. My mother was quiet, watching my face. I sat up straighter. 'Mom, you can't have it both ways. You can't decide that you and Dad want a different life for me with all the opportunities you didn't have, but then decide my future for me.'

'But children are just a part of life! All women have them when they get old enough. *After* they get married, of course. And *after* they've established their careers.'

'According to you. But you are always telling me that my generation of women gets to do things differently. So why not this thing, too?'

'But becoming a mother, that's not what I meant by different!'

I huffed. 'Right.'

'You think this now, but you'll change your mind, Rose.'

She was so sure of herself. It made me so angry. 'I won't. I promise you that.'

My mother laughed knowingly. It made me want to snatch her stupid romance novel from the table and throw it across the kitchen. 'You'll change your mind and one day you'll turn to me and say, "You were right, Mom. You knew it all along!"'

I got up from the chair. 'I'm going to bed,' I announced.

I could practically see my mother's heart racing inside her

chest. The look on her face was alive with a kind of frantic worry. I wondered if she might grab me, place her hands on my shoulders as if she could transfer the desire for children from her body into mine. But then she reached for her book and the moment passed. Her eyes left me. 'Good night, Rose,' was all she said.

I wondered if I had hurt her. Even when I got angry at her, I still didn't want to have hurt her. I leaned forward and kissed her on the cheek. She didn't turn. Just flipped her book and smoothed her fingers across the open pages. As soon as I headed toward my room, her final words of the night came hurtling at my back.

'If you're so against having children, Rose, then you should stop rolling around on the floor with Matthew all night.'

Tears are streaming down my mother's face.

I swallow. 'Mom?'

She looks away. 'What, Rose.'

I've hurt her again and I hate that. I forget sometimes that my mother isn't invincible.

My mother's friends have always described her as a 'tough cookie'. And my mother does have this hard, outer shell. If you don't know her well then you're not likely to realize how soft she is in the middle, how easily she can be wounded. Maybe the thing I admire most about her is how fierce she is, how fiercely she loves. Sometimes that can make her possessive and over-bearing, but it also makes her protective and determined. Back when I was sixteen, I would never have told her that I admired her, or how much I appreciated her. But I also didn't know back then that my mother would eventually take this choice of mine and decide it was a personal critique of her as a mother. That by holding back my admiration of her and how much I secretly wished for her approval, a valley would grow between us, wider and wider.

'I don't think you realize – and maybe it's because I don't say it enough, or maybe because I've never said it' – I close my eyes, maybe to make it easier to get these words out – 'but you are a very good mother. You are a great mother. You always have been.'

'I have? I am?' My mother sounds so surprised.

'Yes. And I do want to please you. I always do. I want you to be proud of me. But I can't do this one thing and I need you to hear me. I can't have a baby.' The house is so quiet. 'I don't want to, I never have, it's just . . . it's not in me. And I can't have a baby to please you or Luke, as much as I want to.' My voice has gotten softer and softer. The last vestiges of sunlight glinting off the oak tree in front of the house disappear, a blanket of darkness falling across the yard, the windows, the furniture becoming shadows around us.

She wipes her face with a tissue. 'But why, Rose? Why don't you want a baby?'

My breath catches. This is the first time my mother has ever asked me this question, rather than simply fought me on the subject. But can I really tell her? 'It's hard to explain.'

'Try. Please?'

I nod, slowly. 'Well, there are the reasons you can probably guess. I like the way my life is. My freedom, my job, my friends, my husband.'

'But those things don't have to go away if you have a baby, you know.'

I give my mother a look that stops her from saying anything else.

'Sorry. I'm listening.'

'It's not just that stuff, Mom. There's something much deeper.' I let out a breath. Her eyes are big and she's watching me intently. 'Everybody talks about how women have a maternal instinct,' I start.

My mother nods.

'Well, it's as though I don't have one. I think I was born without it. And all of my friends, even Jill, will talk about a maternal instinct like they know exactly what it is. Even if they decided not to have kids, they still seem to understand that desire. But I don't. The desire just isn't in me. Like it got left out of my biology.' I stop. There it is. The truth. I'm not sure how else to explain it.

'But Rose, it may be that you discover that instinct only after you have a baby.'

'That seems like an awfully big gamble, Mom.'

'Having a baby is always a gamble,' she presses. 'It's a leap of faith even if you're dying to have one, if you think your whole destiny is to be a mother.'

I turn on the lamp next to the couch. 'Maybe either way it's a gamble. I'm gambling that I'm not meant to have a baby, and most other women are gambling that they are.'

'Maybe,' she says. 'But I think there are a lot of women who feel the way you do, Rose. More than you think. And then they go ahead and have a baby anyway and then they find that they're happy they did it.'

I pull my knees up to my chest. Tilt my head to the side and study my mother. She seems sincere. 'I know you want a grandchild, Mom. It's not that I don't want to give you one. If I could, I would. I hope you know that. And I hope that you'll still love me if I don't give you one, because I think the reality is that I probably won't.'

'Oh Rose, I—'

'—and I wish so badly that the world was different,' I go on, before she can say anything else. Tears are pressing into the back of my eyes. 'That people could think it was just as normal for a woman not to have kids as to have them. It's so overwhelming sometimes, how much pressure I feel to be someone I'm not. I mean, I know I could do it if I had to; I could give Luke a baby. But I'm so certain it's not what I want. I wish I didn't feel like those were the choices in front of me – to do this thing I don't want to do in order to keep my husband, or just . . . let my marriage come to an end.'

'Rose, sweetheart! I'm sorry this has all been so hard for you. I'm sorry that I've made it harder on you, too.' My mother gets up from her chair and sits down next to me on the couch. 'I wish I could go back in time and listen to you better. I wish there was something I could do to fix everything.'

These words. I've been waiting to hear something like this from my mother forever. 'I'm scared I'm going to lose Luke because of this, Mom.'

There is a hand on my back, circling. 'Sweetheart,' my mother is saying in a soothing voice, the one she's always used when I would get upset, or if I fell as a child and bruised an elbow or skinned a knee. 'I'm here. I'm here no matter what.' I let her words form a blanket around me. 'I love you very much, my sweet Rose. I'll love you no matter what, I promise. And if Luke doesn't realize the incredible woman that he has, baby or no baby, then it's his loss.' She sounds indignant during this last part.

As she speaks, my body uncurls until I am sitting up again, soaking up her voice, the way she is looking at me.

'You're your own person, Rose, and I'm so proud of you.'

'You're proud of me?'

'Oh, sweetie. Of course I am. You're so accomplished. Who would have thought that your father and I would have a daughter with a PhD? Maybe I just don't say it enough.' My mother reaches over and plucks a tissue from the box on the table and blows her nose loudly. She dabs at her eyes and then she starts to laugh. Takes a gulp of her white wine and swallows it down. 'Now that I think about it, it's probably better that you don't become a mother. Too much trouble. So much failure!'

'Mom.'

'Really, Rose. I've failed you right where you need me the most. I'm awful!'

'Don't say that. You're not awful. You're my rock.'

'Oh! Rose! Do you mean that?'

'I do.' I start to cry, but I am laughing, too. My mother plucks another tissue from the box and hands it to me.

The two of us grow quiet. In the silence, my mother, she suddenly seems so small, so frail, even, in her ridiculous sweater. I notice the way her pants seem too big for her, the lines in her hands, the veins blue and stark along the back of them. Noticing these things makes me sad, and worried, like I might lose her at any minute. She makes me feel that I'm not alone. Not as long as my mother walks this earth.

Right then, my father comes in the door. 'How are my two favorite girls?' He's wearing his work clothes, bits of sawdust and curls of wood clinging to his shirt. 'Uh-oh,' he says when he sees that our cheeks are streaked with tears.

'We're okay,' my mother tells him. 'We're just having a moment.'

'A nice moment,' I say.

'Well, that's good to hear.' My father leans down to kiss my mother and then me on the cheek. He straightens. 'You've got to enjoy those when you have them.'

11

January 19, 2009

Rose, Life 2

I HEAR THE apartment door open and close.

'Heeyyyyy,' I call out seductively from the bedroom.

Well, I'm trying to sound seductive. I'm not sure I am achieving the desired effect, especially since I am not feeling very seductive. More like dismayed and angry. Even my lingerie is a bit irate. It's a bright, flaming red, the red of fire, the red of rage. I am an angry, lingerie-clad woman.

'Rose?' Luke's questioning voice travels through the apartment.

'I'm right here! In the bedroom! Come and see! You won't be sorry!'

I roll my eyes at myself.

This is obviously the end. The end of everything. The end of *me.*

'I'll be there in a minute,' Luke calls back, oblivious to the sexual delights that await him in our bed, namely his wife, who is currently wrapped in a multicolored, striped, grandma afghan. My plan is to throw it off just before Luke steps into the room, as though I've been perfectly happy to lounge on top of the bed nearly naked in mid-January. It's fucking cold in here. I should have turned up the heat before Luke got home but it's too late for that. I'm not about to traipse out to the thermostat in the living room in this getup. Besides, that would ruin Luke's surprise.

I can hear my husband going through the mail, tossing things onto the kitchen table, opening an envelope, unfolding the papers inside, followed by the silence of reading. Then the process starts over. He may never get here. He may decide to sleep on the couch, never entering the bedroom at all.

Would it be so terrible?

I try not to let myself answer this question, distract myself with other things. The start of the semester is coming up and I haven't finished my syllabi yet. I always start out the December break intending to do my syllabi immediately, but it never happens. Within five minutes of turning in my grades I settle into holiday mode. And this December and January I've done barely any research and writing. Suspecting one's husband of an affair can really do a number on a person's academic productivity.

There comes the sound of another envelope ripping open, another letter being unfolded, followed by the silence of Luke perusing whatever is in his hands. I pull the afghan tighter.

It's been a long time since Luke and I have had sex. Months. Back when Luke made his retreat from wanting a child, I'd hoped that we were on our way to a fresh start, that better times were on the horizon. But lately we only seem to move in different directions, away, away, *away*. This and, well, there's regular life coming between us. Teaching classes, doing research, seeing friends for dinner, Luke's more and more frequent work trips.

And it's not as though Luke has been asking for sex, not like I've had to turn him down. He stopped asking a long time ago.

Maybe because he's getting it elsewhere.

Or maybe he's been waiting for me to make the first move, for me to be the one to reintroduce sex into our married lives, for me to notice how we've grown apart and become the one to start stitching everything together again. To make him, to make sex, a priority. He took a step back from pressuring me about children, now it's my turn to take a step forward toward him. Toward us.

There is a photo of Luke and me hanging on the wall on my side of the bedroom, from the day of our wedding. I am leaning in to kiss Luke on the lips, and his eyes are shining. We look so happy. It's the happiness that makes the photo so hard for me to look at. It hurts to wonder how we've come so far from there to here. I remember the exact moment of that shot from our wedding day. It was taken right after the slideshow of photos we played for our guests, just before the cake was cut. Luke put it together, of course, the official photographer of our life.

Luke led me over to the two chairs in the middle of the dance floor, placed there so we could have the best view of the screen and so all the weddings guests could watch us watching. Two of Luke's young cousins ran over to arrange my dress around the chair, which they'd been doing all day. Someone cued the music and when the slideshow started, Luke whispered, 'I am the luckiest man alive, Rose.'

As the photos appeared one by one, beginning with a few from the first day we met all the way up until just this past week, with a photo of Luke, me, and both sets of our parents, the six of us out for pizza after we'd run around finishing last-minute details for the wedding, I thought about how I'd once been so camera shy. Yet somehow, because of this man who sat next to me now, there I was, smiling, laughing, so unself-conscious. I thought about how Luke was this person who knew the real Rose, the real me deep down, who knew just how to draw her out into the light, just how to capture the person I really am. How, from the moment he handed me that album of my life in graduate school for my parents, I never looked back, couldn't imagine there was a better man in the universe than Luke, a better man with whom to share a life. My life.

The slideshow was perfect, it was us, and when it ended, I leaned in, turned to my husband, and said, 'And I am the luck-iest woman alive, Luke. And I love you. You know me better than anyone else in this world.'

'I know I do,' Luke said, turning back to me. 'You know me, too.'

I kissed him. We were still kissing when the lights went on, and that was when the photographer snapped the photo that has lived on our wall ever since. This photo that I am staring at right now. The sheer magnitude of our happiness in that image, when I allow myself to take it in, makes me want to weep with loss.

Can Luke ever feel that way about me again?

Can I feel that way about him?

I hear the faucet, Luke filling up a glass.

'Hello?' I call out. 'Don't forget that I'm waiting for you!'

'I'll be there in one sec!'

Luke's footsteps sound in the kitchen, then halt in the living room.

I struggle out of the grandma blanket and push it onto the floor. As soon as it's gone, my entire body is covered in goose bumps.

Earlier this afternoon I experimented with different, potentially seductive poses. Lying on my side, head propped with my hand and elbow; lying on my stomach, feet in the air, again with my head propped on my hands and elbows; lying on my back, which I quickly decided against because it made me feel like I was on an operating table, waiting to be opened up.

Luke's footsteps head toward the bedroom. Finally.

I am shivering, shaking with cold by the time he sees me. But I am also shaking with nerves and maybe a little fear. Is this the moment when we start on our way back to that blissful, happy place? Could this be the beginning of that journey?

Maybe?

Luke halts when he sees me. He's not smiling, he doesn't laugh. Just wears a shocked and not entirely pleased look on his face. 'Rose, what is this?'

Luke was supposed to walk inside the room and light up with a smile, get that gleam in his eye he used to get when he wants me, that I used to love seeing but that I haven't seen in ages.

'Um – what do you think this is?' Not the sexiest, most seductive of responses, but I console myself that it's the effort I've made that counts. Given what I'm wearing, that I've been waiting for my husband for the last hour on top of our bed naked, the effort should be evident.

Luke walks toward the bed, rounds it to the other side. Then he picks up the blanket from the floor and throws it toward me. 'You're freezing.'

My skin flushes pink. I pull the afghan so it covers my stomach down to my toes. 'I wanted to surprise you.'

'Rose.' Luke sighs. He sits down on the edge of the bed – far away, far enough that if he extended his arm he wouldn't touch me. 'I don't think I can do this today.'

Do this? This as in sex?

Do the sex?

Do all married people eventually feel this way about sex? Think of this once pleasurable, connective activity as a kind of chore like the dishes or the vacuuming, not exactly pleasant but some- thing that needs to get done?

The way Luke is looking at me now, like he wants to be anywhere but here, anywhere but on a bed with his wife asking for sex. Was I wrong in thinking that we could save our marriage – that we could save us? Am I too late?

'I was thinking.' I inch toward him across the comforter, reck- less. 'Maybe I was wrong, Luke. Maybe we *should* try.'

What are you doing, Rose?

The expression in Luke's eyes grows skeptical. Even slightly cold. 'Try what?'

'You know – to have a baby.' I am getting desperate. Obviously. Luke is up and off the bed in a flash. 'No.' He sounds angry.

I stare at him, unable to move, a rejected heap of blanket and lingerie and wife. 'What do you mean, no? Why not? You pestered me about a child for years. I'm finally telling you yes, and you're saying no?'

'Are you kidding me, Rose? Are you kidding me right now?'

I open my mouth, close it. This was supposed to be a reunion, a rekindling, and instead it's a disaster. Shit.

The cold expression in Luke's eyes, it's as if by doing this today, trying to offer him sex, suddenly offering him a baby after all this time, these things he's so wanted, or used to want – somehow I've made these desired things offensive to him.

Before I can stop myself, I ask him another question, the question that has been zinging through my brain for months but I haven't dared speak.

'Are you seeing someone?' I ask my husband.

His silence is endless.

12

May 3, 2009

Rose, Life 1

'M MMM.' This cake is delicious. Memorable. I eat another bite. I am eating memorable cake with memorably delicious coffee to go with it. The café where I sit is beautiful. Spacious, with tall white tables and tall white stools to go with them. Soft music plays over the speakers. Pale gray concrete floors, tall windows with thin, white metal trim. White and pale gray, pale gray and white. Serene. Clean. Soothing. New.

I'm supposed to be at a conference this week out on Long Island, but after a morning of boring panels and talks I found myself walking out, down the street, through the pretty little town and into this café. I cut a big forkful of the spongy cake and gobble it, let the soft, sugary flavor melt on my tongue before I swallow, chase it with a sip of the rich Americano I ordered to go with it. A sense of peace and well-being spreads from my stomach and my throat to the rest of me. It is a strange feeling, one I wondered if I'd ever feel again. If I'd ever feel it again *by myself.*

My mother promised I would. Jill. Denise and Raya, too.

But it was Frankie, my father's sister, whose late-night phone calls over the last year helped pick me up out of despair and into the land of hope again. Frankie is a painter and she's lived in Barcelona for fifteen years with her partner, Xavi. They fell in love fast, and Frankie fell equally in love with Barcelona. Frankie swears she and Xavi will never get married, and they don't have any children. She always makes me feel less alone in the world, but never more so than since Luke walked out.

For the last eighteen months I've been going out on dates, or trying to. I dated Oliver for a while, but that didn't work out. I wasn't ready, was too clingy, and he had to go back to London anyway. When he did, I bottomed out all over again. Then, after a few more months of wallowing in loneliness, I started dating again and it wasn't going very well. One night, after a particularly depressing evening out with a self-centered man named Mark, I was walking home through the city and I called Frankie.

She answered on the first ring.

'Hey!' Her enthusiasm was evident, even all the way across an ocean. She painted late into the night, so she was usually up despite the time difference. She'd sworn to me that even if I called after she'd gone to bed, she turned off her ringer when she went to sleep so it wouldn't wake her or Xavi.

'I'm glad you picked up,' I say.

'Of course I picked up!'

'But it's so late there.'

'I stay up late. You already know that.'

'Are you working?'

She laughed. 'I'm always working, so you called at the perfect time. I needed a break. How's it going?'

I looked both ways, stepped off the curb to cross the street. 'You know, another bad date.'

'Yeah?'

'Yeah.'

'Oh Rose. It will get better.'

'Will it?'

'Yes, I promise.'

'I'm going to hold you to that, Frankie.'

'That's fine.'

I slowed my pace so I could delay my return to the empty apartment that awaited me. 'I have kind of an intense question.'

'I love intense questions. Ask me anything.'

'Are you and Xavi happy you didn't have children?'

I could hear the scrape of a chair against the floor of Frankie's studio, my aunt settling in for a longer conversation. I wished I could picture her studio better. I'd seen photographs, but I've never been to visit Frankie despite her inviting me to Barcelona many times. Luke and I had considered going on our honeymoon. I'm glad we didn't. I liked the idea that the adopted city of my aunt still lay ahead in my life, untouched by my marriage.

'We are, Rose. But that's easier to say now that we are so far along on the other side of our decision.'

I turned left, down a block lit up with the display windows of expensive boutiques, taking in the elegant dresses as I passed. 'You make it sound like maybe you were once uncertain. I thought you always knew you didn't want kids.'

'We did know. But that doesn't mean Xavi and I didn't have

our moments of doubt. It's not easy making a choice that no one else around you is making. Xavi and I went through all of that wondering if we would regret our decision, if we were making a mistake. I don't think any woman is immune to those questions.'

I halted before a long dress, covered in bright pink flowers, and felt a pang of desire. I tried to hold on to it as long as I could. Desire, even tiny amounts of it, had become rare in my life. 'I'm jealous of your "we", Frankie.'

She let out a breath. 'I got lucky that Xavi and I felt the same way. I know it must be difficult to carry that decision all on your own, Rose. But it's brave of you.'

I continued walking. 'I'm not sure brave is a good way to be. Brave has made me divorced. Brave has made me alone. Brave has made it so my husband' – I halt, backtrack – 'my *ex*-husband is living with another woman, who is probably about to get pregnant any day now. Or maybe she already is.'

'Rose, eventually this is all going to seem so far away.' Frankie's voice went up and up, the force of it growing. 'What I didn't say before is the part you probably need to hear the most, which is now that children are no longer possible for Xavi and me, what a relief it has been not to have them! We love our life. Having children is a fine choice for some people, probably most people, and not having children is an equally fine choice, even if everyone around you is making you question your decision. I'm certain you're going to get to that place, too, where you feel the same kind of relief that I do. I wish I could whisk you to there right now, whoosh!'

I smile a little. 'Me, too, Frankie.'

'Oh, I love you, sweetie,' she said back.

Frankie would tell me she loved me often, peppering our conversations with her love for me, her love for life, her love for the world and for Xavi and for her work. Her love reached for me across the ocean and through the phone and I tried to let it seep into me. During those nighttime calls with my aunt I discovered how much I especially enjoyed hearing Frankie talk about her work, hearing her describe what she was doing and why. There was always a lilt in Frankie's voice when she talked about it, a passion I detected there, her tone suddenly a melody. It would take me out of my sadness for a while.

But there was also something about it that took me back to another time in my life, a time before Luke, when I used to be my own person, when my interests and discussions didn't always revolve around him and whether or not to have a baby, or around what it meant to move forward now that he and I were divorced. Sometimes I imagined these conversations with my aunt as having a tail I could grab on to, letting it jolt me forward into a future where I found that the old Rose was still living inside me like a long-lost friend. Frankie's comments about color and composition, brush strokes and representation and emotion had the power to coax that Rose outside and into the lives of others again, reminding her there was a whole world waiting when she was ready.

I used to so enjoy being alone.

Being an only child does that to a person, teaches her to play alone, eat alone, go out alone. But then love, living with someone, marrying someone, it's like it undoes that part of you, unlaces it from your being so that it floats away. Since Luke and I divorced, I've hated my aloneness, feared it, mourned it, wondered if I would ever enjoy it again. I've tried so hard to be okay. But just when I think that maybe I'm finally there, something comes along to yank me back into sadness.

Now, I eat my very last bite of cake, and I watch as people come in and out of the café in groups, on their own, carrying away tall cups of coffee and wax bags of goodies.

The waitress comes over, studying the crumbs on my plate. 'Do you want another piece?'

Those pangs of desire that used to be so rare, so fleeting, have been more and more frequent lately. 'I do.' *I do!* I shall have cake. Divorce Recovery Cake. More and more cake!

'Good for you,' she says, and heads off to the pretty case that holds the desserts.

Good for me!

I put away my book and pull out my phone. I dial, and it rings twice.

'Rose!' My mother is always extra happy when I'm the one who calls. Usually she is the one calling me.

'Hi, Mom.'

'Is everything okay?' Her tone has dropped to very concerned. I've grown used to her Very Concerned About Rose voice.

'Yes, it's fine. Can't I call just because I feel like it?'

'Of course you can,' she says. 'But you usually don't.'

The waitress returns and slides the plate across the table toward me. I smile up at her and she nods. The slice is double the size of the last one. 'Maybe I should try to call you more often then.'

'I would like that.'

'I'm sorry that I don't.'

There is a long silence. 'Rose, you sound *good.*'

'Mom, you sound *skeptical.*'

'No,' she says quickly. Then, 'Well, you haven't sounded good in a long time.'

'I am good, Mom.' I take a big bite of cake, chew, swallow it, swipe another big bite with my fork and pop it into my mouth. 'I'm eating delicious cake,' I tell her, talking with my mouth still full.

She laughs, the sound of it light. 'Cake is good for the soul. How's the conference?'

'It's fine. Actually, I'm mostly blowing it off.'

'You are? That's not like you.'

'The weather is nice. The town is cute, right on the water. There are all these pretty restaurants and cafés. I decided to enjoy being here. I felt like wandering so I did. I am.'

'Rose, you sound so different. Like maybe you've turned a corner.'

'Maybe I have.' I say this, but then a round knot of darkness opens inside my chest, small but I can feel it there, wobbling, hovering, reminding me of the way it lives in me, constantly. Then, just as quickly it dissipates. 'It might not last,' I add.

'That's okay,' she says. 'Enjoy it while it does. And then it will happen again before you know it, the enjoyment.'

'I will.' The tone in my mother's voice provokes a smile. Because of the way she talks to me, believes in me, encourages me. I hang on to this, trust in it like I might trust in a divine being. My mother always comes through when I need her the most. 'I love you, Mom. I hope you know that.'

'I love you, too, my darling girl. And I do know. But it's always nice to hear you say it.'

The beach is deserted.

The sky is turning pink and orange with dusk. The sand is soft, everything about this town, the weather, the warmth, the sunlight, the breeze, is soft. I slip my sandals from my feet and hook my finger into the straps, dangling them from my hand as I walk, stopping occasionally to inspect a pretty shell, a perfectly smooth white rock, the broken half of a sand dollar. Tiny waves rise, then crash, rise, then crash. There's a cluster of delicate, mother-of-pearl shells, a couple of light orange ones, the others bright yellow, and I pocket three of them to take home. They are my mother's favorite. Then I head closer to the shoreline, dig my bare toes into the wet sand and enjoy the breeze, still cool with spring. The smell of the air tells me that summer is coming.

I stand there, watching the water for a long time.

A burden lifts. I feel it rising from my shoulders, the weight of it lessening, lighter, lighter, until it is no longer there. Tears sting my eyes and I start to cry, but it's not the sad kind of crying.

I don't have to become a mother.

The water runs across my feet, cool and lovely, the tide coming in.

I don't have to have a baby if I don't want to. And I don't want to have a baby. I never wanted to. Never.

Thank God.

Thank God Luke left. Thank God he's gone. Thank God this man who was trying to force me to become someone I've never wanted to be is no longer in my life, in my apartment, in my bed every night. He decided I wasn't enough for him. But maybe the real truth is that he wasn't enough for me.

The freedom of this new reality awakens in my body. Finally, *finally.*

When I move again, when I start on my way down the beach once more, something has changed in me, something permanent, I think. I hope. I wander back to the hotel, a little bungalow not far from the water. I paint my toenails.

It's true, today I am good. Good in a different way, soft, yielding, warm, a fresh ball of dough. I press into it, settle within myself somewhere deep and pillowy.

It might not last.

But it also might.

Part Three

Enter More Roses,
Lives 4 & 5

13

August 15, 2006
Rose, Lives 4 & 5

L UKE IS STANDING on my side of the bed. He never goes to my side of the bed. In his hand is a bottle of prenatal vitamins. He holds it up, shakes it. The sound is heavy and dull because it is full.

'You promised,' he says.

'Sometimes I forget.'

'Sometimes?' His tone is angry. Accusing.

I stand accused. I am guilty.

We both know it.

'I haven't been taking them like I said I would, okay?' I admit my offense, get it over with.

Luke is quiet. Then he says, 'You obviously don't want to take them.'

'No,' I say, another confession. 'I obviously don't.'

*

My will is cracking.

I can feel it, my whole body boiled like an egg and rolled against a kitchen towel so the pieces will fall away.

Luke and I are not speaking. For nearly a week, we have moved around each other, stood in the same room with barely an acknowledgment. The only conversation we've shared is polite – 'Do you want this last bit of coffee or can I have it?' Or logistical – 'I'll be back late tonight because there's a department event.'

But then, day by day, the cold, hard anger between us that started with our fight has softened, left out of the freezer long enough to melt. I can't tell what remains of the ire or what it's turned into. Our minimal interactions have grown a little kinder, a bit more sensitive, sometimes slightly affectionate. It's allowed me to see the future and the future for Luke and me has two distinct paths. Down one road we stay together, have a baby – we stay together *because* we have a baby. Down the other, we don't have a baby and split up – we split up *because* there won't be a baby.

Would it really be that bad to have a child? Can I just close my eyes and will myself to do this? Have a baby and make my husband's dreams come true? Save my marriage?

Maybe it would be fine. Maybe it would be great. Maybe I would look back on this time in my life and think, *Oh Rose, you were so silly! Having a baby is the best thing you've ever done! How could you possibly have missed this?* Isn't that what all mothers think after they've had their children? That this is my magnum opus and all that, like in *Charlotte's Web*?

Maybe half those women are lying. Maybe they just say things like this because they have to because once there is a baby, what, really, can you do? There's no returning it to the store.

Is the fact that I've just likened a baby to a purchase one might return at Bloomingdale's or Nordstrom a sign? A flashing warning that says *Rose Napolitano: You are not fit to be a mother if you are thinking about returning a baby to Bloomingdale's!* Of course, Nordstrom would be the smarter bet. Best to buy the child at a place that will always take things back – isn't that their policy?

As I lie in bed at night next to the man I married, I hold these thoughts inside. In the quiet, a sadness has grown, a recognition, I think. Luke and I are at a crossroads. And at some point soon, one of us is going to have to make a move.

'I give up,' I say.

'Rose, what are you talking about?'

Luke is standing in a towel before the bathroom mirror and sink shaving his face, which is half coated in white, streaks carefully razed across his cheek. I am lurking in the hall just outside the open door. The light of the bathroom is glaring.

'Let's just try, okay?'

'Try what?' Luke asks. But there is a hope, a brightness in his tone that I haven't heard in a long time.

The fact that he's going to make me say it out loud, that he needs me to actually say the word *baby*, let's try to have a *baby*, breaks my last bit of will. 'Nothing, Luke. Ugh! Forget it. Let's try nothing, not now, not ever.'

He puts the razor onto the counter. The white shaving cream

along its edge makes a small cloud on the granite. He knows he's misstepped. 'Just answer the question. Please?'

I shake my head. Slide down the wall until I am sitting on the floor.

'Rose?'

Before I can stop them my hands are covering my face and I am crying. Soon Luke is crouching next to me; his rich, low voice – a voice I used to love, but do I any longer? – is saying, 'Rose, Rose, what's the matter? You can tell me.' This is the first real sign of concern that he's offered since our fight.

I want to soak it up, but I can't. I know he's only offered it because he knows I've caved, because I'm going to give him what he wants. Because he has won. We've been hovering on this precarious threshold for so long and it's about to go his way. Maybe behind that concern in his voice is a little fear, too, that right at the moment I was ready to tell him yes, one misguided question might have ruined his chances.

I look up from my hands, reminded that I am the one who holds the power to give or take this desired thing away. The woman always does. The man can do nothing to change it. Which is why they always find other ways to punish us for this one thing we have that they don't, right?

'You know what's the matter,' I say. 'We're the matter, Luke.'

He pulls the bath mat closer and sits on it, cross-legged, facing me.

'We used to be so happy,' I tell him.

'I know.'

'And now look at us.'

He leans forward, blinking. 'A baby would change that, Rose.

I know it would. A baby would bring us back to the place where we started.'

I stare at him, take in what he's just said, and the moment he's chosen to say it. He can't help himself, not even for a few minutes, not even after I've been sobbing. He wants what he wants and he has to get it from me. What he wants is a baby because I am no longer enough for him. Does he realize this? This implicit message he sends to his wife with so much desperation?

His eyes are a little wild now, a little frantic.

Faced with a choice, I make one. It seems the only real option, because in the other choice I end up alone.

'Okay, fine,' I say, letting out a long sigh. 'Let's try, Luke.'

14

September 25, 2007

Rose, Life 4

M Y FATHER'S CARPENTRY workshop is in the garage of the house where I grew up, though my parents haven't kept their cars in it for years. They park in the driveway or, if it's supposed to snow, under the overhang of the sprawling oak tree that edges the front yard. My mother complains about this, that my parents have to clean off their cars after a big storm, chipping the ice from the windshield or when they have to run out to the car from the front door because it's raining, but she doesn't really mean it. She's proud of my father's talent. He makes such beautiful things.

'Dad? Can I come in?' I push the side door open a crack.

'Rose? Sweetheart? Is that you?'

There is a little screened hallway that connects the house to the garage, and this is where I am. I open the door wider. 'Hi, Dad.'

He looks over, his tall form bent over a table, a piece of sandpaper under the gloved palm of his hand. Dust from the wood covers the floor. Next to him is a bench where he lays out his tools. On the wall behind him there are special notches where he hangs chairs in progress and other unfinished furniture. On the other side of the garage is a big metal cabinet full of varnish, and next to it, stacks of wood. My father is wearing baggy jeans today, and a plain green, short-sleeved shirt. His hair shines gray in the light. 'Come give your ole dad a hug.' He straightens up, takes off his work gloves.

His arms close around me and squeeze hard enough to lift me off the ground. 'To what do I owe the honor of this visit? Don't you teach class today?'

'No. This semester I've got a Tuesday–Thursday schedule.'

My father smiles. 'Tough life you got there, kid.'

I nudge him. 'The life of leisure, Dad.' My father knows how hard I work, so his playful jabs don't bother me. My parents and I have come a long way from the days when they struggled to understand why I wanted a PhD and to become a professor. I relish how we can joke about my career like this now, and I cherish the genuine pride I hear in their tone when they ask me about it. 'I didn't mean to interrupt you. I thought I could just sit and we could talk while you work.'

'You're never interrupting.' My father goes over to fetch the chair he keeps in the back corner of the garage. It's painted the blue of hydrangeas, nearly violet, and it's been my special chair since I was small. He painted it that color just for me. It's bigger than a normal chair, wider. My mother made a thick, flowered chair pad that ties to the spindles at the back. The colors of the cushion have faded.

My father parks it in a spot next to his workspace. 'Here you go, sweetheart.' Then he puts on his gloves and picks up the sandpaper. 'Give me the update. What's going on? How were the first few weeks of school? Any students need a talking to?'

I laugh. 'Not yet, but it's good to know you have my back, Dad.' I tell him about my classes, the department, the new research project I'm hoping to launch.

I've always loved to watch my father work, to keep him company. When I was little, sometimes I'd bring a book with me and stay for hours, Dad and me side by side, him working, me reading in the quiet. My father isn't very talkative, but he's a good listener, a peaceful presence. Sometimes he and I listen to music together. He introduced me to his favorites from the sixties and seventies when I was a kid, and as I got older I forced him to listen to my emerging teenage tastes. He endured it, because it meant more time that we spent together.

On nice spring and fall days, he opens the garage doors while he works so he can breathe the fresh air and hear the birds, but today he has them closed and the air-conditioning is on. It's late September but it's still as hot as summertime.

'What's going on with you, Dad?' I ask after I finish my update, though I've left out the real reason I'm here. I can't seem to get it out of my mouth.

'Oh, you know. Same old, same old. Just making furniture for people. Eating your mother's cooking after I'm done for the day.'

'Any interesting orders?'

This question perks him up. My father tells me about a special series of cabinets he's going to make for a couple who are bringing all the wood from Mexico, some wood I can't pronounce that he's never worked with before. He sounds excited, gives me all the details about the project, and then eventually we shift into a companionable silence. I sit, watching him work, trying to get up the nerve to tell him what I came to say. Occasionally he glances over as his hand moves steadily, back and forth, against the tabletop.

My legs are pulled up, arms hugging my shins. The scratch of the sandpaper against wood is ongoing and familiar. 'I might have an interesting new order for you, Dad,' I say, finally.

'Oh? What would you like me to make you?'

I bite my lip, think about all the things my father has made for me over the years. In high school he made a canopy bed, which my mother thought was spoiling me, but I loved it with all my heart. He made me beautiful picture frames where I put photos of me and my friends at the prom and homecoming, and then Luke and me from our wedding. He made our bedside tables and the desk where I work at home. Half of the furniture in the house I grew up in came from his hands. All of it is beautiful. All of it is special, like him.

'Rose?' My father has stopped working and he is facing me.

I take a deep breath. 'A crib, Dad,' I say. 'I was thinking that maybe you could make a crib.'

I haven't yet told Luke that I am pregnant.

After I promised him I would try, I think I believed that my body would refuse a pregnancy. I'd wondered whether it was really a good idea for Luke and me to have a baby when everything had been so tenuous for so long.

But then, there have been these shifts in Luke – good ones.

125

The first was small and simple. I was sitting at my desk at home, working, and I looked up from my laptop, swiveled around in my chair. Luke was leaning against the door frame, watching me.

'I think we should go out for dinner this weekend,' he said.

'You do?'

'Yes. Like on a date.'

'You want to take me on a date?' I could hear the skepticism in my voice.

But Luke plowed onward. 'I read about this new Italian place. Supposedly they make great homemade ravioli. Maybe we could go this Saturday.'

I studied him. 'I love homemade ravioli.'

'I know. That's why I thought we should, you know, try this place.'

He stood there awkwardly, waiting for me to say yes or no.

We hadn't been out on a date in ages. We were married, we lived together, but for a long time we'd been more like roommates. Roommates who had sex, yes, and who were apparently trying to have a baby, yes, but not people in love. Not like we used to be. I still loved Luke, I always had. But I hadn't felt *in love* with him in a while. All that haggling over a baby, all the pressure from Luke, his parents, was not exactly a turn-on. It was a pretty big turnoff, in fact. Maybe he hadn't felt in love with me much lately, either.

Can married people fall back in love with each other?

'Why are you asking me out, Luke?'

Is this your new prelude to a baby-making session?

'Do I need a reason?'

'Yes,' I said.

Ever since I told Luke I would try to give him his baby, each time he tried to get me in the mood for sex seemed suspect. Like, is it me you really want right now, or the egg that is rattling down my fallopian tube?

Luke stuffed his hands into the pockets of his jeans and rocked back and forth from his heels to his toes. The air-conditioning kicked on, the noise from the fan a rumble above us. 'I just miss you,' he said. 'I miss us. The us we used to be. Don't you?'

I nodded.

'Then why is us going out to dinner such a hard question?'

I got up from my chair and walked past Luke into the living room. Luke followed and the two of us sat down on the couch. I decided to be honest. 'It's hard for me to trust your motives, Luke. Everything you do in this marriage feels somehow related to your need to have a baby. Even asking me out for dinner.'

Luke folded his hands, stared at them. 'I guess I deserve that.' He seemed about to say something else, but I wasn't done.

'Listen,' I went on, 'more than anything, I want your motivations to be simple, for you to be asking me to go to this restaurant because you know your wife loves ravioli.' The sky over the city was turning red with evening. 'But it's difficult to believe that it's not part of some plot to convince me, I don't know, to try harder to have a baby, to track my cycle better, to take more vitamins, ten vitamins a day, twenty of them, or because maybe you read that ravioli is good for fertility or something.'

Luke started to laugh. 'I promise I didn't read that ravioli is good for fertility.'

I glared at him. 'You think this is funny! But I wouldn't be surprised if it were true! I can't believe how much you know about what food is good and bad for a baby and we don't even have a baby. I'm not pregnant, Luke!'

Luke's laughter trailed off. 'Okay, okay. I get it. And I can understand why you feel that way, given how I've acted.'

'You do?' *Please do. Please do, Luke.*

Luke's hand reached across the couch and he left it sitting there, between us. 'Would you believe me if I told you the only reason I want to take you out to this place is because I know my wife, Rose Napolitano, loves ravioli as much as her husband, Luke, loves sushi? And not because I have ulterior motives about that same wife getting pregnant?'

I made a skeptical face and shrugged. 'Maybe?'

'Can you try to believe that?'

I studied my husband in the shifting light.

Could I?

He blinked, then blinked again. I got the feeling that Luke was nervous. Something sparked inside me, the faint memory of a time when I believed that Luke was the only man I would ever and could ever love. What would it be like to feel that again now, after everything we've been through?

Luke's hand looked so lonely there on the couch. 'I can try,' I told him. I covered his fingers with mine. 'I will try.'

'So let me ask you again, then. Rose Napolitano, would you go out on a date with me this Saturday, only because I would like to see you happy and because I am your husband, who loves you very much?' Luke raised my hand to his lips and kissed it.

I laughed, enough that it broke the tension. 'Yes, Luke, I will go out on a date with you, and for no other reason than because

I love you.' When I said this, I felt my body flush. It felt like an admission, something that should be automatic between husband and wife but, given our circumstances, made me feel vulnerable. Like I'd confessed a secret.

But then Luke smiled, too, a bigger smile than mine, and said, 'I didn't have any other ulterior motives, Rose. I just wanted to make my wife happy. Really.'

The two of us sat there, smiling stupidly at each other. Then Luke opened a bottle of wine and we got a little drunk, talked for hours and laughed and forgot, for once, all the troubles that had been plaguing our marriage. When Luke set his wineglass down onto the coffee table and kissed me hard, I let him, I let us fall into loving each other without caring what came of it or what his motives might be. When we went to bed that night a seed of hope had sprouted inside me, and I fell asleep happy.

From that one exchange, Luke and I began the long, slow climb back toward each other. Little by little, the happiness crept back in and began to cauterize the wounds in our love, our lives, our marriage. Enough that when I took that first pregnancy test and saw the two lines that appeared and formed a plus, as much as seeing that positive sign made me afraid, and maybe even a little regretful, I was also able to feel a bit of that hope, too. Maybe after all this fighting and resistance, having a baby with Luke might actually be a good thing. Not just for him or for us, but for me. For me, too.

'A crib?' The look in my father's eyes is uncertain. The sandpaper in his hand crumpled from the force of his grip on it.

He might be the one person in my life other than Jill who has never pressured me about having children, never grilled me about motherhood, about why I've always been so allergic to it.

'I don't like the way Luke has been pushing you,' my father said not long ago, after my mother told him Luke and I had been fighting over having children.

He and I were talking on the phone as I walked home from teaching. Cars passed, honking their horns, people walked by, lugging their things from the train. My father didn't have to spell out what Luke was pushing me about. He and I both knew.

'It's okay, Dad,' I said, even though there was nothing okay about it, which was why Luke and I had been fighting.

'You know what is best for yourself, Rose, and I trust your judgment. You should trust it, too.'

'Thanks, Dad,' I said, and then the conversation shifted to safer subjects, to the storm that was coming and how it was going to rain hard for a full day.

My father is still waiting for me to respond. His eyes are searching mine.

'Yes, Dad. A crib.' I breathe out, and then I say it – I try out the words that have yet to fall from my lips. 'Because I'm pregnant.'

My father is the first person I tell.

'Sweetheart,' he says, then nothing else.

'I'm trying to feel okay about it,' I tell him.

Sweat trickles down my father's brow and he wipes it with the back of his hand. 'Rose, do you think you want to keep it?'

My eyes fill with tears. 'Oh, Dad.' I love that my father is reminding me that I have options, that I can still decide one way or the other if this is the right thing for me. All without flinching while he says it.

In the moments that pass between my father's question and my answer, I think back to the cycle of hope, then doubt, hope then more doubt, which has been rounding my brain ever since I took that pregnancy test, and then the second test and then the third. How I keep rounding back to hope, to this place where my husband and I have found our way back to love and to this new possibility that is a child.

'I am going to keep it,' I tell my father now. 'I am going to have this baby. So will you build me a crib, Dad?'

'Of course I'll build you a crib.' He puts down the crumpled sandpaper, takes off his gloves and sets them on the unfinished table. He holds out his arms to me again. 'I'll build you the most beautiful crib I've ever made in my life.'

That night, after I arrive back in the city, on my walk from the train I decide that I am going to tell Luke what I've just told my father.

'Luke,' I say, the moment I enter the door of our apartment. I find him in the kitchen, boiling water for pasta. 'There is something we need to talk about.'

He turns around, sees that I'm out of breath, looks at me funny, like he doesn't know what to think or what I might need to talk to him about, whether it is a good thing or a not-so-good thing.

'I saw my father today,' I go on.

There is a wooden spoon in Luke's hand, dripping with water. 'Yeah?'

I nod. 'And he told me he's definitely willing to build us a crib.'

When the light appears on my husband's face, the way it shines through his smile and his eyes, so brightly, I think to myself briefly, just a little flutter of thought, *Maybe this was all worth it, maybe everything will turn out all right, maybe someday I will look back on this moment and say that having a baby was the best decision that I've ever made in my life.*

15

September 25, 2007

Rose, Life 5

THE RESTAURANT IS bursting, patrons everywhere, spilling into the street through the glass doors that open onto the sidewalk. The afternoon that is giving way now to evening is perfect, one of those days that aren't quite summer but aren't quite fall. Warm but not hot, breezy but not windy, a faint crispness to the air but not cold. Luxurious. The kind of weather you want to bathe in, that makes you lean into it, that relaxes all of your muscles, soothing your skin. Weather that makes you let your guard down.

My guard is on its way down.

How far will it go?

I push through the happy crowd, the laughter, the flirting, the hands holding wineglasses, the pickup lines flying this way and that, women to men, men to women, women to women, and so on. They seep into me as I make my way to the bar, until I am soaking them in, absorbing their lust into my cells, a little off-kilter, and maybe a little bit out of my mind.

The bar is long, marble, gleaming, wide, packed, save a single open seat next to a man who is alone. He has a magazine open before him, folded so he can read only one page and not take up too much space. His fingers curl around a short, squat glass filled with something golden. Bourbon? Rye? His neck is bent in the act of reading, exposing a sliver of skin between the collar of his shirt and the beginning of his hairline.

I go to him.

The seat is for me.

I climb onto it, without a word, with only the smile on my lips to communicate that I am pleased to be here, pleased to be taking this one particular open seat. Then I am hooking my bag underneath the ledge of the marble bar, crossing my legs, one thigh over the other, knees bared along the edge of my sleeveless green dress, body swiveling in his direction.

Toward this man who is not Luke, this man who is not my husband.

Thomas.

A part of me wonders whether I am dreaming this or hallucinating it.

Thomas looks up, meets my eyes, smiles back.

No. No, I'm not.

The responding jolt in my chest catches me off guard, as though I've been struck by something powerful and sharp.

'You're here,' he says, voice low and steady amid the loud talk and laughter.

I have to lean closer to hear him.

Was that the idea?

'I told you I would be.'

'I know, but . . .'

'But?'

'I thought you might decide not to come.'

'No. That was never a possibility. I was always going to be here.'

His smile deepens. 'Me, too.'

We are grinning now, the both of us, like the high school students I always see when I'm heading down into the subway after school. Couples pressed against each other along water-stained walls, in the middle of platforms, mouths hungry, sucking, licking, making out with abandon. I always take joy in their wild displays of affection, all that desire. I almost feel proud of them for it. I'm nostalgic for that kind of want, the kind that Luke and I had in the beginning but that soon was misplaced amid grown-up life and busyness and decision making about apartments and who would water the plants and take out the garbage. Amid questions about who would have the baby and whether the baby would be had at all.

'It's good to see you again,' I say to Thomas, and it starts to sink in, what we are doing here. My excitement, the thrill in my body at Thomas's proximity is present in every word, every gesture. It's in the flutter of my eyelashes and in my unmistakably flirty tone. I imagine leaning forward, leaning closer, pressing my lips against Thomas's lips, right at this bar, in front of everyone in the restaurant.

Is he imagining the same?

The bartender is standing before me. 'What can I get you?'

'Do you have Sancerre?' I ask him.

'We do,' he says.

'I'll have a glass of that, please,' I tell him.

I don't even hesitate.

I should. In theory I should be horrified by such a casual attitude in the face of catastrophe. But tonight I am feeling reckless, I am being reckless, welcoming all possible catastrophes, calamity that is near and far, some of it so close it is staring at me with a pair of hazel eyes, more green than amber, within arm's reach. Within *my* reach.

And I find my arms reaching.

Fingers brushing a shoulder, moving lightly down a back.

Thomas's back. Thomas who is not Luke.

'It's really good to see you again, too, Rose,' he returns, delayed, as though each movement toward each other, toward all the things we aren't supposed to be doing – meeting up, sitting together at a bar, ordering drinks, touching each other with fingers, hands, bodies – each small step requires another greeting, another acknowledgment, a back-and-forth of approval.

The way Thomas speaks, the tone he uses, tells me everything I need to know. It's a clear and welcoming yes, an opening up to all of this – to him, to me, the two of us together on this beautiful evening in a lovely bar – so full of promise, so pregnant with possibility.

Pregnant like me.

I am pregnant.

'I think I'm going to be sick.'

I whispered this to no one, while kneeling on the bathroom floor, stomach roiling, hands shaking, my entire body shivering

136

as though it were wintertime when it was smack in the middle of summer.

Luke and I were staying at a beach cottage that my parents rented for the weekend, the waves outside roaring because a storm was passing. They mirrored the feeling in my gut, all that white water sizzling, swirling, bubbling along the surface of the ocean, crashing and receding, crashing and receding again. I breathed deeply, let the air out, then breathed deeply a second time. The bathroom tiles glared white, and I nearly had to squint against the brightness. An old pillar sink rose up from the floor next to me, majestic and thick.

I rocked back and forth, gripping my stomach, nearly retching but then never actually doing it. When would this pass? Soon? Never?

There was a soft knock on the door. 'Rose, are you all right?'

No one else was at the cottage, aside from my mother. Luke and my dad had gone to visit a helicopter museum, one of the highlights in this tiny New England town. My mother had given them a list of things they needed to buy at the supermarket afterward, so they'd be gone awhile.

'I don't know,' I said back weakly, my breath as shaky as my voice.

'Can I come in?'

'Yeah.'

I rested my forehead on the edge of the toilet seat. It's amazing what a person will do when she is sick to her stomach – lay her head on the grimy floor, be willing to rest her cheek against the toilet. One's disgust barometer gets out of whack.

'Oh, sweetheart! You look green! Did you eat something that

didn't agree with you? Maybe it was the clams we had for lunch at that little shack. I told your father we shouldn't eat at a shack on the side of the road.'

The mention of clams, the sound of the word itself, hard and ugly, made my body rebel, and I hung my head over the toilet bowl. Still nothing. I slumped backward again, rested my forearm and elbow against the white curving toilet seat and peered up at my mother. 'I don't know what it is.'

My mother plopped herself down, got cross-legged on the floor. 'Don't worry. It will pass. Soon I bet. These things never last long.'

The presence of my mother beside me, so unselfconsciously willing to sit on the bathroom tile and keep me company, brought more solace than I'd expected. It's amazing how an adult can still need her mother. A wave of gratitude spread through me.

'Could it have been the lobster last night?' my mother asked next. 'I hope it wasn't the lobster. You know how getting sick can put you off something for life and I don't want that for you with lobster. You've always loved lobster! Ever since you were little. Remember how you used to love to dig for those tiny shreds of meat from the baby claws? Your father and I would watch you spend ages going through them one by one. We always thought it was so funny.'

'Mom,' I moaned, 'no more food talk.'

'Oh, right! Sorry. Well, let's see . . . what else . . .' There was a silence, but the kind where I could tell my mother was thinking about something.

'Mom, what?'

'Hmmm. I'm not sure I should say.'

I lifted my head slightly, a small tilt, enough to look my mother in the eyes. 'Now you have to tell me. Please, Mom. I can't handle suspense right now.'

'It's just that it might make you angry.'

'I don't have the strength to be angry.'

'You have to promise not to get upset, if I say what I'm thinking.'

'Mom!'

She placed both hands flat on the floor, leaning forward, her chin inches from the edge of the toilet bowl. 'Well, it just occurred to me that this might be morning sickness. Which can happen at any time of day, by the way. But of course, it couldn't be morning sickness because you are against having a baby and you always have been. Unless . . . you and Luke changed your mind and just haven't told your father and me that you've been trying?' She rocked backward now, like she was trying to get out of the way in case I sprang at her. She lowered her voice to a whisper. 'You see why I didn't want to say anything?'

Right then, after all that empty retching, I flung myself over the toilet and vomited. My mother steadied me with her hands, held me there, until it was over. Then she handed me some tissues to wipe my mouth. We sat there, not speaking, the nausea in my stomach subsiding, while the activity in my brain sped and tumbled and sputtered.

Could I really be pregnant?

Yes. Yes, I could.

Shit.

As soon as the suggestion was out of my mother's mouth, I knew she was right. How it hadn't occurred to me during the entire hour I'd sat, draped over the toilet, is incomprehensible. I guess I wasn't looking for it, hadn't truly accepted the idea that this body of mine would succumb to pregnancy, as though the resistance to it in my mind somehow would turn that particular womanly switch to *off* in my reproductive parts as well; as though it were all a matter of religious faith and I was an atheist when it came to pregnancy and motherhood. All that newfound 'openness' to these things, I'd been *performing* it for Luke. But it was mostly just me humoring his need for a baby alongside my attempt to prevent our marriage from ending.

'Sweetheart? What are you thinking?'

'That I might be,' I whispered, but stopped short of saying the word.

'I'm right, aren't I? You're pregnant?'

I could hear it in my mother's voice, just above the concern, the worry, the sense that this was complicated ground and she was walking gingerly, that tinge of hope, a subtle trace of wonder and thrill. I was finally going to make my mother a grandmother. The one thing she wished for yet had been convinced would never, ever happen.

'I think so,' I told her.

To my mother's credit, she responded with a question, not congratulations. 'So how do you feel about that?'

I tried to feel happy then, to turn that baby switch to *on*. I tried to be overcome with that mysterious joy of expectant motherhood.

But what I really felt in that moment?

Regret. Fear. Dismay.

Rage.

What had I done?

The word *abortion* floated in and out of my brain, a little raft of hope.

But could I swim to it? Should I?

If only Luke had been willing to back off with his baby obsession for a minute, the keeping of the calendar for my period, the endless observing of everything that entered my mouth once I agreed to try. If he'd just let us go back to normal, to be the Luke I met and fell in love with during graduate school, who was happy to have sex just because he was having sex with me, Rose, and not because he was having sex with the potential future mother of his child, then maybe everything would feel different. Maybe I would be happier about the fact that I might actually be pregnant.

There came the sound of the front door opening, shutting, and my father's and Luke's muffled voices.

I crumpled the tissues in my left hand. 'Promise me you won't say a word to anyone about this, Mom.'

She leaned forward and kissed my cheek. 'I promise, sweetheart. I love you. It's going to be okay.' She looked at me hard, held my gaze. 'It *is*.'

'I love you, too,' I said.

The bartender delivers my wine and my hands are on it, raising the glass to my lips. I take a big gulp, the crisp tartness of it delicious. As soon as it's down my throat I take another sip, the sharp, tangy flavor perfect in my mouth.

'Good?' Thomas asks.

'Yes. I haven't had a glass of wine in a while,' I tell him. I haven't had one since I learned I was pregnant, but I do not tell Thomas this. I am not showing at all yet, thank God. Soon I will pass that mark where I can still have an abortion. This is my first thought, every single day when I wake up. Abortion. Should I? Will I? But I also know that I won't. I told Luke I would do this baby thing, and I am doing it just like I said. I never said I would do it perfectly, though.

I take another sip and smile into the glass.

Resistance.

This is my resistance, my fuck you to Luke that arrived tonight in a pretty glass, part of a rebellion I've been waging since the moment I read that stupid plastic stick with its double lines, since I found myself in this place where the woman who claimed that she didn't ever want children found out she was pregnant. Preggers. I've always hated that ridiculous word. A man made it up, probably.

But I've only myself to blame, right? This is what I get for being a coward, for being too afraid of my marriage ending, too afraid of Luke leaving me for some other woman who'd give him a baby. This is my consolation prize, those pluses and lines and yeses on plastic sticks soaked in urine. The consequences of my fear of ending up alone.

Thomas shifts his barstool a little closer to me.

This, right here, Thomas, is another consequence. Thomas is part two of my great big fuck you.

Thomas and I met when he gave a lecture on his research that my department sponsored. He is a sociologist, like me, at a university across town. Our connection was immediate, so much that we talked all evening at the reception afterward, until nearly everyone else had gone home for the night, including Jill, who had been at his lecture, too. When Jill said it was late and she was leaving, was I coming?, I shook my head, no, told her I would stay a little longer, which made her eyebrows arch in a *What are you doing, Rose?* kind of way.

That night I told myself I wasn't doing anything other than talking to an interesting new colleague, and wasn't that nice? But as the evening wore on and my sense of Thomas's nearness, his voice, his eyes, and every word from his mouth only grew more acute, I knew I was in trouble. By the time he and I had said goodbye and exchanged phone numbers, a big part of me didn't care if I was.

Thomas stares down into his own glass, like he's debating something.

What could it be? Does it have to do with the fact that he's a single man at a bar with a married woman? Could it be that he's having second thoughts about staying?

I shift a little closer to him now. I shift until Thomas and I are so close that our thighs are touching. Neither one of us moves.

There is a recklessness to everything about me. My body is being taken over by the baby and I gave in to it, and in doing so I've also given in to other outside forces, forces that I've decided are also beyond my control, but these are more enjoyable, more indulgent, and so I indulge. I am gluttonous.

Thomas looks up from his glass and after a beat he turns back to me and smiles.

He's not going anywhere.

I eye the magazine Thomas is reading, the one that he pushed aside on the bar after I arrived. 'So what is the article about?' I ask him. I want to know everything Thomas can possibly tell me. I am hungry for it all, hungry for him.

As he answers I sip my wine. When it's gone, I order another.

The afternoon that I took all of the pregnancy tests, when I ran out to the pharmacy to buy more, gulping down iced coffee and tall glasses of water so I could pee and pee again, Luke was out on a photography shoot. When he came home I was busy in the kitchen, cooking him dinner.

I went through the motions of preparing a lavish celebration for us, and was on the verge of serving it. Steak from our favorite butcher, the expensive one we only went to on special occasions. Truffled potatoes, broccoli rabe sautéed in garlic, champagne to drink, mostly for him, but I would have a sip for the toast we would make to our future child. The steak was still sizzling as it rested on the plate, ready to be sliced against the grain by the sharp knife I'd set next to it. I timed everything perfectly, for the moment that Luke walked in the door.

I was supposed to be excited by this news. I was trying to be.

I was trying so hard my head hurt.

'What's all this?' Luke asked, walking up behind me. 'Wow, champagne – you bought champagne for a Tuesday night?'

I picked up the knife.

'Rose?'

I took the fork in my other hand, stabbed it into the meat, and began to slice it, dark pink blood pooling onto the white china that well-meaning guests had given us for our wedding. I couldn't speak. Couldn't look up, couldn't look at Luke.

He took the knife from my hand, then the fork, and laid them on the counter. Then his hands were on my upper arms, turning me around.

'Why are you crying?'

'I don't know,' I said.

But I did know.

Luke did, too.

'Tell me,' Luke said, the sound of concern entering his voice, but it couldn't quite cover the excitement simmering underneath.

I couldn't speak, couldn't answer him. I wanted to die. I wanted to go back and undo everything we'd done, that I'd done, have that stupid fight about the vitamins all over again, end it differently, with me walking out on Luke, on this marriage. I'd been dumb to think a baby would stop the parting of ways between Luke and me, because having a baby would part us all the same. But even worse, what I hadn't anticipated but should have known, was how having this baby was going to part me from *myself*.

And I could see her, too: the Rose I really was, the true Rose, fighting for air, for her voice, fighting for her life, trapped inside this other, newer Rose who'd gone and gotten herself pregnant with this man who didn't even seem like the person she'd married anymore. This Rose who'd relinquished her will, her own desires, the choice she should have made all along but didn't because she'd lacked the courage.

Which Rose would win out? I wondered.

As I stood there, my husband waiting for me to answer, to say something, anything, I realized that it was always going to end up like this, wasn't it? Luke could only get his way by me relinquishing mine. His joy, his pleasure, would be my end. I was giving Luke what he longed for, but I'd done so by sacrificing myself, my body, my time. Me. I'd sacrificed *me*.

The tears fell harder.

'Rose,' Luke said again.

'I'm sorry,' I said, but the apology wasn't for him.

Stupid, stupid, stupid. How could I have been so stupid? How could I have done this to myself? Why had I agreed? Why hadn't I fought harder for myself, for what I know is true about myself? And now I was stuck. I would have this baby. The alternative would mark me as a monster, a worse monster even than the one I was before, when I simply didn't want to get pregnant. Now that I actually was pregnant, if I aborted this child – this child that was so desired by Luke and his family – I would become the monster baby-killer. And the abortion would obviously be followed by the divorce.

Luke's presence at my back, his arms around my middle, became walls closing in on me, prison bars winding around my body.

I shrugged him off and went to the table I'd set for us so beautifully. 'I took a pregnancy test,' I told him, finally.

He sat down across from me. 'I take it the result was positive.' I could hear his desperation, even as I cried.

And I hated him for it.

'Yes,' I managed.

Then I reached for the champagne bottle, the cork popped before Luke walked in the door, and poured myself a tall glass.

I drank it down, all in one go, like some college student chugging a beer from a keg. The warmth of the fizz in my throat was the first moment of satisfaction I'd had all day.

Luke was looking at me with alarm. 'Rose, you can't do that.'

'Oh yes I can.' I poured myself another glass, topped it off as high as I could without spilling it. 'Tonight I can do anything I want. Tomorrow I'll worry about whatever it is I need to stop doing to make sure this baby turns out all right.'

He reached for my flute but I snatched it away. Champagne splashed onto the floor. The look on Luke's face – worry for the baby, of course, already so much worry – deepened the beginnings of the hatred I felt. It bloomed to a rich magenta, the color of lush red wine.

'Tomorrow then,' Luke said, and got up to serve himself the steak sitting in the bloody pool, half congealed.

Thomas and I talk amid the elegance of the restaurant. We smile at each other. We order food, more drinks, we settle in for the evening.

I couldn't be happier.

People say that motherhood changes you completely, that it remakes you anew. But if that baby growing inside of me really has designs on my being, if she or he plans to do away with that woman, *that* Rose, then I guess this is me fighting back, the real Rose hanging on for her life. I'll change, sure, but I'll change into a woman who cheats on her husband. I'll change into a Rose who rebels against all of it. An antimother.

My first official act of antimothering comes the moment I

decide to kiss Thomas as he and I sit there, sipping our drinks, the night falling like gauze over the crowd, a veil of privacy amid flickering candlelight.

I lean closer, smiling again, eyes on Thomas's eyes, mine half lidded, a dare.

This time, when my smile meets his, my hand is reaching for the back of his neck, fingers on that exposed stretch of skin above his collar. I cross the rest of the distance until our lips meet for the very first time.

And a piece of me, the old me, I feel it return.

16

July 16, 2010
Rose, Life 2

B ARCELONA IS UNLIKE any other city I've ever visited. Its medieval neighborhoods go round and round, circling outward until they are a winding labyrinth of stone, of narrow streets that block out the sunlight, of cobbles underfoot.

'Rose, it's over here. This way!'

My aunt Frankie grasps my elbow and tugs me along. She's light on her feet, the hem of her dress dusting the ground as she floats across it. 'I'm coming, Frankie,' I tell her and laugh. She's so energetic, so excited. The sky above is a perfect streak of blue between the tops of the buildings, the sun not quite overhead but shining bright. The warmth on my face, the warmth of the day, adds to the goodness coursing within. I am good. I feel *good*. I am alive!

'Rose, look at this place, look! Don't you love it?'

The street, so narrow a few paces back that I could almost stretch both arms and touch each side with my fingertips, has widened and wound itself toward a crossing of sorts, a point where three streets meet one another. A triangular building stands at the junction, a restaurant on the ground floor that is open to the air and teeming with lunchgoers. They spill onto the streets. People sit on stools or stand at the tall tables that jut into the open. They chat, they laugh, they're loud as they lift glasses of red wine, of cava, of beer to their lips. Who drinks water at lunch? No one. Not here.

'Ooh, let's grab that open spot over there,' Frankie says, and rushes over, plunking her fringed hippie purse on the round stool. She throws her hand in the air and beckons a waiter, speaks to him in perfect Catalan.

'What did you say?' I ask her.

She pats the open stool next to her and I climb onto it. 'I ordered us a bottle of red, some manchego, some blistered peppers – you know those ones you liked last night? The ones that are occasionally spicy – some *boquerones* and a *bomba*!' Her eyes light up and she grins.

'What's a *bomba*?'

'They're my favorites – but only at this place. They're like, let's see, a giant ball of mashed potatoes with meat in the center. The whole thing is deep fried. Oh, I can taste it already!'

'Deep fried mashed potatoes?' My stomach is already grumbling. This, and the transgressive joyousness of drinking a bottle of wine at two in the afternoon, has made me ravenous. 'I'm glad we've been walking all morning, then.'

Frankie shrugs, still smiling. 'I can't believe you're finally here!' She's been saying this all day.

It feels nice to be so wanted. To be loved with such open enthusiasm. 'I can't either,' I say, because I really can't. Why did

I hold off on this trip for so long? There was always an excuse not to come – I was busy with college, then I was busy with grad school, then I was busy getting engaged and getting married, then I was busy doing research and getting tenure. I was always letting my life choices revolve around work and conferences, rather than deciding to go somewhere just to go, just because I, Rose, felt like it.

Why did I have to get divorced to figure this out?

To let my life open up to new things, new choices?

Maybe Luke did me a favor by cheating. He said as much, but I kept telling him he was wrong. I didn't want to go through a divorce. And I was right not to want to.

The process of getting divorced is the opposite of busy. It's a kind of uncluttering of time and space in a person's life, an un-coupling from responsibility, from meaning and purpose, from obligation to one's spouse. I found myself floating around, unmoored and untethered in this way that was mainly discon-certing. I couldn't quite ground myself or find a railing to grasp. So when Frankie emailed to say that Xavi would be away for a month in the middle of my summer break, I didn't let myself think much before giving her a resounding *Yes, I'll come, I'll come for as long as you'll have me.*

The waiter arrives with the wine, uncorks it, and fills two giant goblets nearly to the top. Then he smiles at Frankie, says some-thing to her in Catalan, and the two of them laugh. He's good-looking, maybe my age. To me, he says, in accented English, 'Your friend's Catalan is perfect.'

'She's my aunt, actually,' I say.

'Your aunt! I don't believe it.' He turns back to Frankie and says something in one long rush and takes off again, winding his way through the packed crowd, bottle opener high above his head.

'Do you always flirt with the waiters?' I ask Frankie.

She shrugs. 'Oh, I wasn't flirting.'

I give her a skeptical look. 'Well, he was flirting with *you.*'

She holds up her wine. 'To your visit to Barcelona!'

We clink glasses. 'Thank you for inviting me. For not giving up on me, Frankie.' I look around; the lively atmosphere is infectious. 'This is amazing.'

'Speaking of flirting, you should try some flirting, Rose.'

'Should I?'

'Yes! With the waiters, with the tourists, with the locals. You're single! How fun!'

A small plate of peppers arrives alongside another of cheese; a different waiter brings them this time. I eat a piece of cheese, then another, then a pepper, wanting to put something in my stomach before I guzzle down this wine. 'Maybe,' I say to Frankie, which makes her light up. 'Don't get any ideas,' I warn, knowing that Frankie is one of those people who will talk to anybody. She doesn't need an introduction to strike up a conversation. That's how she met Xavi. He was at the table next to her, she thought he was cute, and she just started talking to him. 'So do you miss Xavi?' I ask, changing the subject.

'I do, I love that man,' she says. As we munch on our cheese, our peppers, the famous *bomba*, we talk about Xavi's trip this summer, their life together, the renovation they just finished on their beautiful apartment in the Born neighborhood, which has a stunning terrace that looks out onto the top of a medieval cathedral.

'I want my bathroom to be just like yours,' I muse, thinking about the lovely shower I had this morning, with its floor-to-ceiling glass door that opens onto the terrace. Their only neighbors are the birds sitting atop the church across the way, so why not shower in the sunlight every day?

'Rose, you can stay with us as long as you like,' Frankie says, another thing she keeps telling me.

'I'm so lucky my father has such an amazing sister,' I tell her.

'Awww! Rose!' She grabs my hand across the crowded table and squeezes.

The *boquerones* arrive. I take a long sip of wine. I start to feel it in my legs, that pleasant wooziness, that full-body sigh of relaxation. 'And be careful with your offer to stay as long as I want. I might decide to take you up on it.'

'Xavi and I would love that! What else is our spare bedroom for, anyway? You could do your next sabbatical here.'

I laugh. Frankie is so free. She and Xavi travel a lot, have friends over for dinner all the time, have the kind of life that people dream about; live the kind of dream you only see in the movies. 'Maybe I could,' I say. 'Why not? There's nothing really stopping me from spending a semester in Europe.' *There's no Luke to stop me*, I think, unable to prevent my brain from letting thoughts of him enter it. To my surprise the accompanying jolt of pain I usually feel whenever I think of him has faded. It's still there, but it's gotten duller with time.

Frankie raises her glass and we toast again. She makes sure to meet my eyes when she says, 'Why not, Rose?'

I eat another pepper, thinking. 'You know, I haven't cried once since I arrived. It feels impossible to be sad in this city.'

Some of the laughter disappears from Frankie's eyes. 'Do you want to talk about it?' Her voice drops an octave.

Do I? I eye the wine, listen to the happy, chatting patrons all around us, the energy like a soft protective cushion against the sharp edges of what happened. 'I mean, you already know everything.' Alongside Jill, Frankie has been the person with whom I've shared every gory detail of Luke's cheating, Luke leaving me for another woman, Luke divorcing me. 'Cheryl' – I can't help saying her name with a snotty, sarcastic tone of voice – 'is due any day now.' Cheryl, who is making all of Luke's baby dreams come true.

'Oh, sweetie.' Frankie sighs.

'I know. Sometimes I feel like I've ended up living in some bad movie.' I close my eyes, give myself a moment to collect myself. Remember where I am, how I am, how far I've come since that first moment when Luke finally told me about Cheryl and, soon after, walked out the door on me forever. Remember that I am in Barcelona with my aunt Frankie. My breath returns, I open my eyes. 'I'm doing better, Frankie, I really am. You know. Day by day. Time and all that.' Frankie nods. I fiddle with the stem of my wineglass. 'Luke, and everything that happened, feels really far away right now and I want to keep it like that. I mean, he is technically very far away right now, which is honestly such a relief. So . . . new topic. Before I go and get sad on you and on Barcelona.'

Frankie brushes a strand of long, silver hair from her face. 'How's your dad doing these days?'

'You know, he's working a lot as usual. He and my mother are excited about going to the beach for a week this summer. They love the beach.'

'As you do. And I do. I think it runs in the Napolitano blood.'

I pick through the peppers, trying to unearth a really tiny one, wondering if it will turn out to be spicy. 'As does the cooking.'

'Oh, I think that might be from your mother's side of the family.'

'Mom would be happy to hear you say that.'

Frankie gets down from her stool and comes over to stand next to me. She wraps her arms around me, squeezing tight, her cheek pressing against mine. I try not to get teary. 'I see both of them in you! Your father and your mother. What a nice combination.' She lets go, returns to her seat. Raises her glass again. 'Your parents are happy you're here. They're happy you're moving on with your life.'

We clink glasses again, but I barely take a sip this time. 'You're going to get me drunk, Frankie.'

'Getting a little tipsy during lunch is never a bad thing,' she says.

I look around us, at all of the people drinking, laughing, listen to the noise of so much pleasure, feel the happiness in my heart expanding through me, slowly, gently. I eat one of the vinegary *boquerones*, then another, then more cheese, more peppers, followed by more wine. The warmth of the day, the beauty of the city, the vibrancy of my aunt, the round red richness of the wine going down my throat, it's hard not to bask in all of it. It's hard not to be happy in the middle of it, to let it catch and lift me up, open me to anything, to anyone. To life itself. 'I'm going to be okay,' I say after a beat.

Frankie meets my eyes again in that intense way she has when she wants to communicate something important. 'You absolutely are.'

17

October 19, 2007

Rose, Life 5

I AM LYING on my back on the bed, staring at the ceiling, headphones in my ears, listening to a playlist. Thomas made it for me.

We are acting like teenagers. Ever since our first date at the bar, we've only seen each other twice, but in between we've sent each other long, heartfelt emails. Every day I write one to him, every day he writes one to me. This is what I do in my office after I finish teaching class. I sit at my computer and type out my life story to Thomas, I answer the questions from his last letter, and I ask him the things I want to know about him.

At first it was a kind of consolation prize for seeing each other so little, for the sheer difficulty of finding a way to meet up with him in person. Luke is like a parent I need to sneak around. All day I am opening my laptop, obsessively clicking the button that pushes new emails into my account. *Click, click, click.* I do it so much that I had to tell Luke I've been waiting to hear about a grant, then waiting to hear from the review board at my university, then waiting to hear whether I had an article accepted at a journal. The daily wait for something from Thomas is a maddening process, until the moment, the second, that this growing need in me is satisfied and Thomas's name pops up at the top of my in-box. The emails get longer and longer each time, more intimate, more intense.

I love it.

I love being teenage Rose again. It's as if I get to start my life over, take a new path with someone else. I get to pretend that my real life with Luke isn't happening to me. That I didn't really make those choices that got me to the place where I am married and pregnant with his child.

One of my earbuds is yanked out suddenly, startling me.

'Rose.'

Surprise! It's Luke, come home early.

'What are you listening to?' he asks. He's looking at me strangely.

I sit up on the bed, take the other earbud out. 'Nothing much.'

'Really? You had your eyes closed and this dreamy smile on your face.'

'Did I?'

Yes. I did. I know this. I busy myself wrapping up my headphones. I feel caught. Guilty. My cheeks flare. Can Luke see it? Does he notice?

Then, 'Come on,' he says.

'What?'

'We have to go for your checkup.' His eyebrows arch. 'For the baby?'

'Oh. Yeah. I forgot.'

Ha! Right! How could I forget when I am sick all the time? When my boobs hurt constantly? When I am far enough along that I am just starting to show? But not so far along that I've had to tell people yet. Not enough that I've had to tell Thomas yet. I want to preserve this liminal space with him a little longer, this place where I am still just Rose, the sexy, fun professor he's flirting with and not *Rose, the Pregnant, Expectant, Future Mother* who's about to grow big and round with a baby.

Luke sighs, long and heavy. He crosses his arms, impatient, scolding.

My guilt is gone.

Two nights later, Thomas and I are holding hands, walking down the streets of the city.

'I don't want you to go home yet,' he says.

It's late and it's dark and the darkness feels like cover, like safety, like maybe no one can actually see us. We are two children who believe that if we pull a blanket over our heads then no one will notice we are there. I know this is risky, that Thomas and I could run into anyone we know, at any moment. One of Luke's friends, one of mine. I haven't told anyone in my life about Thomas. Not Denise, not Raya, not even Jill.

'I don't want to go home either,' I say, where I'll be reminded about the reality of my life. It's so easy to forget when I'm out with Thomas.

Thomas and I have just had a nice, long dinner, we've talked and talked about our lives, our pasts, why he's single, why I'm not, about his little sister whom he adores, how he grew up near the mountains but discovered as an adult that he prefers the beach, like me, about his work as a sociology professor that is like mine but also totally different. Thomas studies addicts and addiction, the circumstances that lead to addiction, the various kinds of recovery programs that exist to help, the people who run them.

'So I think I won't go home,' I tell him now. 'Not yet.'

'But aren't people waiting for you there?'

Thomas never says *Luke*, not outright. I never say Luke's name either, not to Thomas. It wasn't a decision we made, it's just what we've done.

'I can stay out a little longer,' I tell him.

But what I don't tell Thomas is that Luke is away on a shoot in Boston. That Luke used to always be going on work trips but now that I'm pregnant, he's practically never going on work trips and it's driving me crazy. That I've been looking forward to Luke being away in Boston precisely because it would allow me to see Thomas for dinner, a *long* dinner. That technically I could stay out until morning if I wanted to and nobody would know the difference.

But do I want to?

Yes. No. I'm not sure.

'How long do you have, exactly?' Thomas asks.

'A while,' I say vaguely.

The knowledge of what I might do, what *we* might do if I offer up this information is what stops me from admitting that Luke is gone.

Thomas and I haven't slept together. Not yet. I've thought about it nearly constantly since our first night out, but there's something frightening about taking this step. It's as though, if I stop things at kissing, if I stop them at making out in the dark corner of a bar once or twice, then this isn't really an affair I am having. That somehow this means that I, Rose, am not really doing this, or that I can take it all back. But if Thomas and I cross that line, if I let things go this one step further, then there is no going back. There will be no denying that it's real.

It starts to rain. Thomas pulls me under the awning of the building next to us. His sweater is soft against my arm, and he smells of cedar, of wood and tuberose.

'I was going to suggest we take a walk in the park,' he says. 'But maybe that's not the best idea.' He extends a hand beyond the edge of the awning. Drops of water patter against his palm. 'We could go for coffee somewhere.'

'We could,' I say.

I wrap my arms around him, press my cheek against his chest, breathe him in. When I look up, Thomas is looking back down at me in this way that gives me a rush – of desire, of need. I reach a hand behind his neck and pull him closer, our kiss long and intimate. The narrow street where we stand under the awning is quiet, vacant, aside from the sound of the rain. But when we move apart, I can't help worrying that we are in public. I look around, scan the sidewalks.

'Or we could just go to your place,' I suggest. My heart surges with anticipation, with anxiety. What am I doing?

'We could.' Thomas sounds surprised.

'If you wanted to,' I say.

'I do,' he says.

*

Thomas unlocks the door, opens it, turns on the light.

I've wondered what Thomas's place would be like. Would he keep everything neat and orderly? Would it be a mess? Would he have bookshelves like me, stacked all the way to the ceiling and two rows deep, because of grad school and because he's an academic? Would he have a big bed, a small one? Would it look like a man's room, all navy and gray and dark colors? What new things would I learn about Thomas from what he keeps in the fridge?

A small, orange cat runs up to him and he reaches down to pet him across the head, the back. 'Hi, Max,' he says. 'I'd like you to meet Rose. Now be nice.'

Max glances at me suspiciously, nudges my leg, then meows and runs off.

'I've always wanted a cat,' I tell him. Luke and I talked about it once, twice, but we never actually did it.

'He's skittish around strangers,' Thomas says, 'but he'll warm to you eventually.'

Eventually as in tonight, or eventually as in months from now, years from now? I want to know how long term Thomas is thinking about us, but it's not something I'm ready to ask. And especially since I don't know how long term I am thinking about us either. How could I? I'm having someone else's baby!

I push that thought aside.

Thomas heads into the kitchen, which is open to the living room, takes out a bottle of red wine, a corkscrew, glasses. Meanwhile I look around. On the walls are a series of framed photos of Thomas and what look like his parents, and probably his sister. She is tiny, pretty, with dark features like Thomas.

They have the same smile, big, wide, that lights up their faces, their eyes. There is one photograph of Thomas and a bunch of guys, maybe the friends he told me about from college. The photographs are clearly amateur, not like the ones on the walls of my own apartment. I like them. It's a nice contrast to what I am used to.

His apartment is small, normal, nothing special, a little spare, except for the books against one wall, which are stacked to the ceiling just like mine are, packed into the shelves and overflowing. It makes me feel at home, safe. Books always do. Then I notice a guitar standing against the wall, nearly hidden behind the couch. Thomas comes over and hands me a glass of wine. 'You play the guitar!'

'Not really. It's more that I dabble. And when my sister comes over, she plays. She's actually very good.'

I peer over the back of the couch to see what else is hidden there, and find a couple of soccer balls. 'When do I get to see one of your games, anyway?'

Thomas played soccer in college and still plays on a men's team. He's told me that aside from his work and his family, his other love has always been soccer. 'Anytime you want. You'd just have to get away on a weekend.'

I sigh. 'Yeah.' We both know that will be difficult.

Thomas gestures toward the couch. I set my glass on the coffee table, pull my feet up underneath me. Neither one of us speaks. My heart is pounding.

Thomas and I have never been alone before. Not like this.

He leans toward me and we kiss, moves closer until he can put his arms around me. His hand on my back is firm. I like the feel of his palm pressing against me through the fabric of my dress. I want it on my skin instead. Soon my wish is granted.

Things happen slowly, but they happen and I do not stop them. Kissing, whispering, unbuttoning, unzipping. I let go into all of it, every moment. I am grateful for the darkness that hides the slight curve of my belly, for the fact that it is far too subtle to notice. When Thomas and I finally slide into bed the sheets are cool, our skin is warm, our embrace makes me forget everything but him, but us. I close my eyes.

I don't want this to end.

I don't want to go home ever again.

I don't want this baby.

I keep telling myself: I get to have this.

If Luke gets to have a baby, then I get to have Thomas.

This is the deal. The exchange I am making.

I know that what Thomas and I are doing is wrong. So why doesn't it feel more wrong? Shouldn't it feel more wrong than it does?

It's as though I'm on a seesaw, and pregnancy has made me sink to the ground. Luke holds me there, stuck in the dirt. But every time I see Thomas he steps onto the other side of the plank and lifts me up, balances things so I am above the earth again, so I can get my bearings and see everything around me more clearly.

At some point I have to stop acting this way. Right?

At some point, I have to give Thomas up. Right?

*

Thomas runs a hand across my stomach. Bends down to kiss the skin above my navel. He doesn't even hesitate, but then, why would he? He's never seen my body before. He doesn't have any idea that I am pregnant.

At some point I'm going to have to tell him.

But what will he do then?

He looks up. 'I wondered if this would ever happen.'

'This?'

He kisses his way up my body until we are face-to-face, trails his fingers along my back. Presses himself against me. 'This.'

I respond by wrapping my legs around him, pressing myself into him until we are moving together again. Our lips are nearly touching but not quite. 'Oh, this,' I whisper.

He smiles, closes his eyes, gives in to me.

I'll tell him. Soon. But not tonight.

I don't want the dream of Thomas, of Thomas and me, of the Rose I am when I'm with Thomas, to be over. Not yet. I am not ready.

A month later and I am really starting to show. There's no going back now. I am doing this. I am having this baby.

Luke's baby.

Fuck.

The other thing I am definitely still doing is having an affair with Thomas.

He and I go for coffee one afternoon. He gets a cappuccino, I get a decaf. I hate decaf but apparently it's what women in my situation have to order. I've learned to wear a certain kind of dress that is good at hiding my 'condition'. But I can't keep this from Thomas any longer. I care about him too much. Besides, soon it will be obvious.

We have barely sat down at our table when I blurt it out, 'There's something I have to tell you.' I don't let Thomas get any words in before I continue. 'I'm pregnant,' I say, and when his eyes widen, I add, quickly, 'It's Luke's. There's no doubt. I was . . . I was . . .' I need to say it, get it out of my mouth, my body. 'I was already pregnant when we first went out.'

Thomas's jaw is hanging open. He is blinking quickly. 'But . . .' he starts, then trails off. The hurt on his face makes me want to weep. 'Pregnant?'

I nod. 'I . . . I . . .'

What do I say? How do I put into words what I've done?

I try the truth. 'I didn't want to be pregnant, I shouldn't have let myself get pregnant, and then when I realized I was pregnant, I was angry and I . . .'

Thomas is shaking his head. 'You decided you'd express your anger by going out with me?'

I want to take Thomas's hand, I want to kiss it, but I don't. I can't. This place is too public, the light too bright and glaring. 'No, I decided to let myself have you, even if it was for just one evening.'

'But it wasn't for just one evening.'

'No, it wasn't.' The muscles in Thomas's forearm are so tense, his body so rigid. I hate that I am doing this to him. 'I'm sorry I didn't tell you before. I kept putting it off because I care about you so much.'

He pushes his coffee cup away. 'So much that you kept this major thing from me?'

'But I'm telling you now.' I sound pathetic, I know.

'Why, because you have to? Because eventually I'd notice?' Thomas balls up his napkin and throws it onto the table. 'Jesus, Rose. Is that why when we're together you've made sure that it's dark?'

My eyes flicker down to my stomach, then back up again. 'I don't know.' I sigh. 'Yes,' I admit. 'I'm a horrible person, okay?'

Thomas shakes his head.

No, I'm not a horrible person?

Or, *I'm so disgusted with you, Rose, I don't even know what to say?*

I place both hands on the table now, my fingers so close to his. 'I didn't tell you because I knew it would mean the end and I couldn't bear it. I can't bear it now.'

'You promised me, Rose,' Thomas says, 'that I was the one person you'd never lie to.'

'I'm so sorry,' I say. *I've lost him,* I think. I have. It's over.

'All this time, all those emails, and I was just a game—'

'You were not just a game!' I nearly shout this. I lower my voice. 'You've never been a game. You still aren't. I . . . I . . .' *I care about you so much. I'm falling in love with you. Please don't leave me.*

Thomas leans back in his chair, clasps his hands behind his head, staring up at the ceiling. 'We shouldn't have been doing this before, I've always known that, but now we really shouldn't be doing this.'

Is an affair that much more terrible while pregnant? Not just married? Am I that much more awful a person, a woman? Probably. Yes.

'I know,' I say. But do I?

Thomas stands up, his coffee cup still nearly full. He's barely touched it. 'I need to go. I need time to think.'

'I understand.' But I don't. Or not quite. Does needing time to think leave the door open just a crack? Might it?

'You do, too,' Thomas says. 'You need to think about this.'

I don't answer. I don't need time to think. Not really. I want to keep seeing Thomas, baby or no baby. I could be nine months pregnant and I would still want to see him.

I watch Thomas leave. Watch him walk away through the windows of the café until he disappears down the next block. He doesn't look back.

I assume we are over. I cry all the way back to my apartment and I am still crying when I walk in the door.

'What's the matter?' Luke asks me. He's sitting at the kitchen table, laptop open, working.

'Hormones,' I tell him.

18

October 19, 2007
Rose, Life 4

LUKE TURNS AND smiles at me over the edge of his wine-glass. There is so much behind that smile, so much behind the happiness I see in his eyes. I like knowing why it is there and being the only one in the room to know the reason. I like that he is looking at me like this again. It wasn't long ago that I thought he might never.

'Rose, can I give you another piece of chicken?' Luke's friend Chris is already up, towering over the dinner table, the serving fork in his hand poised to stab one of the remaining drumsticks on the platter. 'You know you want one. You downed that first one fast.'

'I'd love one,' I say.

Pregnancy has made me ravenous.

I turn to Mai, Chris's wife. 'Your husband is a great cook.'

She glances up at Chris as he places a second piece of chicken on my plate. 'Good thing, or nobody would eat in this house.' They are on baby number two, and this is the first time we've seen them since their second child was born. They invited Luke and me over for dinner because they said it was easier for us to come to them after the kids were in bed and so they didn't have to get a babysitter.

When Chris tries to top off my wineglass, I place my hand over it so he can't.

'No?' he sounds surprised.

'I'm fine,' I tell him.

One of the things Luke and I agreed on was that one glass of wine was okay. I was afraid he was going to be more obsessive about things like this, but so far he is respecting my need to make my own choices about what I eat and drink, how I make this transition from antimotherhood to suddenly contending with a pregnancy.

'Okay.' Chris places the bottle back on the table close enough that I can reach it if I change my mind.

Mai eyes me, but she doesn't say out loud what I am sure she is thinking. *Wait, are you . . . ?*

Luke and I haven't told anyone aside from our parents and Jill, not any of my other friends, not any of Luke's. I like hovering in this moment where I am still just Rose, where no one knows I am pregnant unless I decide to tell them. I am not entirely looking forward to the part where we start telling our friends because everyone in our lives knows how resistant I've been to having a child, how sure I've been about not wanting to become a mother. People will be skeptical. I know this because I already went through it with Jill.

*

Every Wednesday for ages now, Jill and I either meet up in her apartment or mine to hang out, drink wine, eat takeout, catch up on things away from the university where we work. It was the wine – my not drinking much, never more than a glass these last couple of months – that alerted Jill that something was up. We were at her apartment this time, there was a third of a bottle left, and Jill kept trying to pour me another glass.

'No, really. I'm good.' Before I was pregnant, Jill and I would easily polish off at least a bottle over the course of the evening, sometimes a bottle and a half. 'I've got an early class tomorrow,' I added. Each week since I learned I was pregnant, I'd given Jill a new excuse – early classes, lack of sleep, lots of work in the morning. Anything to avoid telling her the real reason.

Jill was still holding the bottle, angled, ready to pour, over the rim of my glass. 'That never stopped you before,' she said.

I shrugged. 'New school year, new attitude.'

She set the bottle down on the table. Then she sat back onto the couch, turning to me. 'Rose Napolitano, I know when you are lying to me. Why are you lying? What aren't you telling me?'

I busied myself piling the empty plates on top of one another into a neat stack.

'Hey,' she said, placing a hand on my arm. 'Answer me. Please?'

I kept my eyes on the dishes, the coffee table, anywhere but my friend. 'I don't think you're going to be happy when I tell you what's going on.'

There was a beat of silence. Then Jill gasped. 'Rose. You are kidding me.'

'Did you guess?'

'You're pregnant!'

I grabbed a piece of chocolate from a bowl that Jill kept on the coffee table, unwrapped it, put it in my mouth, and tossed the wrapper on top of the rest. I nodded, chewed, swallowed.

'That asshole,' she said.

'No, it's more complicated actually—'

'Are you getting an abortion? You are, right? I'll go with you, of course. I'll make the appointment if that helps. I know it's one thing to talk about being pro-choice and sometimes another to go ahead and decide to get an abortion.'

This was why I'd dreaded telling Jill. I already knew all the assumptions she'd make about how I was feeling, what I would do next, and that I would have to fend them off one by one. I couldn't blame her. I would do exactly the same if the situation were reversed. This was Jill being the best friend she could be to me.

'Listen,' I said, and took both of her hands, looked into her eyes. 'I'm not getting an abortion, Jill. Definitely not.' When she opened her mouth to protest, I cut in before she could. 'I'm sure about this. I'm having this baby.' I breathed deeply, let out that breath again. 'I want it. I know it must be hard for you to believe that, but it's true.'

'You. Having a baby.'

'Yes, me.'

Jill pulled her hands from mine and filled up her wineglass with the remains of the bottle, then gulped down half of it. 'Whoa.'

'I know.'

'I'm struggling here, Rose. I'm struggling to understand how all of this is possible. This is about Luke, isn't it? He finally gave you the ultimatum, right? A baby or him?'

171

'Yes. No. Well, at first yes. Which is why I decided to try, to give him what he wanted so he didn't leave.'

'I hate that man, sometimes.'

'Don't hate him.' I sighed, already exhausted by this task of defending myself, defending Luke along with me. I knew I'd have to do this, but actually doing it was even harder than I thought. 'I mean, I understand why you feel this way. *I've* felt this way at points, as you know. And I know it's really hard to believe and I can hardly believe it myself, but I'm good with this. Or as good as I can be. And Luke and I are good, too. Much better than we were before.'

Jill huffed. 'Yeah, because you gave him what he wanted.'

'Please don't judge me like that.'

'I wasn't judging you.'

'But you were.'

She drank down the rest of the wine in her glass. 'I just . . . I just don't know what to think, Rose.'

'I get that. But what I really need is not to feel ashamed about this pregnancy. Not when I'm with you. You're my best friend and I need your support.'

Jill gets a look of horror on her face. 'I didn't mean to shame you.'

'Maybe.'

'*Are* you ashamed that you're pregnant?'

I stared down at my hands, at the small round coffee stain in the fabric of Jill's couch. 'Sometimes. Sometimes I worry that I failed myself by doing this, but a lot of the time I'm actually excited. Happy. And I'm trying to stay there.'

'Okay,' Jill said, but I could hear a lingering hesitation in her voice.

'Okay, then,' I said, and we cleared the plates, put them in the sink, and I went home.

'How was your night with Jill?' Luke asked when I crawled into bed. He was half asleep, facing away from me.

'I told her I was pregnant.'

'Oh?' He rolled over. His eyes shined in the dark. 'How did she take it?'

'Not great. It was kind of hard.'

'Give her time. She'll come around. Everyone else will, too. Eventually.'

I was struck by Luke's choice of words: *She'll come around. Eventually.* The same thing that people said to me for years about becoming a mother. They were right and I did. Eventually. But would it take Jill years to come around to the new me? Would it take everyone else in our lives equally as long? First, I had to live through the pressure of everyone telling me that I needed to have a child, that I must, and was faced with convincing people that it was my right to say no to motherhood. And now I'd have to endure people's suspicion about my turnaround regarding motherhood; about the fact that yes, now I was going to have a child. Was this always going to be my life?

Rose Napolitano, damned if she didn't become a mother and damned if she does become one, too?

Chris and Luke get up to clear the dishes from the table. On his way by my chair, Luke leans down and whispers in my ear. 'I love you,' he says. 'You're so beautiful tonight.'

I beam.

Mai is watching me. She raises her own glass of wine to her lips and takes a sip, and I envy this a little, but the moment passes.

She gets up and sits down in Luke's now-empty chair, next to mine. 'Do you and Luke have news you aren't sharing?'

I turn around, glance into the kitchen. Luke and Chris are standing side by side, talking to each other in front of the sink. I give Mai a noncommittal shrug. I am tempted to tell her, *Yes, yes we do,* but Luke is respecting my need to take things slow, so I don't want to steal his chance to share our news first with Chris.

'Hmm' is Mai's response. Then she smiles at me. 'Don't worry, Rose. I won't say anything to Chris. But if it's what I think it is, then I am very happy for you and Luke. And I think you'll love being a mom. I was ambivalent, too, once upon a time. It's hard and all that, but having children can be wonderful. The most wonderful thing,' she adds.

I beam again for the second time tonight.

Maybe I am wrong. Maybe not everyone will doubt me when they find out. Maybe they'll be like Mai instead, and just take it in stride, be happy for me and for us.

Luke returns from the kitchen, puts his hands on the back of my chair. 'What are you guys talking about?'

'That big court case I have coming up,' Mai says. She's a hotshot lawyer, a federal prosecutor, and earlier tonight we'd been discussing that she was about to start a murder trial.

Luke goes and sits in Mai's old chair. She squeezes my hand under the table and I squeeze hers back. Her kindness, her faith, seeps into me. I think about how it's true, that I am still adjusting to this new path in life, that Luke and I are still adjusting to it together. But today is one of the good days. One of the better ones. I soak it up, as much of it as I can, store it away for the harder times to come.

19

March 15, 2013
Rose, Life 3

'ADDIE, GIVE US a twirl,' Joe says.

She obliges. The feathers bobby-pinned to her hair, sewn around her neck and her skirt, bounce and float as she spins.

Cameras flash. Everyone has cameras. My mom, Luke's dad, Luke's mom, Luke. It's like the prom. My mother passes the camera to my dad and now it's his turn to snap a picture. 'Smile for Grandpa,' he says, and she does. It's Addie's first recital, and everyone has come to the little theater where the girls danced their hearts out this evening, none of them in sync, which was all the more endearing. Addie is dressed as a swan.

My mother takes the camera back from my father. 'Show us what swans do, Addie.'

Addie flutters her arms, not altogether gracefully, and more cameras flash. Nancy has her phone out and is taking a video. Addie gives everyone another twirl and produces delight all around. Luke turns to me and shakes his head, with a good-natured expression that says, *What are we going to do with these*

176

crazy grandparents? and I give him a shrug back, a sheepish grin.

Addie is the great unifier of this family. The peacemaker. An entire UN unto herself.

She yawns suddenly, wide and loud.

Everyone laughs.

'I think it's time for swans to go to bed,' Luke says, and scoops our daughter up with one great swing of his arm.

'Daddy, no,' she protests, but her eyes are already drooping.

'What a sweetheart,' Nancy says to me, as though she believes I might actually be doing something right as Addie's mother.

I soak up her approval.

My mother nods, but gives me a quick, searching glance. She knows that things are still strained between me and Luke's parents; we've talked about it endlessly. I look at my mother and smile. *Everything is okay.*

We leave the theater. Joe hangs back, talking to my dad. I hear snatches of their conversation, and realize he is asking my father about his carpentry business. My mother and Nancy are walking ahead of Luke and me, but I don't know what they're discussing. They keep turning to look at Addie, who is nodding off on Luke's shoulder, so probably about her.

During moments like these, I feel lucky that this tiny person has come into our lives to knit everything back together between all of us, great, looping stitches that bind us. I try not to notice how easy it would be to cut those threads. All it would take is one small snip and we'd unravel.

Even though I still don't know how I feel about my in-laws, a tiny part of me is grateful to them.

Maybe. Sometimes.

I don't know.

There are moments when I think to myself, if Nancy and Joe hadn't been so obsessed with their son having a child, with me making sure their son had that child, then maybe Addie wouldn't exist. Maybe we wouldn't have had her. Maybe *I* wouldn't have had her. If they hadn't talked Luke into changing his mind, and if Luke then hadn't talked me into changing my own mind, then she wouldn't be here right now in her little swan costume, charming all of us. Charming me, the woman who once had no desire to be charmed by a child, at least not one who was her own.

But there are so many other days when that lingering anger I have for them creeps out of its little cave in my brain and I find myself wanting to tell them off, to say all the things that Luke forbade me to say to their faces. Which makes me wonder, will I ever forgive them? Will my anger at them poison my life with Luke forever?

'Rose, we want to talk to you.'

Joe was the one who said it first, who started the conversation on his and Nancy's behalf so many years ago. The four of us had gone out to dinner at a very nice restaurant.

'What about?' I said back, glancing over at Luke, who was refusing to meet my eyes. He was staring down at his plate, focusing on cutting up his chicken.

Luke and I had been married for a few years by then and my relationship with his parents was fraying. My relationship with

Luke was fraying, too. Each time Luke wanted to go home for a visit, I became more and more resistant to joining him. I started making up excuses – too much grading, plans with Jill, Raya is coming to town for a visit, my father invited me to have dinner with him that weekend, just the two of us. I'd stopped wanting to see them, Nancy especially. Things had grown awkward between us.

Nancy was always making comments about how intelligent she thought I was, which sounds nice, except she would always add that this meant my children with Luke would also be intelligent. Then the questioning began about when I would be pregnant, when, *when?* She asked this even though she knew Luke and I weren't planning to have a baby.

Joe wiped his hands on the napkin in his lap. 'We want to talk to both of you,' he clarifies. 'About children.'

Luke sighed and set his utensils along the edge of his plate. 'Dad.' He said this like a warning.

Nancy reached over and pressed her hand over her son's hand, a gesture of *Wait, let us finish.*

'We're worried you're making a mistake,' Joe said. I suppose he was addressing Luke and me both, but he was only looking at me. 'We know it would be a mistake for you not to have a baby. You're going to regret it. You will, when it's too late. And then what will happen?'

I was shaking my head, back and forth. I didn't want to have this conversation over dinner at this restaurant. I didn't want to have this conversation at all. I wanted my in-laws to respect my decision – mine and Luke's decision.

It was one thing for Nancy to drop comments when she and

179

I talked, to assume that my opinion about children would change with time, but it was another to stage an intervention. As though Luke and I not having children was something that needed addressing, treatment, a cure.

'I'm not doing this,' I said, folding my napkin and placing it on the table. 'This is none of your business. It's between Luke and me and nobody else.' My chest filled with air. 'I can't believe you'd dare say that I'm going to make your son regret his life.'

'But that's *not* what I said—' Joe started.

'No, but it was implied.'

'Rose.' Luke's tone, the way he said my name, was pleading. 'Just listen to my parents. Hear them out.'

I looked at him, wanted to shake him. Why wasn't he putting a stop to this? Why was he letting his parents do this to us, to me? The blood in my body was rushing through me, my skin growing from warm to hot. Was Luke's pleading to do with his own feelings? I swallowed. Had Luke's parents been talking to him behind my back? 'I don't want to listen to this, Luke. Why should I? Why should you?' I stood up. My chair teetered then righted itself.

'Don't be upset,' Nancy said. 'We just want to talk.'

'Rose,' Luke said. 'Sit.'

I ignored him. 'You already know how I feel, you've all known for years. Why can't you respect that?' My voice was getting louder. Nearby diners were turning our way. 'Why can't you respect me? Why can't you leave me alone about this?'

'We do respect you,' Joe said.

'How can you say that?' My vision grew shiny. I knew somewhere that the rush of rage I felt was outsized for the situation.

But I couldn't control it. I was tired of the pressure that seemed to come from everywhere, ever since the moment that Luke and I walked away from the altar, ever since our marriage began. I stepped around my chair, shoved it underneath the table. 'I'm leaving.'

Luke got up now. 'Rose, you can't leave.'

'Of course I can.'

'My father drove.'

'I'll walk.'

'You can't walk five miles in the dark!'

I left then, ignoring the other diners watching the scene we were making. Let them watch, I decided. I didn't care what they thought. When I pushed through the door of the restaurant, I inhaled, gulping deep breaths of air. I started across the parking lot. Maybe I was being melodramatic, I thought, then I pushed the thought away. Soon I heard footsteps behind me.

'Rose, what are you doing?' Luke ran in front of me, stood there with his arms out.

I stopped. I closed my eyes. Tried to slow my breathing. Was I right to be so defiant, to feel so righteous? Was I wrong? Did Luke's parents know something that Luke and I didn't? That I didn't? Should I listen to them, give them a chance?

But why did I have to?

I walked over to an empty parking spot and sat down on the curb. Luke joined me. I was in a dress, Luke was in a nice shirt and pants. We must have looked strange, the two of us, in our nice dinner outfits, sitting among the asphalt and quiet cars in the dark. 'Did you know that your parents were going to bring this up tonight?' I asked him.

'No,' he said, but I could hear his hesitation.

'Did you?'

'No, I didn't,' he said, more forcefully this time.

'What do you want, Luke?'

The crickets sang in the quiet. A few diners walked out of the restaurant toward an SUV on the other side of the lot. Luke stretched his long legs out, his feet scraping across the gravel. 'What do you mean?' There was a trace of panic in his voice.

It occurred to me that my question was vague, that maybe Luke thought I was asking him about children and whether he wanted them. 'I meant, what do you want to do right now? Are you planning on going back in there to your parents or going home with me tonight?'

'You're really leaving?'

'I am. I can call a cab.'

'Rose, please.' Luke wiped his hands across his face. 'I don't want you to leave things that way.'

'Me? So this is all my fault? Your parents ambushed me!' I started to get up but Luke pulled me back down again. I glared at him. 'And you didn't do anything to defend me, Luke! You just let them do it. You always let them.'

'They're my parents, Rose.' Luke sounded anguished. 'They're your parents, too, and they love you. They really do.'

'No. I don't think they can love me. Not unless I do this one thing. Not until I do. Maybe then they'll love me.'

'Rose—'

'You have two choices, Luke. Either you can go inside and tell your parents that you and I refuse to have dinner with them if they also refuse to respect our choices, or you can let me go home by myself and you'll sleep on the couch tonight. And maybe tomorrow night and the rest of the week.'

'Those choices don't feel fair,' Luke said.

'Well, they're the ones you have, so pick.'

Luke was silent for what felt like forever. Then he got up, told me he'd be right back, and ran inside the restaurant. Later, when he came out and during the cab ride home, we didn't speak, not even when we went to bed.

What else was there to say?

If someone had tried to tell me back then that soon I would be pregnant, about to give birth to Addie, I would have told them to fuck off. I was so tired, so angry, so sick of people pressuring me. And it wasn't as though I simply up and changed my mind about having a baby – I didn't.

One day, Luke and I ended up having this stupid fight about prenatal vitamins – the fact that he wanted me to take them, the fact that I promised him I would but then I didn't. I remember being so angry when I came into the bedroom to find him holding that bottle of vitamins, shaking it at me. A strange, paralyzing feeling gripped my heart in that moment, like someone stuffed it into a box too small for it to beat. I couldn't breathe. I remember thinking, *Why can't I breathe?* I was heaving great, loud gasps of air.

I remember Luke crying out, 'Rose – Rose?'

My eyes blurred and there was a rushing sound in my ears. Soon I was on the floor, my cheek resting against the wood. The gasping continued awhile but eventually it slowed. When my vision sharpened again, I could see that Luke was on the floor with me, his head parallel to mine.

When I found the strength to pull myself up to sitting, Luke took my hands. 'I think you had a panic attack,' he said, studying my fingers, the jagged nails I never took the time to file when they broke. 'This is my fault. I'm sorry, Rose. I'm so sorry.'

Those words – an apology from my husband, an acknowledgment of responsibility – his, not mine, in this mess that had become our marriage, they worked like magic, expanding the walls that had closed around my heart, making new room. Something rolled through my body right then, moving me back toward my husband, toward the possibility of loving him again. I thought about all the conversations we'd had about children, all the arguments, all the anger and hurt, and wondered if we were making things much harder than they needed to be. If only we could stop worrying about what other people thought and wanted, about what Luke's parents thought and wanted, and instead simply worried only about what *he and I* thought and wanted. Luke and me. The us that we used to be before all of this mess began.

'Look at me,' I said to him then. When he did, I allowed myself to speak the words that I didn't know I had within me, words that sounded strange in the air of our apartment, words that ultimately led to the birth of our beautiful, perfect daughter, Addie. 'What if we just see what happens next?'

When Luke and I get home from Addie's ballet recital, finally free of all parents and in-laws, Addie is snoring, the feathers of her swan costume as droopy as she is.

'I'll put her to bed,' Luke whispers.

I study my husband, nod.

He reaches into his bag, pulls out his camera, and hands it to me. 'You should check out the photos from tonight, there are some great ones in there.'

I smile, take it from him. 'I bet,' I say, and watch my husband disappear with Addie into her bedroom. As I look at the photos that scroll across the window of the camera – these images of Addie and the family Luke and I have made together – the difficult things, the awkwardness that has never quite left my relationship with Luke's parents, feel far away. For now. For at least a few minutes, all I see is a beautiful family, and the family is mine.

There is a way that Luke and I have grown further and further apart with each passing year. Parenthood is like treading water. The endless effort of kicking, kicking, kicking, and the exertion of hands, arms, back and forth under the surface, our heads bobbing up and down. A series of constant movements, all of them small, none of them really taking us anywhere in particular.

But as I watch Luke tiptoe across the apartment and I stare at our little girl, asleep on his shoulder, I marvel at how the short puffs of her breathing seem to enter my own lungs, keep the beat of my own heart going; I think about how Addie really is that loose stitch between Luke and me, keeping us together, and I am grateful that somehow the two of us landed here, with her, despite everything that came before the day she was born.

I take off my scarf and my coat, flick on the lights, and sit down at the kitchen table to look at the photos from Addie's dance recital. The first image that comes up on the camera's screen is of the line of little swans across the stage, caught midjump, their feet a couple of inches off the floor, mouths stretched wide, expressions of glee on their faces. There are close-ups of Addie with her arms rounded in first position, pudgy little elbows sticking out at odd angles, photos of the girls in a lopsided circle, their feather tutus askew. I scroll through all of them, smiling and chuckling, until I come to some of the other photos Luke has taken of late. There are a few of me at my desk, working, another bunch of Addie – Addie leaving for school in the morning, Addie in her pajamas before bed in the evening. There is a great one of my mother, standing in her kitchen at the stove, wooden spoon in hand, apron on, smirking at the camera.

Then I come to one of me that I didn't realize Luke had taken. It's from a talk I was giving about my research a few weeks back – I didn't even know Luke had gone to it, he never told me, and I do so many talks it's not like I expect him to go to all of them. There I am at the lectern, looking out onto the packed auditorium, one arm raised. I look so serious, so completely taken by whatever it is I am saying. It's a good picture, it's such a *me* picture. I feel a potent rush of love for Luke as I look at it, as I take in the fact that my husband would do this thing – that he would go to my event and take photos without my asking him to, without his telling me he was there, maybe just because he loves me and for no other reason than he wanted to hear what I had to say. That rush of love moves through my veins and outward to my fingers and toes.

It makes me want to give Luke a kiss; it makes me want to

take his hand and lead him to bed. Luke and I still have sex, once every couple of months, once a month if we are lucky, but it is perfunctory, obligatory, the performance of a marriage, a carrying out of what married people are supposed to do, even if they don't really want to do it anymore. Most of my friends feel the same, gay, lesbian, hetero. After a while, desire wanes and you either make a decision to keep sex a regular thing between you, or you let it go altogether.

If parenthood is like treading water, then marriage is like the sea. It ebbs and flows, with great tidal shifts every now and then, an occasional hurricane shifting the direction of one's feelings this way, then years later, shifting it back in a different direction. Maybe Luke and I could be heading in a new direction right now, a good one. Maybe we could be if I pull us there, if I lead the way.

I keep scrolling past the images on Luke's camera, one by one, taking them in, thinking about how the second Luke comes back from putting Addie to sleep I am going to pull him into the bedroom, how happy this will make him that I am initiating sex for once.

Then I come to a photo that stops my heart.

It's of a woman, head thrown back, laughing. She has on a bright green sweater. It looks like she is in the park. I scroll past it, to see if there are others, but there is only this single image, sandwiched between a few photos from Christmas, and another set of Addie at school.

Cheryl.

The name floats in and out of my mind, a whisper.

There is no indication that this is her name, no real reason to think that this woman's name is Cheryl – no reason other than wifely instinct and the note I'd found in Luke's winter jacket last month when I'd taken it to the cleaners. I was making sure I'd gotten all the change out of his pockets before I handed the bundle over the counter to the man working there. It was a small square of paper, folded carefully, the creases two sharp lines, vertical and horizontal, dividing it into four quadrants. Across it was written, *Luke, you are so talented. Just amazing. Cheryl,* in swirling, perfectly drawn letters. Whoever had written it, this Cheryl, had beautiful penmanship.

I stared at the little slip of paper in my hand, told myself that the note was probably nothing, maybe just a thank-you offered by one-half of an engaged couple whose photos Luke had taken. Even then, I didn't quite believe it, and a cloud of unease formed over my head inside the cleaners. It would reappear now and then as the memory of the note, of the handwriting, of the name, *Cheryl,* materialized again in my brain, hovering there.

I hear the soft sound of Luke's footsteps leaving Addie's room, the creak of her door beginning to close.

Quickly, I scroll back to the beginning of Luke's photos, back to Addie as a swan. Past the photo that made me think my husband was still in love with me, that made me want to take him to bed, an urge that has vaporized, disappearing into the sudden cloud cover of my discovery.

I get up and head to the couch, pull a blanket over my lap. Yawn in an exaggerated way.

Luke pads over and plops down next to me, picks up a corner of the blanket and tugs it over his legs. 'It was a good night, don't you think?'

Luke and I are the perfect scene in a movie – two tired but happy parents, slumped against each other, pleased with the memory of having watched their adorable daughter dance, while their equally pleased parents, Addie's grandparents, looked on. Luke snuggles closer to me on the couch, waiting for me to respond.

'I did think it was,' I say eventually. When Luke looks at me, I wonder if he's noticed that I gave him my answer in the past tense.

20

August 5, 2008

Rose, Life 5

THE VIEW IS spectacular.

'I'm so glad we decided to splurge,' I say.

I'm so glad you forgave me. I'm so glad you came back to me.

I am staring at Thomas as though he might disappear at any moment from my life again, possessively, hungrily. He lifts his suitcase onto the stand and walks over to the glass doors that look onto the ocean. 'This place is perfect,' he says.

'It is.' I'm so happy. Blissful.

Do we feel bliss only when we know the happiness is fleeting? When it will not last, no matter how much we wish it to be otherwise?

'I love that I'm here with you,' I tell him.

I am glowing. I am at my best when I am cheating on my husband. When I have left behind the squalling baby that Luke wanted so badly, the one he convinced me to have despite all the alarm bells going off in me that told me, *No, Rose, don't do it, you*

190

*know yourself well and what you know is that you've never wanted
to be a mother.*

'I read that the restaurant here is wonderful,' Thomas says,
and he puts his arms around me. Pulls me close. 'Maybe we
should go get something to eat?'

I lean into him, let myself be held up by his strong body, let
the equally strong waves of desire move through me until I have
turned my back on the roaring ocean and I am leading Thomas
to the bed. 'Maybe we should go get something to eat afterward,'
I suggest, laughing, pushing him down onto the expensive white
sheets, smooth and cool.

'I like that plan,' he says.

The thing is, I love Addie. I adore her.

On the day she was born, when I first saw her little face, I
felt that wave of motherly love that people talk about. I had all
those thoughts they say you'll have – possessiveness, fear, need,
joy, protectiveness, the desire to hold her tight almost to the point
of suffocation, a combination of emotions that amounted to a
kind of motherly madness – followed by the strong sense that I
would never let this baby out of my sight. It was wonderful and
it was horrible.

All of this was quickly eclipsed by the overwhelming reality
that I was now a mother for good, that there was no giving Addie
back. I had done this and now it was a permanent state. The
daily drudgery of it, combined with a perpetual lack of sleep,
would sometimes overwhelm that love, its magic so fleeting.

The only thing that's been keeping me sane is Thomas. After

he left me at the café that day I wondered if I'd ever see him again. Two weeks went by without a word. But then a long and anguished email showed up in my inbox toward the end of my spring semester, about how Thomas knew it was wrong but he wanted to keep seeing me, that he couldn't stop thinking of me, despite everything. The rush of relief I felt that day was nearly as potent as the love I'd soon feel for Addie. I promised Thomas I'd never lie to him again and I didn't. I haven't.

And so we began seeing each other once more, and when we did, on those nights when Thomas and I managed to have dinner out somewhere, or go to a café for pastries and coffee, everyone assumed that Thomas was the father of the baby growing inside of me, making me rounder by the day. I let them assume this. For one, I wasn't about to correct them and explain, *No, this man is not the father, but the man with whom I'm having an affair.*

But more even than this, I realized that I liked this secret that Thomas and I held between us, the scandal of it, the thought of how shocked people would be if they knew the truth. It made me feel better, as if a little of the person I used to be before I got myself into this motherhood mess were still lurking inside me. Or maybe a lot of her was, and this – Thomas, our affair – was proof of it.

'How's the conference?' Luke asks.

I stand by the window of the room, looking out onto the sea. Thomas is downstairs at the bar in the restaurant, waiting for me. The ocean is a deep royal blue, white caps churning. A storm must be on its way.

'Oh, you know, the usual. Full of men in tweed, going on about their amazing research.' I have gotten good at lying. There is a silence on the other end of the line, a pause meant to remind me of the question I am supposed to be asking Luke without any prompting. So I go there, finally, because I do care, and also to prove that I haven't forgotten that I have a daughter at home. 'How's Addie doing? Is she eating all right?'

'Addie and I are doing fine. But she misses you, I think.'

'You mean, she misses Mother Cow.'

'Rose, do you have to put it that way?'

'Why shouldn't I? It's an apt description.'

Addie begins to cry. I can hear her squalls as though her mouth is pressed to the phone. For a brief second my heart lurches and I wish I could hold her. It is always like this for me with Addie – I resist, but then I can't. When I was pregnant and I could feel her kicking, moving, there were moments that I marveled. But there were plenty when I resented every little twitch that reminded me she was there.

'I've got to go,' Luke says. 'Good luck with your presentation,' he adds, but not like he means it, and hangs up.

I tap in a message to Thomas. *All done. See you in five.*

The more egregiously I cheat, the more I feel like myself. The Rose I was before being thrust into motherhood is struggling to breathe, returning little by little. I can feel her spreading outward and filling up my limbs, pushing away all the motherly bits. I wonder if they'll eventually squeeze through my skin and fall into a pile on the floor. Then some cleaning person will come in the morning and brush them up into the dustbin.

I wiggle into a dress I'm proud of myself for fitting into, seeing that only a few months ago, I gave birth. Then I smile at myself in the bathroom mirror, touch up my lipstick, and head downstairs to have a magnificent dinner with the man I'm in love with, the man who does not happen to be my husband or the father of my child. I don't even feel guilty. I should try to feel more guilty, shouldn't I?

'What are you working on?' Thomas asks.

I look up from the daybed where I've been lounging on the lovely porch of this inn, the closest spot to the deep blue ocean, which is calm this morning, practically a lake after the storm of yesterday evening. Colorful chairs and couches dot the long, wide deck, and at the far end is this daybed. The moment I saw it when we were bringing in our bags, I knew I would live on it all weekend, either with a book or my writing.

Thomas is freshly showered, handsome in jeans and a light sweater. He leans down to give me a kiss and I pull him the rest of the way onto the daybed, nearly knocking my laptop to the floor. 'Be careful,' he says.

'We're already beyond careful, aren't we? We've moved into full-on rebellion.'

'If we have, then I like rebellion,' he says. 'Rebellion is my favorite.' Thomas peers at the screen on my laptop, pushes it farther open so he can see. 'Is this something new?'

'Yes. I started it a few weeks ago. I'm just playing around, though.'

Thomas shifts the laptop in front of him and begins to read.

I lie back against the pillows. The sun reaches underneath the porch ceiling, warming my skin.

Over the last few months, Thomas and I have been reading each other's work. It's something I've enjoyed about our relationship, the way we can share this part of ourselves. Luke stopped talking about work with me – his, mine – a long time ago. Sometimes I go and catch Thomas's soccer game if I can manage to get out, or he'll meet me for coffee with Jill occasionally. I finally told her about Thomas.

She didn't flinch. I don't even think she was surprised. She's been mad at Luke for a long time, wishing I'd leave him. I think she's hoping Thomas will be the reason I finally do. If only it were that easy.

Is the mother of an infant allowed to leave her husband? How long before it's acceptable for her to do so? Then again, I was a pregnant woman having an affair, and now I'm a new mother continuing that affair – how much worse would it be if I left the father of my baby?

Tiny ripples move across the water, fracturing the sunlight. A woman gets out of her car and runs into the little general store on the corner, comes out a minute later with a newspaper and drives off. A girl with a ponytail jogs by.

Thomas looks up from my computer. 'This essay is really different for you. It's more of a memoir.'

I can't read him with his sunglasses on. Does he like it? Not like it?

'I think maybe it is a memoir,' I say. A memoir of every thought I've ever had about motherhood before Addie, all the mixed-up emotions I feel now that I do have her, all my insecurities, my anger and resentment, tangled up in my love for this little person who is now in my life forever. It was hard to start, but now that

I have, it's been pouring out of me. I pick up Thomas's hand, examine the deep lines in his palm. 'But do you like it?' I ask. Before Thomas can answer, I ramble onward. 'It's probably a terrible idea. But I thought I might never work again, you know, after having Addie. At least now I'm doing something.'

Thomas sets the laptop aside on the daybed. He slips off his shoes and puts his feet up so we are sitting pressed together, both of us facing the ocean. 'I do, Rose. I think it's great.'

I look at him. 'Really?'

He nods. 'Definitely. I wish I could write like that.'

'If you did, what would you write about?'

Thomas is quiet a moment, the sun warming us as we lie there, relaxed and basking in it. The thought that soon this moment will be over, that we will have to go back to our lives again, appears in my brain, but I snuff it out.

'I think I might write about my family, my childhood growing up in the mountains. My relationship with my sister. I don't know.' He takes off his sunglasses, wipes a hand across his eyes. 'Or maybe about why I started my research on addiction, what led me there. All the people I went to high school with whose lives ended up so different than mine.'

'I'd love to read that book,' I tell him.

Thomas turns, kisses my neck. 'Well, I'd love to read yours, so we're even. Which also means you need to finish it so I can read it.'

'It feels nice to write again,' I admit. 'Even if I don't do anything with it.'

'I think you will,' he says.

I burrow into Thomas's side. 'I think if I did try to publish it,

Luke would leave me.' This is out of my mouth before I realize its truth.

'Then you should definitely publish it,' Thomas says, and doesn't sound at all like he is kidding.

'But then . . . Addie. What would Addie think when she's old enough to read it?'

'Rose.' Thomas turns to me. 'Addie will think she has a mother who struggled to understand what it means for her to have a child, after so much resistance.'

I sigh. 'That's exactly what worries me.'

I've tried to play house for Luke, for Addie. I've tried to be this domestic person, especially during those initial days after coming home from the hospital. I've endured all the time off from my university, from teaching, from office hours and seeing my colleagues. But I can't wait to go back to school in a couple of weeks. Luke is pressing me to take the upcoming semester off, too, but I keep telling him no – no way. I've never liked the idea that I would use some of my obsessively banked course releases to stay home for another five months with Addie.

Those releases were never intended for having a baby. Releases are for research, for book writing on behalf of that research, for teach-abroad opportunities. Women scholars are always taking leave to become mothers and then struggling to return to academia after having those babies. This was never going to be me – and it wasn't about to become me now.

I may have given birth and now I have a baby, but there's no changing the fact that I'm still a reluctant mother and an even more reluctant wife.

Unlike Thomas, and how I feel about him.

Not reluctant at all.

'Why are you here?' I ask Thomas suddenly.

The sun has shifted. He moves over six inches, puts his sunglasses on again. 'What do you mean?'

'I mean, what are you doing with me? I'm married. I'm a new mother. I literally just gave birth.' I say these things, then wish I could stuff them back into my mouth. Am I trying to sabotage this? Sabotage myself? Weren't we just having a nice, peaceful afternoon, lounging on this lovely porch?

Thomas sits up. 'What brought this on?'

'I was thinking about Addie. How I didn't want her and now I have her and I'm trying to be a good mother and I'm failing at it. Obviously. I'm failing at being a mother and I'm definitely failing at being a wife.'

Thomas has gone still. 'I think the better question is, what are you doing here, Rose, with me? For all the same reasons you just said.'

I shift so I am facing Thomas on the daybed. 'I can't stop seeing you. I couldn't bear it even for those two weeks when we weren't together when I was pregnant.'

'Well, I keep trying to stop seeing you and I can't,' Thomas says.

Panic flickers inside me. 'You're still trying?'

Thomas moves away from me, until we're no longer touching.

'Rose, I told myself that I shouldn't go on this weekend trip with you. That every time we do something like this it only gets harder. I told myself that I should call you and cancel.'

The panic turns to hurt. 'You almost canceled? You really considered missing out on this weekend with me?' My voice rises high, even though I shouldn't be surprised. I understand him completely. I'm a married woman with an infant. What is he doing with me anyway? He's handsome, funny, kind, accomplished – he could have so many other women if he wanted, if he tried.

'But I didn't cancel,' he says. 'Are you crying, Rose?'

I reach up to touch my cheek and my finger comes away wet. 'I guess I am.'

'Do you want to tell me why?'

'The same reason as always.' I think back to the moment of our arrival at this inn yesterday. How the beginning of our time together is always so giddy, so thrilling, that we have somehow amassed two whole nights, forty-eight consecutive hours of just Thomas and me and nobody else. I am brazen, I am happy, I am myself, and it always seems like it will last forever. But then the hours disappear and my happiness dissipates along with them and suddenly I can see it – I can see it right now – the moment that Thomas and I will have to say good-bye again, when we'll go back to our separate homes, our separate lives, when I'll have to be a mother again, a wife again, someone I'm not again. And he'll go back to his friends, his university and his colleagues, the long phone calls he has every day with the sister whom I have yet to meet, with the parents he loves so much who have no idea I exist. Once that bubble bursts, this separateness is all I can see.

Thomas is packing up my laptop, putting it into my bag. Then he holds out his hand. 'Let's go,' he says.

'Where?' I ask him, but I know. We'll go to our room, we'll get into bed, we'll make love and then hold each other. It's what we always do when reality sets in. And it always does eventually.

Thomas doesn't respond, he just leads me upstairs. Before we reach our room, before we unlock it and head inside, he turns to me, looks at me straight on and says, 'I'm not going anywhere, Rose.'

'No?'

'No. I don't think I can.'

'Why?'

'Because I love you,' he says, just like that, like he doesn't even have to think about it. And maybe he doesn't. Maybe there's no going backward for the two of us.

'I love you, too,' I tell him, because I know there isn't for me, either. Of this, I am certain.

The only other time I cry all weekend is when I have to leave, when Thomas has to drop me off down the street from my house. I watch him drive away, back to his own life, this life that is utterly separate from mine. I know I should feel terrible about what I've done this weekend – what I've done to Luke, to Addie – about so much deception. But I just don't. How can I feel terrible about loving someone so much? Someone who makes me remember who I really am?

I am dragging my suitcase down the sidewalk, still two blocks from my apartment building, when the tears come. By the time

I am one block away, I am crying so hard I can barely breathe. I stand there on the street corner, sobbing, people walking by, staring at the crazy woman on the sidewalk.

There is a church near our apartment, small but beautiful, and I duck into it, suitcase and all. The light through the stained-glass windows is red, orange, pink, rays of it across the damp, dark space, specks of dust sparkling and dancing in the air. It is empty at this hour. I roll my suitcase past the font of holy water and sit down in the last pew. I let myself cry until I have nothing left.

Then, when I've finally caught my breath, just as the greens and yellows and violets of the window are illuminated with the shifting sun, I stand up and roll my things back out into the daytime again, to the hustle of the city streets, to the apartment that I share with my husband and my daughter, Addie. I walk in the door to the place where I must become a mother again, the one thing I thought I'd never be in life, the only thing I truly never wanted to be. Yet somehow, here I am.

21

March 2, 2008
Rose, Life 4

'LUKE, SOMETHING'S NOT right.'

I am standing in the kitchen. My hand is gripping the edge of the black countertop, the place where there is a chip in the granite. My thumb digs into the rough valley of it, and I wedge it there.

'Luke?' I call out, louder.

My head spins, and blood rushes in my ears. I finally know what people mean when they say that. I sit down, straight onto the floor, right over the crumbs and other detritus from my attempts to make dinner. My knees bend in two right angles, the great bulge that has become the middle of my body is taut, hardened in a way that is unfamiliar. It's not the normal hardness of a pregnant belly that I've grown used to. This is something different.

I'm about to start shouting when Luke comes around the corner from the hallway, earbuds in, lost in whatever he's listening to. He sees me on the floor and rushes over.

'Did your water break?'

'No,' I say. 'I don't think so?'

Our eyes go to the place between my legs, studying my stretch pants, to see if the insides of my charcoal gray thighs are wet. They're not. Maybe I am just being melodramatic and nothing is wrong.

'Do you think it's time?' Luke asks. His voice has that happy edge I've grown to love these last months, ever since I told him I was pregnant. It encircles the worry in his voice.

I let it encircle me. I need the comfort.

Since the beginning of this pregnancy, Luke's happiness has seeped into me and spread like a medicine I didn't know I needed. It's healed our marriage. Things have never been better.

Who knew that pregnancy could be the answer?

I'd certainly thought it would destroy us before it would make us happy.

Right then, pain like fire streaks across my swollen belly and I scream.

One day, maybe three months or so ago, Luke came home early from work and surprised me – I hadn't expected him for another two hours. He walked in the door to find me talking out loud to my stomach. Well, to the baby. Which yes, I had taken to doing, though I never did it in front of anyone else, especially not Luke.

I usually got home around three from teaching, and sometimes I cooked something lavish. That afternoon I was making a sauce that takes a good three hours of simmering and attention. I was in the process of chopping the ingredients that needed to go into the base.

'Did you know that by using celery, carrots, an onion, and some garlic, that you can make just about anything delicious? Someday, you and Mommy are going to make this sauce together. Maybe I'll have Grandpa make you a special stool or a little ladder so you can climb up and see onto the counter next to me. I bet he would like to do that. We'll cook together and you'll be so proud of yourself when you taste what you've made! My mother, your grandmother, loves to cook, and she gave all that love to me and I'm going to pass it on to you.'

I am not one for sap, and I hate how sentimental everyone gets about expectant mothers, how gooey they're going to feel about the baby, just you wait and you know the drill. Just kill me now.

But it's also true that while I was alone in the house, talking to this baby had become my new norm. It's so strange: you are your own person, separate, individual, but then for a span of nearly ten months, you are two people in one. You don't really feel that part until you start to notice your body changing, when every time you look down you see evidence that something is there, within you. The you that you once knew has shifted. Expanded. Once the baby starts moving around and kicking, then you really know it: you are two people, not one anymore.

It's been kind of nice.

So there I was, chatting away, while I started to chop the pancetta. I was in the middle of a sentence when I heard movement behind me. I stopped speaking, dropped the knife, and turned around. There was Luke, watching me with this ridiculous expression on his face.

'How long were you there?' I shouted. I could feel how red my cheeks were getting. The blood was burning up my neck all the way to my ears and forehead. My teeth were gritted. I felt caught.

An enormous smile broke out on Luke's face. 'Not long—' he started.

'I don't believe you! How much did you hear?' I was shrieking.

'Rose, calm down. Why are you so upset?'

I went to the stove and turned off the gas under the saucepan with one swift twist of my hand. 'You shouldn't spy on me.'

Luke started to laugh, big bellows of it. It made me want to hit him. 'You're angry because you're embarrassed. But you shouldn't be. I wasn't spying on you, I was just listening.'

'Without my permission.'

'Well, yes, I guess. I'm sorry if I upset you. But it was so sweet, Rose, to hear you talking to the baby, and I am just so surprised. I didn't expect it and I couldn't help myself. I wanted to hear what you were saying. Do you do that a lot?'

My hands balled into fists. I tried breathing deeply to calm down. I could still feel the burn on my skin. The pregnancy had been up and down, sometimes nice, but often maddening. Because everyone knew I hadn't wanted a baby, now that I was having one I felt watched, tired of people wondering how I was handling the pregnancy, like it was their right to judge, to observe, to opine on my behavior. So I was sensitive about this.

'Rose.' Luke's laughter dissipated. He took a step closer. I turned toward the half-chopped ingredients on the cutting board. 'It made me happy to hear you,' Luke said. 'Sometimes I wonder if you feel connected to the baby. You don't really show it when

205

I'm around and I never ask you because I know it's been hard for you.'

Luke placed his hands around my upper arms. He leaned in to kiss the back of my neck. 'I love you. I'm sorry I listened without your permission. I'll never do it again.'

'I *do* do it,' I admitted. I couldn't turn around and say this to his face, so I said it instead to the stovetop, into the garlic and olive oil in the saucepan below me. 'I talk to the baby,' I clarified. 'All the time. Okay?'

'Okay,' Luke whispered. His fingers left my arms.

I knew I should trust Luke. Though the people around me could be harsh, Luke had been steady. The pregnancy had loosened things between us, and each day we grew closer again. But I still couldn't look Luke in the eye right then, so I stared off to the left, studying the little cubes of pancetta I'd been cutting. 'I've grown used to her – because I'm certain she's a *she*, you know – being there all the time. She's real. She's already this person to me. I don't know how to explain it.'

Luke may have stopped breathing by this point.

'And because she's this person, I tell her things. But I don't want to talk about it anymore. And I don't want you to tell anybody about it.' My voice was rising again, floating up through the fragrant air of the kitchen. 'Especially not your parents!'

'I won't say a word to anyone,' he promised. 'But I meant what I said. You don't have to be embarrassed about it. Not in front of me.'

But I did feel embarrassed. Like, if other people knew, a ticker tape of *I told you so, I told you you'd come around once you were pregnant. Look at Rose playing at being Mommy already!* would surely be playing through their minds, mocking me. 'It feels private,' was all I said, and then I went back to my cooking.

Eventually, all that resistance ebbed. Luke and I would have long, lively conversations with our future daughter, playful, inside jokes between us. We told my pregnant belly stories, stories from our families and the news and what happened at work to him, or to me, that same day. I taught the baby how to cook and how to get a new study through the IRB at my university. Luke taught the baby how to put together furniture from IKEA. We watched our favorite shows with her, took her on a tour of the neighborhood and all of our favorite restaurants.

My shame melted away.

It turned into happiness, anticipation. Joy.

Blood is pouring out of me, blackening my gray leggings.

'Oh my God,' Luke is saying, 'oh my God, oh my God. Okay, okay, let's get you to the hospital. Can you stand up?'

I can hear Luke speaking, but he seems farther away than he actually is. Muffled. Even though his face is right in front of my face. Why can't I hear him better? Everything is fuzzy, my eyes won't focus. Invisible hands are pressing down on the top of my head, on my shoulders, pushing me toward the ground. I roll onto my side and lay there. Why are so many hands pressing in on me? Whose hands are they? It's just Luke and me at home.

'Rose—'

The wood is smooth and cold against my cheek.

'Come quickly! Hurry up! Rose!'

A million hands are pressing into me, all over my body, trying to make me more compact. They are so heavy. Maybe they are real hands? My arm is lifted away from my side.

Luke. Oh, it's just Luke.

I see him. For a moment I feel peace.

When I open my eyes again I am blinded. The glare is brighter than any sun.

'Hello . . . where am I? What time is it?'

My head is spinning. My body is numb.

'Rose! She's awake!'

That's Luke's voice. But where is he?

'Luke?'

'I'm right here.'

I force myself to turn my head. It seems an impossible task but I do it. Ah. There he is. Right next to me. 'Why are you kneeling on the floor, Luke? Are you crying?'

'Rose,' is all he says. His face is streaked with tears.

Why can't I feel my body?

'Why can't I feel my body?' I ask him, since it seems likely that he should have the answer. Someone must. 'Am I in the hospital?'

There is something I'm not remembering.

A nurse approaches Luke. She is holding a baby. Luke turns to the nurse and takes the baby into his arms.

My eyelids are so heavy but I force them to stay open. 'The baby, the baby. I had the baby?' Memories slide through my mind, slowly, one by one. I am at home. I feel pain. There is blood between my legs. And then there is . . . nothing. A surge of fear roars through me. 'Is the baby okay? Is she all right?'

Luke shifts, reaches his arms out to me, the baby cradled across them so I can see. 'Rose, meet our daughter. She's all right. She's more than all right. She's perfect.'

And she is! Her eyes are scrunched shut and there are her tiny perfect lips, and the littlest, most beautiful nose in the universe. It feels as though someone has ahold of my feet now, though, which is distracting, and they are trying to pull me underwater. 'Hi there,' I manage.

Luke starts to sob.

'Are you crying because you're happy?' I ask him.

He doesn't answer.

I wish he would stop weeping. 'I guess they had to use drugs for the birth, huh,' I say, trying to make a joke. Luke and I had fought about natural childbirth versus C-sections and epidurals. All of it. I said I wanted to be unconscious for the whole ordeal, which always made Luke angry. I guess I got what I wanted, though. I think about saying this to make another joke but Luke is so upset, I decide against it.

Besides, what does any of that matter, now that she's arrived?

'Are my parents here?' I ask. The room spins. 'I want my mother.'

'They're on their way. They'll be here soon, Rose.'

There is something Luke's not saying. I can tell.

I reach out to our baby. Our *daughter*. 'Let me see her,' I say.

Luke obeys, shifting so I have a better view. 'What are we going to name her?' I ask. We'd decided we would wait until we met her to pick a name. This, and superstition, kept us from making a decision, as well as not knowing for sure if she'd be a boy or a girl.

'I think we should call her Rose,' Luke says.

'Rose? But that's ridiculous.' I try to laugh but I can't. My body resists. 'In my head I've always thought her name would be Adelaide. Addie. I know that's old fashioned but . . .'

'Rose—' Luke starts to say something else, maybe to me, but it gets muffled again. Or is he talking to the baby and that's why it's so hard to understand him suddenly?

Right then, whoever or whatever has a hold of my feet finally gets a good grip and pulls me hard. I go right under the water, it drowns out all other sound.

When I was six, or maybe seven, I'd gone into the ocean when my mother wasn't paying attention. The waves were rough that day. A storm had passed offshore, stirring up the sea, the sun shining so the ocean was one great glare of light. I waded right in, fearless, and stupid. My father had taught me to dive under the biggest waves, and I thought I could handle myself. The first one was taller than any wave I'd ever seen. I ducked under it, just like my father showed me, proud of myself, but when I came up there was another one, even taller than the last, right on its heels and hurtling toward the shore. It was on me before I could think and suddenly it had me, had sucked me deep within it. It felt like being swallowed by something tight and dark and fiercely strong. Something that would never let me go – and I thought it wouldn't. But I was lucky that day, and suddenly there was my mother, brave and fierce, putting her arms around me and carrying me out of the sea.

For a single moment, right now, I come up for air, long enough to hear voices speaking. 'Mom, is that you?' I manage to ask, or maybe I don't because no one seems to hear me.

'We're losing her,' a doctor is shouting.

'I love you, Rose, I love you so very much, I'm so sorry,' Luke is saying. I can't see him, so he must be whispering into my ear.

Then another wave comes, bigger than all the others before it and then the world fades and I fade with it and I am gone.

Part Four

Exit Rose, Life 4;
Enter Rose, Lives 6 & 8

22

August 15, 2006

Rose, Lives 6 & 8

L UKE IS STANDING on my side of the bed. He never goes
to my side of the bed. In his hand is a bottle of prenatal
vitamins. He holds it up, shakes it.

'You promised, Rose,' he says, his voice even and slow.

I nod my head, just as slowly. 'I did,' I tell him. 'You're right.'

'I am?' My husband sounds surprised that I would admit this
so easily.

I'm surprised, too, but it's the truth. I did promise him and I
haven't come through. Why not say so out loud? What have I
got to lose? 'Yes. And I'm sorry.'

Luke slumps onto the edge of the bed. If he was photographing
himself, maybe the caption he would give his image would be:
Luke, Portrait of a Defeated Spouse. 'Why haven't you been taking
them?'

I walk over and sit down next to my husband, this man who's
felt like a stranger lately. 'I don't know. Well, I do, sort of. For
one, they kind of give me a stomachache. But mainly, I guess,

because I really just don't want to. Because, as you know, I've never wanted to have a baby.'

'But you said—'

'I said I would take the vitamins. Yes.'

'Which I thought was the same thing as you saying you'd be open to trying.'

'It's never felt the same to me, though.'

Luke turns the bottle round and round in his hands, the heavy, rattling *thunk* of the vitamins filling the silence. The label promises so many things. Folic acid! Iron! The word ESSENTIAL in all caps is repeated over and over. 'Why would you take prenatal vitamins if you still aren't open to us having a child?'

'To make you happy,' I say, then back up. That's part of it, but not the whole truth. 'To make you stop pressuring me.' I pull my legs up and cross them on the crisp, white duvet, the thin one that we put on the bed during the hot, humid summer in this city. I wish for the puffy, lavish one that adorns our bed in winter, to sink into it, comfy and cradled. 'I thought it might stop us from fighting. And it did for a while.'

'Is this a fight?'

'I don't know. Is it?'

Luke turns to face me. He pulls his feet up onto the bed, crosses his legs, so that we are even. 'I don't want it to be. Let's not make it a fight, okay?'

I nod. 'Okay.' We look at each other, uncertain. 'So what's next, then?'

My husband shrugs, the short sleeves of his gray T-shirt lifting a couple of inches, revealing his biceps, strong from the photography gear he's always carrying around. I am struck by how attractive Luke is, something that I seem to have forgotten these last months. It makes me want to kiss him, grip his body to steady my own.

I could kiss him, of course.

As his wife, I probably should.

Right?

Isn't that how spouses make their way through tension, through disagreements, through fights? Makeup sex? Luke and I have never been one of those couples, though, and I've never really understood the concept. Sex isn't something I've felt like doing when Luke and I fight. Mostly I want to throw things, or scream, or pout for a full twenty-four hours.

But what if this one time, what if for just a while, I stop thinking, stop worrying, stop allowing this baby thing to stop me from reaching for him? What if I just let chance and biology decide my future as a mother or as a non-mother? If it happens, it happens, and if it doesn't, Luke and I can say that we tried. I can say that I tried or, at least, that I opened myself to the possibility of motherhood and it simply didn't work out for us, the situation resolved, once and for all.

It would be so nice to be able to say that I tried.

The possibility stretches out ahead of me, beckoning, whispering.

My first small step down this path is a gesture, a single fingertip down the bare skin of my husband's arm. This is followed by a leap, in the form of me, touching his cheek and kissing my husband – really kissing him. There is no talking, no arguing, no deciding.

I give in to it, for now.

An experiment.

23

July 3, 2007

Rose, Lives 6 & 8

'M OM?'

'Yes, sweetheart?' My mother is distracted by the piecrust she's rolling out on the kitchen island. The front of her loose red, white, and blue T-shirt is coated in flour. 'Getting into the Fourth of July spirit!' she claimed, when she showed up dressed like a flag at breakfast. We are away at the house my parents like to rent each summer for the holiday, the one sitting right on the beach.

'Did you and Dad ever think of giving up on having me?'

The handles on the old rolling pin, loose from years of use, clink as my mother presses it across the dough. She pulls off the wax paper, sprinkles a handful of flour onto it. A puff of white rises into the humid air. 'What are you talking about, Rose?'

The plastic cup that contains my iced coffee has sweated through the napkin around it, the ice nearly melted. I take a sip, chew on the straw. The sound of the waves outside the cottage fills the silence. Do I really want to tell her? Am I really going to do this?

Yes.

'When you and Dad were trying to get pregnant, did you ever consider stopping? Just not having kids at all?'

Clink went the rolling pin as it came down onto the flattening dough. My mother stops now, looks up. 'Of course we did. Many times!'

'Really?' I sound skeptical, even though I'm the one who asked her this question.

My mother's brow furrows. I notice a sheen of sweat across it. Both hands still grip the rolling pin. She holds it in the air just across the middle of her body. 'Rose, when you are trying to have a child for ten years, you have plenty of moments when you decide you're going to throw in the towel. It was not for lack of wanting you, though.'

'Sure,' I say quickly. 'That makes sense.'

My mother sets the rolling pin down, brushes the flour from her patriotic shirt. The scrape of a lounge chair travels through the window screens, my father adjusting his position on the deck out front. 'What's this about?'

I consider changing the subject, turning to other, less weighty topics, but then I plow forward. 'This will come as a surprise to you, but' – I swallow – 'Luke and I have been trying to have a baby.'

My mother jerks her arms, her whole body, marionette-like, her hands, elbows flailing and knocking the heavy rolling pin onto the floor with a great crash. 'What?'

'Everything all right in there?' my father calls from the deck.

'Everything's fine, Dad!' I yell back.

'But you don't want children,' my mother whispers. 'You've never wanted children. You've tormented me since you were a teenager about this, informing me that there were no grandchildren in my future,' she grumbles. 'I don't believe you.'

This was obviously a mistake. 'Fine, don't believe me then. I'm sorry I said anything.' I suck down more of my room-temperature iced coffee and start to head out of the kitchen, when a flour-caked hand grips my arm.

'Stay,' my mother says. 'Let's talk.'

I don't turn around. 'It took a lot for me to bring this up, and I'm not going to talk about it with you if you're going to be difficult or make me feel embarrassed.' I breathe in the hot air of the day. 'This isn't easy for me.'

I can hear my mother inhale a long breath. 'Rose, you can tell me anything. I shouldn't have reacted like that. It's just, I'm surprised. I never thought . . .'

'I know.'

'Why don't we go sit in the bedroom? So we have some privacy?'

My mother brushes by me, beckoning me to follow her into the room she and my father are using, with its view of the sea if you stand at just the right angle by the window. Luke and I have the smaller bedroom on the other side of the hall. He's out taking photographs at the bird sanctuary on the other end of the beach, while my father's sunning himself and reading.

My mother sits on the bed and pats the spot in front of her. Then she pulls a pillow to her middle, squashing it with her arms. She's getting flour everywhere, specks of it on the gray quilt, on the pillow. It's even in her hair because she ran her hand through it, but I don't say anything.

I sit down, swallow, try to talk past my anxiety, my second thoughts about having this conversation. 'In the beginning, it wasn't really a decision. Luke and I just . . . became open to it.' My mother gives me a look, like, *Yeah, right.* 'Fine. I decided that I would just stop overthinking things. If I got pregnant, I got pregnant, if not, then oh well.'

'Wow, Rose. Wow. Wow!'

Frustration climbs up my skin. 'Mom, I'm leaving if all you're going to do is express surprise.'

My mother sighs a little, her attention drifting to the window. 'I'm not, sweetheart. You just need to give me some time to adjust. It's a lot to accept at once.' She smiles, claps her hands, gleeful. Then she wipes her excitement away. 'Okay, I've had my moment of joy and I'm calm now, ready to listen. So when was this? When did you and Luke start . . . letting whatever happened happen?'

'Nearly a year ago.'

'Sweetheart, a year is nothing. Especially if you're not actively trying.'

'Maybe this is fate making the decision for Luke and me.'

'Maybe.'

'He and I never actually said out loud that we were going to try.'

This provokes a frown from my mother. 'How is that possible?'

I think back to the day of that fight, which ended in sex. 'I don't know, Mom. But we just . . . stopped discussing it. It's been this unspoken thing. Maybe because Luke is afraid if he

221

says something directly about it, I'll get angry and tell him to forget it.'

My mother snorts. 'Would you tell him that?'

I decide to be honest. 'I don't know. Maybe.'

'Your poor husband.'

'My poor husband? Seriously, Mom?'

'Rose, I think it would be good if you both could be on the same page about this.'

I get up and turn on the air conditioner. The heat is getting to me. This, and I worry about Luke coming home from his photography trip and hearing us talking. The unit rattles before settling into a low roar. The cold air flows over me as I stand in front of it, placing my hands against the grates. 'Luke and I are never going to be on the same page about this.' I look at my mother. 'We're as even as we're going to be right now.'

My mother shifts so she is closer to me. 'Do you think that's fair?'

I turn my back to the air conditioner. The air is freezing, soon it will be too much, but I don't move. I don't like that my mother is asking me these things. I don't really have any good answers for her. 'Well, do *you* think it's fair that I've been pressured to have a child I never wanted, Mom?'

I hear my mother sigh. 'Rose. No. I suppose I don't think that's fair.'

I am shivering. 'Wouldn't you be angry?'

'I don't know. It's hard for me to understand. I'm one of those women you think so little of, who grew up dreaming of having children of her own, and who needed to have a child like her life depended on it, then did everything she possibly could to have that child. Being a mother has been my entire life.'

'Mom.' I return to the bed and sit across from her. 'I don't think little of you.'

She cocks her head, watches me with her dark brown eyes. 'But you don't respect women like me, either. I'm the last person you've ever wanted to become.'

'That's not true.' I say this, but isn't my mother right?

'Of course it's true. You've spent your entire life becoming my opposite, devoting yourself to everything I never did. And I'm proud of you for it! You've become your own person, a wonderfully successful person! And I know you love what you do, which is the best part.' Her eyes drop to the quilt, and she hugs the pillow at her middle tighter. 'But it's sometimes made it hard for me to understand you. I've always thought that maybe if you had a child, it would bring us closer. And of course I've wanted a grandchild. But the real truth is that I've wondered if you had a baby of your own, whether you might need me again? Whether I might be useful to you? That would be nice for me.' She laughs, but she sounds so sad. 'It's not like I can offer you career advice.'

Her words hang in the oppressive August air.

'Mom, I'm sorry.'

She meets my eyes, looks at me hard. 'You don't have to be sorry. It's okay to turn out different from your mother.'

I'm not sure what to say. In a way, my mother *has* always been the model for exactly what I've never wanted to become – a full-time mom, who stayed home to take care of her child, who spent her life cooking and cleaning and taking care of me and my dad. I set myself on the exact opposite path, all the while expressing freely and openly and often how much I didn't want to be anything like her when I got older.

If I had a daughter, would she do this to me, too? Would she try to become my exact opposite and advertise it constantly? Would she disagree with all the choices I've made? And would I be able to endure it? How does any mother endure such a thing?

'I love you, you know,' I tell her. Then, 'I'm such a bitch to you sometimes. I wish I wasn't. I'm really sorry.'

This makes my mother laugh, real laughter this time, devoid of sadness. 'You are not a bitch. Don't ever say that about yourself.'

'I'd make a horrible mother,' I went on. 'Maybe that's my answer, right? I should just listen to those instincts and save my own future daughter the trouble of having a mother like me.'

'Rose! Don't say that either! Besides, I don't believe that's true. I think you'd be a good mother. A *great* mother. And I'd be a great grandmother!'

'I buy the last part, Mom.' I put my hand on the bed, right near my mother's foot. 'But the first part you said, about me being a great mother – I don't know.'

My mother brushes the flour from her cheek. 'You'll never know until you try it.'

'Yeah, well. At the rate things are going, I'll never find out. And maybe that's fine.'

'Maybe it is. But I think you and Luke should keep on trying, just in case it turns out that you love it. And if you don't get pregnant, you could think about adoption.' Her voice is gentle, but prodding. 'You could, right?'

The temperature in the room has dropped, and goose bumps have appeared all over my mother's arms. 'Let's go back to making pies,' I say. 'Dad is probably wondering where we've disappeared to, and Luke will be here soon.'

'Okay, sweetheart,' my mother says after a beat.

The two of us get up from the bed. My mother shuts off the air conditioner and it grows quiet around us.

'Do you really think it's okay, Mom, that I don't know how I feel about having a baby, but I might end up having one anyway?'

'I do.'

'But *why?*'

'Because I have faith in you, Rose Napolitano,' she says, and opens the door.

24

April 22, 2009

Rose, Life 5

MY HUSBAND IS sleeping on one side of me. Addie is sleeping on the other.

All I need is for Thomas to be lying at my feet.

Thomas is here, in a way. He is always here, the memory of him, the wish for him, even when I try to banish his presence. I do it now. I promise myself that I will.

The bedside lamp shines across Addie, but she doesn't seem to notice the light. She is curled up next to me in the hilarious position she likes to sleep in, with her little bum sticking high in the air, doing her funny little snuffling as she breathes. Her snuffling is one of the things I love most about her. It's totally irrational, so irrational that it makes me believe I might be a good mother. Her breath in my ear, the soft sounds of it, so unself-conscious.

Little Snuffleupagus. That's what I call her. It started early, the nickname. I would sit and listen to Addie, like she was the radio. Watch her like she's a television. Those sounds she makes when she's sleeping, it's as though they are on little cords, like church bells attached to my heart, tugging on it each time I hear them. I could listen to her all day, stare at her, like she's a show I want to binge-watch.

'Hello, little snuffly-poo,' I whisper to her, but only because Luke is sleeping. I would never say such a thing in front of him. If Luke heard me, he'd get this smug look on his face, like he's won, like he knew all along that every woman has a baby gene inside her, including me, his reluctant wife. The nickname is my little secret with Addie.

So are the pictures I take of her, on the first of every month, to mark another milestone in Addie's life. Soon she will have lived on this planet for fourteen months.

Addie gives her body a little wiggle, her bum shifting a bit, followed by a big loud snuffling. I have to cover my mouth not to laugh.

Sometimes it's not just my affair with Thomas that makes me want to get out of this marriage. Sometimes it's Addie, the fact that I'd like to be able to be myself with her, not have to parent alongside Luke. Sometimes I want to figure out what it means to be Rose, the reluctant mother, sure, but finding her way into motherhood regardless. I want to be a mother without the judgmental eyes of my husband on Addie and me, day in, day out. If I am feeling insane with love for this tiny snuffling daughter with her bum stuck up in the air, I want to get to feel that way without trying to hide it from him, without having to endure his *I told you so* when he witnesses it. So sometimes the possibility of leaving Luke really has nothing to do with Thomas at all.

I bite my lip.

I've just gone and done what I've sworn not to do, and I've done it twice. I've allowed the name Thomas to float through my mind. Every time it happens, I hurt all over. Like Addie, Thomas also seems to have a set of cords attached to my heart. I wish I could clip them.

Thomas and I are on a break.

It won't last. It never does. Being without Thomas, it's like trying to hold my breath underwater. I can only do it for so long before it starts to feel like I'm drowning.

But I am trying. I am.

'I have to save my marriage,' I told Thomas the last time we saw each other.

This was three weeks ago. I was in bed, gazing at his back, the curve of his muscles, the shine of his smooth skin. Luke and Addie were in bed with us then, too, the ghosts of them, Luke floating next to me and Addie snuggled under the covers, both of them watching the scene that was Thomas and me, naked in a hotel room on a Tuesday afternoon, infecting me with a guilt that only grows more profound by the day, settling into the marrow of my bones. I didn't feel guilty about Thomas before, but the longer this goes on and the older Addie gets, the worse I feel. Luke and Addie are always watching when I am loving Thomas, and I am always loving him, which is the problem.

Thomas turned over in the bed. 'No, Rose.'

'Yes.'

'Not again.'

'I have to.'

His eyes were already red, watery. 'You don't have to. You should do the opposite.' He reached for me. 'You should end the marriage, not save it.'

I let him pull me close. I wanted him – I always wanted him, even when I was trying not to want him.

There was nothing like Thomas's body, the feel of it, the skin of him next to the skin of me. I always let go into us, always gave myself over to this man in the same way I do when I'm swimming in the ocean. I let myself have Thomas like I have nothing to lose, when I have everything to lose. A husband, a baby, a family.

But in the same way that I can no longer bear the touch of my husband, I can't bear not to be touched by Thomas. I long to have more of him, always, wishing I could touch every inch of his skin at once. I can never manage to get enough of Thomas, and I wondered if I ever would.

'I love you,' he whispered into my neck.

I shifted so that we were side by side, so that I could look into his eyes. 'And I love you. But we can't keep doing this.' I said this, my arms around him, my hand in his hair, pressing so hard into his body it was as if I thought I could press through him, or that if I pressed hard enough Thomas and I might finally merge, become one person. I'd never wanted to inhabit a heart like this before, to curl up inside those mysterious chambers. I wanted the inaccessible parts of Thomas to become mine, I wanted the keys, I wanted them handed over to me forever.

I was supposed to want these things with Luke, supposed to feel this kind of incomprehensible love for my child – and I do, in a way, with Addie. Sometimes loving Addie is a form of madness. Terrible, wonderful, frightening.

But loving Thomas is another kind of madness. In Thomas I find myself, I find new tributaries and avenues, I find desire and hope and want and I find quiet and silence and stillness. He is a place where I can come to rest, not move, not even an inch, yet never become fidgety. I can drape myself along his body, close my eyes, and be no one else but Rose, me, the essence of the woman I am. The woman I can't seem to find or be anymore when I'm with Luke.

Thomas's kisses were urgent, then they were lazy, like we had all the time in the world, when all that we had was the already waning hours of the afternoon in this hotel room, the shades drawn to close out the rest of the city for as long as we could keep it away and pretend that it wasn't still there waiting for us.

I would sacrifice everything for this man. I would.

So why don't I, then? Am I just lying to myself, thinking these things? My actions don't reflect this sacrifice. My actions say, instead: *Rose, you are a coward, Rose, you won't take that step to be with this man, you haven't and you won't.*

Eventually Thomas and I pulled apart. I had to go home, Addie would need to eat, Luke would need to go out to his photo shoot, real life beckoned. Thomas began to get dressed, I got dressed. We stood a few feet from the door, barely able to look at each other.

'Please stop crying,' I said. I resisted touching his cheek, but I wanted to. I had to harden myself before I got home, I had to harden my heart to this man, so I could get out of here. But I couldn't somehow.

He wiped a hand across his eyes. 'When will I see you again?'

'I don't know, Thomas,' I said, then, 'I love you,' and hurried out.

*

Luke shifts position, poised to roll one way or the other in the bed. He rolls away from Addie and me, rather than toward us. The tightness in my muscles relaxes.

I've begun to fantasize about Luke dying, about what it would be like to move forward in my life without him. It would be such a relief, and not just because of Thomas. With Luke I always feel watched, evaluated, judged. I am always performing, always trying to get Luke's approval, always trying to do or say the right thing with Addie, about Addie.

I remember the first time I realized my husband was seeing me differently, evaluating my behavior, and I remember the accompanying jolt this provoked in me.

It was a Saturday afternoon in August, not long after the fight we'd had with Luke's parents over dinner about children. We were attending a friend's birthday party for her one-year-old daughter. The air-conditioning in the apartment was a refuge from the steaming air outside. I played with the baby a little, said hello, waved at her, admired her newly acquired ability to crawl with the rest of the guests. But frankly, cooing over a one-year-old is not my favorite activity.

I'd much rather talk to the adults in the room, hear about their work, their travels. Really, anything other than talking about children or to them interests me. I've never been one of those people who plays with the kids, who can make them shriek and laugh. Mostly, what I think when I see a grown-up in the middle of a dog pile of squealing children are things like, *I'm glad that's not me*, and *Why would anybody do that when there are such interesting adult conversations happening around the room?*

In the middle of that party, when I'd just gone to fill up my plate with food, Luke came over. He drew my attention to the children at the other end of the room, jumping and playing and crawling. 'Aren't they adorable?'

I picked up a tiny quiche, homemade, and popped it into my mouth. 'Um, I guess? Sure?' I laughed, but Luke didn't join in.

His face was blank, impossible to read. After filling up his plate, he said, 'I wish you cared about kids more,' and walked away before I could respond.

A kind of panic settled into my chest, my lungs. Had Luke's parents been pressuring him behind my back again? Had his thinking on this issue begun to swing their way?

Now that I knew I was on a stage, I ricocheted back and forth between escaping into conversations with the other adults at the party and the assortment of children they brought with them. I forced myself to sit down on the floor to chat with one, while the birthday baby crawled around us. Occasionally I glanced over and saw my husband watching.

On the walk home, Luke said, 'I could tell you were doing all that just to prove a point.'

I halted. 'Why are you being this way? What does it even matter, what I'm like with kids? It's not like we're going to have any.'

Luke stopped, too, and we stood there awkwardly on the sidewalk, the heat steaming up from the concrete. He seemed about to say something else, but then he didn't. Instead he began to walk.

The panic that had settled into me rose up and expanded. What, exactly, was happening here?

I hurried after him. I fluctuated between anger and fear, but eventually anger got the best of me. I wanted to strike him. 'Who are you to talk, Luke? I didn't see you down there on the floor,' I sneered, 'being all "caring" about the kids.'

We didn't speak for the rest of the evening.

Now, Luke rolls onto his other side in the bed, still asleep. Closer to me this time. I edge away, though not that far since I don't want to wake Addie.

Do other women fantasize about their husband dying or is it only me? Maybe this is a regular part of marriage, of the wish for liberation, for the chance to start everything over again and make different choices this time around. Sometimes Luke dies because he walks in front of a bus he didn't see. Or it's a plane crash if he's gone off on a trip. It's never murder. Just a regular twist of fate that takes Luke from me.

But then I always remember Addie. That would be the worst part. She would miss him. I know she would.

Would I?

Maybe I would be devastated. Maybe it would be the worst thing to ever happen to me. Maybe Luke would be gone and then I would realize that I truly did love him, that I can't live without him, that the tragedy of his loss is real.

But I have a feeling I would be okay. What I do around Addie would no longer be judged as good or bad, as an excellent sign of my maternal instincts or a dismal failure. I could be as vocal as I wanted about how my career fulfills me without any caveats about Addie. I could complain when I'm tired, or be annoyed when Addie is being honestly annoying, or put her in front of the TV for God's sake, without Luke scolding. I could call Addie the sappiest nickname in the history of the world and never worry about who overhears me. I could finally enjoy being a mother. I could *let* myself enjoy it.

God, that would be so freeing!

I study Luke now, the way the lamplight falls across his sleeping form.

I could just ask him for a divorce.

I should, right?

Addie's funny, downward dog makes her wobble over onto the bed. She opens one eye halfway, but then settles again, her breathing growing steady, heavy.

'Good night, Addie,' I say, softly.

I turn off the lamp.

You would miss Luke.

This thought is just a whisper in the darkness.

Even after every other terrible thought about all that I'd gain from Luke's absence, I know this is true, too. I wish that it weren't, but it is.

25

July 14, 2007

Rose, Life 6

'WHAT IF WE adopt?'

This question hangs in the air of the subway after I ask it. Luke and I are on our way home after seeing a band at a bar. It's late, we're tired, but the nice kind of tired after you've had a good time. There are only a few other people in our car.

Luke has had his head resting on my shoulder, but he raises it now, turns to me. 'Adopt a baby?'

I laugh at his surprise, nudge him. 'Um, yeah, a baby.' Did he think I meant a kitten? A puppy? Then again, we've maintained this pact of not speaking about whether to have a child even though we haven't been using birth control for nearly a year. I grab his hand, clasp it. 'Since, you know, this doesn't seem to be happening for us.'

'No, it isn't,' he admits.

'And because maybe I can't get pregnant. Or you know, you can't get me pregnant.' It feels good to get this out finally, to talk about what we've been doing but not acknowledging directly.

'Maybe,' Luke says.

'How do you feel about adoption, anyway?'

He stares down at our clasped fingers. The subway doors open, close, the train moving onward to the next stop. 'I don't know. I haven't given it much thought, really.' He looks up at me. 'Have you?'

'A little.' My conversation with my mother from last week at the beach house has been ringing in my head ever since we had it, how she thought I could be a good mother. That I would be. 'I think I might like it, actually. Maybe it's a good compromise for us. You know?'

Luke doesn't answer.

I decide to keep going. Close my eyes a moment, try to picture it all in my head. 'Maybe if I take pregnancy out of the equation, and all of this trying to have a baby and it not working out, it would take some of this pressure I've felt off me.' The train arrives at another stop. We are almost home. 'But if you and I adopt, we would still have this child we could raise together. You know?'

A big group of teenagers gets on the train, talking, laughing. Maybe they've been out at a party, or maybe in the park that's at this stop. They sit on the bench across from us, lift the mood of the entire car with their energy.

'You almost sound excited,' Luke says.

'I don't know. Maybe. Maybe I kind of am.' One of the girls separates herself from the group, pulls another of the girls down to the other end of the car. Then they start kissing. 'Could you be excited about adoption?'

'Maybe,' he says.

'Can you think about it?'

'Okay. Yes. I guess. Though I think we should, you know, keep trying.' I feel his eyes studying me as we sit, side by side on the bench, the train lurching forward.

Can I agree to that? To keep doing this unspoken thing we've been doing all along, but this time speak it out loud, do it intentionally? My mother's voice floats in and out of my head again, about how she thought I might love being a mother, her faith in me that this could all work out.

'Okay. Yes. I guess,' I say, parroting Luke's earlier words.

This seems enough to satisfy him. He squeezes my hand. Kisses me on the cheek.

Married people are so different than teenagers. The two girls at the other end of the train have their arms wrapped around each other, their bodies pressed tight. No more making out on trains for Luke and me, I guess. But the connection I feel with Luke at this stage in life is gentle, settled. Not bad, just different.

The train arrives at our stop. When we reach our apartment, the two of us go straight to bed because we are so tired. No kissing, no lovemaking, just pajamas then lights out. It's a relief not to have to try to have a baby tonight. Adoption could really be the perfect answer for us, I am thinking, before I finally fall asleep.

Two pink lines emerge on the white plastic stick, side by side.

Pregnant.

I'm pregnant.

It's as if my talk with Luke about adoption last night conjured a baby. Or maybe it was the one with my mother at the beach.

I grab my phone to call my husband, then stop. I'll tell him in person. He'll be so happy.

Am I happy?

The thought of adoption seemed like such a good idea, and like Luke said, I was getting kind of excited about the possibility.

Carefully, I wipe down the stick and place it onto the bathroom counter, lay it across a facecloth.

How will I tell Luke this news? Will I try something casual? *Hi, Luke, how was your day? Mine was interesting. I found out we're pregnant.* Or will I go for a big reveal? There's time to run out for a pretty little box at the store, something plain, not flowery. Tasteful. Maybe a solid aqua blue or a dusty rose or who am I kidding? A sunny yellow or a grass green to be gender neutral. I could set the stick inside, close the lid, wrap the box with a ribbon. Place it in front of Luke on the dining table, make him open it like a present.

Is that gross?

But it is a present, isn't it? Something only I can give my husband, something only a woman's body can offer. I push this thought aside, already not liking the idea that I am imagining this baby as something that can be exchanged, like money. I replace it with other thoughts, of telling Luke, of how I'll tell him.

I could wait until Luke and I are going to bed, maybe write him a sweet note and leave it on his pillow. 'Oh, Luke, what's that?' I could ask. 'Did the tooth fairy pay you a visit?' No, that's cheesy. Also ridiculous.

A strangeness builds inside me as these possibilities ricochet around my brain, a kind of bubbling up, a fizzing up through my middle, my throat.

Happiness.

I am happy. I think?

I shake out my limbs, my wrists, stretch my fingers. Head out of the bathroom and into the living room.

Can this be true? Am I actually pleased to be pregnant? Could it have been this easy all along, a matter of letting myself fall into it, arms wide, allowing the hands of fate to catch me, one way or another?

I halt midstride, just before I reach the kitchen. Stay completely still.

And wait.

Will the excitement evaporate now that I've stopped moving? If I allow the truth of this pregnancy to seep through my body until it reaches my extremities, a slow, antibiotic drip? I stand there a long time, maybe twenty minutes, maybe more. I breathe, I blink, I wonder if the happiness will break apart, atoms into the nothingness. My eyes dart around the house, the long farm table strewn with mail in one corner, the still unread pile of *New Yorker*s, a sweatshirt Luke left draped over the back of the couch.

It takes a long while for the happiness to dissipate, but it does. It turns into something else. Peace, I think.

'Who are you?' I say out loud to the emptiness.

No, I say it to *her*, to my middle, my abdomen. My future daughter, I'm sure it's a daughter, a she, barely the size of a pin.

How strange all of this is to take in.

I grab my purse, slip my flip-flops on, and soon I am running to the drugstore. I buy six different tests. The words *yes* and *no* spelled out on the window of the stick, pluses and minuses, more horizontal lines in singles or multiples. I want to make absolutely sure that I'm right. I don't want to give Luke false hope.

Or do I not want to give myself false hope?

On the way back to the apartment I call Jill. She picks up right away.

'Hey, you, what's going on?'

I take a deep breath. 'You're never going to believe this,' I say, then stop. Jill doesn't know that Luke and I haven't been using birth control. My friends have grown tired of his obsession with parenthood, with how this question of whether I will become a mother or not has come to define our marriage. Jill has even advocated that I leave Luke because of it. She is not a fan of my husband. Not anymore.

'What won't I believe?' Jill asks.

I need to say it out loud to someone who isn't Luke. I need to practice the words. 'So . . . I am . . . I am pregnant. I'm *pregnant.*'

There. There it is.

Jill is silent.

'Say something.'

'Oh, Rose. Well. Are you okay?' she asks, but keeps on going before I can answer. 'Do you need an abortion? Do you need me to come with you? Because you know that I will. I'll be there ASAP.'

'An abortion?'

I press the phone to my shoulder as I unlock the door of the apartment, let myself back inside. Abortion is still an option, isn't it? I hadn't even thought of it until Jill suggested it. But it's true,

I could go and get one before Luke is even home from work later tonight. I could go have an abortion like I might go get an eye exam. No big deal. Luke would never have to know.

I can hear Jill's keys jangling on the other end of the line. 'I'm coming over.'

'No, don't come. I'm fine.'

'Rose, are you sure? Why don't we talk through what you want to do?'

'We're talking about it now.'

'You know what I mean,' she says.

Then I tell her. 'I'm not going to get an abortion.'

'Really?' The doubt in her voice is an anchor, and it drags at my earlier happiness like a fishhook.

I try not to let her reaction tear at me. I shouldn't be surprised. I should expect this from Jill, from everyone who knows me. 'Yeah. Really. I'm going to have this baby. I am.'

'Rose, you sound like you're trying to convince yourself.'

'Would it be so terrible if I was?'

'I'm not sure that you're thinking clearly,' she says.

I pull out a chair from the kitchen table, sit, wanting to be steady, unwavering. 'I think I might actually be happy about this, Jill. I know you're only trying to be a good friend, but I'm serious. Please believe in me.'

Silence again.

Those last words I said to her just now, the way I said them, they almost sound like a mistake. *Please believe* in *me* as opposed to *Please believe me.* What do I want from Jill here, what do I need from her? Is it some kind of faith that I might turn out to be good at parenthood after all, the same kind of faith my mother showed in me?

I press the phone harder against my ear.

Then Jill speaks again, finally. 'Okay – who stole my best friend and replaced her with a woman wanting to be pregnant?'

'I'm still me,' I tell her.

But am I?

There is an unexpected ease to what I am saying, what I am committing to, a sudden slipping into a role that women have been playing for as long as women have existed. I don't shake it off. I let it sit there. Try to get used to it.

I glance down at the dress I'm wearing, flowered, light, flowing, the kind of dress I love to put on when it's hot and I want to feel like air. My feet are bare and brown from the summer sun, my arms, too. I've already been looking forward to going back to teaching at the end of August, to the special seminar I've planned based on the new study I'm going to launch. I was so excited last spring when I got the grant for it.

Will having a baby change any of that? Any of me?

Maybe? Probably?

I realize that I do not care.

At least, not enough to change my decision about this baby.

Classes will be there for me after I have her. My body will go back to its regular size (I hope, I think), and one day I will again fit into this dress (right?). The excitement about my research isn't going to go away, even if the research itself will be a bit delayed.

'I'm coming over,' Jill says.

'I told you, I'm okay.'

'Rose,' she says, my name earnest, sincere. 'I'm coming over

242

because I need to see your face. I . . . I feel a little blindsided. And worried. And I just want to make sure that you're sure – I can't help it,' she adds.

'I understand,' I say to Jill. 'Okay. Come,' I tell her.

I decide on the gift box for Luke, grass green.

By the time Luke gets home, Jill has left the apartment, not entirely satisfied that I am being honest with myself about this pregnancy, but I decide that this is okay and hope that eventually she'll come around. I am standing by the table in the kitchen, waiting for Luke. He walks in and he's barely set down his bag on the chair when I am thrusting the box into his hands.

'What's this?' he asks, startled.

There is this feeling inside me – how to describe it? It's a feeling of certainty, that somehow no matter what, it's going to be okay. I am, Luke is, this little baby is. 'Open it,' I tell him, smiling. 'Open it right now. It's going to change your life. Mine too. *Ours.*'

26

May 2, 2013

Rose, Lives 1 & 2

'YOUR MOTHER ISN'T feeling well.'

My father says this the second I answer the phone. 'Dad?'

'She isn't well. I'm worried.'

My father is not a worrier. And my mother is never sick. She's an iron lady.

'Hang on a sec.' I get up, shut the door of my office. Pick my phone up off my desk again. 'When you say she isn't well, what do you mean? Does she have a cold, the flu, or . . .'

'I don't know, Rose. Last night, she was doubled over in pain, but she doesn't want to go to the doctor. She refused to let me take her. You know your mother.' He sighs. 'She's so stubborn.'

Just like me. This is one way that my mother and I have always been the same. I hate the thought of my stubborn, iron mother in pain. It frightens me. 'Is this the first time this has happened?'

There is a long pause. Another sigh. 'No.'

'How long has this been going on, Dad?'

'A few months, maybe.'

244

'Dad!' My heart quickens in my chest. I swivel around in my chair. Face the window in my office. The pink buds on the tree outside seem wrong suddenly, too much of a contrast to the worry in my father's voice, to the thought that my mother might be sick. 'Where is she now?'

'She's upstairs in bed.'

'And where are you?'

'Sitting on the couch, waiting for her to feel better, to come down and tell me she's fine again. I can't get any work done.'

'It's probably nothing,' I say.

'Probably,' my father says.

My heart beats even faster in my chest. I feel it thumping underneath the fabric of my dress. 'I'll be right there.'

'Don't you have a class to teach?'

'Yes. It doesn't matter. I'll cancel. See you soon.'

'Okay.' He sounds relieved.

'I love you,' I say and hang up. My keys are already in my hand.

When I arrive at my parents' house, my father is sitting in the living room, hands clasped in his lap, staring straight ahead. At first, he doesn't seem to realize that I am there, but then he turns. His eyes are frantic.

'Daddy,' I say – which I never say. Not since I was much younger. But the look on his face is scaring me.

'You need to convince your mother that she has to go to the doctor,' he says. 'Right away.'

I stand in the middle of the room. My big, carpenter father

seems suddenly small. Caved in. 'But if you can't convince her, how can I?'

He is shaking his head back and forth. 'I don't know, Rose. But she's not listening to me. Can you try?'

'Yes. Of course.'

'She keeps saying it's just stomach pains. Maybe it is just stomach pains. But she's been saying it for months now.'

'Maybe it is,' I repeat.

'She keeps telling me I'm overreacting. That I'm being melo-dramatic.'

My father is neither one of those things and we both know it.

We hold each other's gaze. We both want these things to be true, that he is worrying for nothing, that he is being melodra-matic. We want my mother's stubbornness to be right; we want to be in the wrong, so my mother can smirk and tell us she told us so afterward, one of her favorite things to do. Inform us that we made a big fuss over nothing.

I nod at my father then, quick, short bobs of my head.

I go upstairs.

I knock softly. I almost don't want to go in.

'Yes?'

This *yes* sounds hoarse, tired. Not like my mother.

'Mom? It's me.'

'Oh! Rose! Come in!' Her voice has already changed, getting back nearly all of its typical energy.

But is my mother putting on an act? Performing being fine for her only daughter?

246

I open the door. She's on the bed, knees pulled to her chest. She turns toward me, tries to give me a smile, pretends like nothing is wrong, but then she grimaces. 'Mom!'

She gives up the act, lays her head back on the pillow, and moans in pain.

I go to the bed, sit down carefully next to her. 'You're not okay.'

'I'm fine. It will pass. It always does.'

The room is quiet. She hasn't even been watching television while she sits here, all rolled up. 'Mom, stop it. Dad says this has been going on for months.'

'Dad exaggerates.'

'He does not, and you know it.'

My mother goes about the business of shifting her body around so she is facing me, which takes a while. I don't stop her because I know she'll dismiss whatever I say. She's shivering even though it's warm in here, so I pull the covers from underneath her, slowly, carefully, and tuck her in. Then I tuck myself in next to her. She closes her eyes, but I know it's not to sleep.

'Mom, you're scaring me,' I whisper.

'Don't be scared. I'm only allowed to get scared if it's about you.'

Her answer makes me want to pound the bed with my fists. 'You are being so frustrating,' I say, teeth gritted.

'Talk to me about your life. Give me the update.'

'No.'

'Please?'

'Only if you go to the doctor.'

'You're bargaining with me right now?'

247

'Yes!'

'You're as bad as your father.'

'No. It's just that we both love you and want to make sure nothing is wrong. Stop acting like a child.'

My mother huffs. 'Says the child.'

I don't respond, cross my arms as I sit there, waiting for her to make a decision. The right decision.

'Fine, I'll go to the doctor.'

I look at her. Her eyes are closed again. 'Really?'

'Yes. But only if you tell me everything going on with you. I want all the details. Don't leave anything out.'

'Sure. I'll tell you whatever you want.'

'And don't make anything up or our deal is off.'

I laugh – I can't help it. Her eyes flicker open and I see a faint smile in them. This is encouraging. 'Okay,' I tell her, and pull out my phone.

Her fist closes around my arm. 'What are you doing?'

'I'm calling the doctor right now.'

'But Rose, you said—'

'I'll tell you whatever you want to know after I make your appointment.' I peel her fingers away, then scroll through the numbers until I come to the doctor that my mother has had forever, the one I've seen myself, too, ever since I was little. We both love her.

My mother grows quiet, listens as I talk to the secretary at the practice, explain to him what's going on with my mother and that she needs an appointment ASAP. He tells me he can squeeze her in early tomorrow morning and I say yes, we'll be there.

248

When I hang up, my mother dives right in. 'So are you dating anyone?'

'Wow.' I set the phone on the bedside table and shift a little closer to her. 'You want me to go straight to the gossipy stuff, huh?'

'You made a promise to tell me everything. That's the bargain, take it or leave it. Or I'm not going to the appointment you just made at that ungodly hour.'

'All right,' I say, and launch into the update on my life, which isn't much different than when I last updated her. I tell her about the dates I've been on, some of them funny stories now that they are in the past; I tell her that there is no one special, not yet, not since Luke, even though it's been years. That there are entire days that go by when I don't think about him now, something I never thought would be possible when we first separated. I tell my mother that I've stopped going online to look at pictures of Luke and Cheryl, his new wife, and their baby, and my mother tells me that this is a good thing, a healthy thing. She tells me that I just need to be patient, too, that there will be someone special in my life again one day soon, that she's sure of this.

As the afternoon wears on, my mother and I talk and talk and talk, more than we have in ages. There are moments when it almost seems that nothing is wrong, that I've just come for a regular visit. But then I remember why I'm here on one of the last days of classes for the semester, because I can see it on my mother's face, the pain she is in, in the way she curls her body inward, protecting it.

I stop talking when this happens, as she shifts, trying to get comfortable. And in those silences I keep thinking about how much I need my complicated mother, the only person on this earth who has known me every second of my existence. How if there was anything good that came out of Luke leaving, it was this: How it's changed our relationship. How it's made my mother and me closer. Closer than ever.

'I can't lose you,' I say to her now.

'I'm not going anywhere. I'm your mother. Where would I go?'

I don't answer. I don't want to think about it.

'I drive you crazy, Rose,' she says then. 'You're always telling me that.'

'Yes, but in a good way,' I say back.

Her eyes flicker shut again. 'Remember when you were small and you would get scared at night? You would get into bed like this with me. I used to love it.'

'Mom! You loved that I was scared?'

'No. I loved that you'd get into bed with me.'

'But I was always waking you up. You couldn't have liked that part.'

She glances up at me now, eyes wide open. 'I didn't mind, Rose. I loved having you there. I love having you here now. I'll always love it.'

27

December 18, 2009
Rose, Life 8

T HE DECISION TO have sex is going to end me.
The fact of it, the *having to make a decision* – like an
obligation, like it is on the same plane as doing the dishes or
vacuuming the house. It has become drudgery. Whoever thinks
that sex will one day be akin to scrubbing floors? I used to like
sex. I used to love it. I used to love it with Luke. But now I am
filled with dread at the thought of having it, of having to take
off my clothes and lie naked next to this man in our effort to
make a baby. We've been trying for ages. What was once a
nondecision has become a requirement of this marriage that I
loathe with all that I am. And I loathe Luke with it. I loathe his
skin, his body, his mouth, his breath.

Does this happen to all married people? Or only the ones who
are trying to get pregnant – trying and failing? Or, Luke is trying.
I am mostly just allowing him to try.

'Rose? I'm on my way home. I'll be there as quick as I can.'

Listening to this voicemail from Luke sends a shudder through

251

me. He's rushing home because this is a must-have-sex day. We have to do our duty and submit to the schedule my body dictates, my biological clock tick-tick-ticking all the time, my reproductive organs announcing – by way of the calendar, my temperature, the pain I always get in my abdomen on the left side or the right, depending on which ovary is supplying an egg for the month – *Now! Do it right this minute, or risk failing yet again! Risk seeing that single pink line on the plastic stick, rather than the triumphant two!*

Luke has been keeping a calendar. Among the people I know who've struggled to get pregnant, usually it's the woman who keeps the fertility calendar, does the counting of days and marking the ones that carry the highest probability of pregnancy. But in this marriage, Luke is in charge of the daybook, the ebb and flow of ovulation, and while I am sure that some women would appreciate their husbands making this kind of effort, I am not one of them. Luke has become so desperate that sometimes I think he would crawl into my womb if he could, carrying his sperm in a bottle to unite it with one of my eggs, plant it there, monitor its growth, totally unconcerned about my comfort or discomfort.

I wish I could have my ovaries removed. I wish I'd been born without them.

I go into our room and stand there. The bed is a wreck of tangled sheets, pillows half falling on the floor, clothes strewn everywhere. I pull on a pair of gray, stretched-out leggings that sag in the butt and have holes in the knees, along with my favorite oversize sweatshirt that says WEEKEND across the front, the one that hangs down to the middle of my thighs like a dress. I tug my thick, rainbow-striped, slipper socks on my feet because it's freezing, and then I pull my hair into a ponytail. I haven't even showered.

Super sexy. That is me.

Today I didn't have classes so I didn't go into my office, and besides, it's the end of the semester. I have grant deadlines coming up in January and an enormous pile of grading on the kitchen table. Who can be expected to shower under such circumstances? Who can be expected to have *sex* under such circumstances?

'Luke, hi.' I pick up his latest call on the first ring. There is a tiny piece of me that is hoping he's delayed at whatever photo shoot he's doing and is calling to cancel the afternoon's love-making.

'Rose, I'm sorry it's taking me so long to get home, but I'll be there soon. I promise.'

'You don't have to be sorry,' I tell him. 'Take your time. And if you can't make it home before I go to sleep, that's fine. Just don't wake me up. I have a long day tomorrow of teaching.'

'Oh no, I'll be there. We can't miss our window! See you soon!' He hangs up.

'Of course we can't miss our window. Not the window! The fucking all-important window!' I say to the darkened phone in my hand.

Then I think of other things I could say to him:

'Luke, while you were on your way home, I was tossing a baseball around and I broke the pregnancy window. Whoops!'

Or, 'Sweetheart, I was really cold so I closed the pregnancy window and now it's sealed tight. Sorry!'

I pad into the living room, grab my laptop and one of my fat stacks of papers to grade, then I pad back to the bed, prop myself on some of the pillows, get in, and get to work. I may as well do some grading before Luke gets here and we have to window it up.

'As you know, Maria and I do it once a week, on Mondays.'

This was Jill, talking about her sex life with her partner at a bistro near campus, with another married professor friend of ours, Brandy.

'But scheduling sex is the worst,' I moaned, because I was always moaning about sex when I was out with Jill and other friends lately. I gave Brandy an apologetic glance. I'd lost my ability to be discreet about anything. 'I fucking *hate* it.' I took a big bite of my sandwich to stop myself from uttering something else pathetic.

'So what you're saying, Rose, is that things are great with you and Luke,' Brandy chuckled, but not without sympathy. Brandy is beautiful, with wide, dark eyes, and the most gorgeous long dreads. 'I'm with Jill on this one. Just making it happen once or twice a week saves me a lot of headache at home. I mean, I'm trying to get tenure, I've got articles to finish, and I don't have time for relationship issues with Tarik. It's the path of least resistance. Just get it out of the way and then you're good for at least another seven days. Maybe even fourteen!'

'Once a week is what the couples therapist told us,' Jill went on, 'to keep us "bonded".' She said this with air quotes, and a voice heavy with sarcasm. 'I sort of dread it, but then, once we're doing it, it's usually not so bad. Maria was the one who decided it should be Mondays. It works better with her schedule.'

'This is the most depressing conversation ever had among feminists,' I said, and my friends laughed. 'We should call up Gloria Steinem and inform her that the next generation has failed at sex.'

'Or,' Brandy said, 'we could pat ourselves on the back for doing what we need to do to keep our careers on track. I'm not going to lie – it's nice having someone at home when I get there at the end of the day. That, and Tarik does housework! For as long as it stays nice, I'll do whatever I need to do to keep that going. It's only like – what? Ten, fifteen minutes of my time here and there?'

Jill leaned forward, her blouse just shy of entering her soup. 'The real question, Rose, is whether all of this is worth it for you to stay with Luke. Why are you still with him anyway? Do you even know?'

I stared down at my plate. It's not like I hadn't thought about this, or that Jill hadn't asked something like it before. Why *was* I still with Luke, especially after everything he's put me through? Why was I with someone whose touch I'd learned to dread, whose body I'd learned to avoid in our bed?

My only real answer was fear. Fear of change, fear of being alone, fear of the grief I would have to live through because of the loss of Luke in my life. And it would be a loss. I loved Luke. Somewhere deep within me I still hung on to who he was in the beginning, who we were in the beginning back when we were happy. Because we *were* happy. I used to think I'd never be happier than when I was with Luke. I thought he was the love of my life. I thought we would be together forever.

Don't all married people think this, at first? When they're

standing in front of their friends and family after walking down that aisle, their lives so full of hope and promise? When they are so in love they can barely see anything but each other? Even when older couples tell you that marriage will be difficult, that times will get hard, that you might even hate each other sometimes, you never believe them. You never believe that this will happen to you and your beloved. That's only for other people.

How much does a marriage have to endure before two people give up? Before you become willing to turn your back on love that was as real as the hands on your body? When do you know for sure that there is no going back to what you used to have – that you can never go back?

Why don't people tell you how fragile love is? And when they do tell you, why don't you listen harder, so you can try to give it the water and care and sunlight that love needs to survive?

'Inertia is powerful,' I finally said to Jill and Brandy. 'Isn't it?'

'Oh yeah,' Brandy said.

The three of us grew quiet.

Inertia definitely was the thing keeping me in my marriage. I knew it would be painful, this parting of ways, and I didn't want to live that pain. Not yet.

'Inertia also helps with grant deadlines, getting final grades in, getting research done,' I added, trying to lighten the mood. 'Divorce, probably not so much.'

The miscarriage is what caused the maniacal shift in Luke, in our marriage, in our sex lives.

I was pregnant once, briefly, for a couple of weeks. My breasts were hurting all the time, I was nauseated and unusually tired. The test I took to confirm my suspicions was positive. It happened nearly a year ago, which was also well over a year after we'd started trying. My first mistake was telling Luke.

After I got home from teaching that evening, I cooked us dinner. I don't remember what I made, pasta, probably. I was in a daze.

Luke came home and took off his hat, his gloves, his coat. 'It smells delicious.' He joined me at the stove, circled his arms around my middle – something I used to love. Kissed my neck.

Things were still good between us in that moment. For a blissful year after our fight about the vitamins, after I stopped using birth control and opened the door to the possibility of us having a child, we returned to the place I thought we'd lost forever.

I didn't respond.

Luke asked, 'Is something wrong?'

'No,' I said. *Yes.*

'Rose, I can tell something is going on.'

'It's not that anything is wrong. It's just . . .'

'What?'

I may not remember what I was cooking that night, but I remember this moment, how I turned everything off on the stove and went to sit at the kitchen table. Luke followed and sat down opposite me. I'd seen that positive pregnancy test, held it in my hand, knew it was real, but I still couldn't believe the result was true. It might be true for a different woman, but not for me.

'I took a pregnancy test,' I finally said to him.

How can I describe Luke's face in that moment? Joyous? Hopeful?

'And?' His tone swung high with excitement.

'It was positive.' These three words were so quiet amid Luke's taut anticipation.

Luke stood so abruptly that he knocked over his chair. 'We're pregnant?'

There was a brief moment, provoked by Luke's use of *we* – when everything in me twitched. It was like the slight tickle of an allergy. We'd been in such a good place, but in the course of seconds everything shifted. '*We're* not pregnant,' I said. '*I* am. It's my body, not yours, that will have to have this baby.'

'Rose, this is amazing!' Luke was nodding, his hands fidgeting at his sides. He got up and paced to the wine rack against the wall, came back to the table. 'We need to get rid of all the wine in the house. If you can't drink, I won't drink.' He rambled on about all the other things we'd have to remove or fix or do in the house to prepare for the baby. To prepare *me* for the baby.

With every new sentence from Luke, my uncertainty expanded. I wanted to circle my arms around my body, claim it as mine, refuse to let him touch it. I wanted to get up and take all the wine bottles from the rack and bring them to my office, hide them in a cabinet. Drink them between classes. File the edges of the tables and furniture until they were extra sharp.

'I've got to call my parents.' He grabbed his phone. 'Then I'll call the doctor and make us an appointment.'

We went to the doctor two days later and she told us that yes, I was indeed pregnant. Luke had yet to ask me how I felt about this.

Was it because he was afraid of what my answer might be?

I walked around the world, wondering if maybe I would catch

the way that Luke felt about this pregnancy, contract it like a virus, but one that heals uncertainty. For two short weeks Luke was on a high. He sought out photography jobs from pregnant couples and couples with babies. He whistled and sang in the house, came back from work alive with talk of what to do and what not to do while pregnant – no sushi, no more of that cheese I loved because it was sure to end in death for the baby. He told stories about the adorable newborns he'd photographed, about the joys of being a parent.

I tried to let his excitement pull me like a current, tried to step right in so it would carry me. But it wasn't strong enough; I sank to the bottom like a rock.

One morning, after I'd been awake for more than an hour, something occurred to me. I wasn't sick to my stomach today, wasn't tired, my breasts no longer hurt. The last couple of days I'd felt some cramping. I hadn't thought too much about it, assumed it was just another part of being pregnant. But that morning when the cramps started again and I went to the bathroom, I saw blood. It wasn't so much that it frightened me, and the cramping felt like normal cramping. Period cramping.

Had my period arrived? Had the pregnancy been a dream?

Was I free?

Was this my get-out-of-jail-free card?

I walked to the drugstore and bought three more pregnancy tests. Luke was out on a job. When I got home, one by one, over the course of the morning, I took all three.

They were negative.

I remember staring at all of those tests. How I lined them up on the bathroom counter. As if seeing them all at once, in a row, would help me better believe the truth of what they told me. Questions swirled. How could I have been pregnant a few days ago and now I wasn't? What happened to cause the future baby that was there, inside me, to suddenly be gone? Had I done something wrong? How could a child have taken up residence within my body then chosen to vacate it, without even consulting me?

And how did I feel about this?

Sad? Lost? Relieved?

My period, or whatever this was, continued, getting heavier as the day wore on. The only thing certain in me in that moment was that I dreaded the evening ahead, when I would have to share this news with Luke.

He cried. He sobbed. I held his hand across the kitchen table. At one point he looked at me searchingly. 'Why aren't you crying, too?' he asked.

'I cried all day,' I lied. Maybe I would cry, the next day, or the next.

Luke nodded, pulled himself together. 'We need to start marking the calendar.'

I snatched my hand away from his. 'What?'

'We need to figure out *exactly* when you ovulate. We need to keep track of everything.'

I sat there, blinking at him.

'If it happened once,' he went on, 'it can happen again, right?'

When Luke finally gets home from his photography shoot, I don't even hear him come into the house.

I am deeply engaged in the paper of one of my graduate students because it is excellent, and I am busy fantasizing about telling this young woman that I'd love to be her adviser. Not exactly an aphrodisiac for sex.

'Um, Rose? Hello?' Luke is in the doorway of our bedroom.

'Oh, hi.' I look up from my laptop. Take off my glasses.

'I've been standing here for at least two minutes and you didn't even notice.' He sounds annoyed.

'Yeah, sorry. I have a graduate student who is so talented! I was composing the email I want to send to her.'

He doesn't respond. Probably because he has other things on his mind, like the Task Ahead. He comes over, takes off his watch. Sets it on the bedside table. I put my glasses back on, return my eyes to the computer screen. Soon Luke has taken off his shirt, his pants, his underwear, and slides under the covers, whereas I am still fully clothed, still fully unshowered, still fully engaged in my grad student's paper.

'Rose,' Luke finally says – his only advance, if it can even be called one. His tone is slightly impatient, slightly imploring.

Ten minutes, I tell myself, setting my laptop aside. *Fifteen minutes tops. Then it will be over.*

Why did I reach for my husband that day so long ago now, after our fight? Why didn't I push him away instead? Should I have? Would I have been better off just getting up and leaving him, leaving this marriage?

'I'm too cold to take off my sweatshirt,' I say to Luke.

'That's fine.'

He is already pulling at my leggings. I let him, because what else am I supposed to do? Isn't this what I signed up for? For

261

better and worse, and this is the worst of it? Sex is part of the marriage deal, so here it is. The Sex.

Besides, it's not like any of the work is expected of me for this part of the baby making. The rest of it, sure. But Luke is the one who has to have the orgasm. Luke is the one who has to get that sperm out of himself. Thank God I don't have to worry about an orgasm during this whole ordeal, since it would never happen, not like this.

I lie back, my head turned to the side.

Outside the window it's almost dark. The sun goes down so early now that winter is here.

Luke and I don't even kiss; we never kiss anymore. Which is good, because I don't want to. I stopped wanting to kiss my husband the moment he started keeping the ovulation calendar. A peck on the cheek is fine, but those long, lingering kisses we used to give each other? No way.

I catch sight of that photo of me that Luke has always kept by his bedside, the happy Rose, the laughing Rose – where did she go? Is she still somewhere inside me? Will this Rose and that other one ever merge again? Or is that Rose gone forever? Has this marriage killed her?

How long can this go on? Does it ever end?

What if I never get pregnant?

Do I have to do this for the rest of my life? Or at least, until menopause?

To think I once used to wait in this bed naked, excited to surprise Luke with sex the second he got home. I used to be a person who would walk around the city wearing a skirt without any underwear so I could whisper this to Luke as we held hands in the park or on our way to dinner. I used to plan out my seductions of this man – when we dated, while we were engaged, all throughout our early years of marriage. The fact that I used to consider myself a skilled seductress in all things sex seems so laughable now. Like a part I might have played in a movie or television show, a role I took on for a while but that wasn't really me in the end.

What does it feel like to want sex?

I can't even remember.

It's as though there is a switch inside my body that was turned off somehow, and now that it is off – now that I know the switch is there – I can't figure out how to turn it back on. The wires in me have shorted, but the electrician necessary to fix them doesn't seem to exist. Or at least, Luke doesn't have the skills or know-how to do it.

As the minutes pass – three, four, five, surely six by now – I think about those conversations people are always having with college students about sex and desire, about consent and the consequences of not getting it from one's partner, how, just on the other side of want and desire, the territory of assault and the criminal is waiting if we aren't careful.

Even the notion of those well-intentioned conversations with students seems comically absurd as my husband moves on top of me, and I lie here, unresponsive, on my back. What does one call what Luke and I are doing? It's certainly sex of some kind, and technically, I suppose, both of us have consented to it. But wanted? Desired? I can say with total certainty that this sex that is happening to me now is not wanted. I'm doing it anyway, though. I did agree to it, albeit reluctantly. So what does that make it? Semiconsensual? Simply transactional? Am I a kind of prostitute in my own marriage?

Seven minutes have surely passed.

Eight? Nine even? How much longer will this last?

I think about work, my research, the newest project that I've been launching. I'm going to interview young women who've decided they don't want children. Passive-aggressive, much? I haven't told Luke, because I know it will piss him off and I'm too tired to fight with him anymore. But I'm excited about doing this study. I want to know what these women have to say. I think about it all the time. I think about it now.

Ten minutes? Eleven? We must be nearing the end.

Luke grunts and groans.

Oh, thank God, it's finally over.

I'm never doing this again, I think, as the light disappears outside the windows. *I'm done. I'm done.* As these words pass through me, I know that they are true.

Luke falls on top of me, panting, rests his head on the word WEEKEND on my sweatshirt. 'Maybe this will be the time when it finally happens,' he says.

'Maybe,' I say.

'And maybe if it doesn't happen, we should go and see a fertility doctor.'

Luke drops this casually, between breaths, like he is informing me of the weather, that there will be snow tomorrow, and perhaps my classes will be canceled.

No, I think. No. Fucking. Way.

And finally, *finally*, those clandestine thoughts of resistance

I'm always having of late, they make their way back into my throat and up to my tongue and out of my mouth.

'No, Luke,' I say, rolling him off me, grabbing for my under-wear from the floor, then my leggings. I used to be a woman confident saying no to her husband. I need to become her again – she's still in me. I know it. I can feel her waking up. 'I'm never going to a fertility doctor. It was either going to happen or it wasn't. And it hasn't. And it isn't. So it's not.'

'But Rose—'

'No, Luke,' I say again. 'No.'

28

February 16, 2014
Rose, Lives 1 & 2

'D o you want more ice cream, Mom?' I look around for the nurse, but she's left the room. 'I'll go and see if I can find you some. Maybe I can dig up some strawberry?'

'No, sweetie. That's okay.' My mother is nodding off.

I stand up, I sit. I look around.

I don't know what to do. I never do when I'm here.

The nurse arrives to switch the bag attached to the top of the metal pole, nearly empty now. She replaces it with one that is full, and the chemo begins its slow drip into my mother's bloodstream. My mother opens her eyes. 'Oh hi, Sylvia,' she whispers, sleepy.

'Mrs. Napolitano, nice to see you, how've you been?' Her voice is extra loud, extra enthusiastic in the quiet of this room full of people, all of them with cancer, all of them receiving their meds just like my mother, but all of them in different stages of sickness. Some look healthy, their skin still full of color. Others are emaciated, pale, their features, their skin, sagging, drooping. Some patients I've never seen before but a lot of them are repeat customers; they are here each time my mother is. We say hello to one another, how are you, ask how things are going, but that's usually all. Once in a while, someone disappears and we never see them again, often because they are done with chemo. But occasionally we'll find out it's because they didn't make it. Maybe that's why people don't talk to one another much in this room. You never know who you are going to lose next, and with cancer, you've already lost so much.

'Mrs. Napolitano?' Sylvia asks, a little louder this time.

My mother keeps nodding off. She forces her eyes open. 'Well, you know, Sylvia, I'm as good as can be expected.'

'The doctors are trying something new today, aren't they? The other cocktail wasn't mixing well with your system?'

'No,' I answer, so my mother doesn't have to.

Sylvia looks at me, eyes full of sympathy. 'Maybe this one will be better.'

'That's what we hope,' I say, wanting to do something, offer something, anything, even if it's just a few words.

Sylvia taps the bag twice with her fingertip, satisfied. The drip starts. She glances around the room, then back at me. 'Hang on to that hope, okay?'

Denise and Jill are waiting for me at the hospital entrance when I step outside. The rush of frigid air feels good after the stuffy, sterile smell of the hospital.

'Where to?' Jill asks. She's bundled into a purple, puffy coat. Her breath forms clouds that hang there a moment, then disappear. 'What are you in the mood for?'

On the days my mother has chemo, once my father arrives to sit in my place for a while, my friends come to take me somewhere on my break. Sometimes it's Raya and Denise; sometimes it's Denise and Jill, like today; sometimes it's just Jill. We go shopping for an hour. Or sometimes we go to a museum. Occasionally we just walk around the city, to nowhere in particular. 'I think I need to eat something,' I tell them. 'I haven't eaten yet today, actually.'

'Rose, you can't forget to eat!' Denise sounds indignant, motherly.

It makes me love her. 'How about, I don't know, pizza?'

Denise chews on this idea. I can tell she is thinking that pizza is not the healthiest option. Before she can protest, Jill cuts in. 'If you want pizza, that's what we'll get.'

The three of us start to walk. Denise and Jill chatter on, giving me updates on their lives, about how Jill and Maria are planning to go on vacation to one of those all-inclusive resorts, something they've never done before but Maria wanted to try it, about how Denise's new study is going and how nice it is to have grad students helping her instead of having to do everything on her own.

I listen, I laugh occasionally, I ask a question.

We don't talk about my mother, don't talk about her cancer, about the fact that she's not responding to chemo. We don't talk about how all of this happened so fast, how quickly she became sick, then sicker. We don't talk about her prognosis, which is not good. As we walk down the street and I listen to my friends discuss which pizza place is the best, which is the fastest since I don't have long before I need to get back to the hospital, I think

268

about how lucky I am to have such good friends. Between Denise and Raya and Jill and a few kind colleagues in my department who sub for my classes when I need them to, I am able to put one foot in front of the other. I am doing my best, hoping that through my own survival I can somehow help carry my mother through hers and on to the other side.

'How are classes going, Rose?' Denise asks.

It's the first question I've gotten in a while. We are seated in a booth, waiting for our food to arrive. 'You know, it's fine. Teaching is a nice distraction.'

'Are you still running in the mornings?' Jill asks. She's always worried about me getting exercise.

'I am. Every day. It, you know, helps. It's been hard to sleep.' My two friends nod.

The pizza arrives. I don't touch it.

I start to cry.

Denise is sitting on the inside of the booth and I'm next to her on the restaurant side. Jill gets up and joins us, so the three of us are squished together on the bench. They wait while I cry, Denise with her arm around me and Jill with her head on my shoulder.

I've made a pact with myself: no crying in front of my mother. Only strength. It's what she would do for me. It's what she would do for my father. It's the least I can do for her. But I don't have to do it here, now, with my friends.

Denise glances at her phone after a while, checks the time. 'Rose, you'd better eat something. You need to be back soon.'

I nod, Jill slides out and back to her side of the booth. Denise takes a slice and places it onto my plate, then takes one for herself.

The two of them start talking again about innocuous things, how it might snow this week, about the research trip Jill has coming up, about the new colleague Denise has who keeps stopping by her office. 'Is he cute?' I ask, managing to insert myself into the conversation. It's time for me to pull myself together.

She smiles, cheeks flushing. 'He *is* cute.'

'Maybe you should ask him out,' Jill suggests.

'Maybe I will,' Denise says, and stuffs the last bite of pizza into her mouth.

When we arrive at the hospital entrance, my steps are heavy. It takes work to move through the air. 'I don't know how I'd get through this without you,' I tell Jill and Denise when we are saying good-bye.

'Good thing you don't have to find out,' Jill says, giving me a hug.

I turn away from my friends, head back inside, that hospital smell entering my nose, my lungs. The walk to the chemo room where my mother gets her treatments feels never-ending as I navigate myself through the windy halls of this place. The first few times I had to keep asking directions from the nurses and the administrative assistants, but it's been enough times now that I know the way by heart.

My father is sitting next to my mother when I arrive.

This time, my mother is awake, and there is a man I don't know standing on the other side of the chair where she sits. The three of them are talking. My mother seems animated. My mood lifts.

'Oh, there she is, my daughter! Rose!' My mother calls this out as if I haven't seen her in ages, beckoning me.

My father turns, raises both hands in a gesture of innocence. 'Rose, I just want you to know that I had nothing to do with this,' he says in a low voice when I am close enough to hear.

I give him a look. *What?*

He shrugs, then chuckles.

'Rose, I've met this nice professor here' – my mother takes a moment to smile at the man, who is smiling back, probably to be polite – 'who is keeping his friend company.'

I look over at the friend, who is also a guy, and he is cracking up. He gives me a wave. 'Hi, I'm Angel.'

I wave back. 'Nice to meet you.'

'I'm enjoying spending more time with my daughter here in the city,' my mother is saying to both of them. 'She lives just over the bridge.'

I stare at her. This is not how I wanted to spend more time with my mother in the city.

'Have you two ever met?' My mother is talking to me again, gesturing at the man standing on the other side of her hospital chair. 'You two are colleagues, Rose! He's a sociologist just like you!'

I look at him, really look at him now, but don't recognize his face. What I do recognize in his eyes is patience. He is being so tolerant of my mother's craziness, and she already adores him – I can tell this, too. I shake my head, give my mother's shoulder a gentle squeeze. 'We're colleagues?'

The man laughs. 'Apparently. I mean yes, I am a sociologist. And a professor.' He takes another breath, ready to say something else – maybe his name, maybe the name of his university, but who knows? My mother is already speaking before he can get there.

'I've already given him your phone number, Rose. You two should go for coffee and get to know each other.'

'Oh my God, Mom! I can't believe you!'

'I told her not to,' my father says, out of the side of his mouth next to me.

I turn to the man, who is laughing again, then to his friend who is laughing even harder. 'I want to apologize on my mother's behalf,' I tell them. 'She loves to meddle.' I give her a look that says *Stop!* But then I see how happy she is, I take in the grin on her face, and my frustration melts. I turn back to the man. Maybe he understands how hard this is for my family. His friend is here getting chemo, after all. I put out my hand. 'Hi, I'm Rose. And you are?'

He takes my hand. 'Thomas,' he says. 'It's very nice to meet you.'

Right then, I realize that nearly the entire room full of people is watching this scene, the patients getting their chemo, the nurses chuckling, my parents observing us.

'I told Thomas he should go out with you,' Angel says, breaking the silence. 'And now that you're here, I definitely think he should go out with you.'

Everyone laughs. My cheeks are burning, but I find myself joining in.

The pain of the day, suspended.

*

When I was in college, sometimes my mother would come to visit me, just her. She would take the train down to my campus and we would go out to lunch with my friends and she would invade the kitchen and make us pots of meatballs and sauce before she left so we all had homecooked food for the week. But there was this one particular visit when she came because I was brokenhearted about this boy I'd been dating, Arturo.

I remember going to the train station to meet her, watching my mother come walking down the platform to the place where I was standing, waiting for her. I remember her suitcase rolling behind her, how her bob looked freshly cut, how it brushed the tops of her shoulders as she moved. Everything about me felt empty in that moment, blank, like sensation had left my body, my will along with it.

'How are you doing, sweetheart?' she asked immediately, putting out her arms and squeezing me tight. She always smelled like laundry and lavender soap. 'Any better?'

I shook my head and we turned and walked out of the train station, into a cab. It was hard for me not to cry, and I kept biting my lip to stop the tears. My mother studied my face, which I knew was blotchy. It had been that way for days.

'I'm glad you called me, Rose,' she said. The taxi driver gunned the engine and sped through a yellow light just as it turned red. We moved through the city that was home to my university, far away from the home where I grew up. 'I'm glad I could come down for this visit.' She took my hand across the backseat of the car, entwined her fingers through mine. 'This is what mothers are for.'

All sorts of thoughts were going through my mind during that

cab ride. How the second I saw my mother appear on the platform my spirits lifted and I felt safe. That for the first time since
Arturo broke up with me, I believed that I would be okay again
eventually. Even though it was embarrassing that I called my
mother and told her I needed her to come down and be with
me, I was so glad I'd asked her to. Grateful that I had this mother
who literally dropped everything, packed her bag, and now here
she was, holding my hand.

The cab pulled up in front of the apartment building where
I was living at the time, with my college roommate, Raya, who
was away for the weekend. My mother paid the driver and I got
her suitcase out of the trunk. We went upstairs, headed inside
the quiet living room.

'Well, this is nice, Rose,' my mother said, looking around at
the mostly bare walls, at the tables and shelves that lacked color
or decoration, aside from books. This was her first time seeing
the apartment where I lived during my junior year. 'It just needs
a little sprucing up.'

'Maybe.'

I didn't tell my mother that one of the reasons the place seemed
sparse was because after Arturo broke up with me, I purged the
apartment of anything that reminded me of him.

My mother took her suitcase from me and rolled it right into
my room without asking and began to unpack. I followed her
there, watched her hang up her clothes in the closet, next to
mine.

I didn't know before Arturo that hearts could get broken so
badly. I'd thought he was my soul mate, that we'd be together
forever and now that we weren't, I wasn't sure how to go through

my day. I was a bit like a ghost floating around, not sure where I belonged.

My mother zipped up her now-empty bag and stored it in the closet. Then she turned around and surveyed my room. 'Where do you keep the sheets?'

I showed her the closet in the hall. She pulled down a clean set and immediately went about stripping my bed and remaking it, fluffing the pillows and tucking everything in just so, until my bed looked like it could be in a hotel. I remember watching her do this, standing there like a zombie.

'Better, don't you think?'

I nodded. It was better.

Then I followed my cheerful, determined mother into the living room. 'So, here's what I'm thinking, Rose,' she said. 'We're going to clean everything until it sparkles because I know a clean house always makes me feel better. Then you and I are going to go to the store and get a few things to give this apartment a little color. Maybe a nice little rug, some pillows, a few tchotchkes for the tables and the shelves to brighten things up? A bit of a shopping trip to get whatever you might need for this place?'

'Okay,' I said. I was in her hands.

She smiled. 'Wonderful.'

I showed her the closet where April and I kept the Windex, the broom and the mop, the rags and the dusters. The two of us set about cleaning everything, moving little by little through the tiny kitchen until it was spotless and neat, the living room, the bathroom, too.

My mother didn't ask me once about Arturo. Not while we were shopping downtown and picking out things for the apartment, not while we were at the bookstore deciding what new mystery novels I should read, and not when she took me out to dinner afterward. My mother didn't ask me what happened to end our relationship, or why I couldn't seem to get over Arturo. She didn't ask and I didn't offer to tell her, didn't cry to her about how I'd seen Arturo just the other day walking across the quad, holding hands with some girl who looked young, like maybe she was a first-year, or about how he'd replaced me so quickly and my heart hurt so much to know this. My mother has never liked to dwell.

But that day was the first one in ages that I didn't cry.

My mother's energy was boundless, her cheerfulness, too. It radiated from her body and I felt it seeping into my skin, reaching for my wounded heart.

By the time it was dark out and we were ready for bed, I started making up the couch in the living room so I could sleep there. My mother stopped me.

'Rose, no. Your bed is big enough for both of us.' She studied me in this way that made me feel searched, like she was looking around in my brain. 'I thought you might like the company. I know you've been having trouble sleeping and you've always slept better when you know someone else is still awake. I'll stay awake until you're asleep, okay?'

I blinked back at her. Yes, I was having trouble sleeping, and yes, everything she'd said was true, and I found myself yearning for the simple relief she offered, but also resisting it. 'I'm not a child anymore,' I told her.

'No. But can you just let me do this one small thing?'

I didn't answer her directly, but I grabbed the pillows I'd brought out to the couch and headed back into my room, got into bed. My mother slipped in next to me and we each turned on our reading lamps, the two of us settling in with the mysteries we'd bought earlier that day.

There have been times when I've felt like my mother is too old-fashioned and strict. But as I've gotten older and life has gotten so much harder, so much more complicated, I think I've grown to appreciate her more – I hope I have. Who she is and how she is. There are these moments when it occurs to me that I like her as a person, almost as though she were a friend, moments when it strikes me, hard, that despite our differences she is kind of amazing. The older I've become, the more I have these moments, the more I've been able to relate to her like I might to Jill or Denise or Raya. Even though she is so much better than someone who is a friend because she is a mother, *my* mother, and she will love me like no one else in the universe.

But during that one particular visit when I was still in college?

That was the first time I was struck by how much I liked this person sitting there, reading next to me in bed. That I was grateful for this woman who, when I was getting sleepy and reached up to turn off the light next to my pillow, said to me right then, 'Good night, sweetheart, I'm going to keep reading for a while,' like this was no big deal, like she was willing to read all night while I slept the hours away, even though I knew she was tired from the long day we'd had. I could see it on her face.

I can see the exhaustion right now as my mother lies here, propped up in the hospital chair, now that Thomas has returned to sitting alongside his friend and my father has gone off to the cafeteria to get something to eat. It makes me want to climb into bed with her this time around, stay up reading while she dozes off, never leaving her side, so that during the moments when she awakens, when she opens her eyes, she'll see that someone who loves her is right there next to her, keeping vigil, making sure she's all right.

Her gaze keeps drifting over to Thomas and Angel, then back to me. Then she smirks and I see some of her energy return.

I take her hand, squeeze it. 'What in the world did you think you were doing, Mom? Giving my number to some man you just met?' My words sound like they are scolding, but there is laughter in them.

'Isn't it obvious? I was setting my daughter up,' she says. 'And besides, he's not random. He's just like you, Rose – a professor! I think he's perfect! Handsome, tall, willing to talk to your mother.' Her energy grows, as if inserting herself into my love life is helping her return to being the strong woman she usually is, always getting into my business. 'And I want to see you with someone nice, Rose. You've been single for such a long time.'

'Oh, Mom, I'm okay,' I tell her. 'I'll meet someone eventually.'

'Well, I'd like you to meet someone now.'

'Patience, Mom.'

She grows quiet. Then, 'I've got to do what I can while I'm still here, Rose. I want to see you settled and happy before I'm gone.'

A thick lump forms in my throat. 'Mom, don't say that!'

Her breathing is steady. The chemo drips its way into her veins, slowly, always so slowly. 'Sweetheart, at some point soon, we're all going to have to face the truth.'

I inhale, sharply. I get up. My chest hurts. I have to get out of here. 'I need something to drink. I'll be right back.'

I am crying by the time I reach the coffee machine. I dig the coins out of my bag and drop them through the slot, one by one, listening to the sound of metal clinking as they land. A cup falls onto the grate under the spout. There is whirring, followed by hissing, and steaming liquid starts to run into the cup, thick as mud.

That doesn't look right, I think, peering closer.

For a moment, I am distracted by something as stupid as this coffee machine – distracted from the hospital, from the cancer, from my mother and the chemo and the horror of what she is living, what we are all living with her, about the last words she said about the truth, whatever she thinks that is – though I know what it is. Of course I do. The coffee stops dripping, the cup only half full. I decide I don't care and go to take it when it suddenly starts again, explodes really, coffee grinds and steaming hot water everywhere, all over me, my hand, the sleeve of my sweater.

'Shit!' I yank my hand back, studying my skin, angry red blotches already forming. 'Shit,' I say again, softer this time. I shake my head, turn around, lean my back against the wall. 'I just can't,' I whisper to no one, shoulders slumping, thought half finished.

'Yeah, that coffee machine is the worst. The one down on the second floor is way better.'

I look up. Thomas is standing there. 'Fuck,' I say, under my breath. I try to pull myself together. There is coffee all over me, grinds running down my arm. 'Sorry. I'm just, I guess, I'm not having the best day.'

'Well, maybe I can help,' Thomas says. He unzips his bag and starts digging around in it.

'I don't know how to do this,' I say, more to myself than to him.

I don't mean the coffee.

This man, Thomas, is quiet a moment. Then he pulls out a napkin from his backpack and hands it to me. I take it. Look at him, really look at him for the first time since my mother forced us to meet. He returns my stare. In his eyes is understanding. He reaches for me.

'None of us do,' he says.

29

March 2, 2008
Rose, Life 6

S NOW FALLS OUTSIDE the windows.

It collects on the glass in intricate patterns of ice.

In here, it is all warmth and joy.

'Hello there,' I say to the tiny baby in my arms. *My* baby. 'Addie.'

I can't stop looking at her. She is mesmerizing. The trauma of the birth, the exhaustion and pain in my body, seems far away, like it might have happened a few weeks ago and not a mere few hours. Staring at Addie almost makes me forget that I'm in a hospital bed, makes me stop noticing that antiseptic smell, the scratchy sheets, the ugly everything on the walls, the machines. Addie sleeps, eyes shut tight, like she is worried they might fly open at any minute if she doesn't work at keeping them closed, her soft breathing filling the quiet. Maybe Addie will snore like her father. How strange it is to think such a thing, how this baby in my arms might be like her father, or even like me, her mother. And in what ways will Addie turn out like her very own self, unlike either one of us?

The door creaks as it opens. Then I hear, 'Rose?' My father's voice is calling to me, a whisper in the semidarkness.

I see him peering at me from the hallway. 'I'm awake,' I tell him.

He tiptoes in, my mother behind him.

'You don't have to worry – this little girl is out.' I say this, but I don't know if my parents actually hear it. Their eyes are glued to Addie.

My mother is wearing a canary-yellow sweater, the color of happiness, according to her. She put it on the moment she received the news from Luke that all was well, that everyone survived the birth and everyone is healthy. The Napolitanos are a superstitious bunch, which is why my mother couldn't just wear the sweater of joy before the good news was official. She's coaxed my father into a similar canary ensemble.

I laugh, gesturing at his sweater. 'Dad, I like your outfit.'

'I'll wear anything your mother tells me to today,' he says. 'You wait until she's putting you in yellow.'

My mother pulls out a tiny, crocheted hat for Addie in the same color. 'What do you think, Rose?'

'I think the hat is ridiculous,' I say to her, but I'm smiling. 'I love it.'

'You do!' Her cheeks flush pink in the dim lighting. 'And I have a sweater for you, too, of course.' She begins digging through the duffle bag that's hanging on my father's shoulder. 'I thought Luke could take a family portrait for us.'

'I told you, Rose,' my father says, gesturing at the sweater. 'You're next.'

'I'll wear whatever you want me to today, Mom.'

She looks up from her digging and smiles.

How easy it is to make my parents happy – tell my mother what she longs to hear, give her what she's always wanted – yes to a sweater, yes to a grandchild. All that resistance to a baby, what was it for, anyway? Why was I so against this? What was so wrong about inviting all of this love into my life?

My mother hands me the ridiculous sweater and my father takes Addie so I can pull it on over my sore body. I am doing these things like they're all I've ever wanted, like I was made for just this role: New Mother.

Then I sit back in this hospital bed and watch my parents fuss over Addie, noticing the absence at my breast, the warmth that Addie left behind. How quickly the brain, the body adapts to this new presence in life; how quickly the brain, the body develops a sense for it, for her – the ebb and flow of Addie's nearness and farness, the awareness of her location, her safety, her comfort and well-being.

What will happen to my work, my career? Will my brain shift back to my research, my writing, my classes, or will it never be the same again – will I never be the same again?

Does it matter? Do I even care?

I pull the sheet higher.

For now I decide it doesn't matter one way or the other, that I'm allowed to enjoy the bright yellow rapture of this moment.

My father leans down and presses a cheek onto Addie's soft head.

All because I reached for Luke that day.

I hold on to this thought, turn it around, study it. I leaned forward instead of pulling back, I reached out to my husband instead of pushing him away and because of this slight shift in motion, Addie exists. This scene in the hospital that is me, my husband, my parents, my daughter exists. The reality that Addie could so easily *not* be, that her presence in the world is so feather-light, nearly makes me woozy. She is less than a day old, yet the idea that she might not be at all, that she might only be a near miss, seems impossible. Addie's existence is necessary, essential, as important as air and breath and the heart that beats in my chest.

Who would I be today if I'd kept fighting with Luke instead?

There is a strange sense of satisfaction rising in me, that I could do this thing, give the world a new baby, give my parents a grandchild to hold and to love and to spoil.

Luke pokes his head in the door and starts to laugh. 'Nice outfit, Mom.'

My mother looks up, turns to my husband.

He laughs again. 'I meant the other mom, Mom. I meant Rose.'

She leans in and kisses Luke on the cheek. 'I have a sweater for you, too, by the way.'

He rolls his eyes. 'Of course you do.'

'Are your parents here yet?' my mother asks. 'We can lend them our sweaters and take a family photo for you all.'

'That's very thoughtful of you,' Luke says, humoring her. There's no way Nancy and Joe would be wearing any sweaters, and he knows it. Luke takes out his camera, the big one, the one he saves for important shoots.

If there is one thing I am not looking forward to, it's seeing my in-laws, having to listen to all of their advice, their attempts to control everything – control me, control Addie, control their son. I wondered if my having a baby might soften them again toward me. But it's only intensified their need to tell me what to do and who to be. Maybe that time from before, back when we all got along, is gone forever.

'Smile, guys,' Luke is saying. My mother's got Luke in a sweater now, so all of us are matching.

It's the most ridiculous thing we've ever allowed my mother to do to us, but it doesn't seem to matter. All that matters is how happy my mother is today, how her happiness spreads throughout the room, the edges of my vision fuzzy and soft with it, like an old photograph, something that may have happened in the past or the future, but not in the real live now.

Addie sleeps through all the photos – the five of us, with Luke setting his camera to a timer, then my dad, my mom, Addie, and me; then Luke, Addie, and me; then just Addie and me, Addie and Luke. I can't seem to stop smiling, as though if I stop then maybe all of this, my parents, Addie, Luke, everything good in this room, will disappear. We try every combination of people, but then there is a photo that I know I need like my life depends on it.

'Luke, will you take a picture of Mom, me, and Addie? Just us three?'

'Of course,' he says.

My mother sits down on the edge of the bed.

'Mom, you're too far away,' I tell her. 'I want to be able to put my arm around you.'

She looks at me in this way that makes me feel like I am the only person in the world. I soak it up, let it sink into my skin and run through my veins to every part of me. I want to store up this feeling for a rainy day, because rainy days always come, don't they?

'I love you, Rose,' she says.

There is a strangeness to this moment, a way that the scene before me doesn't feel real. My beaming parents, my beaming mother. My eyes settle on tiny, beautiful Addie again, take in this woman who is holding my daughter, my baby, so gently, so comfortably, like she was always meant to hold her grand-daughter.

I try to enjoy it.

But is it a dream? Did all of this really happen?

Will I wake up soon, and all will be different?

30

February 12, 2010
Rose, Life 8

THE DOOR TO the abortion clinic is red, paint chipped, metal.

I study it, unable to take the final steps that will bring me from the hallway and inside its doors, closer to the decision I've been back and forth about since I read those pluses, those parallel lines, those yeses on the pregnancy tests I bought at the drugstore.

Jill is late. She texted that she was stuck on the subway, a sick passenger trapping everyone underground.

The carpet underneath my feet is worn, threadbare, dirty, as are the walls that were once white but are now streaked gray. Only two lights are overhead and one is out.

Everything around me seems to say, *This is what women who refuse motherhood get – dinginess, disapproval, darkness. They do not deserve the pristine labs and the machinery, the bright lights and cheerful doctors for the ultrasound, the happy, pastel-colored delivery wards.*

I go through the door.

The inside isn't much better. There is light, yes, the woman who greets me smiles and is kind, yes, but we talk with bullet-proof glass between us, dotted with small circular holes so we can hear each other. Does getting an abortion really have to involve bulletproof glass?

'I have an appointment at two p.m.,' I say. 'Rose Napolitano.' The woman looks at her computer, then nods, buzzes a door to the right so I can enter. I make my way beyond the bulletproof glass and into the waiting room. The decor here is better than in the hallway. The paint on the walls is a pretty gray, there are stacks of magazines on the coffee table, chairs that look relatively new neatly set up along the walls. I count six women, two of them sitting with partners or friends, the others alone.

I sit down, stare straight ahead, my eyes on a poster that has a list of tips for preventing pregnancy. I wonder if Jill will ever get here, hope that she does, at least by the time I have to go home.

The clock on the wall says 2:10 p.m. I wait for them to call my name.

'Don't let Luke convince you to be someone you're not.'

My mother and I were in the kitchen, hers, and I was keeping her company while she was making sauce and meatballs. I loved the familiarity of it, me standing by while she prepared the ingredients, taking direction from her about what needed chop-ping, what I should pull from the fridge, and could I peel another clove of garlic? It was a scene we'd been playing out since I was small and she began to invite me to cook with her, an art my mother mastered long before my existence. She commanded the kind of authority and ease in her kitchen that I recognized in myself when I was standing in front of the classroom or when I was giving a talk.

I was leaning over the table, chopping parsley, when she'd made this comment. 'What are you talking about, Mom?'

'I can see how unhappy you are with him, Rose. You haven't been happy in your marriage in a long time.' Her voice was stern but sympathetic.

I kept chopping the parsley into smaller and smaller bits. Had I been that obvious?

'You can tell me the truth about how you're feeling. I want to know.'

'Luke and I are having problems,' I admitted.

My mother came over to supervise my work. 'That's enough, you don't want to turn it into mush.' She whisked the cutting board out from under me and tipped the parsley into the simmering tomato sauce. 'When did the problems start?'

'After the miscarriage,' I told her.

She rinsed the cutting board, ran a dish towel across it to dry it, returned it to the table in front of me. Handed me a head of garlic. 'Chop me up eight or nine cloves for the meatballs – tiny.' She leaned down, pressed a kiss into the top of my head. 'I wondered about that.'

I called my mother the day after the miscarriage, after spending the entire evening watching my husband sob. When I told her about the miscarriage, she'd said immediately, automatically, *I'm so sorry, Rose.* Then I heard sniffling and I realized my mother was crying, too. It made me wonder if I should be the one saying sorry to her. First Luke, now my mother, why not me? Why did I feel nothing? Why couldn't I cry? Why didn't it seem like such a loss when I was the one who'd been pregnant and then not? 'Well, if it happened once, it can happen again, you know,' she said next, just like Luke did. 'I don't know if I want it to, Mom,' I responded, and she went quiet. 'I think I'm relieved.' *I know I'm relieved.* When she spoke again it was to tell me to give myself time, to say that I might feel differently as time passed.

And I did. I let time pass, I let Luke take control of everything, of me, my body. But the more time that went by, the more I resented everything about my husband.

I sliced the garlic, chopped one clove, then started the next. As I did this I decided to tell my mother the truth. 'Ever since the miscarriage,' I say, 'it's like Luke can't even see me. All he can see is getting me pregnant. And for a really long time, I let him do whatever he wanted, and then a couple of months ago, I just stopped. I told him no more.' I looked up. My mother was standing halfway between the stovetop and the table. She nodded at me slightly. 'I know a baby isn't what I want, Mom. I don't even think I want Luke anymore. Maybe I don't want to be married either. I'm sorry if that disappoints you. I don't want to disappoint you.'

My mother's hands were on her hips, she closed her eyes a moment, let out a breath. 'Rose. Well.' She wiped her cheek with the edge of her apron. 'I don't want to lie to you.' She sighed. 'I am disappointed, but only because I let myself hope that maybe you'd have a child. So maybe I'd have a grandchild. I've always wanted a grandchild.'

'I know,' I whispered.

She smoothed her apron. Little red dots of tomato stained it.

'But the most important thing to me is that you are happy. And I'm sad to hear you so sad – and angry. I've always liked Luke. And for such a long time, you two seemed good together.'

In that moment I thought about how different this conversation was from the one my mother and I'd had at the beach when she told me she had faith I would be a good mother. Things had changed so much between then and now. From a kind of tentative hope between Luke and me to rage and despair. A distance I didn't think I could cross.

'Maybe you two can salvage things,' my mother was saying. 'Maybe if you just tell Luke that he needs to let this go, that having a child is just not going to happen in your marriage, then you could find a way through.'

I got up, dumped the garlic into the wide metal bowl filled with bread crumbs, parmesan, herbs, where we'd mix the meatballs. Tried to decide whether I had enough courage to tell my mother what else was going on with me.

'Rose, it's okay for you to say no to Luke. "No more," you need to tell him. "Having a baby just isn't going to work for us. I tried and it didn't work out." That's all you need to say.'

'I regret it, Mom – all of it.' I am staring down into the metal bowl. 'I should have left Luke a long time ago, before it got to this point.'

'This point? What do you mean, *this point?*'

I turned to her, decided to say it out loud. 'What if I told you I was pregnant?'

She inhaled sharply. Then she went to the stove, gave the sauce a hard turn. Some of it splashed onto the counter. She stared into the pot. 'Are you?'

I didn't answer.

Yes. I was.

I'd gotten pregnant the last time Luke and I had sex, the same day I'd told Luke I refused to go to a fertility doctor, that there was no way I'd ever go to one. We'd barely spoken to each other since. It was all so ironic. I'd promised myself that I would not have sex again with Luke until I wanted to have sex again with him, and soon afterward I'd come to the distressing conclusion that I was pretty sure I never wanted to have sex with him again. I was fairly certain my desire for Luke was dead and gone forever.

Then one morning about a week ago, I was getting ready for school and I realized how much my chest hurt, how it seemed to have gotten bigger, how I looked different in my dress.

My period. I'm pregnant.

Once these words flashed in my brain, they hadn't stopped flashing.

I began to cry. I hadn't been able to manage a single tear for the miscarriage, but for this pregnancy? I wept and I wept. I cried on my way to work and I cried at my desk when I arrived at my office. I grieved the inevitable loss of my marriage to Luke and I grieved the baby I was sure that I would never give to him or to anyone else. I couldn't. I wouldn't. There was no way.

My mother ripped a paper towel from the roll and sopped up the spilled sauce on the stovetop. 'Oh, sweetheart,' she said. 'What are you going to do?'

I am still in the waiting room when Jill arrives.

'Rose, I'm sorry I'm late!' Her voice is startling, loud in the

292

quiet, but no one else other than me looks up. We hug and she sits down next to me. 'How are you?'

I shrug. Jill's blue dress is bright against the muted colors around us.

'Have you thought anymore about telling Luke?' This is a question that Jill keeps asking me. Ever since I told her about the pregnancy.

I shake my head. Give her the same answer I've given before. 'If I did, he wouldn't have let me come.'

She nods, leans back into her chair.

'I don't know if I'm ever going to tell him,' I say.

Jill hesitates. 'Maybe you should—'

'This is my decision. Not his.' The force of my anger surprises me. 'I stopped caring what Luke thinks a long time ago.' When the words are out, I realize they are true. They are the answer right in front of me – to what I no longer want, which is this marriage.

The nurse appears in the doorway. 'Rose Napolitano?'

'That's me,' I say, raising my arm.

Before I get up, Jill stops me. 'We'll get through this, Rose. Okay? I'm here, no matter what.'

There is a little surge in my chest, hearing her say this, and I think, *Women need one another more than they need men sometimes. What would I do without friends like Jill? How would I survive?*

'I know,' I tell her now. 'I love you.'

As I walk forward, past the other people in the waiting room, I think about what another woman told me when I'd explained to her that I was pregnant, but that I could not have this baby because motherhood was not for me – the woman who is my mother. She'd said that if it is not in my heart to have a child with Luke, then I shouldn't. That it was okay to trust what was in my heart, that she trusted me, too, whatever I decided to do. I think about how hard it must have been for my mother to say those things because of what she would be giving up on my behalf – a grandchild, after so much hoping. I knew right then with such clarity that my mother loved me unconditionally, that this is what people meant when they spoke of the unconditional love between mother and child.

I decide to trust in my mother's love now and those words she said to me, the words that Jill said to me, too. I needed their faith, so I could have faith in myself. 'This is the right thing,' I whisper under my breath. The nurse turns to me, compassion in her eyes. I follow her through the door and I don't look back.

31

May 2, 2010
Rose, Life 5

Thomas and I are seeing each other again – of course we are – and I wait for Luke to catch me cheating. I leave a trail of clues – texts, receipts, late nights, missed calls, laptops left open with incriminating emails on the screen in full view. Nothing I do will turn Luke's head from Addie. Even when I'm practically wearing a sign across my front that says in big, script letters, *Luke, Your Wife Is Having an Affair*, he doesn't notice that something has changed – that I have changed. I wish I could find the courage to just up and leave him, but I keep searching for that brave Rose and not finding her inside me.

'Addie!' I shriek.

My back is turned for thirty seconds and somehow Addie has climbed up onto the table from one of the kitchen chairs and is teetering precariously. I see her falter, tipping forward. Just as she is about to fall, I snatch her up, yelling the entire time. What if I hadn't made it? Would she have cracked her head and ended up with brain damage? Or worse, cracked her head and died? I squeeze her little body tightly, my lungs heaving, and she bursts into tears.

'It's okay, it's okay, Mommy was just scared,' I whisper in her ear, and she cries harder. I carry her to the couch and plop her down in my lap, bend over her wiggly form as she cries. 'It's okay,' I tell her, and she buries her head in my neck. 'But you can't climb up there again, little Snuffles. It's dangerous and Mommy loves you too much to have you playing like that.' *Mommy can't handle losing you ever, my darling girl.*

As Addie's crying subsides and my panic does, too, I plant kisses on the top of her soft head. The sight of her tipping off the table plays over in my mind, each time the table growing taller, until it is ten feet in the air, then fifteen, and my Addie is tumbling off the edge of a kitchen cliff. My heart pounds, I draw her closer, wish I could close my body around hers, my love for her like padding.

Addie grows limp against me, her breathing even.

I once felt this kind of love for Luke. I remember how on our honeymoon I felt it, this possessiveness, this fear that at any moment I might lose him, that he might die, and my heart would be broken forever. We were lying in bed, it was the afternoon. I remember the sheets were white, bright from the sun pouring through the glass doors of our suite. It was the kind of afternoon you could only have on a honeymoon, where every day is a cycle of waking, eating, swimming, relaxing, eating more, sipping wine and cocktails, luxuriating constantly in the beauty and bounty of a pristine hotel, designed expressly for the newly married, to bask in our coupledom, to make love and enjoy ourselves and then make love some more.

Luke and I were laughing as we lay there, talking about what, I can't recall.

But I remember looking upon his face, thinking his face was the most beautiful, most perfect, most special face I had ever seen, that he was the most important person in the entire universe, that I could never, ever lose him, or life would never be okay again. The feeling was a searing flash, burning into me, enormous, scarring, producing a mix of pain and fear and desperation. I remember thinking at the time: I wonder if this is the kind of love parents say they feel for their child, but I feel it instead for Luke.

Now that I have Addie I can answer my own question with a yes, and also a no. It was and wasn't the same. It was the same in that it is exactly that kind of love I feel for Addie, but it wasn't the same at all because that Big Love I experienced on my honeymoon came and went, but with Addie it is permanent. My love for Addie is terrifying, a perpetual state of vertigo, an ongoing condition of living on the edge of an abyss.

I hate it. It's exhausting, this constant terror.

And I love it. I would never trade it, not for anything in the universe. I am a walking cliché and I do not care. Who cares? Who cares when a person finds out that love this big and wide exists and it's yours to live with forever, for better and for ill?

Addie shifts positions, turns her head upward, and opens her eyes, stares at me in that way that has a direct line to my heart. 'Hello, my darling.'

I hear the door open. Luke appears, rounding the corner into the kitchen. He sees Addie and me across the room where we sit on the couch. No, he sees Addie, only Addie, not me. I am just a holder of our daughter. I may as well be made of plastic.

'Hi, Luke,' I say.

'Oh hi. Rose,' he says, my name an afterthought. Something he may have forgotten while he was out shopping, like eggs or milk.

How does one stop a marriage?

It's like trying to stop a slow-moving train, heavy, daunting, something that takes forever to come to a complete halt. Its natural state is forward, its momentum steady, relentless.

Sometimes I think I can leave Luke. I think that maybe I can find it in me to let go, to say to him, 'I don't love you anymore, not the way that I should, not the way I want to love and be loved.' Leaving him is the right thing to do, isn't it? Isn't it about time?

Do I tell him about Thomas? Or do I leave that part out?

I told my father about Thomas. I still can't believe this, but it's true. He had just come in from his workshop and I was waiting for him, alone in the house. He and I had plans for one of our father–daughter dinners. My mother was out at her book club.

I was sitting in the living room where I grew up, hands pressing into my knees, staring at one of the framed photos displayed on a table – of my parents and Luke and me at our wedding. I was trying to understand how it was possible to get from this place where I had once been so happy with this man who is my husband, to the place where I was now: a woman with a child she loves but never wanted, having an affair and cheating on that husband she used to think was her soul mate. I was crying.

'Rose? Sweetheart?' My father was standing in the doorway. 'What's wrong?'

Tears streamed down my cheeks to my lips, my chin. I wiped them away. 'Nothing. Sorry. I'm just having a tough day.'

'What happened? You can tell Dad.' He came over and sat down with me on the couch.

This made me cry harder. I couldn't tell my father what I was really thinking. How does a daughter tell her father that while she was pregnant and then after her baby's birth and throughout Addie's toddlerhood, she's been having an affair? Right under everyone's nose? How could I possibly admit such deception, such betrayal, to one of my parents? The only person who knew about Thomas was Jill. Everyone else thought Luke and I were great, we'd had a child, we were living the dream!

'Did something happen to Addie? Or to Luke?'

I shook my head, tried to breathe. 'No, no. Addie is fine. Luke is fine.'

My father scooted over to the end table and pulled a tissue from the box sitting on top of it, made his way back and handed it to me.

I dabbed at my eyes, my cheeks. 'Thanks, Dad.'

'Then what is it?'

'I don't think I can tell you.'

He looked at me steady, searching. 'You can tell your dad anything.'

'You'll think I'm a terrible person. I am a terrible person.' I started to sob. 'Mom would be so horrified.'

My father's arms were around me and he hugged me tight. 'You can tell me,' he kept whispering. 'I promise.'

I couldn't remember the last time my father held me this way. Maybe not since high school after I'd broken my ankle during track and had to miss the state meet. 'I'm so tired, Dad,' I said to him between sobs, trying to stop, trying to breathe, in and out, slow and steady. I straightened up, and my father's arms retracted. I dabbed my eyes again, blew air out of my mouth. 'I don't know if I want to be married anymore.' I said this suddenly, a bark in the quiet. My eyes dropped to the carpet, studying the tufts of fraying gray fiber. I didn't want to see my father's reaction.

'You and Luke are having a hard time?'

I shook my head. My eyes bore into the floor. 'Dad, I love someone else.' There. I said it. The one thing that was even worse than admitting I no longer wanted to be married. 'I'm a horrible person. Please don't hate me.'

I don't know what I expected from my father – anger, recrimination, disappointment, shock, any number of things other than his actual response.

'What's his name?' he asked.

'His name?'

'The person you fell in love with.'

I looked up, met my father's eyes. 'Thomas,' I said, my voice hoarse from crying.

'How long has it been?'

'A long time.' Shame crept up my spine, my neck. 'A couple of years.'

My father seemed to take this in. I couldn't read his expression. 'Is he good to you?'

I blinked. 'Yes.'

'And you want to be with him?'

300

'Yes.' There was something about saying it out loud to my father that finally allowed me to acknowledge this truth. 'I tried to stop seeing him more than once, but it never worked. I love him too much.'

'People fall in love even when they don't mean to, Rose,' my father said. Then, 'Does Luke know?'

I shook my head.

'You don't think he suspects?' he asked next.

I thought about all the clues I'd been leaving for Luke, carelessly, stupidly, imagining it would be easier to end the marriage if Luke found out about Thomas than for me to do it of my own volition. I was suddenly relieved that Luke was so wrapped up in Addie that he was blind to everything I was doing. 'I don't think so,' I said. 'I think Luke is oblivious. All Luke can see is Addie.'

My father sighed. 'And you don't think you and Luke can fix things?'

I shook my head. 'I think I'm done trying, Dad.'

'Okay. Well.' He looked at me – he looked so sad. 'Then you are going to have to find the courage to end this marriage, Rose.'

'I know,' I whispered.

'I'm sorry you are going through this, sweetheart. I'm sorry that this is the place where you and Luke ended up.'

'Me, too.'

My father reached out, pressed a hand onto my knee. 'I'm glad you told me. You can always tell your dad anything, Rose,' my father went on. 'I know you talk to your mom, but you can talk to your dad, too. I'm here for you, too.'

Tears ran down my face. My father could stand all of this ugliness from me, stand this shameful thing I had done, and still manage to love me. 'I know you are. I see that,' I said, because I did. It was impossible not to.

I wait until Addie is visiting Luke's parents to tell him.

'Hey, have you seen my camera case?' he asks me. 'The small one? I can't seem to find it anywhere. Maybe Addie was playing with it and shoved it somewhere. She loves that thing.'

'Why don't you try under the end table? I found some of my books under there the other day that I thought were gone forever.'

Luke laughs, shakes his head, like our daughter pushing things underneath the furniture is some sort of great comic achievement. *That Addie! Such a goof!*

I am immediately annoyed. The littlest things, the smallest, most insignificant reactions from him make me feel this way. The annoyance, the force of it, reminds me of what I need to do. Tonight. It has to be tonight. Now. No more stalling.

I am in the kitchen as usual, cooking something elaborate, my mother's lasagna, which requires hours of preparation. The pasta, which is homemade, the braciola, the sauce that the braciola simmers in. The more my marriage frays, the more elaborate the things I cook. It is a way to fill the time, the distance, the silence between Luke and me.

Luke is headed into the bedroom to continue his search when I say, 'After you find your camera case, there are a few things I want to discuss.'

'Yeah, sure,' he calls back, oblivious to the fact that his presence has started to bother me, oblivious to the kinds of things I have in mind to talk about.

A shot of guilt cuts through the displeasure. I start scattering the breadcrumbs across the braciola meat and in my haste I dump way too many. 'Shit!' I try to pick them off, press my palms against them so they stick to my skin. I go to the faucet and wash my hands, keep my hands under the water until it burns too hot. I dry them and go and sit at the kitchen table. I put my head down over my arms.

I seem to have lost a war I didn't know I was fighting.

I thought I would be able to take the demise of my marriage to Luke with a kind of grace, the wisdom of years that tells a person that marriages end, even long ones, even marriages that began with an intense love that both people believed would last forever. I used to think I was different, stronger, that I was a woman made of special stuff, a material resistant to the ways that life can batter us. But I'm just like every other person – tired, cowardly, terrible. Capable of reprehensible things, of destroying the life I so carefully built with the man who became my husband so many years ago, with the man who is now the father to my daughter.

I lift my up head. I know that the only way is through, but how in the world does one get through?

I get up from the table, the chair, I walk toward the bedroom. I can hear Luke puttering around, still searching for his camera case, this time at the back of his closet, pulling things from it. Balled-up sweatshirts that have probably been on the floor for ages. Bags of jeans he bought but never wore. I force the words that will start this dreaded conversation from my mouth. 'Luke, I need to talk to you about something serious.'

He doesn't turn around. 'What's up?' He pulls out a stuffed

giraffe, looks at it, and sets it on the bedside table. He goes back to digging through the mess.

I wait. He keeps searching. Anger flares, little sparks at first, that soon turn into a blaze. I let myself soak up the energy of it. 'You can't even stop for a second to talk to your wife?' *Your wife.* This is a phrase I've used a lot in the last few months, talking about myself in the third person. There's something about referring to myself this way, as *Luke's wife*, that if I speak about myself as though I am someone else, Luke might see me more clearly, might hear my words differently.

He throws an old, ripped T-shirt onto the floor behind him, pulls out a lone sock, then straightens up and turns. His eyebrows arch, but he doesn't speak.

'I want a divorce.'

I just say it. This statement, these words that have been simmering within me for ages. I just lob them across the room where they drop to the floor at my husband's feet. It's the impatience on his face that makes me do it.

He crosses his arms, the lone sock still in his fist. 'But what about Addie?'

I close my eyes and breathe. Then I open them again, and start to speak. 'I want to talk about us. Our marriage is about us, Luke. Or it should be. And it hasn't been. Not for a long time.'

He is silent, studying me. Thinking.

I've had so many fantasies about how Luke might react when I finally say these words to him; that there would be rage, yelling, shock, tears, weeping even, begging for us to try to work things out. Silence, stillness, were never on the list.

'But what about Addie?' he asks again. 'Addie needs two parents. You know that.'

What about Addie? What about Addie? I want to scream. Somewhere deep, somewhere in the better parts of myself, there is a Rose who is also saying, *Yes, we need to do this carefully, we need to make sure this is okay for Addie, Addie who is more important than either one of us, of course we need to consider Addie! And besides, won't Addie eventually be happier not to have two parents who are miserable with each other?* But what I say out loud is something else.

'Is Addie the only thing you care about?'

Luke looks at me as though I've just taken the large cutting knife from the knife block in the kitchen and am holding it in my hand, high over Addie's head – Abraham threatening to maim our daughter. 'Addie is not a *thing*,' Luke says.

'God, Luke! That's not what I meant! You can't even hear my question, you're so sensitive about her. You seem to have forgotten that someone else lives in this house – someone who happens to be your wife.'

Your wife! Your wife!

'A wife who apparently doesn't want to be my wife anymore,' he says, voice flat.

I breathe, trying to inject a state of calm into my body. I place my hand against the wall to steady myself. 'No, Luke. I don't. We need to let this marriage go. I need to. I don't even exist for you anymore. I haven't for ages. Ever since I got pregnant.'

'You're only saying that because you wish Addie was never born. You never wanted her in the first place.'

I keep breathing, I remember to be grateful that Addie is at her grandparents' house so that her little ears never hear what her father just said and what I am about to say next.

'You are right, Luke. I didn't want Addie. I only allowed myself to get pregnant because I was trying to keep you, because I wanted to save our marriage. But I think our marriage was already over back then.' I let go of the wall and I take a step closer to him. I want him to see the expression on my face, the truth in it. 'Addie, though – I love Addie and you know it. I'm a good mother. And I may not have wanted a baby before she was born, but now that I have Addie, I couldn't imagine a world without her in it. So don't you ever say that again, and don't you ever say that to Addie.' The more these words leave my body, the stronger I feel, as though they are drawing out a poison that's been living within me. 'I'm glad we have Addie. But the question of her, of having her in the first place, it killed me and you knew it was killing me, but you pushed and pushed anyway. So here we are. We have a beautiful daughter and we have a dead marriage.'

Luke uncrosses his arms. The sock falls and bounces off his left toe onto the floor. He walks toward me, shifts so he can move by me in the doorway without touching any part of my body. He retrieves the suitcase from the hall closet and rolls it back along the wooden floor. Then he begins to pack.

32

June 4, 2014

Rose, Life 3

'I WANT TO go see Grandma. Why won't you let me?'

Addie is standing in the living room, the soft, pink bunny my mother gave her gripped tightly under her arm, pressing into her beanlike six-year-old body. Even though it is warm out, a beautiful early summer morning, Addie is wearing the sweater my mother knit for her last Christmas – thick, oversize, striped in every shade of pink, along with the pink sweatpants her grandmother gave her to match.

Back when Grandma still had enough strength to knit.

But now?

'Oh, sweetie.' I wrap my hand around the coffee mug on the table in front of me, close my eyes, draw in a breath. My mother's cancer hit all of us so suddenly, the news of it, the swiftness of it. I nearly can't watch my little girl go through this, the loss of her beloved grandmother. 'You know why. We've already talked about this. Luke!' I call out his name, I want his help, but I doubt he hears me. He's still in bed. He

307

got home late last night from a wedding shoot. At least, that's where he said he was.

Addie walks past the couch in the living room, toward the table that marks the beginning of our kitchen. That's when I notice she's wearing the shoes that light up in the soles when she walks – also a present from Grandma. She's in an all-Grandma outfit, down to her socks. Addie knows what to do when she wants something. 'Please, Mommy. I need to say good-bye.'

I concentrate on my breathing. I am determined to stay strong in front of Addie, just like I have been determined to stay strong in front of my mother. 'You already said good-bye to Grandma.'

'But Grandma is still here! You keep going to see her. And I didn't say good-bye to her. Not really.'

'Addie, Grandma is different now. Your daddy and I want you to remember Grandma as she was during her life, not how she is today.'

'But Mommy—'

'Luke!' I yell louder this time. I pull out the chair next to mine, pat my hand on the seat. 'Sit down and let Mommy think for a minute, while she drinks her coffee, okay? Can you do that?'

She nods. She does as I say. She waits.

My mother is lying in a hospital bed, unconscious.

We are waiting for her to die. It's no longer a question but a fact, a simple matter of time before she is gone. Her cancer was both fast and slow. At first, it was slow, because it took a while for us to believe it was even there in my mother's formidable body. It seemed like we would all have so much time, so many options, so many possible plans of action. As a family, we could go about carefully deciding what should be done, as if my mother could wait an endless number of years before she got any treatment.

But she's slipped away so quickly. One minute she and I were arguing, laughing, the next my father and I were watching her waste away, her body committing treason against her soul, her mind, her big personality, the gale force in her nature evaporating. Who knew that it wouldn't be cancer that ended her life, but the complications from it, the blood clot that formed in her leg and slowly, clandestinely, made its way to her brain? These last weeks in the hospital have felt like ages but they've also seemed like seconds, that no time had passed before my father and I were making the decision to let my mother go, to remove her from the machines that were keeping her alive, because she was not alive anymore, not really. And now that the doctors have removed all the tubes and the clear mask over her mouth, our job is to wait, to keep vigil, to sit there as her breathing slows, as her pulse goes down to zero.

The grandmother who is lying in the hospital bed is not the grandmother who Addie knows. Luke and I didn't want her to see this grandmother, this woman who is not the woman I know, either. For this last week of my mother's life, her body has become a site of torment, a shell failing her still very alive brain.

'I want you to take my mother's picture,' I said to Luke just yesterday morning. My request sounds grotesque, I know, but I asked Luke anyway. He was sitting next to me at her bedside, the two of us silent, sad, tired. Addie was with Luke's parents, who had been unfailingly kind since all of this started.

'Rose – what?'

I stared at my mother, lying there, took in how diminished she was, the way her skin had gone gray, shriveled, how her limbs seemed so thin and small. But without the machines she had somehow returned to herself, at least a little. There was a kind of peace about her. 'I just, I want to have a photo of her. One last photo.'

'Oh, Rose.' Luke's voice was full of compassion, but also hesitation. 'You don't want to remember your mother like this.'

'Maybe I don't,' I answer. 'But maybe I do. Or maybe I will?'

'Would your mother want that, Rose? And your dad? Are you sure?'

I've heard of women who've lost babies while pregnant, asking the doctor for a photo of their unborn child. Women who wanted that baby, who grieved the loss of their future child, who longed to see that child, to have a keepsake of this tiny person that would have been but is not. A colleague at my university lost twins once, at seven months. She had to give birth to them in order to get those dead babies out of her, to go through that horrible trauma. She keeps a photo of them in her dresser drawer, buried underneath a pile of silk scarves and soft leather gloves. When she told me this, I remember thinking that holding on to such a photo was a terrible idea, that it was a strange and masochistic impulse, a way to keep a person frozen in her deepest grief.

But now I can understand why someone might want such a keepsake, now that I've sat here in this hospital room at my mother's bedside, waiting for the moment when she will take her final breath.

'Can you just do this thing for me? Please? You don't have to agree or think it's a good idea. You just need to do it so it's done. We don't have to tell my dad. I just . . . I think I need to have it.'

After a long silence, Luke said, 'Okay. Okay. Yes. I'll do it.'

Luke returned with his gear an hour later, and I left the room. It was just Luke and my mother in there. When he emerged again eventually, he was crying. 'I love you, Rose,' he said.

'I love you, too. Thank you.' I was so grateful to him in that moment that I nearly forgot that my husband, this person being so kind to me right now, is cheating.

Luke doesn't know that I know about his affair. That I know about Cheryl. That after I found that photo of her on his camera, for a while I went into a period of denial, but little by little I began to notice the signs that Luke was seeing someone – they became too obvious to miss. The late nights, the evasive answers when I'd ask Luke where he'd been, who he was with, why he hadn't called, why he never reached for me in bed anymore. The name Cheryl became an ongoing whisper in my brain, persistent, a taunt.

But then all thoughts of her evaporated once my mother went into the hospital, once we knew that she was going to die – that she was already dying. The affair my husband was having faded into the background given the tragedy unfolding in front of us, in front of Addie. Cheryl, the affair, they would have to wait until later. Until *after*.

'Of course, Rose,' Luke said. 'I would do anything for you. You know that.'

I nodded at him. But I hadn't known that, not really, not for a long time. I felt it now though. It was strong and unbreakable, this connection between Luke and me, as if it had always been there but I'd simply lost sight of it.

Luke doesn't come now, though, when I call out to him, even though I keep calling.

'Come on, Addie, let's go,' I say finally. 'Mommy's going to take you to see your grandma.'

I don't leave a note for Luke. I decide to let him wonder where Addie and I are when he gets up. I've spent enough time wondering where he is, who he's with, what he's doing. I let the door slam on our way out.

'Hi, Grandma,' Addie says, the moment we enter the hospital room.

I put my finger to my lips, ask Addie to keep her voice down, gesture to my father who is sleeping in a chair over in the corner. My father has barely left my mother's bedside, so I'm glad to see him getting some rest.

Addie lets go of my hand and I watch as my daughter walks right up to my mother's bedside. Fearless. Unafraid of the machines that beep, monitoring her breathing, of how slow the beeping has gotten, along with my mother's pulse. I witness the strength of my little girl, the grace she shows in this moment. How did my daughter get this way? Who knew she had this in her? Who gave her this grace? Me? Luke? Some other mysterious force in the universe?

'I thought you might be lonely, so I brought you some company, Grandma,' Addie whispers, and places her bunny on my mother's chest.

I resist the urge to turn around, to face the door. I don't know if I can watch this. But of course I have to, I'm the mother, so I do. My mother would do it for me, so I need to do this for Addie.

'I have plans that you'll like for this summer,' Addie goes on. 'I'm finally going to learn to swim like you showed me before you were sick.'

My father shifts in the chair, opens his eyes. He straightens up the moment he sees Addie there, but doesn't say anything, knows not to interrupt the one-sided conversation she's having with her grandmother. I go to him, bend to kiss his cheek. He gets up, grasps my hand, and the two of us stand there together, quiet, careful not to disturb this delicate moment. I listen as my daughter tells my mother about her life, what she's been doing in school, what she wants to do in the near future this summer, this fall. Addie talks and she talks, even though my mother can't answer, and maybe can't even hear her. I'd like to think that she can, though. As Addie speaks, I realize that Luke and I were wrong to keep her from seeing my mother. That this is the right thing for her, to be here now. That she can handle it.

Eventually Addie stops speaking.

My father and I join Addie at my mother's bedside.

'Hi, little Gnocchi,' my father says to Addie and she turns around, wraps her arms around his waist. 'It's good that you're here to see Grandma. I'll give you girls a moment alone with her, okay?'

Addie nods, lets go.

The tears are getting harder to swallow back, so difficult that I can barely tell my father thank you, but he gives my arm a squeeze and pads away, quietly opens the door then shuts it again, leaving Addie and me to our good-byes.

I place my hand on my mother's arm, and Addie places her hand next to mine. The warmth of my mother's skin strikes me, along with the reality that this may be the last time I touch my mother while she's alive, the last time that I feel the warmth of her body. We stand there a long time, our breathing the only sounds in the room.

'Are you ready, sweetheart?' I whisper, finally.

Am I?

How does a person say good-bye to their mother forever?

How does a little girl walk away from a beloved grandmother?

Addie nods, tiny and sharp.

I bend over my mother's body, kiss her papery cheek. Then I lift Addie up so she can do the same. 'I love you, Grandma,' she whispers.

I love you, Mom.

Addie doesn't start to cry until we leave the room.

Neither do I.

The two of us clutch each other in the hallway. We sob together, without saying anything. *Like mother, like daughter.* This thought passes through me as Addie and I weep. I see the truth in it, relish the truth of it. The way that my mother lives on in me, the way that she and I both live on in Addie.

'You're so much like your grandmother,' I tell Addie. 'I see her in you, Addie,' I say, and I do. I do.

The funeral is three days later. My father made the casket. Frankie flew in all the way from Barcelona to be with us.

It is strange to stop thinking of my mother as being everywhere at once. The second she is gone, I miss her unbearably. I want her back, I want her to be overbearing, I want her to drive me crazy. The secret love I've held for this part of her is no longer a secret to me. I know full well what I have lost and that I will never get this back.

That's what it is to be loved by a mother, isn't it?

To have someone in your life so absorbed by whatever you are doing, however small and insignificant, who cares so deeply about each and every thing about you, that she raises these tiny details to the level of tremendous significance; she likewise smooths over the pain for you, the failures, the letdowns, the challenges of life, doing her best to help you move forward. Overdoing it, sometimes, maybe even often, but in this way that communicates to you, deep down, that you are not alone.

I don't want to be alone. I want my mother to help me through whatever comes next because I know it won't be pretty. I am going to have to pay attention to my husband again, to my marriage and its crumbling state, to the fact that it is deteriorating at a rate that isn't fixable and I am going to have to somehow get through its end without her there alongside me.

But I have Addie.

Isn't it funny, how I only agreed to have my daughter because Luke wanted her? I did this to save a marriage that was going to end regardless, it was only a matter of when. I gave Luke the very thing he wanted, but ultimately he still wasn't satisfied. If only I had known that nothing I did would ever be enough for him. If I had known this, I'm certain I would have made different decisions, I would have let my marriage end

315

before Addie came into our lives, before my mother could meet and fall in love with her beautiful, passionate little granddaughter.

I'm so glad that I didn't know.

33

April 8, 2015
Rose, Life 6

'GRANDPA, WHEN DID you decide to become a carpenter?'
Addie is munching on her fries, dragging them through
a giant pool of ketchup on her plate. She loves ketchup.

'When I was not much older than you are, Gnocchi,' he says.
'I was only about twelve. But I already knew that I loved working
with my hands.'

We are sitting at my dad's favorite diner, the one affectionately
nicknamed the Greasy Spoon by the people in the neighborhood
where I grew up. We come here once a month – my father, Addie,
and me. It's become a tradition since my mother died. The three
of us make a triangle at our table, my father and me on one side
of the booth, Addie on the other. Lately she likes to have the
entire bench to herself. As we eat and talk, there is the occasional
sizzle of a burger hitting the grill behind us, or the cook calling
out an order to one of the waitstaff.

Addie glances at me, then takes the tall squeeze bottle of
ketchup and proceeds to squirt it directly over the fry pinched

between her fingers. She's waiting for me to tell her to put the bottle down, but I just start to laugh. She pops the ketchupy fry into her mouth and starts the process over.

'So, Grandpa,' Addie says, now that she's confident I'm not going to scold her. 'If you were a kid again, like me, would you still decide to be a carpenter?'

My father follows Addie's lead, takes the bottle she hands to him and squirts a line of ketchup across each of the fries he eats, making her giggle. They both keep looking at me like I'm going to take the bottle away.

'Go ahead,' I say. I love seeing my dad with Addie. I love how he plays with her. I love that he has Addie and not just me. It's interesting how having a child and a grandchild can heal a person in ways you'd never expect. You always think a child is going to be all take, then suddenly they are the ones who are giving, without even realizing they're doing it. Just by being.

The lights in the diner are bright, they emphasize the lines that have grown deeper on my father's face. I try not to see how he's aged this last year, but sometimes it's impossible to miss.

'If your gramps could be young again today,' my father is saying, 'he'd definitely go to college first. Then maybe I'd still become a carpenter later on. But I wish I'd gone to school, even if I didn't need to in order to do my work. Just like your grandma went, and just like your mom and dad did.'

The waitress arrives with three ice cream shakes and sets them down in front of each of us. Strawberry for me, a black and white for Dad, and chocolate chip for Addie. She immediately pounces, trying to suck the thick liquid up the straw.

Then Addie asks, 'Grandma went to college?'

'Yes, she did,' I say. 'She studied to be a teacher.'

'But was she a teacher?'

My father is stirring his shake with his straw, trying to thin it. 'She was for a while, before she got pregnant and had your mom.'

'Why did she stop teaching when she had you, Mom?'

'Because it was another time,' I explain. 'And also because your grandma was so excited to have me she wanted to stay home and take care of me full time.' These words are out before I realize what they might convey to my daughter.

'But you're a teacher now,' Addie says.

Here it comes.

My dad dips a fry into his shake, something he's always loved to do, that he taught me to do even though my mother thought it was disgusting. 'Your mom isn't just a teacher, she's a professor because she got her PhD and teaches college students. Your mother got a doctorate, so she has a different title. Your grandpa has always been very, very proud of her for all that education.'

'Aw, Dad,' I say as I swipe a fry from his plate and dip it into his shake, not mine, because fries with strawberry shake are not my favorite. I turn to him, next to me on the bench. *I love you*, I mouth.

Addie is still trying to suck down her very thick shake. 'But, Mom, you don't stay home with me like Grandma stayed home with you.'

'I do not, little Gnocchi.'

'Why?'

'Because I love my work, Addie. I love my work and I love

319

you all at the same time. And we live in an age when women get to do both.'

My dad is watching Addie. So am I.

The wheels in her brain are turning. She's stopped eating fries and drinking her shake. The waitress comes over to ask if we need anything and we tell her no, send her away.

Then, 'Did Dad think about staying home with me instead of you?' Addie asks.

My father glances at me, eyebrows arched.

'He did not, Addie,' I say.

Addie is still studying me. The older she gets, the harder it is to give her vague answers. 'Does Dad love his work as much as you love your work?'

I consider this. 'I think that's a question you need to ask him, Addie. I can tell you that your father loves what he does, and he's very, very good at it.'

Addie is nodding. 'That's why he's away so much. Because people love his photographs and they ask him to travel all over to take them.'

'You're exactly right,' my father says.

Or, it's because your parents' marriage isn't going so well these days. Because, even though it's been wonderful that you came into both of our lives, having a child together wasn't enough to save our relationship.

The conversation moves on to other, less fraught topics: Addie's favorite subject in school, which is history, along with an invitation from my dad to take her to one of the history museums in the city that she hasn't visited yet, to more questions about Grandma and her life, a subject Addie has taken to asking about a lot. Addie wonders whether we are all going to rent a house again over the summer at the beach – probably, my father and I tell her. *Though maybe not with your dad along this time, Addie,* I add privately. Eventually the fries and the shakes are gone, we pay the check, and we head back to my father's house for another part of this monthly tradition we've established. Maybe my favorite one.

My dad flips on all the lights in his workshop, I go and pull up my chair to the spot where I like to sit. But Addie doesn't join me.

'Put on your gloves,' my father tells Addie.

She complies; they're pink, of course. Grandpa found them for her, who knows where. 'It's almost done,' she says, proudly.

'It is, sweetheart.'

For the next hour, Addie and her grandfather sand the study desk they are making together for Addie's room. He's been teaching her to work with her hands, just like he does, and it turns out she loves it. The two of them can do this for hours, hang out in his workshop, banging and sanding away, not talking much, my father occasionally stopping to show Addie the proper way to do this or that, music playing softly in the background. Sometimes the three of us will chat, but often I just sit here and watch.

Addie's hand stops a moment, she looks up at my father. 'Can we make something else after this is finished?' she asks.

My dad beams. 'Of course, we can. Whatever you want!'

'How about a chair to go with the desk?'

'A chair sounds perfect.'

'We can paint it the same color pink that Grandma loved,' she decides.

My dad and I share a look and a chuckle, since the only reason my mother tolerated the bright pink that Addie loves so much is because Addie loves it so much.

'I'm sure your grandmother would approve,' my father says to her.

Before Addie returns to sanding, she glances over at me. 'Do you think Grandma can still see us? Do you think she knows that we're here, talking about her? Do you think she knows that we miss her?'

I consider all of Addie's questions. I know that it's only wishful thinking to say that my mother is here, that she somehow knows what we are doing in life, how much we love and miss her now that she is gone. But I also decide that I do not care if this is wishful thinking, because it is a wish that I share with Addie. I've wished these same kinds of things about my mother every day since the day she died. 'Yes, sweetheart,' I tell her now. 'Yes, I do think that.'

34

April 8, 2015

Rose, Lives 1 & 2

'DR. NAPOLITANO, I really loved your book.' A young woman who looks like a grad student stops me in the hallway of the conference hotel. It is bright and warm inside, a contradiction to the freezing, snowy Colorado weather outside.

'Thank you,' I say. She is about my height, stylish, with black hair and a sleeveless red dress that shows off her muscular arms and calves. 'Did you read it for a class?' I asked her.

'Actually, no.' People from the conference pass us on both sides, tweed-clad fish, heading to the various rooms set up for a panel, a talk, or toward the stairs that lead to the book fair. 'I read it because I don't think I want to have children. I read it for me.' Her statement comes as a confession, like the admission of a crime.

This makes me want to lean in and hug her, put my arm around her and walk her to a place where we can sit down and have a coffee. I want her to know that she is not alone, that there are more of us, more than you would think. 'I wrote that book for me,' I tell her. 'And ultimately, for people like you.'

The project grew out of a decision I made a while back – partly for survival's sake, post-Luke – to seek out other women who don't have children and won't, who maybe never wanted them and stood their ground. I wanted to meet my women peers who had lived through something similar, something that perhaps cost them their marriages, too. It turns out there are a lot of us. But most of us live in hiding.

I am grateful to that book. It's turned out to be a helpful distraction, the way its promotion has consumed my attention since my mother died. I've thrown myself into every possible opportunity on behalf of it, said yes to all of it.

'What's your name?' I ask the young woman.

She looks up again. 'Marika,' she says.

'You don't have to be embarrassed that you don't want children.'

'I know.' She shifts from one foot to the other, her spiky heels sinking into the carpet. 'But it's one of those things that's really hard to talk about with other people. No one ever believes you if you tell them. Or they think something is wrong with you.'

'I know exactly what you mean. I used to feel really alone.' I think about how nice it is to be recovered from that part of my life, happy in my work, fine in my singleness. I have wonderful friendships and colleagues, Dad and Aunt Frankie. 'Thank God I met all of those women I interviewed for the book,' I tell her.

Marika nods. 'That must have been nice.'

'It was.' The hallway is growing quiet, the next section of panels about to begin. I dig around in my cavernous bag, past the thick books that hang heavy inside, the conference program, my wallet, and come up with the thin blue leather pouch that holds my business cards. I hand one to her. 'If I don't see you again, you can email me sometime if you want, and we can talk more. If I didn't have to go to a meeting, I'd say we should go get coffee right now.' Marika takes the card. 'It was wonderful meeting you.'

I start on my way, closing the little leather wallet, letting it slide back to its place at the bottom of my purse. A gift from Luke that he presented to me at dinner on the night we celebrated my first academic job. He wrapped it carefully in matching blue paper, my favorite color, the bright color of the sea on a sunny day, tied it with a green bow, my second favorite color. Wrote in the card, *To my forever-love, Professor Rose, at the beginning of what will be a long and successful career. Love always, Luke.* I remember this so clearly. As I walk down the hall, I marvel at how this memory doesn't cause me to wince, it doesn't hurt, not in the sharp way it used to. I feel a kind of peace instead, a peace that I didn't know was possible to feel about this man who was once my husband.

Somehow, despite the pain of the divorce, of Luke moving on with someone else and having a child, we have found our way to a kind of friendship.

It was my mother dying that did it.

I'd texted to give him the news that she didn't have much time left. I figured I should. Luke had known my mother for years, had called her Mom, had loved her, and she'd loved him, too. Luke messaged me back, nearly immediately.

I'm so sorry, Rose.

Then a second message arrived.

325

Would it be okay if I come and say good-bye?

His request startled me. I was sitting in her room at the time, reading a mystery novel in the chair where my father usually slept. I'd made my father go home for a few hours. I was worried about him; being there constantly was taking a toll. It took me a long time before I replied to Luke. At first, I didn't know what to say. Luke and I hadn't seen each other in years.

Divorce is so strange. You're with someone all the time, you live with them for a decade, share everything with them, and then – if you don't have a child between you – suddenly you are nothing to each other anymore, or you don't have to be anything if you don't want to be.

But after so many days of sitting in that room and staring at my mother, on the verge of losing this person who had loved me every second of my life, my perspective began to shift. Facing death will do that to a person. It will make everything you do seem different. It will take the dramas that you've lived in the past, all that rage a person might feel toward someone else, and make it seem small and insignificant.

As angry as I had been at Luke for so long and as good as it was to be out from under our marriage, I didn't want him and me to be nothing. We'd lived too much. And I was touched he wanted to see her.

I typed out a message back.

Yes. But come soon. She doesn't have much longer.

Two hours later, he was knocking on the door. The sun had dropped in the sky outside the windows, the room darkening except for the lamplight near my mother's bed. I hesitated a second. A brief moment of panic flickered in me. *Why had I said yes to Luke?*

Then I got up and let him in.

'Hi, Rose.'

'Hi.'

We stood there looking at each other. Then Luke pulled me into a hug. At first it was awkward, like neither one of us was certain if it was a good idea. But then it became familiar, a kind of comfort. Something I recognized, something Luke and I had done for years without thinking when we were together. 'I'm so sorry about your mom, Rose,' he said into my shoulder.

We pulled apart.

'It was nice of you to come,' I said. And I meant it. I'd been uncertain about this decision moments ago, but now that Luke was here, I wasn't any longer.

We went and stood at my mother's bedside.

She seemed so small, so withered, so not like herself. Every time I looked at her there, really took her in, I wanted to weep.

'I still miss your mother's lasagna on Christmas,' Luke said.

I smiled a little. 'Really?'

'Oh yeah. No one makes lasagna like your mom.'

I sighed. 'Yeah.'

'Do you remember how mad she got when we told her we weren't going to have the big Italian cookie table at the wedding? Or the Jordan almonds as favors?'

I laughed. 'How could I forget? She acted like we were murderers.'

'This lady can really hold a grudge.'

'Tell me about it.'

Luke and I stood there for an hour, trading memories of my mother, good ones, funny ones, difficult ones, laughing about the things my mother said and did. The ways in which she wove her way into our lives, our marriage, our wardrobes with her crazy sweaters, whether we liked it or not. The more we talked, the easier it was for me to be there, at my mother's bedside, as though our words held the power to transform her back into the woman we knew, to give her back her life, even if only for a very few minutes.

'I'm really glad you came, Luke,' I told him when he was getting ready to go.

'Of course I came. I loved your mother.'

'That's nice of you to say.'

'It's true,' he said. His voice grew hoarse. 'I know you're going to miss her, Rose. I know you and your dad must be going through hell.'

'These last weeks have been awful.' I looked over at him. His eyes were still on my mother so it was easier to say what I told him next. 'It's nice to see you. I didn't realize how nice it would be, or could be, to have you here.'

He turned to me. 'It's nice to see you, too.'

We held each other's gaze. 'I'm glad you found your happiness in life, Luke,' I said. 'I'm glad you met someone who wanted a child as much as you did.'

There was a beat of silence. 'Thank you for saying that,' he said. Then, 'Rose, I know that it hasn't been easy between us for a long time, but I want you to know that I'm still here for you. I really mean that. If you ever need anything, or just want to talk.'

His words hung between us. We suddenly stood on a precipice, Luke and me, not sure what would be there to catch us if we jumped, if there'd be anything at all. But it felt as if Luke had offered me his hand. I decided to take it.

'Okay,' I told him. 'That's good to know.'

Luke said good-bye to my mother, then to me, and he left.

A few days later my mother died, and I sent him a message to let him know. He asked if he could come to the funeral.

I said yes to this, too.

We didn't speak that day. I barely was aware of Luke's presence. I vaguely remember glimpsing him in the way back of the church when I got up to give the eulogy. But I've thought a lot about how this loss of my mother, how knowing that Luke felt this loss in his own life, too, had forged a truce between us after all that division. How this fragile truce had inched its way toward something like a friendship, albeit a tentative one that consisted of a phone call now and then.

I think my mother would have liked this.

To know that even though she is gone, she is still influencing the decisions I make, the relationships I am in, negotiating a peace that I thought would never be possible between Luke and me. Butting in still, to my life.

I think I like this, too.

The meeting is packed when I arrive.

People are milling around, taking their seats, setting their bags next to them on the carpeted floor, removing laptops from sleeves. I spot an open seat and place my bag on it before someone else can grab it.

'Hi, Cynthia,' I say to the woman on my left, a colleague from the West Coast who I only see at conferences.

'Hi, Rose, hope this doesn't run over like last year.'

'No kidding.' I look to my right at the man sitting there. He's staring at the screen of his laptop and I am staring at him. 'It's you!' I practically shout, then lower my voice. 'Thomas, right?'

He looks up. Then smiles at me. 'Rose!'

There is something about seeing Thomas now that strikes me, that causes a rush in my veins, my body. Something I haven't felt in a long time. 'I can't believe you're here.' I laugh. 'How funny that we're on the same committee.'

I haven't seen Thomas since that day we met at the hospital, back when my mother was still in chemo, though not for lack of his trying. He texted me for a while; sometimes I texted him back, but then my mother was dying and that's all I could see. I stopped returning his messages. Then there was the grief and the attempts to move forward, everything with the book, all that travel.

'We were bound to run into each other at some point,' he says.

I pull out my chair, take my seat, settle in. Thomas closes his laptop. We turn to each other again.

'How are you?' I ask. 'How's your friend, Angel?'

'I'm good. He's good. Angel is cancer-free for now, so that is excellent news.'

'Wonderful. I'm so glad to hear it.'

'And your mom?'

I shake my head. A lump forms in my throat. No matter how many months she has been gone, this still happens, no matter how hard I try to avoid it.

'Oh, I'm sorry,' Thomas says.

I breathe in, breathe out, wait to speak again until the lump starts to dissipate. Concentrate on getting more of my things out

330

of my bag, putting my notepad on the table, a pen next to it. When I look at Thomas, he is all patience. The connection I feel between us is immediate. 'Thank you. And I'm sorry, too. It's still really hard to talk about her, even though it'll be a year in June.'

Thomas's eyes are strange, beautiful, his gaze seems to reach inside me, right past the grief. 'A year is nothing,' he tells me. 'I still have a hard time talking about my dad, and it's been almost ten years that he's been gone.'

'I'm sorry you lost your dad,' I say. Then, 'God, there really isn't anything good to say to someone about losing a parent, is there? "I'm sorry" is just so lame.'

Thomas and I share a bit of a laugh.

'You were so nice that day in the hospital when my mother was getting chemo,' I say to him. 'I don't think I ever told you that, back when we were texting. But it's true – you were.'

'It was easy,' Thomas says. 'Your mother kind of lit up our day. She made Angel and me laugh so much.'

'She was like that.' My eyes fill again, I wipe my hand across them. Do the breathing thing again to collect myself. I smile at Thomas, a bit embarrassed that I'm still almost crying. 'Sorry, sometimes I'm such a mess about her.'

'It's okay. Really. It's normal to feel that way.' His lifts his arm, and for a moment I think he's going to place his hand over mine or touch my shoulder. But he doesn't. 'This is kind of a strange place to be having such an intimate conversation,' he says instead.

I look around the committee room, at all of the academics around us, busy typing on their laptops, shuffling papers, trying to impress one another. 'Yeah, but it's also good to talk about something other than work. Something real.' My gaze settles on Thomas again. 'It's so nice to see you again.'

'What are you doing tonight?' he asks. 'Got any plans?'

Thomas is about to invite me to go out.

This thought brings with it a rush of pleasure. Then I think, *My mother would be so pleased by this.* 'Just the usual,' I say. 'Reception hopping. What about you?'

Before he can respond, the chair of the committee shouts above the din that we will begin in five minutes. More people vie for the last remaining chairs.

A photograph of a young girl lights up the phone on the table in front of Thomas. She is skinny, smiling, with long dark hair flowing past her shoulders.

I didn't realize Thomas had a daughter. My eyes seek his hand. There isn't a ring on his finger. But maybe I was wrong before – maybe he wasn't about to ask me out. Maybe that day in the hospital, all those texts afterward, was just Thomas trying to be nice because of my mother.

Thomas grabs his phone, picks up, says, 'Honey, is everything all right?' Pause. 'Okay. I need to call you back later. Love you.' He sets the phone face down on the table and turns back to me. There is a sheepish grin on his face.

'Your daughter?' I guess.

He nods. 'Yeah. She's adorable, though I am kind of biased. She used to run around after me like I was her hero, but she's started locking herself in her room lately. I thought it would be a few more years before she was doing that.'

I smile. Nod, like I understand, even though I don't. Of course I don't.

'Do you have children?'

'Actually, no. I'm not married. No kids.'

'Me neither – I'm not married either, I mean,' he says, and I feel myself rejoicing. 'My old girlfriend and I got pregnant, gave it a go for a while, but it was never meant to be. We're friends now, though, and we do a pretty good job of parenting together, I think, which is nice. Anyway!' Thomas smiles again. It reaches his eyes, his entire face, lights his body. 'I was about to see if you wanted to skip all the receptions tonight and have dinner with me instead. What do you think?'

'I think yes,' I say without any hesitation. 'I'd definitely like that.'

'Great.'

The two of us sit there, grinning at each other. Then Thomas's phone vibrates with a message, which, when he reads it, produces a grimace – a very handsome grimace. 'My daughter thinks she can convince me that she should stay over with her friend for an entire weekend, but her mom and I keep telling her no. She's always trying to wear us down, and sometimes it works.' He shrugs, places his phone down on the table again.

'What's your daughter's name?' I ask him.

When he looks at me again, he turns and says with a big smile on his face, 'Her name is Addie.'

Part Five

Enter More Roses,
Lives 7 & 9

35

August 15, 2006
Rose, Life 7

LUKE IS STANDING on my side of the bed. He never goes to my side of the bed. In his hand is a bottle of prenatal vitamins. He holds it up, shakes it.

The sound is heavy and dull because it is full.

'You promised,' he says.

'Did I?'

'Rose.'

My name, a statement from Luke's mouth. Ominous.

I sigh. I don't have it in me to do this today. Or any other day for that matter. I'm tired of fighting with my husband over having a baby. Will we? Won't we? Will I ever come around? Why am I not like all the other women in the universe whose entire purpose is to make babies? Why am I the one woman out of everyone who isn't interested?

'Yes, Luke?'

'I thought this bottle would be nearly empty. I thought I would have to buy you another.'

I open the dresser drawer, take out some underwear – hot pink, a thong. 'I guess not,' I say, and shut the drawer with a thud.

'You guess not.'

If Luke keeps repeating my sentences, I might start screaming. I swivel around, the underwear dangling from my hands. 'How about we just split the difference and I'll go down to the doctor's office and freeze my eggs?'

Luke's mouth opens. Nothing comes out.

'Then we can table this conversation for a while,' I say, hopeful that Luke will agree to this compromise, wanting to pat myself on the back for my brilliant plan.

My husband finds his words again. 'But freezing your eggs isn't the same as having a baby, Rose.'

'You're right, it's not. But freezing my eggs is the best offer you have right now, from your wife, who never wanted a baby in the first place.' I go to my husband, set the thong onto the bed, trading it for his hand. I look up into his eyes, attempting to read them. 'Take it or leave it, Luke. Which will it be?'

36

May 22, 2020
Rose, Lives 3 & 6

'ADDIE, IF YOU don't pick up your phone and call me back right now, you are grounded for one month!'

I hang up after leaving this message, slump over onto the kitchen table.

The apartment is dark except for a single light above the stove. The sun has drained from the sky, dimming the world around me. I've been sitting here, still as stone, staring at the phone, willing Addie's face to appear on the screen. I get up and turn on some of the lamps until a rosy glow fills the living room and kitchen. Luke and I always maintained that overhead lights were too stark, too glaring, while lamps provided lovely mood lighting, the two of us proud we'd decorated our apartment with romance in mind. Now the soft shadows and halos around me are a taunt.

I bang my phone against the table, as though I can knock Addie loose. Then I slam it down with a scream. The screen cracks – of course it cracks. I'm such an idiot! 'Look what you made me do, Addie!' I shout into the empty apartment.

I remember when I was young and defied my mother. How angry she got, how she would shriek at me like a maniac when I got home. I remember telling her this. 'You're a crazy person!' I would yell, then stomp up the stairs to my room, knowing that soon I would hear her footsteps followed by the pronouncement that I was grounded. Then I would shout back and slam my door as loud as I could. Sometimes I would do this thing where I would open it back up and slam it again, multiple times, while screaming with rage.

If my mother were alive, I would call her up and apologize profusely for all that I put her through. If my mother were alive, I could tell her this, and we would laugh about it, we would recall some of the worst times I misbehaved. Then I would explain to her how Addie has been acting lately and she would offer motherly advice. The world is so lonely without her.

Sometimes I want to shout this at Addie. *You'd miss me if I were gone! You would!*

Parenthood really does turn people into maniacs.

My phone lights up, but it's Luke, not Addie. 'Has she been in touch with you?' I ask.

'No.' His sigh is heavy, tired.

I know what he is thinking without him having to say it. 'Even though I am so mad at her right now, I still don't think we should follow the tracker on her phone. She needs her independence. She *does*.'

'I agree. You know I do,' Luke says. Then, 'I think we should cut her some slack.'

'No way. Her behavior is unacceptable.'

'Rose.' Another sigh. 'Her behavior is because of us.'

I don't respond.

'It is. You know it, too.'

'It's been more than two years, Luke, and we were separated even before that,' I say, but he's right.

'Divorce is hard on a kid.'

I know he's right again, but then panic grips me. 'But what if something horrible happened to her?' My voice rises and I move with it, until I am standing. 'What if someone took her?'

'No one took her, Rose. She's fine. She's just acting out.'

I deflate. 'You really think so?'

Luke chuckles, he actually chuckles. 'I think she'll end up grounded once we find her, but yes, I think she's absolutely fine. She's just pushing back against her evil parents.'

I walk into the living room and lie down on my back on the rug, between the couch and the coffee table, staring up at the ceiling. 'When did we get evil? We never used to be evil.'

'If we're comparing, I think I'm probably more evil than you are.'

There is a trace of playfulness in Luke's voice. 'Are we having an evil contest right now?'

'I think we are. And I win.'

I put my hand over my mouth to stifle a laugh. How can I be laughing? Addie is missing! Luke and I are divorced! 'I think you do win, actually.'

'Oh, definitely. I went and had a baby with a woman who isn't Addie's mother.'

'Yeah, that's pretty evil.'

'Mega-evil.'

'For your birthday, I'm going to give you a special cape and mask to represent the depth of your evil and your evil escapades on this earth.'

'I'm way ahead of you. I already have my supervillain attire. I bought it on sale after Halloween.'

A siren rises outside the windows, then fades. I am giggling. I can't stop. 'Then I'll buy you a spare villain suit to wear while the other one is at the dry cleaner.'

Luke is laughing hard. I haven't heard him laugh like this since well before we separated. 'Where are you right now?' he asks suddenly.

'If you must know, I'm lying in front of the couch on the rug, staring up at the ceiling. I bought a new rug since you left and it's really nice. I never liked that scratchy one you made us get because it was on sale.' A breeze floats through the windows and across the living room. I sit up and lean my elbows on the coffee table. The curtains are moving softly. 'I miss you, Luke,' I say, without thinking. 'I mean, not in an inappropriate way. I miss your sense of humor. I miss our friendship, I guess. We used to be such good friends.'

'I miss our friendship, too.'

'Do you think we could become friends again one day?'

'I think it would be good for Addie if we were friends.'

'Yes. But maybe it would be good for us, too.' What am I saying? Do I even mean that?

'I think so, too.'

I think I do mean it. But maybe only because Luke and I are agreeing on something, and we haven't agreed on anything for such a long while. Or maybe it doesn't matter why.

I pound my fist on the coffee table. 'Where the fuck is Addie?'

'Whoa, whoa. Language, Dr. Napolitano.'

'My language doesn't fucking matter because our beloved daughter is ignoring us and rebelling against your evil ways so she can't hear me right now!'

'I think we're making a lot of progress this evening, Rose.'

'What the fuck are you talking about, Luke?'

I hear the scrape of a chair in Luke's apartment. The rustling of him sitting down. 'I think we're fast-tracking the friendship effort. We haven't talked like this in' – he pauses – 'I don't remember the last time we talked like this. Or that I laughed this hard with you.'

I decide to be honest. 'Me, too. It's nice.'

'Maybe that was our daughter's evil plan. To put her parents under duress so we can bond again. Maybe Addie knew that this was exactly what you and I needed. So she decided to take off with her other preteen evil minions in order to test her experiment.'

'Well, if that's true then it's only because of you. My daughter is a little angel. Loving and sweet and perfect.'

'That's not what you were saying earlier.'

I get up off the floor and retrieve a glass from the cabinet. Fill it with water. 'I'm saying it now. I've decided that if I focus on the positive and only think about the version of our daughter who adored her mommy, then perhaps that version will return and swap herself out with the newly preadolescent version that her evil father's been molding her into.'

'I told you so,' Luke says.

I sit back down and set my glass on the coffee table. 'Now what are you talking about?'

'I knew you'd love being a mother.'

'Oh my God, shut up with that right now. I do not love being a mother. I love Addie. There's a difference.'

'What are you talking about, Rose? How is there a difference?'

'I'm not the motherly type and I don't think I ever will be. Just because I caved and became one doesn't mean that I've become a convert. But now that I have a daughter, I love her like a crazy person.' I gulp down some of my water. 'It's horrible to love someone this much. I fucking *hate* it.'

Luke is laughing again. 'You're totally a good mother.'

'Of course I'm a good mother. I'm very successful, you know. I have a PhD and I've published many books. I can pretty much do anything.'

'Stubborn, impossible woman.'

'Just a minute ago, you were giving me a compliment,' I remind him.

'Can I ask you something?'

His serious tone makes me hesitate. 'Um. Maybe? Yes? It depends on what?'

I hear Luke exhale. 'How's Thomas?'

This, I am not expecting. 'Do you really want to know?'

'I do.'

Luke and I agreed that I would tell him if I started dating someone because it would affect Addie. But mentioning that I was dating someone was very different than having a full-fledged conversation with my ex-husband about the state of the relationship. 'This is the weirdest postdivorce conversation that you and I have ever had.'

'I like it,' Luke says.

'Me too,' I say, then, 'Thomas is good. He's great.'

Thomas and I met at one of my book signings. He'd tagged along with a few colleagues from my department. Just about everyone I knew was at the bookstore that night. My father was there, Addie, Jill, Maria, Raya and Denise, a big contingent of parents from Addie's school. It was really nice, but in ways I hadn't expected – in the way that it also turned out to be the night Thomas and I met.

'Hi, what's your name?' I asked automatically when it was his turn at the signing table.

'Thomas,' he answered.

I looked up, immediately realized that the man with the nice voice standing before me was very handsome.

He smiled, which only made him more attractive. 'Congratulations on the book. I'm really looking forward to reading it. Your colleagues think very highly of you.' He looked around, gestured over to the group of professors standing around the wine and talking. 'I'm a sociologist, too.'

'Really!' I said, a bit too enthusiastically. 'I'd love to hear more about your work!' I could tell that the man waiting behind Thomas was getting impatient. He kept peering around Thomas and making a grimace. 'Are you able to stick around? A bunch of us are going out to drinks after this is over. Then we'd have more time to talk.'

Oh my God. What are you doing, Rose? Asking out random men?

'Sure, I'd love that,' Thomas said.

I signed Thomas's book and handed it back to him. 'Thank you for coming tonight. It's always nice to meet another person in my field.' *Especially when he is as handsome as you.*

345

'It is,' he said, smiled again, and I watched him walk away toward the rest of my colleagues.

We ended up talking all night. Then we went on a date a week later, and then another, until one day I woke up with Thomas next to me in bed and realized that all of those dates were piling up into a relationship. A relationship that was actually making me happy.

'It's still early with Thomas,' I say to Luke now. 'We haven't even been together for six months.'

'You sound like you like him.'

'I do like him,' I admit. My call waiting beeps and I pull the phone from my ear for a second to look at it. 'Ohmigosh that's Addie—'

'That's great! But go easy on—!' Luke is in the middle of saying this when I hang up and answer Addie's call.

'Addie! Are you all right?'

'*Mom*, I'm *fine*.' She is full of attitude. Like it pains her to have to talk to me.

'Addie, you scared me to death!'

'Mom—'

'Don't you dare Mom me! I love you, I love you so much, and because of that I am so happy to hear your voice and know that you are fine, thank God, but your father and I have been frantic and you are so grounded! You are grounded until you are twenty!'

37

May 8, 2023
Rose, Lives 1, 2, 7 & 8

'ADDIE, ARE YOU ready to go?'
My voice echoes through the house and up the stairs. A door creaks open, then shut, footsteps sound across wooden floorboards – slow, unhurried, the walk of a teenager. Thud, thud, *thud*. Addie descends slowly, boots heavy, thick soled, loud, just the way she likes them, the way she likes everything. But the girl who appears, first her feet, then shins, knees, and jean-covered legs, followed by the hem of a flimsy, silky, *sexy* pink tank top that Thomas would kill her for if he was around to see it – this girl is smiling. Addie somehow intermingles this don't-care, don't-mess-with-me, I'm-going-at-my-own-pace teen attitude, with also being the loveliest and friendliest young woman I've ever met.

'Hey!' Her brown eyes are as wide as her grin. Her cat, Max, weaves around her legs and into the other room. 'I'm so super excited about shopping today!'

I laugh. Addie loves the phrase *so super*. She prefaces everything

347

she can with it – so super hungry, so super upset, so super intrigued, so super into this girl who's so super hot. 'I'm so super excited, too,' I say.

We hug. She's so skinny. I detect the narrow ridges of her ribs underneath her top. It makes me want to feed Addie fat hamburgers and plates piled high with pasta, thick with Bolognese sauce, but alas she's been a vegetarian since she turned thirteen. This urge to feed Addie, though, it makes me want to roll my eyes at myself as I realize that I am my mother sometimes. This thought always gives way to a kind of bittersweet warmth, a sad pleasure to realize that my mother left her imprint on the person I am now. She'd be pleased to know this.

'Are you hungry?' I ask Addie. 'Maybe we should start our day with lunch?'

Addie cocks her head, thinking, short, spiky hair tilting but stiff with gel. The day she cut off her long hair was shocking. One minute it nearly reached her waist, the next it was shaved close to her skull, exposing her neck. She didn't ask permission – she just did it. Her father freaked out, but it made her eyes seem even bigger. It suits her. 'How about we go to one store, then to lunch,' she bargains. 'I'm not hungry yet.'

'But maybe you'll get hungry if we sat down with a menu. We could go to that vegetarian diner you like! The one with all the crazy, homemade veggie burgers?'

Addie grabs a sweater off the back of a chair in the living room, also pink, but a paler shade than her tank top. She snorts. 'You are always trying to feed me.'

I laugh. 'Am I?'

'Yessss. *Rose*,' she adds, my name a heavy downbeat, heavy as the soles of her black lace-up boots that her father also hates. She's smiling as she says it, liking how using my first name makes her feel like the adult.

This is new, Addie calling me Rose. She takes every opportunity she can find to say it, and lately her use of '*Rose*' is nearly as frequent as her use of '*so super*'. *Rose, can you tell my dad that it's okay that I stay out late to go to the dance? Rose, do you know if we have any of that cereal I like? I can't find it in the closet. Rose, do you think we can go shopping this weekend? There's this girl that I like. I need to impress her.* The use of my name is much preferred to the initial anger and resistance she showed when she found out that I was dating her father. But she was so young then, young and possessive of her dad, whom she did not want to share with anyone else. Now that she's turned fifteen, she really does seem like she is becoming an adult. I like her. A lot. And not just because she is the daughter of the man I love, the man with whom I've been talking about sharing a house.

Who could predict that I would end up with a daughter, without ever having a child myself? And one who is so much fun, so smart, so wonderful?

It's way better than I thought. A compromise I would never have imagined.

Addie picks up her bag. It's black with fierce metal spikes on it. 'Do you think my dad will let me stay out until midnight next weekend?'

I eye her. 'You'll have to ask him that.'

'But do *you* think it would be okay?'

I don't answer. Her eyebrows arch. She already knows that I

agree with her that it would be fine, but I won't say it out loud. It's still not my place to decide these things.

Whenever Thomas is on the verge of a meltdown over Addie's latest drama at school, with her friends, over curfew, or the newest girl she wants to date, I try to remind him that he got very lucky with Addie, that the teen years could be horrific – that's what all my friends who are parents say, at least.

'How about *I* ask him,' Addie goes on, 'then *you* talk to him about it.'

'I'll think about it,' I tell her.

She grins, opens the door. She knows she has me. 'Thanks, *Rose.*'

38

June 18, 2022

Rose, Lives 3, 5 & 6

'A DDIE!'

I am screaming and waving. So is my father, next to me. Addie turns our way as she walks down the aisle with the other eighth graders graduating today, and she gives me a pleading look that says *Mom, calm down!* But I can't. She rolls her eyes. Even the budding, teenagery attitude in my daughter can't dampen the pleasure of seeing Addie in a cap and gown, walking onto the stage with all of her friends.

'Woo! Woo-hoo!' I clap as hard as I can, my palms stinging.

My father leans in. 'Rose, if I'd done that when you were young, you would've gone a week without speaking to me.'

Jill nudges me from my other side. 'Addie is definitely going to give you a talking-to later. You might want to take it down a notch.'

'I don't care,' I tell them both. 'She'll have to endure her embarrassing mother.' I look around at the packed auditorium. I see Luke's parents all the way on the other side, carefully avoiding catching my eye. We haven't spoken in a very long time. 'Besides, all the other parents are doing the exact same thing.'

'Well, that is true.' Jill pauses, then, 'So, is Luke going to make it?'

I glance across the auditorium again at the empty seat next to Luke's parents. 'I hope so.' He was coming back from a work trip, was worried about flight delays, train delays, traffic overall. He doesn't always do too well, juggling the responsibilities of his job and also having one daughter with me and two others with Cheryl.

'But this is Addie's middle-school graduation.'

'I know. I *know*.'

'Maybe he'll surprise you,' my father says, ever the optimist.

My friendship with Luke is, to say the least, imperfect. Since he had his second baby, he has not been as attentive to Addie as he used to be. But we plod forward, the two of us, doing our best to parent together, to be there for Addie, to even, sometimes, be there for each other. I would be lying, though, to claim there isn't a kind of freedom in his absence, in the ways it liberates me to be Addie's mother however I want to be. I know that's selfish, I know Addie needs her father to be as present as he possibly can be, but it's also true. I am relieved, sometimes, when Luke isn't here.

The junior high band's rendition of 'Pomp and Circumstance' starts over again. Kids are filing into the bleacher seats on the stage. My eyes are glued to Addie as she sits down in the second row, four in from the left, next to her best friend, Eve.

My father is shaking his head. 'I can't believe I like that haircut, but I do.'

Addie chopped all her hair off to within two inches of her head. I was highly opposed to the idea, but I let her do it – and it does look good on her. Luke hates it.

Principal Gonzalez asks everyone to sit and we automatically do, like we are also her students.

Jill leans over. 'Can you believe we're at Addie's graduation? I remember when she was just a tiny little Gnocchi.'

I nod. I glance over at my father. I can see that his eyes are already teary. I know that if I speak I'll start crying and then I'll really be in trouble with Addie later on when we have her party. If I were capable of speech, I would tell Jill that I can't imagine a world without Addie in it. To think I came so close to living in that world. A tear runs down my cheek anyway. I wipe it away with my hand.

'Is Thomas coming to the party?' Jill asks.

The cake is at the center of the table. It's chocolate, no frosting – Addie doesn't like frosting – except for the thin, scripted stream of lemon icing that says, *Happy Graduation, Addie!* I adjust it so it's at the exact center of the rest of the food – cookies, brownies, cupcakes on one side, bowls full of salads and pasta, Addie's favorite meatballs, and a deep, rich dish of my mother's braciola, which I spent hours making and Addie also loves. 'No.' I switch the placement of the spinach salad with the broccoli pasta. I'm not sure why. 'Addie would be upset if Thomas came.'

Jill grabs my arm when I go to move another bowl, stopping me. 'It's fine. No more fussing. The table looks great.'

I retract my hand.

She's right. It does. Just off to the side against the wall is a tall wardrobe – beautiful, simple, with a big, bright pink bow around it and a card tucked inside. Grandpa's gift to Addie as she heads into high school. It matches the rest of the furniture that the two of them made together for her bedroom. Addie is going to love it.

Jill and I move over to the island in the kitchen. She pops the cork of one of the bottles of white wine I bought for the parents who are coming to the party. Jill fills two of the glasses sitting on the countertop and hands me one. 'I thought Addie and Thomas were making progress.'

I take a sip, enjoy the cool, sweet-bitter liquid in my throat. 'They were. They are. It's much better than it was, since the beginning was terrible, as you know. But during the last few months they seem to have made friends. I knew they would, he's wonderful with her, and he's been so patient. More than I would be if it was me and I was dealing with someone else's kid, that is for sure.'

Jill laughs. 'I bet.'

I check my phone to see if Luke has texted, but there's still no sign of him. I sigh, swirl my wine in the glass. 'Addie is going to be heartbroken if Luke doesn't make it to this party.'

Right then, the door buzzes and my phone buzzes, too.

'I'll get the door,' Jill offers.

I grab the phone. 'Luke!'

'I'm on my way! I'll be there soon!' he says. Then, 'Does Addie hate me?'

'Of course not.' *A little.* 'She'll be happy when she finds out you're going to make her party.'

'And I'll be her friends' personal professional photographer.'

I smile. 'She'll love that.' *She really will.*

'Do you think she'll ever forgive me?'

'Yes.' *Yes.*

'Good.'

I hear Luke leaning on his car horn. 'Drive safe!'

We hang up.

Your daughter needs you, I think then. *She needs both of us.*

She always will, won't she? Even if she doesn't realize it yet, even if her newest favorite thing to do is roll her eyes at her parents. I hope Addie will need her mother forever, because her mother does so love to be needed by her. Maybe all mothers do.

My eyes fill, and I wipe the back of my hand across them.

I know mine did.

39

August 15, 2006
Rose, Life 9

L UKE IS STANDING on my side of the bed. He never goes
to my side of the bed. In his hand is a bottle of prenatal
vitamins. He holds it up.

I take a step closer. I make sure to breathe, in and out. 'I
stopped taking them, okay?'

Luke's shoulders slump. 'Rose. You *promised*.'

'Luke, I—'

But he isn't done.

'Rose, you promised and you *lied*.'

I stare at him, standing there, slouched, the portrait of a victim.
As though somehow I've done something to him – hurt him.
'Oh really, Luke? Did I? Well, tell me, are there any promises
that *you've* broken? Any at all that you can remember? Any lies
you might have told?'

'Rose.' He sighs, a big exhale of air and space. 'Don't be like
that—'

'Don't be like *what*? Don't be like I've always been – honest with you about this whole issue? From practically our first date, Luke, I warned you that I didn't want a baby. I told you so many times. And you know what you said back to me?'

More sighing. Heavier this time. My husband is diminishing before me, melting onto the bed. He sinks down onto the edge. 'Rose—'

'That question was reciprocal, Luke,' I say, my body, all of me, expanding, taking over the room, pulsing. 'What you said, every time I reminded you that I was not having kids, was that you didn't want them either. That you'd never wanted them. You told me this over and over before we walked down that damned fucking aisle and married each other. So who's calling who a liar?'

'I didn't *lie*—'

'Stop. Just stop the fucking bullshit because I'm tired of it. I'm tired of being blamed for disappointing you and every single person in your family. I'm tired of thinking that I'm some failed woman, some terrible person, some selfish, awful bitch.' I pause for a breath, and as I do, I see the shock strike Luke's face as though it is my hand reaching out to hit him. 'Did it every occur to you that *you've* failed me? That *you're* the failed husband in this marriage?'

'Rose, that's not fair.'

My laugh is bitter. I walk over to my husband, stare down at him, collapsed there on our bed, and right then I *know*. Luke tilts his head upward, meets my eyes. A flicker of fear passes across them. 'This whole time, this whole torturous time of you and your family telling me I'll regret not being a mother for the rest of my life, that we'll regret it, that I'm a horrible person, a terrible, selfish woman, that I'm ruining your life – I've just taken it as truth. When really the truth is that *you* are ruining *my* life.'

'Rose?' My name, strained, almost shrill from Luke's mouth.

I bend down, place my hands on either side of Luke's face and kiss his forehead. He blinks, I see confusion settling into his gaze. I let go, straighten, turn, and march out of the bedroom, through the living room and to the hall closet where the suitcases are stored, high up on the shelf. I struggle to take the biggest one down, so big we've always joked that it could fit a dead body. It bangs against the closet door before crashing to the floor.

'Rose?' My name, a second time.

I right it, wheel it back to the bedroom, straight to the drawers where I keep my bras, my underwear, my socks. I lay it on the floor, unzip it, and begin the work of piling all of it across the bottom. Stacks of bras tip and mingle with pajama tops, but I don't care. I am a machine, twisting one way and then the other, over and over, my bent arms small forklifts doing the work of emptying the containers of this life, of my marriage.

Bare feet pad over to me, Luke's feet. 'What are you doing?'

I drag the bag across the floor to the closet, open the door, and begin pulling things from the hangers and dumping them on top of the underwear, tank tops, fleece pants for sleeping, colorful socks with tiny dogs on them. Sweaters, T-shirts, dresses.

'I asked you a question.'

'What does it look like I'm doing, Luke?'

'What's your plan? Go to Jill's for the night?' He sounds hopeful.

I don't want him to have false hope, so I tell him the truth.

'I'm done,' I say. 'I love you, I do, I always have, but I'm not letting you ruin my life.'

'Seriously?'

I zipper the bag, the sound overly loud. 'Yes, seriously. I'm leaving. And I'm not coming back.' I breathe deeply, then I say it. 'I can't do this anymore. This marriage.'

A rush of relief, like wings, lifts me up, all the organs in my body lighter, floating, no longer pulled and pushed by gravity. My shoulders uncurl, my neck lengthens, my chin tilts upward.

This question of motherhood, of *if* I will become one, and if so *when*, and *what if* I don't become one, *then what*, all of them intimately laced into who I am as a woman, if I am a good or bad woman, a fulfilled or unfulfilled one, selfish or selfless, happy or not, and all of this tied up in marriage, work, divorce – it's formed one enormously heavy boulder. I've been carrying it for years, dragging it, shoving it, a shapely Sisyphus in heels, in running shoes, in work clothes, in pajamas and jeans.

I tip that boulder away from me now, just slightly, watch it tumble down the mountain and smash to bits in a ravine.

Would that I not had to carry that boulder at all.

I heft the suitcase until it is standing, handle up. I grab it, tilt it, and roll it toward the doorway. Luke is walking behind me the entire time, his footsteps seeming to echo his shock that I am actually doing what I am doing. 'Good-bye, Luke. I hope you find a mother to make you happy someday.'

I say this, then I turn the lock and walk out the door.

40

August 23, 2024

Rose, Lives 1–3, 5–9

'Please tell me Addie isn't going to hurt herself, diving off those rocks.'

Thomas leans forward in his colorful beach chair, blue, green, and pink stripes at his back, hand shading his eyes, voice half kidding, half serious.

Teenagers of all ages, maybe even a few college students, are clustered on the summit of the biggest rock that juts out from the end of the beach. It's at least twenty feet tall. A girl with long red hair squeals with glee on her way down to the water after leaping.

'Oh, don't worry.' I brush the sand off my feet and hands. 'Addie will be fine. She's having fun. I used to dive off those rocks when I was her age. I did it for years.'

'But parents are much more stressed out and vigilant these days,' Thomas says. 'I'm surprised jumping off those rocks hasn't been outlawed by the local PTA. The two of us should propose a law to prohibit this kind of behavior, Rose.'

'You're ridiculous,' I tell him, then I kiss his shoulder. Addie's friend Tim is calling down to the girl in the water to come back up for another round.

'I'm not even kidding! Look at that thing! It's Mount Fucking Everest but on a beach in New England!'

I nudge him. 'It's not that high. And the water's plenty deep around it.'

'Exactly!'

My beach chair is tilted too far back to watch Addie climb up the rocks, so I shift the metal slats until I am sitting straighter. Like Thomas and me, other people on the beach are watching the kids swim out to the rocks, climb up, and dive off, only to repeat the sequence. The atmosphere is festive, owing to the heat wave and the weekend and the fact that it's August. The beach umbrellas dotting the view are red, pink, orange and yellow and violet and green, striped and polka dotted and flowered. The towels and bathing suits are another riot of color and patterns against the backdrop of burning-hot white sand and cold blue ocean.

Ever since I was small, my mother instilled in me a love for the beach, nurtured it as I got older. Like all mothers, she could be judgmental, aloof, inaccessible, but she could also be wonderful and fun and loving and giving; a person who encouraged me to take risks, to follow my heart's desire. I miss her, now especially, because being at the beach was her own heart's desire.

'Oh my God. Addie's getting ready to jump.' Thomas puts his hands over his eyes. 'I really can't watch.'

'It's going to be okay,' I tell him, my eyes glued to the tall, skinny-legged girl in the lime-green bikini, long wet hair hanging down around her face. For a long time Addie wore it short, but then she decided to grow it out and now it's past her shoulders again. Addie peers down into the deep, dark water, and my heart flutters with fear – Will she really be okay? What if something terrible happens? How could I live with myself for letting her go up there – and all because I'd plied her with stories of doing exactly this when I was her age? 'Now,' I go on, 'if Luke were here, he'd be sermonizing about how no child should be allowed to put her life in danger like that, aka, no child should be allowed to have any risky fun.'

Addie swings her arms back, bends her knees.

'I might be with Luke on this one,' Thomas says, eyes still covered.

'You are not.'

'No, really. I mean it.'

'There she goes,' I cry out, watching as Addie flings herself off the rock, straight down into the water. A second later she pops up. The other kids cheer for her. 'She did great!'

Thomas finally uncovers his eyes. He lets out a giant breath. Then he looks at me. 'Uh-oh. What's that grin for, Rose?'

I stand up from my chair and grab a towel. 'You just watch.'

'You're going to go join her? Are you crazy?'

'Don't worry! I'm an expert in jumping off that rock—'

'You mean cliff.'

Thomas's hand is reaching for me. I grab it. 'It will be fine. *I* will be fine.'

'Great. Now I get to stress about two women dying a horrible death today.'

Thomas won't let go of my hand. I shake it a little, and my fingers slide from his.

362

'Yes, fine, go and be with Addie,' Thomas says, shaking his head. 'I don't like the idea of her up there alone anyway. If something terrible happens, then you can save her.'

I put my hand on my hip, pretending to be offended. 'And what if something terrible happens to me?'

Thomas laughs. 'Then Addie will save you, obviously.'

'I'm sure she's going to be happy when she sees me coming,' I say.

'She'll probably be secretly thrilled.'

'I guess we'll see!'

The walk up to the diving rocks takes a little over five minutes. Kids playing in the water, building sandcastles, people laughing, the surf coming in and out of the beach provide the soundtrack. By the time I get there, I am sweating. It must be ninety-five degrees.

A boy, tall, muscular, maybe sixteen or seventeen, in aqua swimming trunks, cannonballs into the water and all the remaining kids waiting for their turn shout and clap. Eventually, some of them see me standing there, about to swim over to the spot where everyone starts their climb. Addie is deep in conversation with her friend, Tim. He says something and she laughs.

I wave my hand wildly. 'Addie!'

She looks up. Right when she smiles, I dive in, the ocean cold and swirling. It's refreshing in the heat. I swim the breaststroke, the slurp and slap of the water against my body a music I've missed. Sharp memories flood my brain as I arrive at the ledge and place my wet hands against wet rock – images of the first time I dared do this when I was thirteen, standing tall and high in my bathing suit, as Ray, the boy I had a crush on, called to me from below. That was right about the same moment that my dad found out I'd disobeyed him, and he showed up to drag me home and ground me.

'Dr. Napolitano, do you need a hand?'

Tim is yelling down to me, and I look up at this tall young man Addie seems to like, having recently declared herself bi to us one night over dinner. Maybe this is the boy who helped her discover this detail about herself, because before this, she was only into girls.

'Tim, I told you to call me Rose,' I call back to him.

'I can't, though. You're like, a professor and stuff.'

'Suit yourself, then,' I say, laughing, staring up at Addie's friend, at Addie. It turns out that I really like her friends. That I genuinely like kids when they are teenagers.

Along the edge of the rock is a kind of staircase, a series of natural slate steps. Tim is peering down at me, probably wondering what this old lady is doing swimming up to this massive rock to be with the kids. Addie is next to him. She seems nervous, like she's sending me mental telepathic strength to help me climb to where they stand, waiting. When I am close to the top, Tim offers his hand and I take it.

'Thank you, sir,' I say, and he laughs.

'I can't believe you came up here!' Addie's expression is disbelieving, but also happy. Or maybe she's relieved that I didn't tumble to my death off the side. I hope Thomas has managed to remove his hands from his face and is relieved about this, too.

I give Addie a squeeze. 'I figured it was like riding a bicycle and all that.' I turn to Tim. 'I hope you don't mind, but I think this next jump is for the two of us.'

Tim gestures toward the ledge. 'Be my guest.'

'Come on, Addie. Let's do this.'

'Seriously?' She sounds shocked.

'Sure, why not? What did you think I was coming up here for, anyway?'

'Okay!' She is nodding.

I want to throw my arms around her again, but I resist.

The two of us, Addie with her skinny, tanned legs and lime-green bikini, and me with my bright purple one-piece, walk over to the edge. I can feel the other kids' eyes on us, the sound of their chatter disappearing as they watch. We grab hands.

'Ready?' I say, and then, laughing, together we jump.

41

May 23, 2000

Rose, Lives 1–9

L UKE IS DOWN on one knee.

It happens so suddenly that at first I'm confused.

'What are you doing, Luke?' I stand there, arms at my side, fingers curling toward my palms and uncurling, jittery.

He is looking up at me, smiling, glowing, but not speaking. He wobbles a bit, then rights himself. Begins to dig around in his back pocket.

Oh. *Oh!*

As Luke fumbles, grasping for the small box wedged into his jeans, my heart begins to race, goose bumps rise all over my skin, even under my sweater. My lips part, I remember to breathe. I think I'm smiling. I've been waiting for this moment, anticipating it, hoping it would be soon.

Luke comes out with the box, opens it, and takes out an engagement ring. He holds it up to me and begins a speech. It shimmers and sparkles as it moves in his trembling hand. 'Rose, you are the love of my life and you always will be . . .'

As he speaks, I hear his lovely words, but I also hear something else, a voice inside my head, and it has its own opinion about what is happening. I try to silence it, but it's such a strong, annoying, interrupting voice.

Rose, it says, *why is Luke down on one knee? It's so* traditional. *And you told him a million times – no, a billion – that you did not want some traditional proposal, some traditional engagement, that would be followed by a traditional marriage. You* specifically *said you never wanted someone to get down on one knee and ask you to marry them. You joked that if Luke ever did this, your answer would be a big loud no.*

'I want to live the rest of my days with only you . . .'

Luke's words are so sweet, so beautiful, how can I not love them? How can I not simply melt in the face of such a declaration? I mean, so what if he's on his knee and I told him never to do this? So what if I'm a feminist? Feminists can enjoy a good declaration of love, right? I mean, anybody can. It's a nice tradition! So why can't I? I have the right to enjoy this. Don't I?

But what if this is a sign of other things to come?

'Rose Napolitano, will you do me the honor of becoming my wife? Will you marry me?'

What if there are other ways that Luke didn't listen?

Luke is beaming and most of me beams back.

Most.

There's another Rose inside of me, and she's worried. I wish she'd shut up and let me enjoy this.

Rose . . .

Shut. UP.

Luke is waiting. He bobbles a little on his knee again.
I reach out and steady him.
The other Rose grows silent.
I smile, open my mouth, and say, 'Yes.'

42

December 12, 2025

ROSE

THOMAS IS CALLING from the other room. 'Rose, your phone is buzzing! It's Luke.'

I am stringing lights up on the tree. Meera, our new cat, is pulling at them from the box of Christmas decorations. We miss Max, but Max has gone on to a better place. I snatch Meera up in my arms and she mews in protest as I head into the other room.

Thomas is sitting on the bed, holding my phone out to me. I take it, putting it to my ear. 'Luke, how are you?'

'Good. Any news?'

Thomas reaches for Meera. I pout, but let him take her. 'I got the grant!'

'You did! That's great! I'm not surprised.'

'Thanks,' I say. I am touched that Luke would call for no other reason but to ask about my work. 'What about you? What's up with the awards this year?'

Luke sighs. 'I'm trying not to think too much about it.

Maybe if I pretend I don't care then I'll get one of the big ones.'

I laugh. 'You usually do.'

'Shhhh. Don't jinx me.'

I head back into the living room and kitchen, passing the half-decorated tree, and see Addie at the kitchen table, head bent over a screen. 'Listen, I've got to go. I have Christmas cookies in the oven and I don't want to burn them. *Someone* is supposed to be watching them but is immersed in her phone instead.' Addie doesn't even look up when I say this – probably doesn't even hear me. 'Then I have to start on all the other holiday goodies.'

'Stop, you're killing me,' Luke says. 'I still miss that part of our life. Cheryl doesn't even know how to boil water.'

'Don't want to hear that, happy holidays, bye now!' I hang up before Luke can say anything else.

The buzzer sounds – Addie still doesn't look up. I hustle past her to the oven, open it, see the perfect golden color on the tops of the cookies. I grab a pot holder and pull them out.

They smell delicious. They smell . . .

My mother.

For one brief, searing moment, she is here, with me, right now. We are in this kitchen together, I am small, maybe six, maybe seven, and we are baking cookies – these cookies, together.

I've been thinking lately, when I am in bed at night or when I am headed to teach or just walking around the city, about my mother's life – the life she lived before she had me. What it was like, what she dreamed of, if she ever had doubts about her choices, about her choice to have me. This longing to have known her, really known her, as a woman, before motherhood changed her, has grown and expanded and flourished inside of me. I wish I had.

That longing, this need is what led me to apply for the new grant, the one that Luke asked about. This time I'm interviewing mothers, mothers who are later in their lives, with children grown and out of the house. I want to know about the before and after of motherhood for them. I'm going to ask them all the questions I wish I could have asked my mother, that I would ask her now if she was still alive. I want to know who they were before this sea change occurred in their existence and I want to know how they see their choice from such a distance, in the present of their lives today. Would they have done anything differently? Do they miss any part of their old selves? Do they ever wonder who they would be if they had chosen otherwise about motherhood? Do they ever wish they could meet that other woman, the person they would be if they had chosen differently?

Spatula in hand, one by one I pry each cookie from the baking sheet, transferring most of them to the cooling rack and a couple onto a plate. I wonder, as I do this, about the other lives I might have lived, lives where I might have chosen not to have a child, and some lives where I had one, or tried to. Either way, whether I am the Rose who said yes, or the Rose who said maybe, or no, never, absolutely never, or some combination of those Roses, I am here, there is a child, whether she is technically mine or not doesn't matter, I decide. There is love and friendship and family, and that is enough to carry us through the harder times, the days and months and years of loss, the inevitable grief of being alive. There is a peace in that, a certain kind of happiness. That is as much as anyone can hope for, I think, from a single life.

I slide a plate of cookies, still hot from the oven, across the kitchen table toward Addie. She looks up, startled. Then she smiles. 'You want one?' I ask, and smile back.

ACKNOWLEDGMENTS

To Miriam Altshuler, my agent, who is a tremendous supporter of women (in general) and of this woman in particular, I'm lucky to have found such a wonderful, enduring 'professional marriage', and that you have stuck with me through thick and thin (and so much thin), without ever losing faith.

To Pam Dorman, for falling in love with my book overnight and making my writerly dreams come true in so many ways; for your wise editorial insight, for your faith in Rose and in me, and for deciding something that I have written is worthy of your imprint – I am honored, and grateful, and I have learned so much working with you. Having you publish this novel has been one of the highlights of my professional life. And to Martha Ashby at HarperCollins, my UK editor, for your gentle prodding, your kindness, and your initial excitement after first reading my book, which produced a document from you and your colleagues that I still look at when I'm feeling blue. I am so lucky to have such a dynamic duo of Book Mothers looking out for me and for Rose.

To everyone at Viking and Penguin who took a chance on Rose. To Jeramie Orton and Marie Michels, for your patience and diligence, and most especially to Leigh Butler and Hal Fessenden, for your extraordinary support, for 'getting' this book, and for your designs on world domination – between you two and Pam, the three of you made last summer into one of the most exciting summers of my life.

To the editors across the world who also fell in love with Rose, I am so grateful and excited to be published by you, and thrilled that you believe in this novel and in me. I have loved getting to know so many of you, and look forward to continuing the conversations that this novel started between us.

To my wonderful friends, Marie Rutkoski, Daphne Grab, Eliot Schrefer, and Rene Steinke, who read drafts and helped me talk things through, and Rebecca Stead, who kept me steady at an important moment and gave excellent advice. To Kylie Sachs, still my friend even now (how is that possible after so many years?), who is my confidante on all-things in this novel, big and small, rage-filled and happy. To my dad, who is the best, and my husband, who, when I was writing this book, every night would ask over dinner, 'What happened today with Rose Napolitano?'

To the women who've never wanted children, who society and culture have made to feel broken, and small, and less than, and like there must be something wrong with them for not wanting to bear children and for maybe never wanting to do this, even from a young age – this book is definitely written with you in mind. *I see you.* I hope I have done your experiences justice.

To the mothers in my life of all types – mothers to their own children, writing mothers, and the women who have mothered me at different points when I have needed mothering. To the mothers I meet in the future and the ones who read this book.

There are so many ways to be a mother and so many of them don't actually involve birthing a baby. We don't acknowledge this enough in the world.

Finally, to my own mother: I will end this book and its acknowledgments by acknowledging my mother again, to whom I dedicated this novel, but I will give the full dedication here since I have more room:

Thank you, Mom, for giving me this life. I wish I could have said that to you while you were still conscious enough to hear it and take it in. I said this to you – these exact words – the day before you died, but you couldn't hear me. I've spent the last almost sixteen years thinking about how you couldn't hear me say those words on that day, and how unjust this is. Because you deserved my thanks and my eternal gratitude. Giving someone life is no small thing. Being a mother is no small thing. But it is often thankless. I wish I had thanked you to your face, specifically, for this life, my life. I like to think that you did hear me somehow, that maybe you still can, even in death. It's probably just a fantasy, but sometimes fantasies are all we have, and this is mine. I love you. Thank you.